# Tomorrow's Promise

Here's what reviewers say about *Yesterday's Shadows*, the second of the ***Pinkerton Lady Chronicles***.

"A romantic mystery. . . . It should please readers . . . with a subtle message of faith. Recommended, especially where Christian mysteries are in high demand."

*Library Journal*

"Laurel's double life haunts her. Should she tell Granger the truth—that she's not the newspaper reporter he thinks she is? More important, does her secretive work honor the God of her Christian faith? *Yesterday's Shadows* is by accomplished novelist Lee Roddy."

*The Bookwatch*

"Torn between her past work as Pinkerton spy for the Union and the former Confederate cavalryman whom she loves, Laurel Bartlett struggles to both find happiness and honor God."

*Civil War Book Review*

## The Pinkerton *Lady* Chronicles

# Tomorrow's Promise

# LEE RODDY

**Cook Communications**

Faithful Woman is an imprint of
Cook Communications Ministries, Colorado Springs, Colorado 80918
Cook Communications, Paris, Ontario
Kingsway Communications, Eastbourne, England

TOMORROW'S PROMISE
© 2000 by Lee Roddy

Editor: Susan Reck
Design: Bill Gray
Cover Illustration: Matthew Archambault

**Published in association with the literary agency of Alive Communications, Inc., 1465
Kelly Johnson Blvd., Suite 320, Colorado Springs, CO 80920.**

1 2 3 4 5 6 7 8 9 10 Printing/Year 04 03 02 01 00

**Library of Congress Cataloging-in-Publication Data**

Roddy, Lee,
    Tomorrow's promise / Lee Roddy.
        p. cm. -- (The Pinkerton lady chronicles ; 3)
        ISBN 1-56476-688-8
        1. Private investigators--West (U.S.)--Fiction. 2. Women detectives--West (U.S.)--
Fiction. I. Title.

PS3568.O344 T66 2000
813'.54--dc21                                                                          99-054260

To My Literary Agent,

*Greg Johnson*

of Alive Communications, Inc.,
with deep appreciation.

# Chapter 1

H e sat unnoticed in the ebb and flow of humanity at the Chicago depot that muggy July day, 1867, staring at her over the top of an open newspaper. From the time she and her spinster aunt stepped off the train and the tall man with a slight limp met them, his loathing rose. So did his determination to render the ultimate punishment.

For that, he was glad she had returned. Now that he knew the truth of what she had done, it would be easier for him. After all, it was her fault. Yet in spite of how much he detested her, he swallowed hard.

*She's so pretty. Petite, barely five feet tall and not over a hundred pounds, yet she's all woman. She's easily more lovely than any of the others. . . .*

"Stop it!" he whispered to himself in stern rebuke. *She's a Jezebel; an Athaliah, or worse. She fooled everyone, including me, but now that I know. . . .* He left his thought unfinished and angrily glared at her.

A hundred feet away, Laurel Bartlett impatiently tapped a foot under her hoop skirt. *What's keeping him*? Suddenly, she felt a tingle of gooseflesh at the back of her neck. She was used to having men steal appreciative glances at her, but this time it was different.

It gave her a vague sense of concern, like the time she was returning from gathering military intelligence behind

Confederate lines and a picket had her in his musket sights. She had sensed something and turned just before he fired.

Since the war ended fifteen months ago, she had briefly visited in Virginia and was just now returning from California. She casually let her violet eyes sweep the crowd. A couple of young men gave her discreet glances as they walked past, but she didn't see anyone really looking hard at her. Still, the feeling remained.

Subconsciously, she lightly touched her tingling neck where her brunette hair was pulled back slightly behind the ears. Cascading curls from under the pert traveling hat enhanced the whiteness of her throat. Her gaze stopped abruptly on a short man wearing spectacles.

She sucked in her breath. Sam Maynard!

He rose from a bench and headed toward a side exit without looking in her direction.

"Laurel?"

Startled, she whirled around. "Oh, Ridge!" she exclaimed in relief while her heart gave that same little leap of excitement which he always aroused in her.

"Something wrong?" he asked with a hint of Southern drawl.

"What? Oh, no. It's nothing!" she exclaimed.

"Don't try to fool me," he said firmly. "I can see it in your face. What happened?"

She hesitated, looking up into his pale blue eyes. He wasn't quite handsome, but she found his looks very appealing. A three-inch long scar over the bridge of his nose and right cheekbone, along with a slight limp from a Yankee minie ball in his left leg, testified to his four years of war as a Confederate cavalryman.

"Well?" he prompted, taking her arm and starting to walk toward the exit where she saw hacks lined up.

She was unwilling to again mention the fear that someday her war-time missions might come back to haunt her. However, to insure honesty in their relationship, Laurel had revealed to Ridge both her spying past and her present work as a secret Pinkerton Detective operative. She had to admit what had startled her.

She told Ridge, "I just saw Sam Maynard."

"Here? Are you sure?"

When Laurel nodded, Ridge added, "I'm surprised to hear that. He was so glad to get home alive after the war that he said he'd never leave Virginia again."

Ridge stopped and looked down at Laurel from his six-foot height. "You're not concerned about him, are you?" She hesitated, so he continued. "There's no need to be. I told you in Virginia that even if he ever did recognize you from what you did to him at Petersburg, he's not vindictive."

Laurel was unconvinced, but looked around and changed the subject. "Where's Aunt Agnes?"

"She's waiting with the hack. I've got your trunks loaded. Do you want to see Sarah first, or your father?"

Laurel considered that. She and Sarah had grown up together. She was the only one outside of Allan Pinkerton and Ridge who knew of Laurel's spying. Sarah had often assisted Laurel with disguises and places to hide highly sensitive military information which she had to smuggle from behind Confederate lines.

After a moment's reflection, Laurel said, "She should have had her baby by now, so naturally I'm eager to see them both, but I'd better stop at Papa's first."

"Whatever you want." Ridge smiled down at her. "I'm just so glad to have you back."

"Thank you. It's good to be here. How was Nebraska?"

"If those settlers keep rushing in and buying land, I'll soon have enough money to build our house. All you have to do is set our wedding date."

*No, that's not all I have to do.* The thought made her

stomach lurch when they stepped outside the depot where Agnes waited in the hack. Laurel turned and looked back, but there was no sign of Maynard. She dropped her voice. "We'll have time to talk about that after I see Papa and Sarah."

Ridge glanced sharply at her. "You're not having second thoughts again, are you?"

Before she could answer, her thin-faced Aunt Agnes exclaimed irritably, "Would you two hurry? You can talk later."

"Yes, later," Laurel agreed, but she wasn't looking forward to that as Ridge helped her into the vehicle.

Ridge and Agnes chatted amiably, but Laurel was mostly silent until the hired hack turned up the long, tree-lined driveway. Laurel smiled at the sight of the two-story red brick home where she had grown up. It silently testified to the affluence of her father, a retired manufacturer who had made railroad wheels and other iron parts for the Federal's war-time rolling stock.

The hack driver lifted both trunks from his vehicle and followed his passengers toward the front door. It opened before anyone could ring the bell.

A matronly woman in a servant's black dress and white apron scurried out. "Miss Agnes! Laurel!" she exclaimed, hurrying to embrace them in turn. "We got your wire, so everyone's here to welcome you both home."

"It's good to see you, Maggie," Laurel said, readjusting her perky hat after the embrace. "You remember my fiancé, Ridge Granger?"

Maggie's brown eyes briefly glittered with disapproval. "Humph!" she muttered, glancing up at him.

He didn't take offense, but grinned at her. "Maggie, that's a lot better greeting than I got the first time I came here and you threatened to set the dogs on me."

"Ain't got no dogs," she said disdainfully. "Never did have. Just wanted to see if it was true that all you Rebels run from your own shadow. . . ."

"Maggie!" Laurel said sharply. "The war's over!"

"Not for some people!" she muttered, then motioned to the hack driver. "Take that first trunk upstairs. Second door on the right. Leave the other inside this front door."

Laurel lowered her voice as Maggie stepped back to hold the door open. "I'm sorry, Ridge. She's been with our family so long she's become very impertinent."

"It doesn't bother me," he said truthfully. But he recalled that Laurel had been uncomfortable when she came to visit him in Virginia. His family was dead, so his friends had welcomed her. Later, Laurel told him about sensing their resentment of a Yankee in their midst. It had troubled her, but he was unmoved by Maggie's and Laurel's sister Emma's disapproval of a former Confederate cavalryman as a prospective member of the family.

Ridge's gaze took in the stairs, the tall case clock standing against the wall, and the long hallway leading toward the back of the house. A door opened there, and Laurel's family rushed forward with outstretched arms.

Hiram Bartlett, who was now sixty-two, hugged Laurel and lightly touched his sister on her shoulder. Agnes did not like to be hugged. He then warmly greeted his prospective son-in-law.

Harriet, at twenty-two, was the family's middle daughter. She tentatively offered Ridge her right hand as she glanced out of the corner of her eye to see Emma's reaction. The oldest sister, in her early thirties, did not offer to shake Ridge's hand. She gave him a cool, semi-tolerant look out of dark, critical eyes.

Everyone except Ridge seemed to be talking at once, commenting on health and asking questions of the two California travelers. Maggie gave Ridge a scathing look, then announced to no one in particular that she was going to make tea.

Momentarily forgotten, Ridge admired the parlor with its fireplace, quality dark furniture, scenic pictures, and an oil painting of Laurel's late mother, Naomi. Beside her there was a photo of their only son in his Federal infantry uniform. Ridge knew that Laurel's only brother, Dorian, had been killed in the war at age sixteen.

"Sit down, Ridge," Hiram Bartlett said, turning away from the women and motioning toward a Victorian love seat with its ornate scrolls. He studied Ridge with shrewd blue eyes. "Laurel wrote that you're speculating in land along the route the transcontinental railroad will take when it's finished. I trust it's going well for you?"

"Very well, thanks." Ridge's eyes reluctantly moved from the women. He envied the way Laurel was welcomed with loving words and embraces. He wished his family had survived the four years of invasion and destruction.

Bartlett lowered his six-foot frame into the wingback Louis XVI Bergere chair before pressing Ridge for details. "I understand that you lost everything in the war, even the land on which your family plantation had been for generations."

"That's right," Ridge replied shortly. It was a sensitive area for him. He steadfastly refused to petition President Andrew Johnson for amnesty which was required for Confederate lands to be returned after being seized under the Union's war-time confiscation acts.

"Pardon me," Bartlett began tentatively, absently touching his forehead where the gray hair had given way to baldness to the top of his scalp. "I don't mean to pry, but after you and Laurel became betrothed in California, she didn't write me about when you two expect to be married, or where you'll live. I'm sure you can appreciate a father's concern for his daughter's welfare, even after she marries."

"I can certainly appreciate that, Mr. Bartlett," Ridge replied. "I'd do the same if it were my daughter. The truth is that we didn't work out those details before I had to leave Sacramento for Omaha to begin my business venture. There hasn't been time to really talk about such matters since meeting her and your sister at the train."

Laurel broke free from the other women to come stand by her father's chair. "Papa, I couldn't help overhearing what you just said. Please give Ridge and me a little time to talk. When we've come to our decisions, I promise that you'll be the first to know. All right?"

Her father smiled fondly at her and took her hand. "Of course. I just want you to be happy and to know you'll be cared for."

Laurel quickly bent and kissed him on his clean-shaven cheek. "I know that." She glanced at her sisters and aunt still huddled in animated conversation before lowering her voice. "I wish Emma and Maggie would accept Ridge as Aunt Agnes and Harriet have."

"They'll come around," Bartlett assured Laurel. "Now, tell me about your trip to Sacramento."

She didn't want to do that because of a secret that she and Ridge shared. She was an agent for the Pinkerton Detective Agency where terms of employment required that no one know the truth of what her work really was. She had been sent to investigate a case involving the building of the transcontinental railroad. The Central Pacific was headquartered in California's state capital. They were laying tracks east from there toward a future meeting of the Union Pacific which was building west out of Omaha.

It hurt her conscience to represent herself as a female correspondent for the *Chicago Globe*. She felt even more shame at misleading her father and sisters, so she deftly shifted the subject to Ridge.

"Tell Papa how you recovered a stolen railroad payroll and used the reward money to buy up land."

Ridge sensed why she had deftly switched the topic to him. "Well, the only part that's really of interest now is that since Nebraska has changed from a territory to a state, homesteaders are rushing there in great numbers. At first, they were my customers. But now I'm in Chicago to try to persuade some businessmen to open offices or stores where the railroad will pass. I hope to sell them business property on land which I bought on speculation."

Bartlett nodded approvingly. "There's more money in selling to businesses than individual homesteaders. Say, I have some commercial contacts in this city to whom I could give you letters of introduction."

"Thank you," Ridge replied, "but I hope you'll not take offense; I'd like to do this on my own."

"No offense taken." Bartlett's mouth crinkled with a pleased grin. "I felt the same way when I was courting her." He glanced toward the oil painting of his late wife.

Excited exclamations which erupted from the women caused the other three people to look in their direction. Harriet cried, "Papa! Did you hear that? Aunt Agnes has a proposal of marriage!"

Bartlett's eyebrows shot up in surprise. He asked his sister, "Is that true?"

She snapped, "You don't have to look so surprised, Hiram! Just because I never married doesn't mean that a man couldn't want me to share his life!"

Her brother grinned good-naturedly and took a few quick steps, reaching out his arms to her. "I know you don't like to hug, but I claim a brother's prerogative to give you one anyway."

"Don't muss my hair!" Agnes complained as he pulled her into his arms and Emma and Harriet pelted her with questions about her suitor.

Agnes always reminded Laurel of a dried-up apple core of a woman. At fifty-five, she was slight, thin-faced, and famous for having a sharp tongue. She was also the self-appointed guardian of family and public morals. She had been highly critical of Laurel's periodic war-time disappearances. Agnes had never guessed the real reason for Laurel's absences.

When Laurel introduced Ridge to the family, Agnes had joined Emma in trying to thwart a relationship with an ex-Rebel. After Ridge unexpectedly showed up in Sacramento, Agnes had gradually come to view him as an acceptable family member.

In flustered tones, Agnes told about meeting Horatio Bodmer on the stagecoach ride to California where she had been Laurel's chaperon. In Sacramento, Bodmer, a widower, had courted Agnes in spite of her initial attempts to rebuff him. Bodmer's height and bony facial features reminded Laurel of the late Abraham Lincoln.

"But," Agnes told her family, "I haven't made up my mind. I'd have to sell my place here and move to California. I'm not sure I want to do that."

Laurel reminded her, "He said he would write you every week until you said 'yes.' Oh!" Laurel turned to her father. "Why didn't you write me when Sarah had her baby?"

"I did. Emma, you posted that for me, didn't you?"

"Of course, Papa." She pivoted to Laurel. "Then you don't know that she lost her baby?"

"Oh, no!" Laurel's face contorted with grief. "What happened?"

"The cord was wrapped about his neck at birth," Emma said. "Sarah and her husband were devastated. Papa's letter must have reached Sacramento after you left."

"Poor Sarah!" Laurel cried. "I'd better go see her right away."

"Letter!" Maggie exclaimed, entering the parlor with a tray of cups and a teapot. "I almost forgot. Laurel, one came for you a couple of days ago."

"A letter came here for me?" she asked in surprise. "I haven't lived here since I turned eighteen!"

Emma said sarcastically, "It's probably from one of those soldiers you dallied with during—"

"Emma!" her father broke in sharply. "Not another word! Not a word! Do you understand?"

Emma shrugged and glanced at Ridge, who gave her a wink that flustered her. If she had hoped to plant a suspicious thought in his mind, it obviously failed.

Laurel smiled to herself, aware that her sister had no way of knowing that Laurel had told Ridge all about her war-time absences.

Maggie said, "If you can pour your own tea, I'll get the letter." She set the tray down and left the room, leaving a strained silence behind her.

It wasn't just the cruel and unjustified comment by Emma that caused the tension. Laurel was stunned at the loss of Sarah's baby, and ached to comfort her friend.

Agnes had almost finished pouring the tea when Maggie returned and handed an envelope to Laurel.

She didn't recognize the handwriting. Tearing it open, she found no letter inside. Instead, she saw a strip of paper torn from the top of a newspaper page. There was no headline or story; not even the name of the paper. There was simply the page number and publication date showing.

"Well?" Emma said. "Who's it from?"

Frowning, Laurel started to remove the item, then gasped as the date registered on her.

"What is it?" her father asked, coming toward her. "What's wrong?"

"Uh? Oh, nothing! Nothing!" She hastily shoved the piece of paper back into the envelope and crumpled it in her hand.

Emma scolded, "You're not a good liar! Your face says it's something important! We're family, so tell us!"

Laurel ignored the demand as the significance of the date fifteen months ago seared into her mind.

Ridge quickly but gently took her into his arms. She yielded, still clutching the crumpled envelope in her hand. "What is it?" he murmured in her ear.

She whispered, "He remembers!"

"What?"

"I'll tell you privately. Please take me away from here!" she replied in a low, hoarse voice.

Ridge turned to the anxious family. "I'm going to take her outside for some fresh air. Be back later."

Laurel vaguely heard the protestations as Ridge took her by the hand and led her outside. He didn't say anything until they were well out of sight of her family. Then he asked, "What do you mean, 'he remembers'? "

She handed the envelope toward him. "Here. Read it."

He took it, glanced at the torn piece of paper, and handed it back. "April third, 1865," he said musingly. "That was the day Petersburg and Richmond fell. What's that got to do with you?"

"I was there." What had been an exciting adventure for her as a Union spy now seemed filled with new danger. She couldn't stand still, but started walking. Ridge joined her. "Two days before," she explained, "I had been in Petersburg. That's where I met Sam Maynard."

Ridge laughed lightly in relief. "Oh, that! I told you before: he probably wouldn't remember you."

"Oh, he remembers! Otherwise, why would he send me this?" She opened her palm, showing the envelope.

"You're making too much out of this."

"I don't think so, Ridge. He sent it, knowing that I was coming back from California, and I'd go see my father. He wanted that letter to be waiting for me so I'd know that he now has recalled what I did to him."

"You didn't do anything except smile at him and make him feel important."

"That's not all, and you know it! I told you what happened. He told me things; showed me the weakness in the Confederate lines—"

"Yes," Ridge broke in, "but he has no way of knowing who passed on that information to the Federals. I'm sure Sam didn't send that letter, so there's no reason to get upset."

"Then who else would have?" she challenged.

"I don't know, but seeing him at the depot awhile ago is just coincidence."

"No!" she shook her head vigorously. "I can still see him with those spectacles on his nose, proudly showing off to what he thought was a wide-eyed, innocent Southern belle.

"He told me, 'If our right flank here at Petersburg is penetrated, not only would this city fall to the Yankees, but Richmond would be threatened. What's more, even General Lee's entire retreat route might be cut off. Then we'd lose our army of Northern Virginia, and probably the war.'"

Ridge shook his head. "You remember too many things from back then. Forget it."

"I can't. The very next day after I smuggled this information on to Federal officials, they used it to seize Petersburg. I had already reached Richmond where I saw the Confederate government officials evacuating. I couldn't get across the bridges that day, but the next, while the city was burning, I mingled with the thousands of people fleeing from the capital. Union troops marched in right behind us and occupied Richmond."

"I remember," Ridge said softly.

"On the following Sunday, after General Lee's escape was cut off after leaving Petersburg, he surrendered at Appomattox. The war was over, but apparently not for Sam Maynard; at least, not after he found out what I did."

"Laurel! Laurel!" Ridge said softly, stopping to put both hands on her shoulders and look down into her eyes. "What do I have to do to convince you? I've known Sam since we were boys. He would not do this."

She sighed heavily. "All right, suppose I'm wrong and it wasn't Maynard. Who else would have sent me this envelope with nothing in it except a date?"

"I don't know, but why do you insist on reading some sinister aspect into it? You're not an easily frightened woman. You deliberately wanted excitement and danger in the war. That's why you became a spy."

She cringed. "Don't use that word! I hate it! I was a courier, and I became one only after my brother was killed!"

Ridge knew she had been a spy, not a courier, but it wasn't worth disagreeing with her. He said, "Nobody else except Pinkerton and I know that."

"There could be files somewhere."

"There probably are. But they're confidential."

"I'm sure they're supposed to be, but maybe Maynard somehow got access to them."

"I don't see how Sam could have done that."

"Sarah also knew."

"Yes, but you said she's good at keeping secrets."

"Maybe she told her husband, and he told—"

"Stop it! You're scaring yourself! But if it'll make you feel any better, let's go ask her right after we return to your family and try convincing them that there's nothing important in this letter."

"I'd rather catch a cabriolet and ride over to see Sarah right now."

"Your family will be concerned until you give them some explanation for the way that letter upset you."

"I know, but I need time to think of what to tell them. I don't want to lie to them, but neither can I tell them the truth about this letter."

"All right, we'll go see Sarah right now." Ridge glanced down the street. "If you don't mind walking, we'll be more likely to see a hack if we go a few blocks to a more-traveled area."

"I don't mind." She slipped her arm through his and matched his steps. "Riding a stagecoach for fifteen days and nights, then having to change trains five times after we crossed the Missouri, gave me enough sitting to last a long time."

He said approvingly, "You're sounding more like yourself."

"That letter still bothers me though."

Ridge didn't comment as he hailed a passing hack. It delivered them to the front of a small single-story frame house in one of Chicago's poorer districts. A dry leaf skittered across the tidy path between lawns, making Laurel jump.

"I thought it was a mouse," she said with a nervous laugh. "I guess I'm more jittery than I thought."

"I'll protect you from monster leaves," he assured her with a teasing smile as they neared the front door.

"That's strange," she said, frowning. "The door's open."

"Maybe the wind blew it open."

"It's not that strong. Besides, Sarah is a very careful person. Back when she helped me make places to hide things in my hair, my shoes, even my chemise, she always insisted on locking her doors."

They stepped upon the small wooden porch where Ridge knocked.

Laurel cocked her head, listening. "Better do it again. She may be in the kitchen."

After Ridge complied, they both listened.

Laurel shook her head. "I don't hear any footsteps." She pushed the door open enough to stick her head in and call. "Sarah! It's Laurel and Ridge. May we come in?"

They listened but heard nothing.

"Maybe something's wrong!" Laurel exclaimed. "Let's go in."

They stepped inside and glanced into the parlor to the right. It was silent with only a straight-backed chair and sofa in sight.

"Sarah!" Laurel called again. "It's Laurel and Ridge. Where are you?"

Silence.

Alarmed, Laurel motioned for Ridge to follow. She started down the uncarpeted hallway, passing the massive framed picture of Sarah's late parents who had willed this house to her. Calling again, Laurel entered the spacious old kitchen she remembered from years ago. Two embroidered Scripture verses hung on the wall next to the open cupboard with Sarah's rose-patterned tea cups and saucers.

Laurel passed the wooden table on which a dish towel had been dropped. But the ladder-back chair at the far end had been knocked over and a broken dish lay on the floor.

"Something really is wrong!" Laurel exclaimed. She raised her voice in alarm. "Sarah, where are you?"

When there was no answer, Laurel took a step toward the closed back porch door.

"Wait!" Ridge reached out and took her hand. "You stay here." He passed her, slowly opened the door, then stopped dead still.

Seeing the sudden stiffening of his body, Laurel started toward him. "What's the matter? . . . ."

"Stay back!" His voice stopped her. "Don't come any closer!"

"Why? What is it?"

He turned somberly toward Laurel. "Go tell a neighbor to get the police. Sarah's been murdered!"

Two days later, as Sarah's pastor concluded the mid-afternoon graveside service in sweltering heat, the church bell tolled slowly and mournfully. Still in shock, Laurel gripped Ridge's hand and peered through her black veil from eyes dimmed with tears. Mourners pressed around Sarah's grieving widower, then began to break up into small groups.

Laurel looked up at Ridge. "We need to speak to John, but let's wait until the crowd thins out some."

"Of course, but I've noticed several people looking at you, so I expect they'll come over to see you."

"I've known most of them all my life. So did Sarah. I dread the thought that they're going to ask questions about us finding her."

Ridge gave her hand a squeeze. "I'll try to head them off. Uh . . . who's this man coming toward us?"

"I don't know. Maybe the husband of one of the girls who married soldiers they met during the war."

The bell's final peal faded into the distant trees as the stranger strode purposefully past the headstones to where Laurel and Ridge stood. He was good-looking with clean-shaven cheeks, a heavy brown mustache, small goatee, and hair that covered his ears.

He gave a slight nod to Ridge but spoke to Laurel. "Miss Bartlett, I know this is a bad time, but I must talk to you as soon as possible about her." He motioned toward the grave where workmen were slowly lowering a plain casket into the open grave.

Ridge frowned. "You're right, sir. This is not the time."

"Forgive me," the stranger replied, extending his right hand. "I'm Vance Cooper, a correspondent for the *Chicago Globe*. You must be Ridge Granger."

Ridge nodded and briefly shook hands. He resented the reporter as an intruder, just as he resented all the press coverage which had been given to Sarah. From what Ridge knew of her, she would not have liked it. She had been a quiet, retiring woman.

Cooper added quickly, "I've vainly tried to reach Miss Bartlett at her father's home."

Laurel explained, "Papa asked me to stay with him until I can find suitable lodging for myself."

Cooper shifted his gaze to Laurel. "I'm interested in seeing your friend's killer brought to justice."

"So is everyone," Ridge said crisply. "Now, if you'll excuse us. . . ."

Laurel interrupted. "It's all right, Ridge. Mr. Cooper, I appreciate your interest, but I've already told the authorities everything I know. So talk to them."

"I've done that. I'm the crime reporter for the paper, so I've read all the detectives' reports—"

"I'm sorry, Mr. Cooper," Laurel interrupted. "I've said all I have to say."

She was distressed that the *Globe* and other area daily papers had all interviewed Sarah's neighbors. Each indicated that she had no enemies. No one could think of a motive, or even suggest a possible suspect. However, reporters like Cooper were obviously still digging for something sensational below the story's surface.

Ridge took Laurel's arm and started to lead her away, but

Cooper exclaimed, "Please wait! Miss Bartlett, the reason I must talk to you is because I'm new in Chicago, but I have covered two similar types of murders in New York where I last worked."

Laurel stopped. "Similar types?" she repeated.

Cooper nodded. "Yes. I mean, in the unusual way your friend was tied up and then smothered."

Laurel raised her eyebrows in surprise. The papers had reported on the cause of death, but there had been no mention that Sarah had been bound and gagged.

Cooper seemed to read Laurel's mind. He explained, "The detectives asked correspondents not to report on that aspect of the crime. They suspect it might be a clue to the perpetrator's identity. In the war, some soldiers were punished that way, even though rarely so. It was known as being 'bucked and gagged.' "

Laurel closed her eyes, trying to shut out the memory of seeing how Sarah had died.

Cooper rushed on, "Since that's such an unusual way to bind someone, some detectives speculate that an ex-soldier might have killed her."

"Mr. Cooper," Laurel said coolly, "almost every man around here served in the war. That's a lot of possible suspects, but which one had a motive?"

"That's what I want to talk you about, Miss Bartlett. If you'll let me do that sometime soon, perhaps I can be of help in bringing this killer to justice."

Laurel hesitated in confusion. She had been certain that Sarah had been slain because of her part in helping Laurel's wartime spying missions. But Cooper's mention of two victims in New York being bound as Sarah had been might mean she was wrong.

Laurel said firmly, "More than anything, I want Sarah's killer caught and punished. So call at my father's home this time tomorrow and we'll talk."

"Thank you very much. I'll be there."

After Cooper walked away, Ridge asked under his breath, "You know Sam Maynard was in the military, but do you still think he had anything to do with this?"

"I . . . I don't know what to think." Laurel looked toward the mourners. Some were crossing the cobblestone street, following the fragrance of food emanating from the fellowship hall of the church. Others stood in small groups, eyeing Ridge with open hostility.

Laurel knew that each man there had worn the Federal uniform, but she chose to ignore the enmity shown in their faces. The war was history, but, as with Ridge, it wasn't over for some of them. There were so many terrible memories that some could not easily forget.

She had sensed similar antagonism directed toward her during a brief visit to meet Ridge's friends in Virginia. They had been polite, but the subsurface tension was so real it was almost tangible.

She fleetingly wondered if Ridge would change his mind about petitioning President Johnson for amnesty. Only if that were done could the Granger family plantation land be reclaimed. Of course, the house and out-buildings had been destroyed, but Ridge could rebuild.

However, Laurel wasn't sure she wanted to live where resentment against a Yankee like her was so strong. She didn't think the feeling was as marked against Ridge here in the North, but she couldn't be sure. Would they be happy together in either area?

She realized that Ridge was speaking, so she snapped her mind back to hear his words.

"There are fewer people around Sarah's husband. Let's try to get to him before more come."

They had only taken a few steps when a young woman wearing all black and a matching full-length veil broke away from the other mourners.

"Oh, no!" Laurel exclaimed under her breath. "Here comes Adeline Curry; well, it's Crawford now. I was her bridesmaid. Sometimes she's rather tactless and is the worst gossip of all the girls Sarah and I grew up with."

Ridge said, "I can cut her off."

"Thanks, but I've got to face her."

Adeline's pregnancy showed as she approached. She didn't look at Ridge, but smiled and hugged Laurel.

"It's so good to see you again!" Adeline exclaimed. "I'm just sorry it's under such tragic circumstances."

"So am I." Laurel could see through Adeline's veil as her eyes swept Ridge. They briefly lingered on the scar where a Union cavalry saber had sliced his nose and cheek. Laurel started to introduce him, but Adeline spoke first.

"So, Laurel, this must be your Rebel!"

Laurel cringed at the thoughtless use of the term. She hated it as much as she did being thought of as a former spy.

Laurel introduced them, aware that Ridge's jaw muscles twitched, indicating his controlled emotions.

"How do you do, Mrs. Crawford?"

"Oh! I love your accent," she cried. "It seems so strange to hear a Southern drawl up here in the North." Then, without pausing, Adeline exclaimed to Laurel, "Isn't it perfectly awful about Sarah? I still can't believe it. She never had an enemy, so why would someone kill her?"

Laurel didn't feel like replying to a question which Sarah's widower, the police, and others had already asked her. She shook her head without speaking, but Adeline didn't seem to notice.

She dropped her voice. "How awful that you had to find her. . . ."

"Excuse us," Ridge broke in, protectively putting his arm around Laurel's shoulders. "We were on our way to extend our sympathies to Sarah's husband." He hurried Laurel away.

She said under her breath, "I suppose that seemed rude to her, but I don't think I can stand many more of these morbid questions. Oh, I know everyone is dying to know more, but I can't even stand to think about it."

"Funerals are always hard," Ridge mused. "It seems to be something that brings out both the best and the worst sides of people."

"People!" Laurel exclaimed, looking quickly in all directions. "Seeing all of them here makes it hurt even more because it brings back other memories. We lost three of our classmates in the war, but Sarah's the only one of the girls to die."

Ridge didn't answer. He had not allowed himself to dwell on how many of his boyhood friends had fallen in defense of the Confederacy, including his only brother.

Laurel continued, "Sarah, like most of the girls we grew up with, married men from the neighborhood. That was usually just before they went off to fight in the war, or when they were home on leave. I was a bridesmaid four times. Now all the girls are married and most have at least one child. I'm the only one still single."

"That can be changed as soon as you set the date."

Laurel wondered why he didn't seem to sense her continued doubts about how a former Union spy and an ex-Confederate cavalryman could be happy together. She had thought a lot about that on the long ride back from California, but she dreaded mentioning it. She put that aside as she and Ridge approached Sarah's widower.

John Skillens was as tall as Ridge, but his black suit sagged on his skinny frame as he opened his arms and Laurel walked into them. His tears brushed her cheek as he held her, his shoulders shaking.

"Why, Laurel, why?" he moaned brokenly. "Why would anyone do such a terrible thing to my Sarah?"

She fought back her own tears. "I don't know, but I won't rest until whoever did this is caught."

He didn't seem to hear. "She never did anyone any harm in her whole life! She was a wonderful wife, a good church member, and would have been a wonderful mother if our baby . . ." He broke off, his body trembling.

"I know." Laurel gently freed herself from his embrace. "I know how much it must hurt you, John. Sarah and I were best friends. We shared a lot together."

She paused, knowing that Sarah was such an honest woman that she surely had told John about her war-time involvement with Laurel's clandestine ventures. But now wasn't the time to mention to him her theory about why Sarah had been killed.

Other sorrowing friends gathered around, giving Laurel an opportunity to say a few comforting words to John before Ridge led her away.

He said, "Laurel, you told him that you would not rest until Sarah's killer is caught. I hope you're not planning to get personally involved in that aspect."

"Of course I am!" Laurel stopped and looked up at him in surprise. "I've been trained . . ." she hesitated, glancing around to make sure that nobody was close enough to overhear. She added in a low voice, "You know what I do for a living, so why shouldn't I use that knowledge to help apprehend whoever did this?"

"Pinkerton doesn't take murder cases."

"I know, but if he won't let me do this, then I'll resign and do it on my own."

Ridge's face contorted in a disapproving manner. "You know I want you out of that agency and in our home."

"We do not yet have a home!"

Puzzled at her tone, he reminded her, "I'm working hard to

get the money to build it. It'll be ready when you are."

"You mean you've applied for amnesty?"

He wished she hadn't said that. He didn't want to discuss that now, so he said, "No, I haven't. Besides, you still owe Pinkerton one more job before you can resign. You promised him that when we were in California."

"Yes, I did, but Sarah is more important to me."

A wan smile touched Ridge's lips. "I love you, but sometimes your stubbornness and self-reliance bother me."

"It's not just Sarah this time," Laurel protested. "Whether you believe it or not, if I'm right about what happened to her, then I'm also in danger. I'm not just going to sit around and wait for him to do to me what he did to her."

Ridge tried to keep the fear in his heart from showing in his eyes. He needed to assure her, not make her more concerned than she already was. Neither did he want to let the tensions between them rise any higher and possibly lead to another argument.

He suggested, "Let's get something to eat and then get away from . . ." He left that thought unfinished at the sight of Laurel's father pushing his way through the mourners.

He hurried up to Laurel and Ridge. "I've been trying to find you, sweetheart. Maggie just hired a hack to come here." He glanced around before reaching into his suit pocket. "She brought this."

He extended an envelope to her, saying, "It's the same hand-writing as on the other one."

Licking her suddenly dry lips, Laurel took the envelope and confirmed her father's statement. She started to open it, but hesitated, again visualizing the first envelope with the enclosed newspaper clipping bearing an ominous date.

Ridge asked softly, "Do you want me to open it?"

"No, thanks." She turned her back to the people to shield the envelope from their view. Tearing off the end, she reached inside, feeling around. Frowning, she held it up before her eyes. "It's empty!"

Ridge gently took it from her and confirmed the truth of her statement. There was no newspaper clipping, no piece of paper, nothing.

"What do you suppose happened to it?" Laurel mused, glancing from Ridge to her father.

He guessed, "Maybe it was accidentally left out."

"Maybe," Laurel agreed. "Or it could have been deliberately sent this way to make me worry about what might have originally been in this envelope. Such as another date which ties me to something I did in the war. Anyway, the unknown is usually frightening, and even more so in this case because it's obvious that the handwriting is the same as on the first envelope."

Ridge lifted his eyebrows in a kind of shrug. "You can't let it bother you, Laurel, no matter why it came empty. Come on. Let's get something to eat."

She shook her head, making the dark curls bounce. "I'm not hungry, so let's just leave."

Her father protested, "You'd better eat something. You've hardly touched a bite in two days."

She stood on tiptoes to give him a quick kiss on the cheek. "It's all right, Papa. I'll be fine." She turned to Ridge and took his hand. "Now, please."

He quickly led her toward the lot behind the church where his rented rig was waiting.

"Ridge," Laurel said as they passed the back end of the church, "this second letter means I've got to do something right away, not only to see that Sarah's death is avenged, but to protect myself."

"The safest way is for me to take you back to Virginia until this is over."

"That won't work!" She stopped to look up at him. "The war's been over nearly a year and a half, but this is the first time anything like this has happened. So whoever is behind this—Maynard or someone else—has waited this long. He won't quit now. Don't you see? . . ."

She interrupted herself and lowered her gaze from Ridge to someone behind him.

"What is it?" Ridge asked, turning around.

She dropped her voice. "Porter Armistead. He's sitting in the buggy tied under that tree. I haven't seen him since sometime during the war."

"Armistead?" Ridge focused on the short man sitting alone in a black buggy. His back was turned toward the couple while he held a newspaper in front of himself. Ridge added, "I don't recall your ever mentioning him."

"There was no reason." She kept her tone low. "Growing up, he was unmercifully tormented because he was the smallest boy in the class. He was always withdrawn and quiet and alone. He had no real friends, but he was the most intelligent one in school. Yet he never liked the teacher to call on him. I'm really surprised that he came to the funeral."

"You want to speak to him?"

Laurel hesitated. "I suppose I should. In some ways, he and Sarah were alike. Maybe he identified with her. I'll introduce you, then we can go."

Armistead didn't move until Laurel spoke to him. He turned and lowered the paper. His hazel eyes widened behind wire-rimmed spectacles. He didn't smile, but somberly regarded her from a face pitted with smallpox scars. "Laurel," he said in a raspy voice. "It's been a long time."

"A very long time, Porter," she agreed, thinking that his voice always sounded as if he were talking around dry sand.

"How have you been?"

"Fine, thanks," he replied.

She remembered the pain in his eyes in their teen years when he once bashfully asked her if she would sit with him at a church picnic. She had tried to spare his feelings in declining, but the hurt had shown deeply on his sallow face. She had never forgotten.

"This is my fiancé, Ridge Granger."

Armistead nodded but didn't extend his right hand until Ridge reached his up into the buggy. "Nice to meet you, sir," Armistead murmured.

"Thanks for coming to the service," Laurel said, feeling uncomfortable without quite knowing why. "Sarah would have liked that."

Armistead shifted uneasily in the buggy seat. "She was such a nice girl. I can't understand why anyone . . ."

Laurel thought he was going to cry. She quickly changed the subject. "What are you doing now?"

"I'm a clerk and relief telegrapher in a railroad office near the *Globe* building."

"Really? I did some correspondence writing for them while I was in California."

"Yes," Armistead replied. "I saw your byline. You're a good writer." He glanced at Ridge. "I suppose you won't want her to write much longer."

Ridge said with a grin, "You suppose correctly."

Laurel rankled and took a quick breath to reply, but stopped herself. She had a very hard time relinquishing her strong, self-reliant nature to be the submissive wife that Sarah and others had accepted as natural.

An awkward silence started to build while Laurel vainly tried to think of what to say. Ridge spoke first.

"Well, Mr. Armistead, Laurel's had a trying time, as I'm sure you have. I'm going to take her home."

Armistead shoved his spectacles higher on his nose before saying, "It was good to see you, Laurel."

"Thank you. See you again, Porter."

"Yes." He picked up the newspaper while the couple walked away.

Nearing Ridge's rented rig, he mused, "He's not quite like anyone I've ever met."

"He's different, all right." Laurel let Ridge take her hand to help her into the hack. "Back when we were in our teens, it was rumored that he was a Copperhead with Southern sympathies. He left Chicago, saying he was going to New York to enlist in the Union army."

"He doesn't look like he'd make much of a soldier."

"I don't think he ever was. During the war, one of my father's friends came back from a trip to New York saying he had seen Porter there, dressed in mufti."

Laurel settled into the seat and waited until Ridge had joined her before continuing. "Father's friend told Porter that he was surprised that he wasn't in uniform. Porter claimed he was on 'detached service,' so didn't have to wear one."

"You mean, he was with the intelligence service?"

"I'm sure that's what Porter meant. But nobody around here believed him. We all figured that he had either totally evaded the conscription act, or had hired a substitute to fight in his place. That was allowed."

Ridge loosened the reins and clucked to the horse before saying, "So I heard."

"But I don't know where he would have gotten the money. His father ran off when he was little, and his mother lived hand-to-mouth. She was a big woman and Porter was always little. He's only about three inches taller than I am. Anyway, he sometimes came to school with black and blue marks on his face."

Ridge guided the horse out of the yard filled with other carriages and onto the cobblestone street. "You mean she beat him?"

"That was the speculation. Anyway, he was away most of the war. I feel sorry for him."

"It was nice of him to come to Sarah's funeral, even though he apparently didn't mix with any of the others."

"It's a little ironic, because Sarah and he were both rather plain looking. She never had many beaux, although she finally did marry. So far as I know, Porter never did. But she had friends, and he didn't."

"My only concern is for you. Let's get you to your father's house where Maggie maybe can coax you to eat something. Then I hope you'll go to bed and rest."

"Rest?" Laurel shook her head. "I'll never really do that again until whoever killed Sarah is behind bars."

"Let's hope that's soon. But if you're going to be up this evening, we need to talk. So I'll come back and take you to dinner about seven."

The flat statement was like a barb to Laurel, making her want to remind him that she liked to be asked—not told. A sharp reply leaped to mind, but she bit it back. Maybe he wasn't being presumptuous, but just wanted to be protectively close to her. He was right. They needed to talk alone because there hadn't been time since her return. Yet she was uneasy about the direction their conversation might take.

Still, sooner or later, she had to tell him about the doubts that had troubled her since she last saw him. She might as well get it done. "All right," she said. "We can talk over dinner."

Ridge changed clothes and headed back to the Bartlett home shortly after dark. His hired hack passed a house where a man sat in a rented second-story bedchamber with pen in hand.

He looked up from the desk and glanced out the window. Laurel's bedchamber was dark. Sighing softly, the man used his free hand to move the coal-oil lamp a little closer to the journal page to re-read the brief entry while the ink dried.

*She's hurting over her friend, but not nearly as much as she will. She deserves to also pay the ultimate price. But not yet. That would be too easy.*

He lowered the pen and scribbled three more words: *So, not yet.*

# Chapter 3

"That was a good dinner," Ridge commented to Laurel who was sitting to his right in the buggy. "But there were too many people around. I want to be alone with you for awhile, so let's drive along the shore. We can enjoy the full moon and watch the waves coming in."

She wasn't sure that was quite proper under the circumstances, but she longed to be held in the comfort of his arms. Maybe that's what was missing earlier. They had talked freely about Sarah and everything except what secretly troubled Laurel deeply: their future, if they were to have one together.

Ridge turned the horse off the main cobbled road and onto a small sandy one paralleling Lake Michigan. The few carriages moving through the night by the faint glow of coal-lamps were left behind. Ahead, Laurel could see the silhouette of two parked buggies facing the lake. Their lights were extinguished, indicating sparking occupants in the shadowed shelter of the buggy tops.

Ridge stopped the horse, facing the waves illuminated by a rising summer moon. They erupted into white spray as they were driven toward the shore.

"This is a beautiful spot," he mused, sliding his arm around her shoulder. His voice dropped as he gently pulled her close. "But you are more beautiful, and I've wanted to have you alone like this for such a long time."

She felt a tingle of pleasure at his words and touch, but she didn't look at him. She gazed out over the moon-dappled water, fighting with her emotions.

He whispered, "You're a perfect woman in every way."

She felt his hands gently touch her hair. A little shiver rippled over her, but she did not turn or move. His breath was on her neck, warm and pleasant. Very tenderly, he moved curls away from her left ear. She tensed when he blew faintly behind it. That was a new experience for her, and so was the delicate nibbling on her ear lobe that followed. She couldn't control a stronger shiver.

He laughed happily, a low rumbling sound like a satisfied cat purring. "That's good," he whispered, his hands moving to her face. Carefully, as though handling something precious and fragile, with one hand on either side of her face, he turned her toward him. "But," he added, "this is even better."

Light as a butterfly landing on a blossom, his lips touched hers. They lingered, slowly becoming firmer, more urgent, more demanding.

She yielded, her pulse throbbing, her lips responding to his. Her mind wanted to push him away, but her heart would not listen. *I love him, but I'm torn up inside. It won't work, yet how can I give him up?*

He lifted his head, his breath coming hard and fast. "Oh, Laurel! Laurel!" It was a moan of pleasure. "I love you so very much!"

His face was barely visible in the shelter of the buggy top, but she could see the desire in his eyes as he again bent to kiss her.

She scolded herself. *We shouldn't be doing this! We can't make this marriage work. I'm too independent! Even if I could change that, other people would make it impossible for one of us, no matter where we lived.*

She turned her face so his lips brushed her cheek.

He drew back. "What's the matter?"

She didn't turn around. "Nothing."

His tone became husky. "Don't be frightened by what we feel for each other."

"I'm not!" She said it with firmness, but she knew that wasn't the truth. No man had ever made her feel the way Ridge did, and she wasn't sure how to handle those emotions. She wanted to respond, but she resisted, keeping herself a little rigid and aloof as his lips again sought hers.

With an effort, she pushed against his chest and drew her head back. "Stop! Please stop!"

"Why?" he asked, his fingers caressing her hair. "I just want to enjoy the delight there is in holding you close and tasting your sweetness."

"I know, but we mustn't even do this!" She absently patted her hair, re-arranging the curls and trying to beat back her surging emotions.

His voice hardened. "There is something wrong. What is it?"

The answer leaped to her lips. *I love you, and you love me, but that's not enough! We could never overcome the obstacles that others place in our way!* She said, "Please take me home."

"Not until you tell me what's troubling you."

"I can't, not tonight, anyway. So, please!"

He hesitated, then abruptly turned and released the reins from the buggy whip socket.

"Ridge, please don't be angry!"

He ignored her, lifted the light whip from its socket, and snapped it sharply over the horse's back. "Get up!" he called.

The horse leaped forward so suddenly that Laurel's head snapped back. She closed her eyes, shutting out the moonlight on the water, but she could not block out the anguish that suddenly flared in her heart.

After a fitful night of tossing and fretting, Laurel threw back her covers as dawn touched the window in the bedchamber where she had grown up. She didn't want to risk Maggie or her father sensing something at breakfast, so she decided to dress, skip eating, and slip down the back stairs hoping she wouldn't be seen.

She forced her thoughts away from last night to focus on what had to be done today. She wanted to know what progress the authorities had made in solving Sarah's murder, and she must report to Allan Pinkerton that she was back from California.

*But I'm not ready to do that,* she told herself as she washed in the flowered white ceramic basin on the marble-topped nightstand by her high bed. *First, I've got to talk to the police.*

Even after she was dressed, the Queen Anne mirror with its graceful scrolls over her Chippendale chest of drawers mocked her efforts to hide the surface signs of a restless and tearful night. But, satisfied she had hidden the evidence as best she could, she put on her bonnet and left a note on her door. She slipped out unseen into the fresh morning air.

It took some time to find a hack, but when she was on the way to the police station in Sarah's neighborhood, Laurel was fully composed and self-assured.

The precinct was housed in a brick building that reeked of cigar smoke, stale perspiration, and un-emptied spittoons. It took a strong mental effort to keep from wrinkling her nose while identifying herself to the gruff desk sergeant. Though he was twice her age, he swept her petite figure with appreciative eyes before calling the lead detective on Sarah's murder case.

Laurel had met Ulysses Kelly at the murder scene. He was a heavy-set man of about thirty, with a perpetually flushed face and red hair. He approached her with a package in his big hands.

"I'm glad you came in, Miss Bartlett," he said, making the ends of his reddish mustache quiver. "I need to ask you some more questions."

"Of course. I'll do anything I can to help."

She followed him into a small windowless room. "Have you made any progress in solving my friend's murder?"

"Not yet." Kelly motioned for her to sit in one of two badly scarred chairs across from a battered table. His pale blue eyes flickered over her before returning to her face. "I want to review your statement."

She waited while he opened the package and pulled out some papers. He laid them on the table and tapped them with freckled fingers that were thick as sausages.

"Miss Bartlett, are you sure that you and your beau didn't touch anything before the beat officer got there?"

"Not a thing." She suppressed a shudder and closed her eyes, seeing the whole ghastly scene all over again. Opening her eyes, she continued, "After Ridge checked her pulse and confirmed what we already knew, we closed the door to the back porch and waited outside her house until the first officer arrived. We started to follow him inside, but he told us to wait until the detectives arrived. That's what we did."

"There's something very strange about this," Kelly mused. "I mean, it not only happened in broad daylight, but from evidence at the scene, the perpetrator obviously spent some time there."

"He did? How can you know that?"

"I'll ask the questions, if you don't mind." Leaning back in his chair, Kelly thoughtfully studied her face for a few seconds before continuing. "What do you know of her husband?"

"John Skillens? Surely you don't suspect him!"

"I suspect everybody until I've checked them out."

Laurel briefly told about John having worked in the local funeral parlor before the war, and then on a lake boat after he returned. "He's a good man," she concluded. "He loved Sarah. He wouldn't hurt her."

The detective made a non-committal grunting sound. "How about her neighbors? She ever have trouble with any of them?"

"Not to my knowledge. She lived there all her life. When her parents died, they willed her the house."

"What about her beaux?"

"She really didn't have any serious ones. I think she was about ready to accept herself as a spinster when John began courting her."

"What else do you know about her background?"

Laurel quickly dropped her eyes and hesitated. She could not tell about Sarah's part in helping her prepare for her clandestine spying trips into the Confederacy.

"Well?" Kelly demanded sharply, leaning across the table. "Don't try to hide anything from me."

Calling on the skills she developed during the war to disarm a suspicious man, she smiled at him. "What makes you think I'd do that?"

"I saw it in your face. Now, what is it that you don't want to tell me?"

Laurel tried to keep her smile in place while she scrambled to find words that would evade but not be outright lies. That was not easy because in her teens she had rebelled against both her father and God, and telling lies hadn't troubled her. Her spying activities and detective work also required falsehoods.

However, after she met Ridge, and both made recommitments of their faith, her spiritual life had changed. She had also been reconciled to her father. Still, telling falsehoods was so easy that she struggled with her conscience over being fully truthful all the time.

Before she could reply to Kelly, the door behind her burst open. She whirled around, eager to have a diversion.

A burly man in a rumpled dark suit glanced from Laurel to Kelly. He regarded Laurel with cold gray eyes but curtly asked the detective, "What've you got here?"

Kelly rose to his feet. "'Morning, lieutenant. This is Miss Laurel Bartlett. She and her beau found the body of Sarah Skillens. I was reviewing her statement. Miss Bartlett, this is Lieutenant Seth Pierce."

"How do you do?" she replied with a little smile, noticing that his nose had been broken and grown back with the end slightly twisted to the left.

He glanced briefly at her, then glowered across the table. "Kelly, why didn't you go to her instead of having her come in here?"

Before he could answer, Laurel exclaimed, "I came in on my own, Lieutenant. Naturally, I want to do everything possible to solve my friend's murder."

Pierce gave her a cold stare. "Thanks for your concern, Miss, but hereafter, stay away from here. We have work to do, and I don't want any distractions."

Laurel felt herself flush. "Sir, I'm just trying to be of help—"

"Don't help!" he interrupted sharply. He shifted his eyes to Kelly. "Didn't you get her statement at the scene?"

"Yes, sir, but I wanted to clarify some—"

"Then do it in the field!" Pierce broke in. "Go interview all the neighbors."

"I already did that, and nobody knows anything!"

"I don't believe that! This happened in broad daylight, so

somebody must have seen something. Go back over the crime scene!" Pierce's voice rose angrily. "Maybe you overlooked something!"

Laurel felt sorry for Kelly being criticized in front of her. "Lieutenant," she said sharply, "please don't be angry with him over what I did."

He shot back roughly, "Who asked you?"

Laurel leaped from her chair. "Sir! I am not used to being spoken to in such a tone!"

"Then get out where you can't hear me!" He stepped aside and held the door wide.

Laurel stared in open-mouthed surprise. "What?"

Kelly protested, "Lieutenant, that's no way—"

"Not another word from you Kelly! I know your ways. You saw another pretty face and wanted an excuse to talk to her. Your job is in the field, not here!"

Pierce turned to glare at Laurel. "The door's open, Miss."

Humiliated and angry, she protested, "Sir, I am going to help find whoever killed Sarah! I was—"

"Good-bye, Miss," Pierce interrupted. "And Kelly, if you or anyone else wants to interview this woman again, do it outside this office. Whatever you do, don't tell her anything more. I don't want this investigation hindered by meddling outsiders. Is that clear?"

Laurel didn't hear Kelly's reply because the lieutenant slammed the door in her face. Stunned and in a frustrated fury, she started to reopen the door but the desk sergeant's voice stopped her.

"I wouldn't do that, Miss," he said quietly.

She whirled toward him, about to vent her fury on him, but she hesitated upon seeing an attractive young woman standing across the counter from the sergeant. She had a round, pretty face and blonde hair pulled back in the current style, yet it didn't make her look severe.

She said, "Sergeant Kerston is right. It's not a smart thing to do. But you musn't mind the lieutenant. His wife died not that long ago. He's mad at the world."

Instantly mollified, Laurel whispered, "I'm sorry!"

"He's a good detective," the woman added. "So's Kelly. They'll find your friend's slayer."

Laurel frowned, trying to place the woman.

She said, "My name's Charity Dahlgren. I saw you at your friend's funeral where you talked to Vance Cooper. I work for the *Illustrated Press*. Do you have time for a cup of tea?"

The question made Laurel realize she hadn't had breakfast, but she wasn't in the mood to talk with a newspaper correspondent after the unexpected encounter with the lieutenant. "Sorry, Miss Dahlgren," she replied, "but I've got to see somebody right away."

"How about lunch? And please call me Charity."

Laurel started to decline, but Charity said quickly, "You're not going to be welcome around here, so the only news you'll hear from now on is what's in the papers."

She paused, winked at the sergeant and then added to Laurel, "Unless you have a friend who works the police beat and can give you inside information."

Laurel nodded in understanding. "Lunch sounds good."

"Good! How about the Excalibur Hotel at noon?"

"All right. I'll see you there." Laurel left to find a hack for the ride to Pinkerton's office.

The summer's heat beat upon Chicago's streets as Laurel

paid the hackman and headed for the door under the sign of the all-seeing eye. It read, "The Eye that Never Sleeps."

She rehearsed what to say as she entered the building and headed for Allan Pinkerton's office. She wanted to help solve Sarah's death, but Pinkerton didn't handle murder cases. Laurel hoped he would make an exception for her.

A powerfully built and bearded man in his forties, Pinkerton rose from behind his desk and greeted Laurel warmly. "Welcome back! I knew you got in Monday, and expected you to report in the next day. After I read the newspapers, I understood why you didn't come in. Sorry about your friend."

"Thank you." Laurel shifted uncomfortably in the chair and laid her reticule on the desk. "It was awful."

"Isn't she the same one who helped you during your war-time trips south?"

"Yes." Laurel hesitated, her mind snapping back to how it had all started.

Even before the war, Pinkerton was known as America's most famous detective. When the hostilities began, he had formed and headed up the first U.S. Secret Service and spy ring under General George McClellan.

Laurel's sixteen-year-old brother had volunteered for the Union Army and was killed fighting the Confederacy. Wanting to avenge his death, Laurel had persuaded Pinkerton to let her spy against the South once she turned eighteen. With Sarah's help, she had been very successful. Now Laurel debated whether to tell Pinkerton that she was concerned Sarah's death might have somehow been connected to those clandestine war-time activities.

Pinkerton broke into Laurel's thoughts. He asked, "Who's the detective on the case?"

"His name's Kelly."

"Ulysses Kelly?" Pinkerton inquired. When she nodded, he

added, "He's a good man, but has a weakness for the ladies."

Laurel suppressed a smile, knowing that Pinkerton had the same reputation. "You think he'll find Sarah's murderer?"

"Let's hope so." Pinkerton leaned back and laced his fingers behind his head. "Did you know that I was the first police detective in Chicago?"

Laurel's eyebrows arched in surprise. "No, I didn't."

"I was elected deputy sheriff of Kane County in 1848, and two years later moved to Cook County to join the police force as its first and only detective."

She smiled, trying to charm him into letting her do what she secretly had in mind. "I guess there's a lot I don't know about you."

He seemed pleased. He was a man who delighted in keeping secrets which could be revealed at opportune times. "Did you know I was also an abolitionist and had a way station on the Underground Railroad?"

"I didn't know that either," Laurel admitted. "But I do know that after a series of express and railroad robberies, you opened this business."

"The Pinkerton National Detective Agency," he said proudly. "I pioneered this business, and we solved a lot of railroad crimes before the war interrupted that."

He paused, then said quickly, "You did a good job on that California railroad case. I've still got your wire saying you wanted to resign to get married. I hope you've change your mind by now. Have you?"

The same doubts that had often troubled her made Laurel hesitate. She hedged, saying, "I promised to do one more job for you. I'll do that, and then we'll see."

He fixed her with shrewd eyes. "Having some second thoughts about marrying that ex-Confederate?"

Laurel had no intention of discussing such personal matters with her employer. "Before I ask what assignment you next have in mind for me, I'd like to ask a favor."

He shook his head. "The answer is 'no.' "

"But you don't even know what it is!"

"I can guess. You want to be assigned to work on your friend's case."

Laurel wasn't really surprised that he knew her objective. He had a reputation for making shrewd observations. "Yes, I do," she admitted.

"I can understand that, Laurel, but I have another case pending where a woman should be more effective than a male operative. I'm going to hold you to your promise."

"But I owe Sarah so much! I've got to help solve her murder!"

"I also understand that, but let Kelly and Pierce do it. I need you to get on this next case."

Stalling, trying to think of how to avoid that, she asked, "What kind of case?"

"I have a client who has a substantial monetary stake in the success of the last major railroad tunnel being cut through a quarter-mile of granite in the Sierra Nevada Mountains."

"You want me to return to California?" she exclaimed with indignation.

"Yes, since the Central Pacific Railroad is headquartered in Sacramento and you know some of their people. You also know something about their rush to quickly lay as much track eastward as possible. I believe the C.P. had just started on that last tunnel while you were in California."

That was true. She knew about the thousands of Chinese workers who were hand-drilling the Summit Tunnel through the mountain's backbone of solid granite.

Pinkerton continued, "Getting that tunnel built is part of the race to remove the last major obstacle before tracks are laid across the Nevada-Utah deserts to link up with the Union Pacific working west from Omaha. There are huge financial rewards given by the government for every mile of track laid. So, when can you leave?"

His self-assured attitude aggravated her. She snatched her reticule from the desk top and abruptly stood. "I've never broken my word, but you leave me no choice! I resign!"

She spun toward the door and took a few quick, angry steps before his voice stopped her.

"Laurel, wait!"

She didn't turn, but rested her hand on the knob.

"You're the right person for this job," he said, coming around the desk to stand behind her. "So let's compromise."

Hopefully, she faced him. "What do you have in mind?"

"I'll have to convince my client that you're the only person for this case, but you have some pressing personal business that will take you, say, a week. I'll give you seven days leave of absence to work on your friend's case."

She shook her head. "Thirty days!"

"Two weeks."

Hesitating, she asked, "What if it's not solved by then?"

"Ask me then. Now, do we have an agreement?"

She hoped it wouldn't take any longer than that because she would have no income and her savings were limited. "All right," she replied, "we have an agreement."

Walking out onto the street again, she paused under the sign of the all-seeing eye. Charity Dahlgren might be able to funnel some inside detective information about Kelly's investigation, but that wouldn't be enough. There had to be a way to circumvent the lieutenant's order for Laurel to stay away from the precinct.

*But how?* she wondered, glancing up and down the street for a hack. She didn't see one, but her gaze fell on the building housing the *Chicago Globe*. An idea popped into her mind. She started walking toward the *Globe*.

# *Chapter 4*

A gnawing sense of concern that he could not shake followed Ridge down the hotel stairs the next morning. In the lobby, the desk clerk handed him a wire. Ridge took it to a chair by the outside window, his thoughts still on Laurel.

He had not slept well after leaving her at her father's home. The warm glow of pleasure at the memory of her lips was offset by trying to understand her abrupt insistence that he take her home. He also recalled that she had been somewhat aloof when he mentioned setting their wedding date shortly after she and her aunt arrived from California.

While opening the telegram, he wondered, *Did something happen after I last saw her in Sacramento? Or is she worried that somebody might try to kill her, like Sarah?*

Ridge forced his mind back to the wire. It read, "Investment capital ready. Important we talk. Please wire arrival date." It was signed *Griff*.

Jubal Griffin, Junior, and Ridge had been friends since childhood. At twenty-four, Griff was a year older than Ridge, still single, and expected to remain so. A Yankee bayonet wound near the spine had confined him to a rolling chair for life.

Gold was a rare commodity in the post-war South, but when Ridge had seen Griff months ago in Virginia, Griff confided that he had some hidden away. He wanted to invest in Ridge's business venture as a silent partner.

Griff reasoned that this was sensible because Ridge was doing the physical work in the field and needed to be free to make quick decisions. Investing also made Griff feel that he was not helpless and could make a living.

At the time, Ridge had declined in order to prove to himself that he could start with nothing and earn enough to build Laurel a fine home. Since then, his land buying venture grew beyond what he had envisioned. Prospective Chicago investors with big money were interested, but demanded control, which Ridge refused. Griff would not make such a demand.

*I should go see Griff again,* Ridge told himself as he walked out into the sunny summer morning. *But Laurel will have to come along. I don't believe she's in any danger, especially from Sam Maynard. But I don't want to take a chance on leaving her here alone just in case she's right about why Sarah was killed.*

He would have to discuss the trip with Laurel before answering Griff. He knew she planned to see Pinkerton when his office opened. Perhaps he could catch her before she left there. He stepped to the curb and hailed a hack.

Laurel's past association with the *Globe's* publisher allowed her to bypass the editors and be admitted into Orville Seymour's office. A man in his fifties with a receding hairline, he stood in front of a large glass window which gave him a view of the workmen in the editorial department.

"I heard you were back," he said by way of greeting. "Sit." He turned to face her. "As a stringer, you did a good job on those stories you wrote for us from California."

"Thank you." That was a good sign. She seated herself in the chair across from his desk. As usual, she tried to avoid showing her distaste for the smelly dead cigar in the ash tray. She added, "I liked writing for you."

He sat opposite her, absently reached for the cigar, then stopped to ask bluntly, "What can I do for you?"

She gathered her thoughts, marshaling the words in a way she thought most likely would make him agree to her plan. "Mr. Seymour, I believe I can benefit your paper by something I have in mind."

He raised gray eyebrows that matched his heavy mustache and bushy sideburns. "You want to offer me a benefit? That's a novel opening to what I suspect is going to be something you want. Right?"

She was momentarily disarmed by his perception, but she smiled confidently. Her eyes dropped to his clean-shaven chin which showed above the tight white collar and broad-lapelled jacket. "Perhaps we can both derive some benefit from my proposal."

He smiled, obviously intrigued. "Let's hear it."

She took a quick, short breath, inhaling the good smell of paper and ink along with the cigar's stench. "I've noticed that the *Illustrated Press* has a woman correspondent on staff. I'm sure that's caused quite a bit of controversy among other publishers."

She stopped speaking, leaving the words as bait while she closely scrutinized his face for reaction.

It showed nothing, so she continued. "I would think that women readers would identify with her, and so gain more circulation for the *Press*."

His smile returned. "So you want to become the first female correspondent on the *Globe*, and to do that simply to boost our circulation?"

She ignored the hint of sarcasm in his words and avoided a direct reply. Instead, she reminded him, "You have indicated satisfaction with my ability to write as a stringer. Now I'd like to show you what I can do as a staff member here in Chicago."

He half-closed both eyes in thought. "I see. And I suppose you have a particular beat in mind that you'd like to cover?"

She sensed that he was ahead of her, so she plunged ahead with a brief nod. "Yes, I do."

He leaned back in his chair and grinned at her. "The police beat, no doubt?"

She blinked, aware that he was farther ahead of her than she realized. "I'd like that."

"I'll bet you would! Then you could work toward helping solve your friend's murder while getting paid by this paper." He abruptly leaned forward across the desk. "Miss Bartlett, you are the most audacious young woman I've ever known. I'll give you credit for that. But the answer is 'no,' and you should know why."

Laurel tried to keep her disappointment from showing. "Yes, I do. Vance Cooper was recently hired to report on police activities. But the way this city is growing, he probably could use an assistant."

She saw no point in mentioning that Vance had made an appointment to interview her this afternoon at her father's home.

Seymour slowly shook his head while a faint smile touched his lips. "You're a saucy one, all right. Quick with answers, and you don't quit. You'd probably make a good correspondent. But you're also likely to marry, move away, or otherwise leave me right back where I am now." He stood, indicating the interview was over.

Laurel also rose to her feet. "Mr. Seymour, I understand your position, and I respect it. But I assure you that I would bring different insight to reporting than Mr. Cooper or any other male correspondent would. I would like you to think about it. I'll be back tomorrow."

He picked up the cigar, then replaced it. "Don't you understand what I said, Miss Bartlett?"

She turned toward the door. "Yes, but I also know what I can do for this paper. So I'll be back."

"Just a minute."

She turned expectantly.

He scowled thoughtfully. "You have no police beat experience, and Vance Cooper does. He would probably resent having another correspondent on his beat, especially a woman. So how about serving a short probationary period as his assistant? Standard pay."

She tried to control her rush of relief. "That would be fine with me."

"Then I'll give you a week."

"Two weeks." The words popped out.

He chuckled. "I hope you can do as well with Cooper and the police as you have with me. Especially Seth Pierce. He eats correspondents; swallows them whole."

"He may try, but he won't swallow me whole."

Seymour grinned. "I hope you're right. Report here to Cooper at seven o'clock Monday morning. I'll let him know you're coming and what your responsibilities are."

She nodded, deciding that she would say nothing about this when she met with Cooper. "Thank you, Mr. Seymour," she said, and left.

🌑

Ridge's hired hack passed the railroad station on the way to Pinkerton's office. Ridge's eyes casually flickered over the carriages arriving or departing the busy depot. His thoughts were still on Laurel, so the hack was past the long, barn-like structure when Ridge suddenly whirled around to look back.

Sam? A man just turning away from a hotel omnibus was short like Sam Maynard. Ridge couldn't see the face, but a temple piece along the side of his head showed he wore spectacles. "Driver, stop here!" Ridge ordered.

He leaped out, shoved a greenback into the driver's hand and ran as fast as his limp would permit across the cobblestone street and into the station. As when Laurel and her aunt had arrived, it was a mass of shifting humanity with baggage. It moved in two general directions: toward the cars on the tracks or outside where carriages waited at the curb.

Ridge's height allowed him to see over the tops of most people's heads. *There! Heading for the cars! But I can't be sure it's Sam.* Ridge hurried after him, working his way through the travelers and their baggage, trying to close the distance between him and the short man.

"Watch where you're going!" a pear-shaped matronly woman snapped at him as his leg brushed her carpet bag. She jerked it back so suddenly it fell open. "Now look what you've done!" she cried indignantly as her comb and hairbrush clattered to the floor.

"I'm sorry. It was an accident." He bent to pick up the items. "Here. Let me help—"

"Don't touch it!" She glared at him. "Rebel! I hear it in your voice! Get away from me!"

Ridge choked back the angry response that leaped to his lips. Wordlessly, he turned away and pushed through the small cluster of passers-by who had stopped to watch.

He glanced hurriedly in the direction the short man with spectacles had been heading. There was no sign of him. Ridge rose on tiptoes for a better look over the shifting crowds. Nothing. He widened his search, but with no better results.

Moving as rapidly as possible, he left the depot and hastened along the platform, his eyes skimming passengers boarding a train on the tracks. He walked as fast as he could along the cars, straining to peer into the windows. He reached the last car as the train began moving.

Not a sign of him! Ridge gave up the search and slowly re-entered the station. *It couldn't have been Sam. But even if it was, that doesn't mean he had anything to do with Sarah's death. But if I tell Laurel I think I saw him, she's going to be unnecessarily concerned. If there was some way I could be sure it was Sam. . . .*

"Of course!" he muttered aloud. *Ask Griff!* Ridge turned toward the telegraph office, then stopped. If he took time to send a wire, he would miss Laurel at Pinkerton's. Maybe he already had. But it was worth a try. Ridge again changed direction and moved toward the street exits.

❧

Laurel walked away from the *Globe* building with mixed emotions. She was grateful that Seymour had agreed to let her work a police beat. Now she could legitimately have direct access to inside police information which might help solve Sarah's murder. Charity Dahlgren was surely right when she said that Kelly and Pierce were good detectives.

But, Laurel reminded herself, I can't tell them what I think the killer's motive might be, because then I'd have to admit what Sarah and I did during the war. I've got to keep that to myself.

Out of the corner of her eye, she glimpsed a horse suddenly swerve toward her. Instinctively, she started to step back before she realized the animal had been turned so that the hack it pulled could stop at the curb.

"Laurel!" Ridge's voice from the back seat made her look beyond the horse.

"Good morning," she called as he stepped down.

"You sound cheerful," he replied, turning toward her with a grin. "I assume your meeting with Pink . . ." he broke off at the sudden warning look in her eyes.

She glanced around at people passing both directions, but nobody even looked at her.

"Sorry," he said, lowering his voice and taking her elbow to guide her back out of the foot traffic and near a store front. "I mean, how did your meeting go?"

"Wonderful! I got a leave of absence."

"That's good, I suppose, but you'll need some money while you're off, so I'll give you . . ."

"No, please!" She stopped him as he reached inside his suit coat. "I don't need anything."

"Don't be offended, Laurel. We're going to be married, so what difference does it make if I help out a little now?"

He noticed something flit across her face, alerting him to some reservation. Before he could comment, she spoke.

"Thank you, but I wouldn't feel right about that. Besides, I got a replacement job with the *Globe*."

He frowned. "I think we should go somewhere and talk."

She stalled. "You're not going to be angry with me for working again, are you?"

"Not angry, just puzzled. Do you want to take a hack someplace quiet so we can discuss everything, or just find a restaurant close by?"

She didn't want to get into a heavy discussion this morning for fear it would lead into the one area she did not want to deal with, at least, not yet. "A restaurant," she decided. "There's one right down this street."

By the time coffee was served at their table, Laurel had told Ridge about her three meetings that morning. He reported receiving Griff's wire, but deliberately avoided mentioning his possible sighting of Sam Maynard.

"So," she said when he had finished. "Are you going to Virginia to see him?"

"I really need to, but not alone. Come with me."

She took a slow deep breath. "You know I can't do that. I've only got a few weeks to help the police solve Sarah's murder."

She saw his jaw muscle twitch and a flash of anger in his eyes, but his voice was level when he replied. "If I didn't know how much we love each other, I'd say you're having second thoughts about getting married."

It was obviously a statement meant to draw her out, but she refused to let that happen. She said, "This isn't the time or place to speak of such a matter."

His eyes narrowed slightly and a hard glint showed in them. "Are you saying that you're not sure about us?"

She impulsively reached out and laid her hand on his. "Please don't make an issue of this right now. I am so concerned about what happened to Sarah." Laurel looked around hastily and lowered her voice. "And what I'm afraid it might mean to . . . you know. So don't you understand that all else must wait until this awful tragedy is resolved?"

He glanced down at her hand lightly resting on his, then lifted his eyes to hers. "I love you, Laurel, love you with all my heart."

"And I love you, Ridge. But sometimes love has to wait."

He didn't want to hear that. But having possibly seen Sam awhile ago made Ridge admit to himself that Laurel might be right about her life being in jeopardy. Still, he wouldn't allow himself to really believe that his boyhood friend could do such a thing until he learned from Griff if Sam had been off the peninsula the last few days. Even if he had been, that didn't mean he was involved in murder.

"Let the police handle her case," Ridge urged. "You said that woman reporter, Charity, what's her name? . . . ."

"Dahlgren."

"Charity Dahlgren. She told you that both detectives you spoke to are good men. Let them do their job. You come with me to Virginia where you'll be safe while I talk with Griff."

She withdrew her hand from his and picked up her cup with both hands. Slowly, she lifted it to her lips but stopped there, looking at him. "I'd like to, Ridge, I really would. But I just can't."

"I see!" His tone turned hard. "After we're married, are you going to disagree with everything I suggest?"

She resented the tone. Her voice rose as she replied hotly. "I have been self-reliant since I got separated from my father at the first Battle of Manassas!"

"Yes, I know that," he replied wearily. "Back when you were barely fifteen."

"Then you also know that I am not the average submissive Southern woman that I've heard so much about."

"I'm not asking you to be submissive!" The angry words spewed out of him. "I respect your opinions, but I also have mine, and common sense tells me that getting you away from here is the safest and wisest thing for both of us! Now, doesn't that make sense to you, too?"

She glanced nervously around and saw that the few other patrons had turned to stare. "Please, Ridge," she whispered, "keep your voice down."

His gaze swept the onlookers who promptly turned away

from his disapproving scowl. Swinging back to her, he said, "Please answer my question."

She sipped from her cup, eyes downcast from his, her mind whirling. She knew he was right, but running away for awhile would not solve the problem if she was right about the motive of Sarah's killer. Besides, she had a tight deadline from both Pinkerton and Seymour.

"Well?" Ridge prompted.

"I am not going to sit here and discuss this any longer," she quietly told him. "We can be alone tonight to finish this discussion."

He didn't answer for several seconds, but drained his cup while his eyes remained locked firmly onto hers. "I think," he said at last, lowering the cup, "I have already heard enough. There's no need to waste any more time talking tonight."

He rose so abruptly that his chair tipped over. As he grabbed and righted it, Laurel warned, "Don't you walk out on me again as you did that time in Virginia!"

Wordlessly, he strode off without looking back.

Laurel placed her right hand on her forehead so her palm covered her eyes. Nobody could see the hurt and frustrated tears that suddenly formed there.

The Excalibur Hotel was as ornate as any Laurel had seen, but the elegant marble walls in the lobby and the massive matching pillars were wasted on her. She would gladly have skipped this meeting, but there had been no way to reach Charity to cancel. Laurel forced a smile and walked across the luxurious carpeting to where Charity rose from a Louis XV wingback sofa to greet her.

After they were seated in the hotel restaurant with its spotless tablecloths and black-suited waiters, Laurel said, "I should tell you right away that since we met this morning, I've accepted a position with the *Globe*."

"Congratulations! I didn't think that Orville Seymour would ever hire a woman correspondent."

"It's probationary," Laurel explained, then added quickly, "I hope you and I won't be competitors, but it's only fair to let you know I'll be working with Vance Cooper on the police beat."

Charity's pale blonde eyebrows arched in surprise. "What did Vance say about that?"

"He doesn't know yet, at least, he didn't when I left Mr. Seymour."

"I see." Charity waited while the waiter placed the napkin in her lap.

"You don't think Vance will like it?" Laurel asked as the waiter also fixed her napkin.

"I've only know him a short time, but I've heard that he can be difficult. But tell me, why did you hire on to a newspaper?"

Laurel thoughtfully regarded the woman sitting across from her. Charity was attractive and likable. Laurel decided to cautiously explore how much she could be trusted.

"Well, after the lieutenant ordered me not to interfere with Sarah's case, I appreciated your offer to help keep me apprised of what's going on inside the police department. But Sarah was my dearest friend, and I decided that I could best help solve her murder if I could have direct access to police records. I hope you're not offended."

"Not at all. I know what it's like to scratch and claw in a man's world. But I hope you won't think of me as a competitor. I would prefer that we be friends."

"I'd like that, too."

The waiter brought bills of fare which they studied in silence until their choices had been made. When the waiter left to fill their order, Charity lowered her voice and leaned across the table.

"Don't look now, but do you know that man eating alone in the corner?"

Laurel casually glanced around the room, ending up by letting her gaze sweep past the corner. "Oh, yes," she said, turning back to Charity. "That's Porter Armistead. Why do you ask?"

"Because he kept looking at you, but the moment you started to look around, he turned away. Is he an old beau?"

Laurel laughed lightly. "Hardly! But I have known him since we were little. He was at the funeral. That's the first time I'd seen him since early in the war."

"I see. Speaking of the funeral, would you like to hear what I learned from Kelly after you left this morning?"

"I'd like very much to know that."

"All right, but first, you should know that I have read your report given to the police at the time her body was discovered. I also read what Kelly wrote after he interrogated you. He said something that I found rather curious."

"Oh? What was that?"

"He thinks that you're not telling him everything."

Laurel licked her lips in sudden concern before asking, "Why would he think that?"

"The report doesn't say. But he's an experienced detective, good at reading people's mannerisms. He must have seen something."

Charity paused, her eyes probing Laurel's before she asked softly, "Did he?"

Laurel knew she should not have looked away, but she did.

"So!" Charity exclaimed. "What is it?"

Laurel didn't reply while calling on her quick and capable mind for a disarming answer. But Charity spoke first.

"If we're going to be friends, and we're going to work together to help Kelly solve your friend's murder, we need to be honest with each other. Don't you agree?"

Laurel absently dabbed at her lips with the napkin, trying to decide what she should say.

# Chapter 5

L aurel decided to trust Charity with a limited bit of information to see if she would betray it. Replacing her napkin, Laurel said, "All right, I'll tell you, but only on condition that you keep it between us."

Charity shook her head. "I can't do that if it's something Kelly should know to help solve this case."

"It's related, but it's only my suspicion. I have no proof, yet I'm concerned that I may be right. That's all I can say unless you promise to keep this confidential."

For several seconds, Charity sat silently, her face puckered with lines of concentration. Finally, she nodded. "As a reporter, I'm probably going to regret this, but as one woman to another, I understand. You have my word."

Laurel looked around, making sure no one was close enough to overhear. Porter Armistead had a newspaper in front of him. He lowered it to take a bite of food from his fork, then replaced the paper, ignoring the women.

"Not here," Laurel whispered to Charity. "Walk with me after we eat, and I'll tell you."

Charity's face showed disappointment, but she agreed. "Fine, but in the meantime, will you answer some questions about your friendship with Sarah?"

"Of course."

While they ate, Laurel replied to Charity's queries. Sarah was a buxom woman, plain-featured, and had few beaux in her teen years. Except for being active in her church, she was otherwise a quiet, retiring person with no known enemies.

She had met John Skillens before the war when he worked in the local funeral parlor. He had sailed on the Great Lakes until the conflict ended but had not served in the armed forces. Laurel didn't know if he had hired a substitute or been physically exempt. He had returned to the mortuary after he and Sarah were married. Their first child had died while Laurel was in California.

"I think that's about it," Laurel concluded, placing her spoon on the empty desert plate.

Charity mused, "There doesn't seem to be any reason why someone would kill her. Yet the police think it was premeditated, and not a random act of violence."

"How did they come to that conclusion?"

Glancing around, Charity commented, "There are some details that Pierce and Kelly don't want to be general knowledge, so why don't we finish our conversation outside?"

"That's fine with me," Laurel said, rising. "But first I'd better speak to Porter. He's too shy to come over to our table. I'll introduce you to him."

When she did, Armistead asked, "Are you the one whose name I've seen in the *Illustrated Press*?"

"Yes, and I'm pleased that you've noticed."

"I always read the crime stories. Unfortunately, there's so much of it lately."

"I agree," Charity replied. "There is a lot of it."

He cleared his throat. "Excuse me if I'm out of line for asking, but I've known Sarah since she was a little girl. How are the police doing in catching her killer?"

Charity said, "I'm sorry there's nothing new."

"Too bad. I hope they soon catch her slayer."

"So do I," Laurel added fervently.

She and Charity said good-bye to Armistead and walked out of the restaurant together.

Sauntering along the sidewalk, Charity spoke above the sounds of carriages and horsemen passing in both directions. "Did he ever court Sarah?"

"Not to my knowledge. Why do you ask?"

"Idle curiosity. Now, you were going to tell me something confidential."

"And you were going to tell me why the police think Sarah's murder was premeditated."

"You first," Charity suggested.

Laurel hesitated. She considered herself a good judge of human nature, and had taken an instant liking to Charity. But training and experience made Laurel decide to be discreet in how much she told about her suspicions of Sam Maynard. She had to choose her words carefully.

Ridge looked around the small, dingy second-story office with a small sign on the door: "Emory Brush Private Investigations." Ridge's anger which had caused him to abruptly walk out on Laurel had cooled. His feelings toward her hadn't changed. He had come to provide a means of protecting Laurel when he couldn't be near her, if she would forgive his stalking out on her.

The dark-complected man in his middle thirties across the desk from Ridge looked as if he needed a shave, although there was no sign of stubble. He shifted his two-hundred-plus pounds in the squeaking chair and listened until Ridge finished speaking.

"That's it?" he asked when Ridge fell silent.

"That's it, Mr. Brush. As I told you, the desk sergeant at the police station highly recommended you. He also said you had discussed the case with your former partner, Kelly. I think your detective experience and reputation for working quietly is what I'm looking for."

Emory Brush waved the compliment aside with his large hand. "All you want me to do is keep an eye on her to protect her, yet not let her know what I'm doing?"

"Basically, yes. Make sure nobody follows her, or bothers her in any way. I don't really think she has any reason to be concerned because of this fellow she saw at the train station. But after I thought I saw him there today, I can't take a chance. I'm not so concerned about Sam Maynard as somebody else; someone we don't know about."

"Right. But if she does get suspicious, I'm to say that I'm a private detective investigating the murder, but I can't say who hired me."

"Right. Let's hope she thinks it's her father or Sarah's husband."

"Whoever killed the victim," Brush commented, "took an awful risk of being seen, doing it in daylight after first taking time to tie and gag her that way. I only heard of that in the war when it was used as a kind of punishment for some soldiers. I saw it done a couple of times."

The murder scene flashed into Ridge's mind. Sarah, obviously already gagged, must have been forced to sit on the floor. She had been required to raise her knees so a three-foot long stick could be placed under them. Her arms were extended so the stick rested on the bend of the elbows. Her hands were tied together, resulting in very limited movement and prolonged pain before she had been suffocated. Sarah had not died quickly or easily.

Ridge forced the image away and reached for his wallet.

"Does that mean the police think Sarah's killer had a military background?"

"It's a possible clue because he got the idea from somewhere outside of civilian life." Brush stood and came around the desk, taking slow, deliberate steps, a holdover from his uniform days of walking a street beat. He was two inches taller than Ridge and outweighed him by fifty pounds, yet there was no sign of flab on him.

He extended a large hand and took the greenbacks Ridge held out. "Thanks, Mr. Granger. Now you can go about your business without worrying about her."

"I'm depending on that." Ridge walked out to begin mentally composing a reply to Griff's wire.

Charity stopped so abruptly that a matronly woman following almost bumped into her. "Are you sure?" she asked Laurel after the other woman passed, muttering.

"No, I'm not. It looked like him with the glasses and his short stature, but I couldn't be positive."

"So you don't have any solid reason to suspect this Sam Maynard, except that you think he might be angry with you and Sarah because of something that happened in the war. And that's something you won't tell me about?"

"I can't tell you, Charity. But I feel strongly that whether it was Sam Maynard or someone else, his motive goes back to the war."

"There were a lot of very hard feelings during that time. I recently interviewed two brothers who fought on opposite sides. Each did what he felt was right at the time, but now they put it behind them. Yet I've heard of others for whom the war isn't really over."

Laurel knew that was true. Ridge had signed the loyalty oath required at the end of the conflict, but he still stubbornly refused to petition the President for the amnesty needed to reclaim his ancestral land.

Charity continued, "Even with many people still angry over the war, I've not heard of anyone carrying a grudge strong enough to want to kill someone over what happened then."

"Neither have I," Laurel admitted, "but I can't shake the feeling that there's something behind this."

Charity stopped and faced Laurel. "Are you saying that you think your life might also be in danger?"

"I know it sounds silly, but I've thought about it."

"Yet you won't tell me what it is?"

"As I said, I can't." Laurel started walking again and Charity fell into step with her. "How about telling me why the police think Sarah's murder was premeditated?"

Charity abruptly reached out and gripped Laurel's arm, then dropped her voice. "Later. Here comes Vance Cooper, and I don't want him to know what we've talked about."

Laurel felt a twinge of concern. She wondered if he knew that Seymour had hired her to work with him on the police beat. If Cooper didn't know, should she say something? If she didn't, would that pose a problem when she showed up for work Monday morning?

Laurel watched the good-looking *Globe* correspondent striding purposefully toward them on the sidewalk. She speculated as to why he still wore the goatee. Some men still had beards or mustaches after the war, but most had shaved off such affectations as chin whiskers.

"Ladies," he greeted them with a hint of mockery in his voice. "Charity, I see you're trying to beat me to Miss Bartlett's first-person account of the murder."

"I shouldn't tell you this," Charity told him, "but Laurel and I were just getting around to that when you came along."

"Good! Then I still have an opportunity to beat you to the story." He turned to Laurel. "Will you be at your father's home at our scheduled meeting time?"

Laurel glanced from him to Charity, sensing that there was more than suppressed animosity in their semi-pleasant exchanges. Laurel wished she hadn't agreed to let him interview her about Sarah, but her curiosity had overridden that at the funeral when he mentioned "similar types" of murders in New York. Laurel didn't think it at all likely that there was a tie-in, but she had to find out. So she nodded to Cooper.

"Yes," she said, "I plan to be there."

"Laurel," Charity said, "I really should be getting back to work, so maybe you and Vance can talk now?"

"Suits me," Cooper said, looking at Laurel. "You?"

She hesitated. She didn't want to leave Charity until she got the explanation as to why the police believed Sarah's murder was premeditated. Also, after four consecutive meetings, Laurel wanted a break. Yet she was eager to learn about the New York murders.

She told Cooper, "I guess that would be all right."

"Fine!" he replied. "I'll hail a hack so we can ride and talk." He stepped to the curb, looking up and down the street.

"Sorry about running off, Laurel," Charity said. "We must get together again real soon."

"Yes, I want to finish our conversation."

Charity glanced toward Cooper whose back was to them. She said, "I hope you won't tell him everything. Save something so I can give my paper something the *Globe* won't have."

"I'll do that," Laurel replied with sincerity.

Under her breath, Charity said, "If you get a chance, try to get him to tell you about his interest in the criminal mind."

"The what?"

"What makes some people kill other people, beyond the usual motives. His interest in what goes on in the minds of killers is deeper than covering a police beat. Ask him about his father, who was murdered. That's what got Vance started on trying to understand. . . ."

Charity interrupted herself as Vance turned around and a horse-drawn hack pulled toward the curb. Giving Laurel's hand a quick squeeze, she said, "I hope we can become good friends."

"So do I," Laurel replied. "I enjoyed the lunch."

Cooper gave her a hand up into the hack. Before he released her hand, he held it a moment longer than Laurel expected. She hoped she hadn't made a mistake in agreeing to the ride.

"Driver," he said, "just drive around for awhile." He turned to Laurel. "It was a surprise running into you with Charity. In fact, this is the second surprise about you I've had today."

She saw something in his brown eyes that warned her that he wanted to do more than interview her about Sarah's murder. *He knows we're to work together, and he doesn't like it!*

But she smiled and spoke casually, "This is the first chance I've had to look at the city since I got back from California."

He did not return her smile.

Ridge entered the small telegraph office at the train station. He was a little annoyed at himself for not wiring Griff before he hired Emory Brush. Griff would know whether Sam Maynard had been off the peninsula the last few days.

Standing before the stack of blanks, pencil in hand, Ridge debated whether to add anything about Laurel. He didn't want to leave her now, but he had not been able to convince her to go south with him. Yet he needed to talk business with Griff. More working capital meant greater profits possible. It took money to make money, especially along the route where the transcontinental railroad would someday carry a nation's future. Griff would benefit from those profits, and Ridge could build a grand house for Laurel. A house with a garden, as she wanted.

He frowned, recalling her aloofness. Yet when he had first kissed her, she had responded warmly. Then she had changed. *I've got to find out what she's thinking!*

With an effort, he forced his mind back to the wire. He absently tapped the paper, fighting for the right words to set down. They wouldn't come. He slapped the pencil down and looked up.

He blinked and looked again, hard. Less than halfway across the long, barn-like depot, Sam Maynard was pushing through the crowd toward the exit.

Ridge whirled around, yanked the door open and hurried across the station as rapidly as his left leg permitted.

The hack driver had turned to drive along the river when Laurel decided to confront Vance Cooper at once instead of waiting for him to broach the subject to her.

"Your second surprise," she began, "is learning that I called on Orville Seymour this morning. Right?"

"You're a pretty woman, Miss Bartlett. I can see why he hired you, but—"

"My looks have nothing to do with this!" Her tone was like a slap, making his head snap back. "He knows and likes my work from the stringing I did for him while I was in California. I'll earn my money. But I didn't mean to do anything to make you unhappy."

"Well, you failed miserably in that, Miss Bartlett! I don't need an assistant, especially one personally involved in a story to be covered. But when I calmed down after Seymour told me, I figured out your motive."

She modified her voice. "Oh?"

"Kelly told me about Pierce ordering you to stay away and not interfere with the investigation of your friend. You're stubborn enough that you figured a way to outsmart him. Well, if you think I'm angry, wait until the lieutenant gets ahold of you."

"That's one of the risks I had to take. If he hadn't been rude and upset me, it wouldn't have happened."

"You're saying it's his fault?"

Laurel took a deep breath before answering. She kept her words soft and calming. "No, of course not. But I cared too much for Sarah not to do what I can to help bring her slayer to justice."

"Oh, so now you're qualified as a detective!" The sarcasm was heavy.

Laurel ignored it, fearful that if she lost her temper, she might blurt out something that would expose her experience. She explained, "I'm qualified because I will do anything I can to help solve this case."

"Well, in my opinion, you're going at it all wrong." His words were also softer. "You're making enemies where you could be making friends. That's too bad."

Sensing an advantage, she dropped her eyes and asked, "Do you blame me for trying to do whatever I can for Sarah?"

"No. I guess not. So I apologize for speaking sharply. When I approached you at the funeral, I just wanted to interview you for the paper. I still do. That is, if you're willing?"

Glad that the air had cleared, she smiled in relief. "Of course, but maybe we could make an exchange."

"What do you have in mind?"

"I'd like to hear your thoughts on what kind of a person you think did this terrible thing to Sarah."

"I see that Charity told you about me."

"Only that you're interested in the criminal mind, especially what makes some people kill others, as happened to your father."

Cooper was silent for a long moment before speaking again. "That's what got me started studying the subject. I couldn't find much published material about it, but on my New York police beat, I got a chance to talk with several convicted killers. I began to form some ideas about what goes on inside their brains."

"Like whoever killed some people back east in the same manner as Sarah?"

"No. That's still a mystery because whoever did those crimes was never caught. But I have some pretty strong ideas—no, convictions—about what went on in that killer's head to make him do what he did."

"You know his motives?"

"It's more than that. Much more."

Intrigued, Laurel looked expectantly at him, but she saw a change in his eyes.

"You're good," he said admiringly, "very good. You not only got me over being rightfully angry with you, but you even switched me away from my interview to where you're interviewing me."

He didn't sound upset, giving Laurel the impression that she could learn more. "I told you my motive," she reminded him. "Whatever I do, that's my reason."

He grinned at her. "I haven't met a really fascinating woman in a long, long time. Certainly I haven't met anyone as pretty as you."

She tried to give her answer a light tone. "Now, Mr. Cooper, flattery won't get you anywhere."

"Please call me Vance. And I'm not trying to flatter you. I'm an honest, blunt-speaking correspondent. I'd like to interview you, but there isn't time to do that and answer your questions about the criminal mind. So let's continue this conversation over dinner tonight."

Laurel hadn't expected that, but she had a ready excuse. "Oh, thank you. But I'm betrothed."

"Oh? Well, you're not married yet, are you?"

"No, but—"

"I don't suggest you might be making a mistake," Cooper interrupted, "but I would be if I just quit trying to get a chance to know you better. So how about it?"

Laurel's tone stiffened. "Really, Mr. Cooper, I'm going to marry Ridge Granger. You met him at the funeral. I won't do anything that a betrothed woman shouldn't."

Cooper stroked his goatee. "Fair enough, but you offered an exchange. You want to know more about what kind of person killed your friend, so I'll tell you—but only over dinner."

"That's unfair!" she exclaimed.

He grinned, obviously pleased with himself. "Right now, you think I'm a terrible person. I admit what I just did lacked class, but I meant it when I said that I want to know you better. As long as you're not married, I'm not going to give up trying."

When she didn't answer, he added quietly, "I hate getting off on the wrong foot with you, but I hope you'll come around to thinking more favorably of me."

When she still remained silent, he shrugged. "It seems I've lost this battle, but I don't plan to lose them all. I'll ask you again sometime."

Laurel didn't know what to say. She should have been upset by his insistence on courting her, yet she was rather touched. And he might be right about Ridge. She had thought about it often enough lately. It wasn't that she didn't love him; she did. But was that enough to withstand the outside pressures that threatened to destroy their marriage even before it began?

Cooper broke into her thoughts. "Tell me where you want me to go, and I'll have the driver take you there. On the way, I'll just talk about the weather or something innocuous so as not to distress you more."

Laurel decided to return to her father's house where she could be alone to sort out her thoughts. She didn't like some of them; didn't like them at all.

# Chapter 6

Fairly certain that he was following Sam Maynard, Ridge quickly threaded his way through the train station crowds. This time, he was determined not to lose sight of his quarry until he had confirmed his identity.

As the man exited the door to the street, he turned his head enough that Ridge got a good look. *That is Sam!*

Seconds later, Ridge pushed through the outside door, leaving behind the echoing murmur of people in the station. Outside, the distinctive clip-clop of horses' hooves and rattle of vehicles on cobblestones competed with the rising wind and the stentorian cries of hotel runners seeking passengers for their omnibuses.

Ridge's gaze swept the carriages lined up at the curb and settled on Maynard entering a hack. Ridge raised his voice and called over the heads of people in front of him. "Sam! Sam Maynard, wait!"

When Maynard gave no indication of having heard him, Ridge ignored the startled look of the people closest to him and cupped his hands together. "Sam!" he shouted through them. "Sam! Wait!"

Maynard didn't look around, but sat down in the hack which pulled away from the curb and blended with other vehicles on the street.

For a moment, Ridge stared after him, then turned toward

the line of hacks. He hurriedly got into the first one. He ordered the driver, "Don't lose sight of that hack!"

As the reinsman picked up the lines, Ridge stared at the cab ahead. His mind whirled. Had Sam pretended to not hear him? If so, why? Well, one thing was certain: Sam Maynard was in the city. But, Ridge reminded himself, that didn't mean Sam had anything to do with Sarah's death.

Noticing that Maynard's vehicle was pulling away, Ridge leaned forward and tapped the driver on the shoulder. "I must speak to that man ahead of us, so please try to catch up."

"It'll cost you extra," the driver replied, and picked up the whip.

It was a mistake for Laurel to return to her father's house. She realized that as soon as she opened the door and heard her sister's voice down the hallway.

"She'll never marry him, Papa! She's going to end up a spinster like your sister!"

"Now, Emma, don't be so sure!" Laurel's father answered quietly. "She's strong-willed and independent, but she'll change when—"

"No, she won't!" Emma broke in. "She thinks the whole world revolves around her and what she wants! That's why all her friends are married—most already have children—and she's still single! Eventually, that Rebel will realize she's a lost cause and walk out of her life. Not that I care about him, but . . ."

Laurel didn't hear the rest because she closed the door so hard the scrolled glass pane rattled.

"Hello," she called as if she had not overheard. She stopped at the bottom of the circular staircase and looked down the long hallway. "I'm home."

Her father stepped from the dining room into the hallway. "Oh, Laurel! I'm sorry you didn't join me for breakfast this morning." He approached to kiss her on the cheek.

"I had an early appointment," she said, shifting her gaze toward her sister as she entered the hallway.

Emma glared from dark eyes. "You overheard, didn't you? Don't deny it!"

"I heard," Laurel admitted, placing the drawstring of her reticule over the newel post and letting her father help her off with her cloak. "But you're wrong. I'm not going to end up like Aunt Agnes. Besides, you know that she's going to be married."

Emma snorted. "Yes, thirty-some-odd-years too late!"

"Now, Emma," her father chided, "that's enough."

"Excuse me," Laurel said, glancing up the stairs. "I'm going to be in my room."

"That's right," Emma said sarcastically, "run away from anything that'll make you face up to your problems!"

The women's father exclaimed sharply, "Emma, please!"

Laurel choked back her resentment toward her oldest sister. Instead, she asked with controlled calm, "As long as we're talking about flaws, have you ever wondered why you are so critical about everyone, especially me?"

Emma blinked in surprise, giving Laurel time to hurry up the stairs and into her bedchamber. Angry and hurt, she jumped up on the high, four-poster bed and flopped down to stare up at the white lace canopy.

She silently fumed, *Why can't she mind her own business?* But an unwelcome thought began gnawing at the back of her mind like rats on an ear of corn. *I know she's wrong, but why did I distance myself from Ridge when he mentioned my setting our wedding date? Why did I make him take me home when we kissed at the lakeshore?*

She frowned, wondering, *Did I unconsciously make him so angry that he walked out on me at the restaurant this morning? Am I really afraid to let myself love him enough to marry?*

Her mind jumped. *Will he go back to Virginia to see Griff? If he does, Varina will* . . . Laurel shook her head, vainly trying to shake off the memory of what had happened months ago when she had gone there to meet Ridge's friends. That had included Varina, to whom Ridge had been engaged before the war. But upon his return, he found that she had married an older man.

When Laurel had angered Ridge at a picnic on the peninsula, he had walked off in the same way as this morning. Varina, now widowed, had promptly moved in to try rekindling Ridge's romantic interest.

Laurel silently warned herself, *She'll do it again if he goes back there without me.* . . .

Her thoughts were interrupted by a knock on the door. Sitting up, she said, "Yes?"

"It's your father. May I come in?"

"Of course." She slid to the edge of the high bed and let her feet dangle over the sides as he entered.

He looked at her with troubled blue eyes. "I'm sorry about what happened just now. Emma went home to her children. She means well, but that doesn't stop the hurt I'm sure you're feeling right now."

She motioned for him to sit in the Boston rocker where her mother had held her and sung lullabies when Laurel was a baby. In her teen years, Laurel had rocked in that chair and thought about someday holding her own children.

"You want to talk?" her father asked, gently starting the old chair in motion. It squeaked very slightly, making a noise that

Laurel had never found offensive. Rather, it was a soothing, comforting sound.

Laurel hesitated. There was so much she could not tell, secrets about war-time spying and now being an operative for the Pinkerton Detective Agency. She had blamed her father for causing her teenage rebellion because he had been so domineering. Lately, she sensed he had changed and finally accepted her as a woman, realizing she was not his little girl anymore.

She thought of what she could safely tell. "I'm concerned about who killed Sarah, and why."

He studied her in silence, making her uncomfortable. There was something about his eyes that had always seemed to look inside her heart, although he had never pried into her life after she turned eighteen and moved out.

He asked, "Are you saying that you know something you're not telling?"

The discernment unsettled her. She glanced around the room, trying to think how to answer him. Vaguely, she noticed the familiar furnishings: her bedside table with a blue and white pitcher and basin for washing. A small chamber pot in matching colors rested on a low shelf underneath. Across the room stood the walnut wardrobe for storing accessories and clothing.

"Yes," she finally admitted, fixing her gaze back on him. "But I can't talk about it."

"I see. Well, your mother and I used to talk about why you weren't like your sisters or even your friends. Emma insisted you were wild, but your mother described you as 'colorful.' Anyway, you were different. But if you can't discuss what's troubling you, can you tell me this: does it have anything to do with unexplained absences during the war?"

She smiled in spite of her concern. "Papa, I've only recently realized what a wise man you are."

He returned the smile. "Thank you, but I wish I were wise enough to know how to help you right now."

She slid off the bed and stooped to kiss him on his forehead. "You can," she assured him. "Tell me honestly: is Emma right about why I'm still unmarried?"

He parried, "What do you think?"

She turned and walked to the high, double windows behind the bedside stand. Her gaze drifted over the familiar sight of shrubs and trees splashed with the colorful flowers that adorned the garden. Absently, she thought she noticed a crouching shadow move, but her mind was on her father's question.

"I don't know, Papa," she said over her shoulder. "I really don't know."

"Yet you're one of the most strong-willed persons I've ever met. From the time you were about fifteen, you made up your mind what you wanted to do, and you did it. That caused your mother and me many a restless night."

She turned, touched. "I'm sorry, Papa! Really!"

"You turned out all right, Laurel, and that's all parents hope for when children are finding their own way into adulthood."

"You think I've found my way?"

"Most of it, yes. But you've come to the single most important crossroads in reaching adulthood: marriage. Oh, it's not always just a decision like my sister to remain single. It's more a matter of choosing the road that leads to a long life of happiness as man and wife."

"Do you think Ridge and I can be happy together?"

"Do you want that?"

She hesitated, remembering the doubts, the fears. "In one way, yes, I do. With all my heart. But I'm afraid of things that Ridge and I can't control. Like Emma's dislike of him. Maggie, too. And I saw it in the eyes of some of those I grew up with when we were at the funeral. Oh, it's not just here, either. When I visited Ridge's friends in Virginia, I felt the same resentment directed toward me."

"I know it may sound trite, but love is the most powerful force in the world. If you love each other enough, you'll overcome those difficulties in the same way that you must surmount those obstacles that are common to every life."

She thoughtfully bit her lip, thinking. "Are you asking if I love Ridge that much?"

"That's a question only you can answer. But let me make a fatherly suggestion that you might consider. Is being with Ridge the rest of your life more important than having your own way? Your own independence?"

She frowned, knowing he wasn't prying, yet she felt a rush of resentment because she sensed that he was in agreement with Emma. *I think the world revolves around me? Well, that's wrong!*

Her father stood. "I've said too much." He walked the few steps to where she stood and took both her hands in his. "I see it in your eyes, and I'm sorry I hurt you or made you angry. I love you, Laurel, love you with all that's in me. I'm just trying to help. Remember that."

He released her hands and walked out, his shoulders very slightly slumped. It made her heart ache, but she didn't try to stop him. She watched the door close behind him, but his words echoed in her mind.

*Is being with Ridge the rest of your life more important than having your own way?*

She didn't know. In sudden frustration, she turned to the bed and plunged both fists into the long white pillow. The impulsive act surprised her, making her back up, shaking her head. *What's the matter with me?* she wondered.

Sighing heavily, she turned again to the window and looked out across the shrubs and the lawn. A movement near a huge tree trunk caught her eye. She focused on the spot in time to see a man's foot just before it vanished behind the tree.

*Someone's been watching!* The thought made her spin away and dash across the room. *That's what I saw a few moments ago! Well, let's see who it is!* She jerked the door open and ran down the hall to the staircase.

Ridge urgently told the hack driver, "We must go faster! He's pulling away!"

"I can't go any faster without risking an accident. This Chicago traffic has been getting worse every day since the war, and half of these drivers don't know how to . . . whoa!"

He pulled back hard on the reins as a team of heavy draft horses plodded into the crossing intersection ahead. They pulled a load of large beer barrels. "Hey!" Ridge's driver yelled at the offending drayman. "Why don't you watch where you're going?"

The other man was nearly as round as his cargo. He called, "You can stop faster than I can!" Then, with a smirk, he leaned back slightly, tightening the reins so that the ponderous draft horses slowed, forcing the hack to a full stop.

While the two drivers shouted at each other, Ridge inwardly groaned at the sight of Sam Maynard's vehicle disappearing around a corner two blocks ahead.

*That's twice I missed him!* Ridge told himself. *But at least I know for sure that he's in town. Now what?*

Darting out the front door, Laurel turned to her left, lifted her long hoopskirt above her ankles, and ran as fast as possible through the yard. She raced around the corner of the house and stopped, her eyes focusing on the huge old maple where her swing had been as a child and where she had glimpsed the man's foot moments before.

Forcing herself to be more cautious, she slowed and headed for the tree but at an angle that would take her past it. Her pulse had speeded up, and she was breathing hard, but not so much in fear as excitement. She felt the same exhilaration that had often gripped her when she slipped through both Federal and Confederate pickets during the war.

She circled wide of the tree, watching carefully to see if the man she had glimpsed was still there. As she passed the trunk, she saw nothing. But she remembered that squirrels always moved sideways around a tree trunk when she chased them as a girl. To make sure that the man wasn't doing the same, she suddenly jumped back a couple of steps hoping to surprise him as she had the squirrels.

There was nobody there. Hurriedly, less carefully, she approached the tree and quickly circled it. She stayed safely out of reach in case anyone was there. There wasn't.

She turned in a slow circle, violet eyes probing the bushes and other trees. In her childhood, she had played all around them, but now they were so grown that if someone hid in them and didn't move, he couldn't be seen.

*But I know what I saw!* she told herself. *There was somebody there, watching. But who? And why?* She decided not to mention the incident to her father. There was no sense in alarming him. *I can take care of myself!*

Instantly, she recalled her father, Ridge, and Sarah all having chided her for repeatedly saying that. Just before Laurel had left for California, she had made that same confident declaration to Sarah. Throwing up her hands in mock despair, Sarah had exclaimed, "Oh, how many times have I heard that from you?"

Laurel swallowed hard. That had been the last time she had seen Sarah alive. *Well, it's still true,* Laurel told herself as she re-entered her father's house. *And I can help find whoever killed her.*

She didn't intend to add the words that instantly leaped to mind: *But if I'm right about who did, and why, I've got to prove it before he comes after me.* She climbed the stairs to her bed chamber to think how best to go about doing that.

🦋

Ridge didn't want to alarm Laurel about twice seeing Sam Maynard, but he decided that she should know. He felt awkward after directing the hack driver to the Bartlett home. Ridge wasn't sure how she would react when he showed up unannounced after having walked out on her at the restaurant hours before.

He had felt somewhat the same way the first time he had ever called there, back when he was still wearing his Confederate jacket. He had come with a letter which a dying Union infantry-man on a battlefield had made him promise to deliver after the war. That soldier had turned out to be Laurel's sixteen-year-old brother.

Ridge mentally rehearsed his apology as the vehicle headed up the long-tree lined driveway on Elm Street. He hoped she would accept it gracefully so he could tell her about Sam without unduly increasing her alarm.

Ridge paid his fare and walked toward the front door of Hiram Bartlett's red-brick home. It combined elements of Federal and Georgian architecture, but was not as grand as the manor he planned for Laurel and him, although her father's home was still imposing.

Ridge rounded a hedge and glanced up at the curving facade over the entrance which was supported by four white columns. Taking a deep breath, he knocked and waited.

The matronly Maggie in black dress and white apron opened the door, her brown eyes showing disapproval. "Yes?" she said coolly, shaking a gray-brown lock of hair away from her stern face.

"I've come to see Laurel," he replied, unruffled by the servant's manner. "Is she home?"

Maggie asked haughtily, "Whom shall I say is calling?"

Ridge's instant reaction was that which he had used with blacks in his own home. He couldn't get over the impertinent manner of Northern servants, but he checked the sharp reprimand that leaped to mind.

Instead, he said quietly, "Maggie, I'm going to marry Laurel if she'll have me, and I'll take as good care of her as you or her father ever did. Meantime, I would like it very much if you would treat me as you would have any of her previous suitors."

Her mouth dropped slightly, then she recovered. "I ain't treating you much different. Never did like any of them, not that she brought many around here."

Ridge suppressed a grin as Maggie added, "Too picky, she was. But I guess it's better for her to have a Rebel than end up a bitter old woman like her Aunt Agnes. Come in. Wait in the parlor while I tell her."

Ridge smiled to himself as Maggie went mumbling up the curving staircase. *Well, I hope Laurel is as easy to charm as Maggie was,* he thought, stepping past the tall case clock against the hall wall and into the parlor.

He thoughtfully studied the photo of Laurel's only brother hanging on the wall beside the oil painting of Laurel's late mother.

Ridge wouldn't have recognized the brother. In their brief encounter in a cornfield the morning after a battle, his face had been black with powder from the fierce hand-to-hand fighting of the previous afternoon. He wasn't a drummer boy, but a tall, gangly teenager in blue. Even though Ridge was in gray, the boy, barely alive, had asked for water. Ridge had given it to him, averting his eyes from the bloody bayonet wound through which his life was draining away.

Then the boy had made his dying request: take a letter from his pocket. When Ridge did, the boy made him promise to deliver it after the war. Ridge never forgot the boy's strange little smile of gratitude.

"Good afternoon, Ridge."

Laurel's voice behind him jerked him back to the present. All the words he had carefully formulated vanished at the sight of her. He could only stare, aware of what a foolish thing he had done, how downright stupid it would be for him to ever let her get away.

She misread his silence and motioned toward the portrait. "He had that taken shortly after he enlisted. He was so proud, so young." She sadly shook her head. "So very, very young to die."

Ridge found his voice. "I know." His younger brother had also died in battle.

The doubts and fears about their future relationship made Laurel shift her gaze back to Ridge. She waited silently.

He said hastily, "I was wrong to walk out on you as I did. I came to apologize and ask your forgiveness."

She sat in the Victorian love seat and motioned for him to join her. "That's twice you've done that, counting the time in Virginia." The moment the words were out, she regretted them. She caught a flash of temper in his eyes, but he sat stiffly and took a slow, deep breath.

"I know. I regret both times, but I'll try not to do it again."

"That's not good enough!" Her words were sharper than she intended, but they were honest ones. "It makes me wonder if we're ever really going to be able to be happy together."

"Of course we are!" He reached out and took both her hands. "We're just going through an adjustment period as I'm sure all young couples do when facing marriage."

She hadn't intended to get into such a discussion right now, but it was probably just as good a time as any. "I'm not so sure, Ridge. After you left Sacramento for Omaha, I thought a lot about us. It's only fair to tell you that I'm having second thoughts."

Ridge realized that the conversation was veering far away from what he had come to tell her. But he knew that what she said had to be dealt with promptly.

"I see. So that's why you seemed cool when I met you at the train station and suggested you set a wedding date?" When she nodded, he added, "And that's why you suddenly made me take you home when we kissed at the lake."

She freed her hands and stood up to take a couple of quick steps before turning to face him again. "It's not just that, Ridge. Oh, it started that way, then Sarah got killed, and you walked out when I'm hurting. . . ."

He quickly rose and approached her. Placing both hands on her shoulders, he looked down into her eyes. "I have no excuse, Laurel. I love you so, yet I consistently seem to show no more sense than an army mule!"

She smiled in spite of her distress. "Right now, I'm not going to argue about that."

Encouraged, he returned the smile. "Then am I forgiven?"

She sobered. "Yes, but that still doesn't make me any less concerned about the other things I mentioned."

"We'll work them out. We have to, because I'm never going to give you up."

She looked up into his eyes and realized he meant what he said. Then she glimpsed concern flit across his face. She asked, "What is it?"

He carefully considered his answer, trying to phrase it so that she had a minimum of alarm. "You were right about Sam Maynard being in town. I saw him twice."

"You did?" Her voice rose. "Where? When?"

He told her, including losing Sam in traffic a short time before. "But that doesn't mean he had anything to do with Sarah's death. I don't believe he's capable of such a terrible thing."

Laurel stepped back and sank down again on the love seat. "But if I'm right about why Sarah was killed, Maynard is the only person I can think of who had any possible motive."

"He's the only one you can think of, but that doesn't mean somebody else didn't do it, someone you don't suspect, or maybe even know. Don't you see that?"

"I understand the logic of it, but I believe he's a logical suspect. Now that I know he's here, I'm going to find out."

"No! That's too dangerous! Even if it's not Sam, if you go prying around, the real murderer might think you're onto him, and he could. . . ." He broke off, unwilling to voice what he had thought.

A frown puckered Laurel's forehead. "How long ago did you last see your friend, Maynard?"

"I don't know; maybe forty-five minutes or so. Why?"

She thought of the man who had been watching and tried to estimate how long ago that had been. It would have been difficult but not impossible for Maynard to have gone from where Ridge had last seen him to here in such a short time. "About thirty minutes ago," she said, "I saw someone watching from behind a tree."

Ridge suspected it was the detective he'd hired, but he didn't want Laurel to know about that. She might think of it as spying instead of trying to protect her.

He asked, "Did you get a good look at him?"

"No. I only saw his foot as he pulled it back behind the tree trunk. When I ran out to get a closer look, there was no sign of him."

"I see." Impulsively, Ridge said, "I've got to go back to Virginia to see Griff. Come with me!"

"You know I can't do that! I've got a job starting Monday at the *Globe*, plus Pinkerton's deadline."

"We could take the cars down tonight and be back the first of next week."

"I just can't. I plan to use the time between now and Monday morning to investigate Sarah's murder."

"I understand that, Laurel, but I'd feel safer if you went with me. I can't stand the thought of leaving you alone while I go see Griff, although it's very important that I talk with him about some business. Part of our future depends on what Griff and I can work out. Come with me!"

Laurel looked up into his face, undecided. Slowly, she stood. "Give me a few minutes to think about it," she said. "You talk to Papa until then. He's in the back."

Without waiting for Ridge's reply, she walked out and climbed the stairs.

# Chapter 7

Safely back in his rented upstairs room, the man smiled in satisfaction. He removed his spectacles and breathed heavily on them, then wiped the moisture away with his handkerchief. He glanced around the furnished room. It was spacious with a chair at the desk, a high four-poster bed covered with a handmade quilt. He knew that the elderly widow who owned the place would express regret when he left. He was such a quiet, mannerly guest. They all said that wherever he lived.

He was exhilarated because Laurel had caught sight of him hiding behind the tree. He enjoyed the close encounters; it gave him a tangible way of proving his superiority. He took chances but avoided detection. Greater risks were required now to give him the flush of satisfaction he craved. In coming to Chicago, he was taking the greatest risk yet. He was already sensing the rush of excitement that usually only came later.

He had added to that anticipation by striking in daylight. After the first two victims in New York's darkness, he had changed to the more daring daytime. But he still found the nights more effective in creating a sense of creeping terror in his intended victims.

Replacing his spectacles on his nose, he walked to the window and looked out. Idly, he fingered the windowsill before him and marveled at how easily he had prepared the one at her father's house for his return.

With the back of his hand, he wiped a trickle of saliva from the corner of his mouth. Tonight he would demonstrate to Laurel that the threat she had begun to feel was only the beginning of dread.

Ridge waited until he heard the door close to Laurel's upstairs bedchamber before he sauntered down the long hall toward the kitchen. He hoped she would be sensible and go with him to Virginia, but he didn't have much confidence of that happening unless he pushed hard.

"Stubborn!" he muttered to himself, shaking his head as he passed the library door. "Pretty, but stubborn!"

"Let me guess," Laurel's father said from inside the library, "who you're mumbling about."

Ridge stopped and peered inside the room. One dark-paneled wall had a small unlit fireplace. Two walls had windows with open bookcases above and below. The fourth wall was entirely devoted to glass doors through which heavy, leather-bound books stood in stately array.

"I hope I'm not intruding, Mr. Bartlett. Laurel wanted some time alone and said I'd find you in back."

"Come in. Sit down," the older man said heartily. He motioned Ridge to a leather wingback chair that matched the one where he sat.

"You're sure I'm not interfering? . . ."

"Of course not!" Bartlett interrupted. He carefully placed a tasseled leather bookmark in the volume he was reading and turned to replace it on the shelf behind him. He said over his shoulder, "How's your business going?"

Ridge sat down, catching a faint whiff of fine leather. "Fine, thanks. In fact, it's going so well that I need to return to Virginia to confer with an old friend who wants to invest."

Bartlett settled into his chair. "So that's why you were muttering to yourself; I mean, because Laurel won't go with you."

"She might. She's thinking about it right now."

Bartlett regarded Ridge with thoughtful eyes before speaking again. "She's a strong-willed woman, Ridge. A little like her mother was when I courted her. I'm sure you've lived long enough to know that all women have flaws, just as men do. In this house filled with women, as you saw, I have one outspoken daughter; one quiet one; a sister who speaks her mind; Maggie, who vexes me with her insolence, but she's a great housekeeper; and Laurel.

"Laurel," her father repeated softly, then sighed. "I'm speaking bluntly because you're entitled to know what kind of a family you're marrying into. Laurel was quite a handful when she was growing up, but what you might now consider a character flaw is something that will change, in time."

Ridge didn't know what to say, so he waited, guessing that the older man had seen or sensed some tension between Laurel and himself.

"Her mother changed," Bartlett added somberly. "That's why I know Laurel will, too. So don't give up if you truly love her."

"Oh, I do! And I'll marry her as soon as she sets the date."

"But she hasn't set it, has she?"

Before Ridge could answer, Maggie stuck her head in the door. She looked at her long-time employer and spoke accusingly. "I told you that if you didn't get those windows fixed before winter, they'll start giving 'way before you get the shutters up and the first wind blows. I just now found one already unlocked in back and partly open." She turned away, adding, "You'd better fix it right away."

Ridge rankled at her tone, but Bartlett smiled and called after her, "It'll keep until tomorrow, Maggie. I'll see to it then." He brought his eyes back to Ridge. "Now, where were we?"

Ridge shifted uneasily. "You guessed that Laurel hadn't set the date, and you're right."

"Don't rush her, Ridge. Give her time. She'll come around."

"I'm counting on that, Sir."

"Good! Now, tell me more about your friend who wants to invest in your new venture."

Ridge nodded and began explaining, feeling almost as comfortable with Laurel's father as he had been with his own before the Yankees invaded Virginia. Ridge silently wished that all Northerners would treat him as well.

He paused in his narration when he heard Laurel's footsteps overhead. He wondered if she would decide to accompany him to Virginia. *She must!* he told himself. *I can't risk leaving her here, even with Emory Brush hired to look out after her.*

※

Laurel entered her room with the same calm self-confidence she had possessed ever since she was a teen. She looked at herself in the mirror. *I can't go with Ridge,* she decided. *I can't, whether it's Sam Maynard who killed Sarah or someone else, I've got to stay here and find out who did that awful thing.*

She stared into the reflection, aware that if she was right about the killer's motive, she would be better off to go with Ridge. She might be snubbed or treated with cool disdain, but at least his friends wouldn't try to kill her.

Her thoughts jumped to Sarah. Laurel gripped the edge of the vanity so hard her knuckles hurt, but she seemed not to notice. She had not yet grieved for Sarah, had been too shocked and too busy making plans of how to bring her friend's slayer to justice. But a series of memories flickered in her mind's eye, faster than summer lightning streaks: their first day at school together, picnics, hay rides, ice skating, graduation. Their first giggling awareness of boys. Then the war. Laurel's brother killed in action. Her seeking revenge by applying to Pinkerton for spy missions, being refused because of her age, and then accepted when she turned eighteen.

It was Sarah who cleverly created secret places to hide maps and other documents in Laurel's clothing, her shoes, her hair. . . .

Laurel took a deep breath, willing the memories to vanish. But they were replaced by the post-war train ride when Sarah met a tall, sort of mysterious railroad messenger and introduced Laurel to him.

"Ridge Granger," she spoke the name aloud, and closed her eyes. She was suddenly overwhelmed and whirled around. Passing the six-foot-tall walnut Chippendale highboy, she threw herself face down across her bed and dissolved into painful, wracking sobs.

She tried to stop, but the tears seemed to erupt from her very soul, and she finally let them flow freely. A tiny bit of her mind told her she was grieving for Sarah, and that was true, yet in her heart, Laurel knew it was more than that. She wept for Ridge and a life that common sense told her they might never know together.

She didn't know how long she wept, but when she was empty and dry, she slowly sat up. Pouring water from the ceramic pitcher on her bedside stand into the matching basin, she washed her face and dried her eyes.

*If I don't go with him,* she reminded herself, *and he goes alone, Varina will work her magic on him as she did so brazenly before, even with me right there. But I must stay here and do what I can for Sarah—and me.*

Then, with as much of her facial damage repaired as possible, she adjusted her skirt and lifted her chin. She braced herself for what Ridge's reaction would be when she told him her decision and walked down the corridor hoping no one would guess what she had just gone through.

Laurel had nearly reached the top of the stairs when there was a heavy knock at the front door. Stalling as long as possible from having anyone see her face, she called, "I'll get it."

Maggie grumbled from the parlor, "It's about time somebody else did something around here besides me."

Laurel peered through the frosted floral design of the front door. In the gathering dusk, she recognized Ulysses Kelly, the detective assigned to Sarah's case.

Laurel opened the door. "Mr. Kelly! I thought you'd be home with your family this time of day."

"I'm trying, Miss." The end of his reddish mustache quivered as he spoke. "I have been interrogating all the victim's neighbors, and I have to ask you a few questions before I can go home and put my feet up."

"Of course. Come in!" Laurel opened the door wide and motioned toward the parlor. "Take a seat. Is this to be private, or may I have my father and fiancé join us?"

She involuntarily flinched at the use of "fiancé," but it had come automatically. Technically, she reminded herself, that was still true.

As Kelly stepped into the parlor, Maggie pushed by him with a suspicious glance of appraisal. "I'll go fetch the men," she whispered to Laurel, then waddled down the long hallway toward the library.

Laurel lingered in the doorway until she saw her father and Ridge head toward her. Then she entered the parlor and sat demurely on the loveseat.

The heavy-set detective dropped wearily into the upholstered chair. His already-flushed face seemed to color even more, as though he was angry at her for not trusting him to be alone with her. He growled, "You don't need witnesses, if that's what you're afraid of."

"Oh, Mr. Kelly! I didn't mean to imply! . . ."

"Don't mind me," he broke in, waving big hands in a dismissal of her apology. "I'm just bone-weary and a little sore from being blasted by the lieutenant over this case."

She sat on the love seat facing Kelly. She asked hopefully, "Any progress?"

He smiled without humor. "Remember what I told you at the station? I'll ask the questions."

"Sorry." She introduced her father as he and Ridge entered the room. She added, "Mr. Kelly, you remember my . . . " she hesitated before adding quickly, "uh, Ridge Granger."

Kelly shook hands with Laurel's father but merely nodded to Ridge. "Glad you're both here," he said, glancing from Laurel to Ridge. "It'll save me another trip. Would you mind if I ask each of you some more questions?"

"No, of course not," Laurel said. She looked at Ridge who nodded.

The detective turned to the older man. "Sir, is there someplace where I can talk to them separately?"

Laurel blinked in surprise. "Why don't you want to talk to Ridge and me together? We both found her. . . ."

"Remember what I keep telling you?" Kelly asked with a hint of annoyance. He turned to her father. "Well?"

"The library," he replied, "but I would prefer to be with my daughter while you question her."

"Most fathers would," Kelly snapped. "But that's not how

interrogations are conducted."

Laurel stirred uneasily. "Are you suggesting that Ridge and I aren't telling you the truth?"

A scowl brought thin reddish eyebrows down over pale blue eyes. "I told you at the police station that I know you're keeping something from me, Miss Bartlett. I hope you're ready to tell me what that is."

Laurel's father asked her, "What's he talking about?"

"Nothing I can't handle, Papa."

He threw up his hands in mock dismay. "You always say that!"

Laurel rose from the loveseat and moved toward the door. "The library's this way, Mr. Kelly." Her voice didn't betray any of the sudden concern she felt.

Laurel stood watching as the detective gave the library a cursory look. When he motioned for her to sit, she sank into her father's big leather chair in front of the bookcases. Kelly remained standing.

"You ready to tell me what you're holding back?" he asked bluntly.

Laurel tried to keep any sign of her concern from showing in her face or voice as she replied. "I've told you everything I can."

"Not everything, and we both know it. So then let's do it the hard way." He sat down and reached inside his coat pocket to produce a small note pad and pencil. "Now, start again from the very beginning, and don't leave anything out."

"But I've already told you! . . ."

"Tell me again!" His mustache ends quivered with controlled anger. "And if you don't tell me everything this time, then we'll keep doing it until you do. Is that understood, Miss Bartlett?"

She met his cold glare without blinking, knowing she could not tell him about Sarah's and her war-time roles. Without that information, he might never be able to solve the case. She would have to do that herself.

"Well," she began, "Ridge and I walked up to Sarah's front door. . . ."

She described every action they had taken until finding the body, then stopped, dropping her head as the awful scene on the back porch again filled her memory.

Kelly urged in a quiet voice, "Go on, please."

Nodding, she raised her head and fought back the tears that fogged her eyes. She reluctantly held the scene in her mind and softly repeated everything she saw.

When she had finished, Kelly's pencil stopped moving. "That's it?" He flipped back in his notes and skimmed them. "Except for the body, everything looked normal, the way you remembered it from previous visits."

"Yes, except for little things that wouldn't have been left from before. Like the newspaper."

"It was beside her body, you said?"

"Yes, next to her right hand. She must have been carrying it out to throw away or something when whoever it was surprised her."

"You didn't pick it up?"

"No, of course not. Anybody knows you're not supposed to touch anything at a murder scene." She saw something in his eyes that suddenly alerted her. "Why? Was there something special about the paper?"

"You honestly don't know, Miss Bartlett?"

"How would I know? Neither Ridge nor I . . . "

He brushed her protest aside with a quick sweep of his big hands. "I believe you, so let's go on." He looked down and reached inside his coat pocket.

Laurel involuntarily licked her lips, abruptly sure that it had been an old newspaper—maybe dated April third, 1865.

Kelly held out a small object toward her. "Did you see this?"

She leaned forward to examine it more closely. "No. What is it?"

"You really don't know?"

"No, I don't."

"It doesn't matter." He returned the object to his inside coat pocket. "Well, I'll give you one last chance to tell me what you're holding back."

"I told you that I have no idea what that is!"

"I don't mean this." He patted his suitcoat where he had replaced the unfamiliar object. "I meant what I first mentioned at the police station."

"I've already answered that, Mr. Kelly."

He sighed and heaved his weight from the chair. "Very well. Let's walk back to the parlor where you can visit with your father while I ask Mr. Granger what he knows about your secret."

Involuntarily, Laurel started to gulp, knowing that Ridge knew what she was keeping back. Even though she stopped the throat reflex, she saw from an instant glint of triumph in Kelly's eyes that he had detected her automatic fear response. That also confirmed that Ridge knew that secret, too. Kelly chuckled and motioned for Laurel to precede him down the hallway.

❧

Ridge regretted that he and Laurel did not have a chance to even mention what happened in the library before Kelly trailed Ridge back there. He took the chair opposite the detective and waited. But Ridge was ready, having already cautiously fended off Bartlett's questions about what the detective had meant when he told Laurel that he knew at the police station she was keeping something back.

Kelly took out his note pad and pencil. "I feel certain that a young couple contemplating marriage would have shared many secrets about their past. So I would appreciate it if you'll confirm what Laurel just told me about what she had held back at the police station."

*You're a liar!* The words leaped to Ridge's lips, but he checked them. He knew Laurel would not have confessed to either her war-time clandestine activities or her employment as a Pinkerton agent.

"Mr. Kelly," Ridge said evenly, "you may think I'm a fool, and I may be in some respects, but not in this. She didn't tell you anything that you don't already know, and we both know that. So let's cut the foolishness."

"Now listen, Granger! . . ."

"No, you listen!" Ridge rose, towering over the other man in his chair. "We all want this murder solved and Sarah's killer brought to justice. But don't try any of your police interrogation tactics on me!"

Kelly jumped to his feet, his ruddy face flushing with anger. "I'll arrest you for interfering with a murder investigation!"

"I'm not interfering, and you know it! You ask the questions and I'll answer them truthfully, as best I can. And I sure hope you didn't try to bully Laurel this way."

Ridge saw that Kelly realized he had made a mistake in the tactics he used on Ridge, because the detective kept his blustering manner but softened his voice.

"All right. Sit down and let's go over everything again. Tell me every detail of what you saw at the murder scene."

Ridge sat on the edge of his seat. "Do we have to do this again? I've already . . . oh, all right."

He leaned back in the leather chair and closed his eyes, unwilling to see again what he must. "We found her just as I said before, on the back porch. . . ."

He continued without being interrupted until he had repeated everything he could remember. When he fell silent and opened his eyes, the detective reached into his coat pocket.

"You didn't mention seeing this." He held out the same object he had shown to Laurel. "Why not?"

Ridge scrutinized the object closely. "Because I never saw it before."

"You sure?"

"Certainly. Where did you find? . . . Oh, yes; I heard you tell Laurel that you ask the questions."

"You're a good learner, Granger. How about the newspaper you mentioned being beside her body. Did you look at it closely?"

"What? The woman was murdered! Why would I stop to look at something like a paper?"

"Don't get your liver in an uproar! I'm just doing my job."

Ridge nodded and relaxed.

"I understand your feelings. From what you both told me at the scene, the dead woman was a friend."

"Yes. She introduced Laurel and me."

"I remember hearing that. I know you were in the Rebel cavalry—"

"I was in the Confederate cavalry!" Ridge broke in sharply. "I didn't consider myself a Rebel any more than George Washington or any of those men did when they broke away from England's tyranny."

Kelly asked quietly, "Is that why you haven't petitioned President Johnson for amnesty?"

Ridge stared. "So you've been investigating me? Well, to answer your question: No, I haven't. And yes, I know the war is officially over, and the Union won."

"But it's not over for you, is it?"

Ridge continued as if the question hadn't been asked. "I know that everything I had in the world is gone—family, home, everything. Well, except for what I have up here." He tapped his forehead. "That, and the willingness to do what I must to make Laurel happy the rest of her life. But I did not kill Sarah, and neither did Laurel. So look elsewhere for your suspects."

Kelly didn't say anything for a few seconds. Then he nodded and got to his feet. "I'll do that, Granger. And I'll keep looking for what you and Miss Bartlett are trying to keep from me. Now, let's rejoin the others."

Ridge took a deep breath and stood up, but he didn't feel good because he knew Kelly meant what he said. Sooner or later, just as he had checked on Ridge's lack of amnesty petition, he would delve into Laurel's past. Ridge hoped Kelly would not find the secret she and Sarah had shared.

# Chapter 8

The post-midnight air was sticky and muggy, but he shivered from excitement. After making sure that everything was quiet, and there were no lights in the house, he gripped the gunnysack and took another quick glance around. Satisfied, he slipped from the bushes and made his way through the darkness toward the back window. He made no sound as his fingers explored the bottom of the sill and eased it up.

When it was high enough, he placed the sack inside on the floor and crawled through the window. With every nerve taut, he crept across the room, into the hallway, and along it to the foot of the stairs. The methodical ticking of the tall case clock was the only sound.

He placed his left foot on the first step next to the railing where there was less chance of the wood creaking. Trying to keep his breathing under control, he climbed to the top of the stairs. The thrill of what he was doing sent his blood surging.

He paused to listen to the heavy snoring from the front bedchamber. Satisfied that this was her father's room, the intruder tiptoed on down the hall, stepping close to the walls. The door to the middle chamber was closed, but he had seen her lamp light up the window the past few nights.

There was no sound from within as he eased his free hand onto the white porcelain knob and gently began to turn it. By now, his exhilaration was intense. It was this feeling of danger mixed with power that drove him. There was a thrill in knowing that her life was in his hands.

It was this, mixed with frustrated vengeance against one woman, which had made him claim his first victim. He had been very badly frightened, but after that, it had been easier. Every triumph sent him into days and sometimes weeks of reliving the moment when he chose to exercise his power. But the need for that feeling had become more frequent, and he had yielded to it on an accelerating basis. He had learned to heighten the anticipation by terrorizing his victims before the final moment of gratification.

He glided into her room, gripping the sack tighter while listening to her slow, even breathing. It was too dark to even make out the four-poster bed which he knew was there, near the window. He paused, knowing that he was in absolute control. She could not escape the fate she had earned.

But not yet! he reminded himself as he felt his way along the wall by the door. When he gingerly touched the first piece of furniture, he cautiously explored it until he determined that it was a highboy. Good! She'll see it first thing in the morning!

He slid his fingers along the highboy's polished side until he reached the top. Ever-so-carefully, he felt around until satisfied that there was no knickknack there. Slowly, he eased it onto the top. Then, almost bursting with a sense of achievement, he retraced his steps.

Only when he was again outside in the protective darkness did he allow himself to raise both hands overhead in a silent gesture of exultation.

Ridge awoke early Friday morning in his hotel room. He

thought about shaving before going downstairs for breakfast. But his eyes fell on the letter where he had left it on the nightstand.

He picked it up to re-read, having hastily done so last night after the desk clerk handed it to him. His mind hadn't been on the contents because he was still stewing over Kelly's declaration that he intended to keep looking for what secret Laurel and he were trying to keep from him.

Sitting on the edge of the bed, Ridge held the letter closer to the lamp and focused on Griff's irregular handwriting.

Dear Friend Ridge: This is to advise you that I am well and trust you are the same. Also, I want to again stress the importance of your coming here to discuss our business venture.

Naturally, I would come to you, but this rolling chair I'm in all day long doesn't travel well.

There isn't much news here, except that Simon Turner has applied to President Johnson for amnesty. This leaves you as the only one of our friends who is still holding out. I keep hoping you'll change your mind so you and Laurel can rebuild on your family property and we'll be neighbors again. It's lonely with so many of those we knew now gone forever. My parents reminded me to say you and Laurel are welcome to our hospitality anytime, so I hope you'll both be here soon.

Maybe I shouldn't mention this, but my mother tells me that the women at church are still convinced that Varina will end up marrying you. It seems the only thing that will stop their wagging tongues is for you and Laurel to marry and move onto your old property.

Ridge impulsively crumpled the page in his hand, his mind

leaping back to Varina. They had grown up together and had been betrothed early in the war. He and Varina had never really quarreled until after she embarrassed and hurt him by marrying an older man during the years Ridge had been away fighting the invading Yankees.

Widowed after the war and in desperate financial straits, Varina had openly tried to re-kindle Ridge's romantic interest. He had not succumbed, and didn't feel he would, not even if he was often near her. He loved Laurel, but did she love him? She had been acting so reserved since returning from California.

In spite of himself, Ridge started recalling the happy times with Varina before he rode off to war. He quickly checked himself. *Stop it! You know what she's really like, deep down inside! I'm fortunate that we broke up when we did.*

Ridge knew his business success required him to see Griff in person. Today, Ridge decided, he would push Laurel to accompany him to Virginia.

It was full daylight when Laurel awakened. For a moment, she lay still, regretting that she had distressed her father last evening. He had asked what she and Ridge were keeping from Kelly. She had refused her father as politely as possible, but she could see he was hurt and troubled.

Sighing, she sat up in bed, stretched, yawned, and reached for the Bible on her nightstand. She had tried to develop the habit of reading a chapter each morning before getting up. As she rearranged her pillows behind her back so she could sit up comfortably, she noticed the sack on the highboy.

She blinked and looked again. *I don't remember seeing that before.* Curious, she lowered her bare feet until they touched the hard wooden floor, then padded across the spacious room to look closely at the sack.

She started to reach for it when Maggie's scream from the first floor froze her hand in mid-air. Laurel whirled around to the foot of the bed, grabbed her dressing gown and ran barefooted down the hallway.

Taking the stairs two at a time, she heard her father's voice trying to calm the housekeeper. But Maggie's voice was high with fear and indignation.

"I tell you, somebody was in this house last night while we were sleeping! Came right through that window! We could have all been killed in our beds!"

"Get hold of yourself!" Bartlett ordered sternly. He turned to Laurel as she entered. "Are you all right?"

"Yes. I just woke up—"

"I told you yesterday it was open!" Maggie cried, "but nobody listens to me! No, siree! So this what we get! We been robbed, and could all be dead!"

"Stop it, Maggie!" Bartlett ordered sternly, turning toward the window where Laurel was already headed.

"It has been forced, all right," her father mused, pointing to fresh pry marks. "See?"

Laurel nodded without speaking, her thoughts jumping to Sarah and Sam Maynard.

Bartlett stepped back from the window. "We'd better check everything. Laurel, run up and make sure that nothing is missing from your room, then check your sisters' old rooms, too. Maggie, you take a quick look through this end of the house. I'll take the front, then check my bedchamber before we call the police. They'll want to know what was taken."

"No!" Maggie shrieked. "You ain't going to leave me down here by myself! He might still be here!"

"By thunderation, you stop that squawking right now! Whoever did this was gone long before day—"

Laurel interrupted. "Maggie, did you leave a sack in my room?"

The housekeeper looked at her in disbelief. "A sack? You ask a fool question like that at a time like this?"

"Sorry." Laurel turned to her father. "Did you? . . ."

"No, of course not!" He looked sharply at her. "What kind of a sack?"

"I don't really know. It was on top of my highboy. I noticed it when I awoke and heard Maggie. I'll go take another look." She headed toward the stairs.

"Wait, Laurel!" her father called. "I'll go up with you."

Maggie declared, "I'm coming, too!"

Laurel tried to tell herself the sack probably meant nothing as she followed her father up the stairs. Maggie trailed them, muttering in fear.

Ridge had a busy business schedule planned, but he used his shaving time to think. He swirled the brush in the mug, stirring up a thick white lather.

*No matter which way it goes,* he told himself, *there's a problem. If she agrees to accompany me, maybe we can talk through some of the things that are troubling her. But after we get there, that could all be undone if she thinks my friends are being cool toward her. And if Varina pulls another of her stunts. . . .*

Ridge shook his head, the thought unfinished. But the alternative immediately demanded his attention. *Yet, if I leave her here and something happens. . . .*

His thoughts were snapped off by a knock on the door. He

glanced at his pocket watch where it lay face up on the night stand. Seven-thirty. Who could that be at such an early hour?

"Just a minute!" he called, rapidly rinsing the razor in the soapy water and giving it a quick wipe on the towel hanging by the mirror. He crossed the floor and opened the door.

"Mr. Kelly!"

"Granger."

Ridge commented, "I'm surprised to see you out so early in the morning. Don't you ever sleep?"

"I can't sleep when I've got a case that bothers me, and this one sure does. Besides that, the lieutenant is putting the spurs to me because I've got other cases that he says I'm neglecting."

Ridge suspected the detective was trying a different tactic; making himself seem sympathetic after yesterday's blustery attempt to interrogate him. Ridge pointed to the single comfortable chair. "I'm sorry about that, Kelly. Sit down. Mind if I finish shaving? I've got a busy day ahead of me."

"Shave away, Granger." Kelly sank heavily into the chair. "There's something missing in this case, but I can't put my finger on it. Maybe you can help."

Ridge moved the mirror so he could see his visitor in the reflection. "I hope you're not going to bring up that idea from yesterday about something you think Laurel and I are keeping from you."

"Oh, I'll work on that, but I'm not here for that reason. I've repeatedly gone over your sweetheart's and your statements about what you saw when you first arrived at the murder scene. But when I got back to the precinct last night and again examined the pictures our department photographer had taken, I noticed something."

"What was that?"

"You seem to forget who asks the questions."

"Sorry." Ridge rinsed the razor in the wash basin, carefully dried it on the towel, then folded the blade inside the handle. "Ask them, then."

"Think back." Kelly took out his pad and pencil. "Who else was there besides you and your lady friend?"

Ridge sat at the foot of his bed. "You took both of us out into the parlor so Laurel wouldn't have to look at Sarah. You asked. . . ."

"No! No! Before that. Who was there besides me and the uniformed beat officer the neighbor summoned?"

Ridge shook his head. "I didn't pay much attention, beyond noticing a couple of newspaper people. A woman, Charity, I think her name was. I was introduced to her yesterday."

"Charity Dahlgren of the *Illustrated Press*. She was at the station when I got the call. So was Vance Cooper, the new crime reporter for the *Globe*."

"He was the last to arrive at the scene. I met him at the cemetery when he introduced himself to Laurel and me."

The detective cocked his head. "From your tone, I gather that you weren't favorably impressed with him."

"I thought it was a very inappropriate time to approach Laurel about an interview."

"Sometimes newspaper people are like that. They also like to hang around the station house even when there's no real news. Anyway, besides them, who else do you recall seeing inside the house at the crime scene?"

"Just you and the police photographer."

"His name's Darius Barr. He's good at what he does. I was looking at the crime scene photos he took and noticed something."

Ridge opened his mouth to ask what he had noticed, but closed it before he could be reprimanded again.

Kelly noticed and smiled before asking, "Did any neighbors get in?"

"No. Not that I noticed. Nobody even came near until after Laurel had a neighbor go find a policeman. When neighbors started coming, I wouldn't let them inside."

"You sure? Not even one?"

"Positive. When the uniformed officer arrived, he took over until you and your team arrived. Why? What's this have to do with? . . ."

Ridge caught the disapproving look on Kelly's face and left the question unfinished. "Sorry, Kelly; I keep forgetting."

The detective stood and replaced his note pad. "I'm glad you're cooperating with the investigation, Granger."

"I'm afraid I wasn't much help."

"Ah, but you were!" Kelly said softly.

He left without another word, leaving Ridge frowning in perplexity. *How could I have helped him?* he wondered, then he hurriedly made a decision. His business would have to wait while he went to see Laurel.

Laurel's father stepped inside her bedchamber and stopped, forcing the two women to do the same in the doorway. He glanced at the sack on top of the highboy, then scanned the room. "Laurel," he asked without looking at her, "does everything else look normal in here?"

Her eyes swept the chamber. "I think so."

"Maggie, you ever see that sack before?" he asked.

"No. Never." There was a tremor in her voice.

Laurel started to push by her father. "I want to see what's in . . ."

"No!" he broke in. "I'll do that. You stay here."

She waited impatiently as he approached the six-foot-high walnut Chippendale highboy with brass ornamentation on its seven drawers. The sack was of coarse material which Laurel recognized as something called gunny. It had collapsed upon itself and seemed empty, but that didn't seem logical to her.

Of course, Laurel thought, the burglar must have brought it to carry off whatever he stole, and either forgot it or got scared off somehow.

Her father carefully felt the sack. "Seems empty," he said, lowering it in front of him. "No, wait! There's something at the bottom."

Laurel joined him as he slowly opened the top and looked inside. "What is it?"

"Looks like a photograph."

"Let me see."

He reached in and retrieved it, holding it up as Maggie joined them. "That's what it is," he said, "a tintype of a park or something. No people in it."

Laurel took it, glanced at it, then turned it over. "Nothing on the back, so it was probably not made by a professional studio. They usually put their name on these things."

Maggie shook her head. "Well, you two can stand there all day looking at that, but I'm going to check the rest of the house."

Bartlett asked in a teasing tone, "Aren't you afraid he might be hiding somewhere and carry you off?"

"Not likely! Any thief stupid enough to leave his bag instead of carrying things off in it don't scare me much. Still, it won't hurt to take my rolling pin along."

"If you find anything missing, call me, then go find a policeman." Bartlett looked at his daughter. "What's the matter?"

"What? Oh, nothing, Papa."

"Don't try to fool me. You were thinking of something that frightened you."

She gave his arm a quick pat, silently conceding that she had thought that maybe there had been a dead mouse or something in the bag. But now she understood that the intruder had done this to prove a point.

"It's nothing for you to fret about, Papa. But I'm concerned because somebody was in this room last night while I slept."

"Not necessarily. When Maggie told me yesterday about that window being open, I should have checked around. He probably had been up here, left this, and then got away before Maggie noticed the window."

"That would mean he did this in daylight, with Maggie and you in the house. Besides, I'm sure I would have noticed this sack last night before I went to bed. No, Papa, somebody did this last night."

He set the sack on the floor and put his arms around her. "I hope you're wrong, but if you're right, does this have anything to do with what you won't tell me about Sarah's murder?"

Laurel suppressed a shiver, not wanting to alarm him any more than she already had. "I don't know. But it doesn't make sense. Why would a burglar have a photograph in his sack?"

"Maybe he didn't realize it was there."

Laurel freed herself from her father's arms. "Let me see that photograph again."

He held it out so they could examine it together. "Hm?" he mused. "I seem to remember seeing something like that, but I can't remember when or where."

"I was thinking the same thing. There's something vaguely familiar looking about that tree on the right. May I keep this for awhile? I want to study it."

"Of course. Now, I don't want you to be frightened. I'll have all the doors and windows checked, and then I'll personally make sure they're locked each night before bedtime."

"Thanks, Papa." She gave him a quick kiss on the cheek.

"Now, if you'll excuse me, I'd better get dressed."

After he had gone, she took the photograph to the window. She raised the shade and pushed the lace curtain aside to allow the morning sunshine to fall upon the photograph. For a long moment, she scowled thoughtfully, yet she couldn't place the scene. But something else clicked into her mind. "Of course!" she exclaimed aloud, her mind suddenly racing.

*He didn't forget his sack. He deliberately left it as a warning that he could have murdered me. He wanted me to know that he was in my room. But he must have overlooked this picture. Well, it's not much, but it's all I've got.*

Laurel hastily dressed, knowing what she had to do.

From his rented room, the man with the spectacles watched Laurel push the curtains aside to hold something to the light. He smiled with satisfaction, confident that he was fully in control of both Laurel and the police. Yet neither knew that.

He had carefully chosen the sack to mislead the detectives. It meant nothing, but it would cause them to waste time, just as they were now doing because of a miscue he had deliberately left at the murder scene. These would give him time to carry out his carefully-thought-out plan for Laurel.

*Now she'll do just what I want her to do,* he assured himself. *She's not yet really frightened, but slowly, she will be. When she finally knows what stark terror is, it'll be too late.*

# Chapter 9

Ridge's reasons for going to see Laurel were forgotten when he learned about the break-in. That was of more concern than speculating what Kelly might have meant by saying Ridge had been of help to him. But the brazen intruder's action was a strong new reason for Ridge to insist Laurel accompany him to Virginia.

Standing outside with Laurel and her father, he examined the window where entry had been made. They were careful to avoid getting too close because the authorities had not yet arrived to investigate.

Bartlett said, "It's my fault because I didn't close this window yesterday after Maggie said it was open."

"Papa," Laurel protested, "don't blame yourself. It turned out all right; nothing's missing and no harm has been done."

He straightened up to look at her. "I would like to believe that, but after those two letters and now this, it's obvious that you and Ridge are keeping something from me and Kelly. It's time you told me about it."

She shook her head. "I can't, Papa. I just can't."

He turned to Ridge. "How about you?"

He stood up and brushed dirt off his hands but did not reply.

"I see," Bartlett said softly. "Well, then I'll be blunt. So far, there's been no real danger that we know about. But this thing shows signs of escalating into something worse than a break-in.

Ridge, are you willing to risk that with the woman you love?"

Ridge's jaw muscles twitched in his struggle to control his emotions. He turned to face Laurel. "Your father's right. For your safety, we should leave for Virginia at once."

Laurel knew he was right, but she shook her head. "I can't. I've told you why. Besides, that would be running away, and I'm not going to do that."

Ridge cried in exasperation, "You are the prettiest, the most wonderful woman I've ever known! But you are also the most stubborn. I love you too much to stand by and not do what my heart tells me. You must go with me! We can leave today—"

"I must?" Laurel exploded indignantly. "You are not my husband, and even if you were, you cannot tell me what to do! Is that clear?"

Instantly, Laurel regretted her words and realized she had gone too far. Even looking at him in her anger, she felt the same strong attraction she always had when he was near. But she couldn't make herself apologize.

Ridge's words spewed out in an angry stream. "It certainly is clear! I also now understand why you have been reserved since you got back from Sacramento. You obviously want out of our engagement."

He paused, waiting for her to protest, but when she stood mute, he snapped, "I told you that I wouldn't walk out on you again, so I'll give you the opportunity to do that to me instead."

He held her eyes, silently imploring her to turn him down. He wanted to take her in his arms and express regret for his outburst, but he resisted and just waited.

Her heart suddenly ached, silently trying to cry out in surrender, but her stubborn nature bound her tongue.

Bartlett protested, "Now, just a minute, you two! When you're both angry is no time to act rashly!"

"It's all right, Papa," she said in a whisper, her eyes still on Ridge. "Marriage would never work for us." She whirled, lifted her skirts, and hurried toward the backdoor. When he did not call for her to stop, she broke into a run to get inside before she began to weep.

By the time Kelly arrived to take Laurel's statement, she had regained her composure and wrapped her heart in a protective covering of anger. She turned some of that on the detective when he again asked her what she was not telling him.

"I'm not going to answer that question again, Mr. Kelly!" she replied irritably. "Now, if you've got all you need, please leave. I must go talk with my father."

The detective's face tensed, but he spoke quietly. "I will overlook your bad manners this once because I have been around police work long enough to know what kind of stress you're under. But I must advise you what common sense tells me this means."

He paused, absently fingering the photograph in his right hand. He held the sack in the other. "Nothing was taken, which indicates to me that this break-in was meant as a warning. It proves the perpetrator could enter your bedchamber while you were asleep, and leave these."

He held up the sack and the photo. "It also proves that he could do so undetected, but it's even more than that. Since the window was known to be open yesterday, it shows the responsible party was so sure of himself that he didn't break and enter at the same time. Instead, he came twice. That's either daring or foolish.

"Either way, this is very unusual behavior. It's not the work of an ordinary burglar. I'm satisfied that it somehow ties in with the death of your friend. My guess is that you are also a potential victim, Miss Bartlett. So if you value your life, you must cooperate and tell me what I need to know."

*Of course I value it, but I can't tell you what you want!* Laurel silently protested. Frustrated, she moved away from the highboy and approached the window. Shoving the curtains aside, she looked out without focusing on anything while her thoughts raced. She was trying to justify walking out on Ridge.

That had severely torn up her emotions, but one factor was unchanged: if she told Kelly she suspected Sam Maynard, she would have to tell him why. Kelly would then surely access her confidential Federal documents file. Sarah and Laurel's war-time activities would be known. Kelly would have to make a written police report which newspaper correspondents like Cooper and Charity would read and perhaps report. Laurel's carefully-guarded past would no longer be secret. She couldn't risk that.

*But what if it's not Maynard?* she wondered. *What if it's someone else, someone whose motive I can't guess? But there's one thing I do know: Kelly's right. Whoever was in this room last night will probably come again, no matter how carefully Papa tries to lock the house. That could put him and Maggie in danger, and not just me.*

She shuddered, thinking about how easily last night's intruder could have killed her. *I still can't risk staying here anymore. But where can I go to be safe until I figure this out?*

She dropped the curtain into place and turned away from the window. "Mr. Kelly, may I keep that photograph?"

"Sorry, it's evidence."

"How could it be? If the burglar is as clever as you say, he wouldn't have been careless enough to leave something like that. It has to be an oversight."

"Maybe, or maybe he wanted this to be found." He glanced down at the picture. "You ever see this place?"

She stepped closer for another quick look. "Both my father and I seem to remember it from somewhere, but we can't place it."

"I see." He slid the photo into his pocket. "You going to continue to live here?"

"I think I'll take a hotel room for a few nights."

"Good idea. Just make sure your father knows where you are so I can reach you if I want."

She said she would, and he left. Laurel returned to the window and stood silently looking out, though not really seeing. She knew that she should move out at once. She wasn't a little girl to be protected by her father.

"Little girl!" she whispered aloud. "That's when I saw that tree!"

The mental image came sharply into view. *Sarah and I were about twelve when we went on a hayride with our Sunday School class and the team passed that tree. Ghost Tree, that's what we called it.*

It had been topped twenty feet above the ground and turned ashen gray with time. The broad trunk extended up past two opposing limbs so that the tree resembled a headless man with outstretched arms but no hands.

*It's the angle in the photograph that fooled me,* she told herself. *It was taken off to the side, instead of straight on. Now, where was that? . . . Oh! Yes, of course!*

She headed to her armoire for her reticule.

🍂

Standing back from his bedroom window so that he could not be seen, the man watched the curtains close behind Laurel for the second time. The detective had earlier passed in front of Laurel's window holding the sack. It was a reasonable assumption that he now also possessed the photograph. Shortly before, Ridge had been observed walking rapidly away from the Bartlett house. A faint smile touched the man's lips. He headed for the door.

Ridge leaned forward in his chair to look across the desk of Emory Brush's small and dingy office. "Are you sure?"

"You doubt my word, Granger?"

"No, of course not. I thought I already knew the answer, but I wasn't sure, or I wouldn't have asked."

"Now you know." The dark-complected man shifted his two-hundred-pound body in the protesting chair. "It was not any of my men she saw behind that tree yesterday."

"And your man last night didn't see or hear anyone enter or leave her house?"

"He failed. Even the best of us sometimes do that."

"I know. I'm just trying to figure out what kind of a person we're dealing with."

Brush raised his left hand and scratched at the stubble of dark beard. Ridge noticed the scar, recalling the police desk sergeant saying it was one of three wounds Brush received in the late war. He had blocked a Confederate bayonet thrust with that hand. After the war, he had briefly returned to plain clothes work before opening his own agency.

A good man, the sergeant had assured Ridge.

Brush told Ridge, "I hate it when one of my men fails to do his job right. I wish I could guarantee that it won't happen again, but we both know that's not possible. So if you want, I'll give you your money back."

Ridge shook his head. "I just want her protected."

"The only sure way to do that is to take her away from here until this thing is solved."

Ridge stood up. "I've tried. To make matters worse, she and I . . . well . . . as of a little while ago, we're not planning on getting married. But I still want her protected around the clock."

Brush also got to his feet. "We'll do that. Wherever she goes, one of my men will be close by. We'll keep better watch at night, too."

"Thanks." Ridge walked out, but he didn't feel the confidence he had hoped for.

❧

In the half-hour ride after Kelly left, Laurel's thoughts drifted from the Ghost Tree to Ridge. *I was wrong to speak so sharply to Ridge before walking out on him this morning. I probably shouldn't have done that, either, even when he made me so angry. But it's just as well; we both know it would never work out for us.*

As the hack rolled away from the city, Laurel sank so deep into recrimination that she didn't notice when the horse stopped.

The driver's voice roused her. "We're here, Miss."

She raised her head and glanced around. *It's changed a lot,* she thought, *it's overgrown, but there's that strange tree.*

The end of the right limb had broken off, but there was no doubt it was the same tree. Laurel clutched her reticule and started to step down to take a closer look.

"Excuse me, Miss," the driver said. "It's none of my business, but I wouldn't want my daughter to get out here, not even in daylight."

She hesitated, one foot on the step. Glancing around, she saw that he was right. There were no houses nearby, and the wind moaned mournfully in the trees. "Maybe you're right," she conceded. "Could you just drive around so I can see the whole place?"

"All right, but I wouldn't linger, if I was you." He clucked to the horse and the vehicle crunched over gravel as it began moving.

Laurel's gaze skimmed the area, bringing back memories. This had been open area when she and Sarah were on that hayride. Laurel tried to recall who else had been along, but she could only remember Porter Armistead. She had been surprised that he had come along because his stern mother rarely allowed him to go on social events. Even on those few occasions, he had kept to himself, retreating from tormenting remarks by fellow classmates. It had been worse on the hayride because he couldn't get away.

Laurel took a deep breath, remembering. *That was a long time ago. So much has changed, but it's not pretty or anything worth taking a picture of. Unless . . .*

An abrupt thought made her chop off her question. She swiveled in the seat and looked back. Some distance behind, a cabriolet had stopped by the side of the road. The driver sat out openly in the front, but the folding top over the two-passenger vehicle prevented her from seeing if anyone was seated inside.

"Driver," she asked softly, "did you notice how long that cab has been there?"

"Sure, I noticed. Made me a little nervous because he's been behind us for some time. Stopped when we did."

Concerned, Laurel declared, "I've seen all I need. Is there any way we can go back without turning around?"

"There used to be a side road up ahead." He lifted the light whip from its socket. "Hang on to your bonnet!"

When the hack turned the corner, Laurel took a quick look back, then sighed with relief. The cabriolet had not moved. She shook her head. *This whole thing has set off my imagination. It's probably just a coincidence. But what if it isn't?*

Ridge was miserable as he forced himself to go through his business day. He managed smiles and hearty handshakes with prospective investors to whom he gave glowing but honest reports of what profits were to be made along the route of the transcontinental railroad.

He had learned that if he made enough calls, he would average enough sales for a profitable day. So he kept driving himself from business to business, in spite of the ache in his heart about Laurel.

*One more call,* he promised himself, *then I'll call it a day, and I'll have the whole weekend free.* He chose a large grain distributor because it was closest. He pushed open the front door and stopped.

"Sam?" he asked, peering closely at a man sitting in the outer office reading a newspaper.

His friend lowered the paper and peered through the spectacles. "Ridge Granger!" He leaped up, smiling and extending his right hand. "I thought you were in Omaha!"

"Just got back. What are you doing here?"

"Trying to see the buyer here before I head back to Virginia. And you?"

"Hoping to interest the owner in some prime real estate out west." He sat in the chair opposite his old friend. "Say, didn't I see you earlier this week at the train station?"

"Might have. I go there sometimes, wishing I was through here and on my way home."

"You sound lonely. You have a lady friend back home?"

"Not really. I want to get home because I don't like the big city. As for women, you know me. I never seem to have much success with them. But you—I heard you turned Varina down in favor of that pretty Yankee."

Ridge tried to not let his feelings show. "Varina made her choice when she married and I was off fighting the Yan—" he checked himself and glanced around to make sure nobody was listening. "Fighting the war," he finished quietly.

"Everybody's still talking about that. But it seems all of the women folks at home still think she'll end up marrying you."

"That's not likely." Ridge deftly moved away from the sensitive subject, his thoughts quickly turning to how best to frame a question that wouldn't arouse Maynard's suspicions. "How about during the war? Didn't you meet anyone you'd like to know better?"

Maynard slowly shook his head. "Not really. Once, while the Petersburg siege was going on, I met one who seemed to really like me. I mean, maybe it was the uniform, but she seemed genuinely interested in me. But . . ." he shrugged. "She left just before the Federals breached our lines, and I never saw her again."

Ridge phrased his question carefully and cautiously. "Did you get her name?"

"Wilson."

Ridge flinched, remembering that Sarah had first introduced Laurel to him as Laurel Wilson. It was the name she used when working for Pinkerton.

"Charlotte Wilson," Maynard mused. "She was so little and cute, with the softest Southern accent. . . ."

Ridge suppressed a sigh of relief. Charlotte, not Laurel. He thought carefully before asking, "Would you remember her if you ever saw her again?"

"I'm not sure. It was just that short time together. But you know, when I first saw your friend Laurel on the train pulling into

Richmond, for just a moment, I thought she was Charlotte. I got up courage to say something stupid like, 'Haven't we met before?' but of course we hadn't. So, how is she?"

"Laurel? She's fine. I saw her this morning."

"She's sure pretty, but I hear she's very saucy." Maynard grinned. "It'll take a man like you to keep her in line, but she'll be worth the trouble."

"She's saucy all right," Ridge agreed, mentally forming his next remark. "I hope you didn't get into any kind of trouble over this . . . Charlotte."

Ridge saw Maynard flinch before he turned away. Ridge waited expectantly, but the inner door opened. A balding older man stood there.

"Which one of you is Sam Maynard?" he asked.

"I am." Maynard quickly stood. "Ridge, it's sure good to see you again."

Ridge grasped at a fading opportunity. "How about meeting for supper tonight? We could . . ."

"Sorry, Ridge. As soon as I finish here, I'm heading straight for the train station." He turned and hurried toward the older man. "Sorry to keep you waiting, Sir."

Ridge scowled in frustration as the door closed behind the men.

❧

Laurel hated going to the undertaker's parlor where Sarah's widower worked, but she had to talk privately with him as part of her investigation. She had never been in such a place before. Every funeral she had attended was either in a home or church.

"Wait for me," she said to the hack driver who had brought her back from seeing the desolate place recorded on the photograph. "I'll only be a few minutes."

He nodded as she turned and took a final look back. There was no sign of the cabriolet she had seen earlier.

Taking a mental grip on her emotions and a firmer one on her reticule, she approached the funeral parlor's front door. She pushed it open. This activated a tiny bell that was intended to discreetly announce visitors, but somehow jarred Laurel's nerves. She closed the door behind her and stopped uncertainly on the thick carpet.

There was a wide door ahead of her and one on each side of the entry area. All three were closed, shutting her in. She was tempted to leave, but reassured herself that there was no reason to be uneasy.

Her nose wrinkled at the faint but strange smell that seemed to cling to everything, even the heavy gray curtains over the entry way windows. They added to the sense of gloom which was not eased by the light from a single kerosene lamp with a brass reflector mounted on the right wall. She reached toward the front door.

"Good afternoon . . ." a voice from behind made her whip around, her draw-string reticule swinging in a sudden wide loop. Her right hand flew to her mouth to stop the startled scream that almost escaped.

"Oh, John!" she exclaimed with a nervous laugh. "You startled me!"

"I'm sorry, Laurel!" he said in a low, soft voice which she suspected he practiced in his profession. "Are you all right?"

She nodded a little too vigorously. "Oh, yes! Fine!" She gave him a brief hug, adding, "I . . . uh . . . I hate to bother you at work, but . . . "

"It's no bother," he assured her, opening the door to her right. "Come in. We can talk privately in here."

She thanked him and entered a small room furnished with a clean desk, two chairs in front of it, and one behind. There were two windows on the left with white curtains which sunlight penetrated. She swept her skirts aside and discretely sat on the edge of the nearest chair.

He took the chair behind the desk and hunched forward, causing his black suit to sag over his bony frame. He regarded her with dark eyes.

"Thank you for coming, Laurel. So many people always gather around right after a death, but most seem to forget that the days that follow are sometimes even more sad and lonely for the bereaved."

Laurel squirmed uneasily at his misinterpretation of her call, but she didn't correct him. Instead, she gave a casual glance to his thinning light brown hair parted in the middle, his clean-shaven face, light skin, and freckles on the backs of his delicate hands. She seemed to recall that Sarah had said he was twenty-four.

She asked, "How are you holding up?"

"About as well as can be expected, thanks."

He spoke calmly, but his eyes suddenly misted, giving away his true feelings. He quickly turned his face away.

"If there's anything I can do. . . ." she began, knowing it sounded trite, but was somehow always the right thing to say under such circumstances.

Without looking at her, he replied, "Thank you, but no. It just takes time." He swung back to face Laurel. "Oh, Sarah was such a wonderful woman! Everyone loved her. She was a good friend to you, active in our church, a loving wife, and would have been the best mother, so why would? . . ." His voice cracked and he looked away.

It was obvious to Laurel he had no inkling of the thoughts that were troubling her. Sarah apparently had no warning or hint of her jeopardy.

It was awkward for Laurel, but she said, "Forgive me, but I have to know some things."

He swung his gaze back to hers. "I can guess. I told you that first awful night that I don't know who would have reason to kill my Sarah. Especially after she just lost the baby. . . ." He clamped his jaws tightly.

Laurel gave him time to regain his composure by saying, "I remember. But I've been wondering, did she . . . did she tell you much about what she and I did in the war?"

"Yes, all of it. She was very patriotic, and I'm proud of what she helped you do."

"Uh . . . did you ever tell anyone else?"

"No, of course not! She made me promise before she even told me, and I will keep that promise."

Controlling a relieved sigh, Laurel pressed on. "Did she receive any strange mail or anything unusual in the days before . . . it happened?"

"No. Why?"

Laurel didn't want to tell him about the two mysterious envelopes she had received, or the break-in last night. "Just curious," she explained, adding, "Sarah didn't act anxious or anything?"

"Well, she was certainly depressed about losing our baby, but the doctor assured us that was normal. You know, just going through the grieving period."

"I see. Did the detectives give you any indication of what they found? Any theory on who did it, or why?"

"No. Nothing."

"I hate to ask this, but I must: Did Kelly tell you why they think she was tied up like that?"

"No. But they did say she was in the kitchen when whoever it was surprised her. He must have slipped up behind her and clamped a cloth or something soaked in chloroform over her mouth."

Laurel sucked in her breath. "She was chloroformed?"

"Yes. The coroner told the owner of this place, not me. He said she passed out so quickly that she didn't have a chance to defend herself. She must have either dropped the dish she was holding, or knocked it off the table when she fell."

"Chloroform," Laurel mused. "That was in such short supply during the war. But I guess an apothecary might have a supply now."

"I suppose. Anyway, whoever he was then dragged her onto the back porch and tied her up in that strange way."

Laurel frowned. "Why would he do that?"

"Kelly doesn't know. It's lighter out there, which seems like a foolish thing for the man to do because it was daylight, and there are more windows out there. But Kelly says he checked with the neighbors, and they said the hedges are so high that they can't see our back porch."

Laurel's frowned deepened. "That's really strange." She stood slowly, feeling she had asked all the questions that she should at this time. "Well, I have to go, but I want you to know that I'll do anything I can to help see that Sarah's murderer is brought to justice."

"Thank you." He rose and reached for the door knob. "Oh, I almost forgot." He turned back to the desk and opened the top drawer. "This must be yours." He held out a single earring set with a black stone.

Glancing at it, Laurel said, "No, that's not mine."

"It isn't? Well, I know it's not Sarah's. I found it in the coal scuttle after the police left. It was empty that morning, so I filled it for Sarah before I left for work. So far as I know, you're the only other woman who was there that day."

Curious, Laurel touched the stone. "Would you mind if I took this along?"

"Take it. I certainly don't want it, or anything else that reminds me of that awful day."

Laurel's fingers closed around the piece of jewelry. *It might not have anything to do with the murder,* she silently admitted, *but I want to think about it.*

She gave Skillens another brief hug and walked out. She was already deep in thought as she entered the waiting hack. She didn't notice another one parked a couple of hundred yards away.

# Chapter 10

When Laurel returned to her father's house, she moaned inwardly upon entering the front door to find both her father and Aunt Agnes sitting in the parlor. Laurel instantly had to refocus her concerns from being followed and thinking about the earring that John Skillens had found after Sarah's murder.

Agnes turned cold blue eyes on her niece. "Where have you been, Laurel?" she asked in her tactless manner. "Your father and I have been worried sick about you."

"There was nothing to worry about. I stopped by the undertaker's parlor to see how John was getting along." It was partly true, but Laurel still felt a slight twinge of conscience. It was hard telling the whole truth after years of lying as a Union operative and then a detective sworn to keep her employment a secret. Sometimes the recent recommitment of her spiritual life was a problem, especially when nothing seemed to be going right.

"Humph!" Agnes exclaimed, plainly indicating her suspicion. "Your father told me everything that happened today. I'd like to hear what you have to say."

Laurel tried to keep her annoyance from showing. She set down her reticule before answering. She asked, "Everything?"

Her father nodded. "About the break-in, the sack and photograph . . ."

"And about your walking out on Ridge," Agnes broke in.

"Plus whatever it is that you and Ridge won't tell your father or the police about that murder."

Laurel took a deep breath before replying. "I don't feel like going over any of that. I'm moving to a hotel."

"What?" Agnes exclaimed. "I'm surprised at you, Laurel! You didn't show very good judgment in walking out on Ridge, and now you're showing even less by going off alone where you can't be protected."

Hot anger surged through Laurel. For a long time, Agnes had stoutly protested the idea of having a Rebel in the family. But she had changed after getting to know Ridge in California, and was now on his side.

Laurel managed to remain politely calm. "You're entitled to your opinion, but I can take of—"

"Don't say that again!" Agnes broke in sharply. "You are obviously in some kind of jeopardy. . . ." She took a quick short breath and finished quietly, "So you need to be where those of us who love you can help. I understand why you're reluctant to stay here after that break-in, no matter how carefully my brother has tried to prevent it from happening again. You should come stay with me."

Laurel's eyebrows shot up in surprise. "With you?"

"Yes." Agnes dropped her eyes. "You can help me get ready for my wedding."

All of Laurel's anger flowed out in a spontaneous burst of excitement. She impulsively reached out to hug her aunt, but stopped, remembering she didn't like to be touched. "Oh, Aunt Agnes," Laurel cried happily. "I'm so glad you decided to marry Horatio Bodmer!"

Bartlett protested, "Well, I'm not! It's not wise for a woman your age to move clear out to California to marry someone you've only known a short time!"

"My age," Agnes answered crisply, "is what gives me the wisdom to know that I missed one chance at marriage many years ago, and I'm not going to miss this one." She turned to Laurel. "I hope you're not making the same mistake now that I did when I was young."

Laurel wasn't really surprised by her aunt's blunt remark, but she decided not to say the angry *it's none of your business!* thought that leaped to her mind. She rationalized, *When Sarah's murderer is caught, Pinkerton is sending me back to California. That might be good, being as far away from Ridge as possible.*

Laurel admitted, "I also hope I'm not making a mistake."

"That's a good start," Agnes commented. "I asked your father if he would go to Sacramento to give me away, but he can't. So would you be my bridesmaid?"

Laurel was surprised by the unexpected invitation. *Well, why not?* she asked herself bitterly. Another wedding, and again a bridesmaid but never a bride. She tried to push away the painful lump that formed in her heart at the thought of losing Ridge. "Thanks for asking," she said sincerely. "Let me think about it."

"Of course. But do that at my house tonight."

A slight frown touched Laurel's forehead. She was reluctant to do that for two reasons. She didn't want to risk undoing the tenuous but improved relationship with her sharp-tongued aunt. Laurel also didn't want to chance having somebody follow her to Agnes's place and maybe put both their lives in peril. But she could go at night and make sure she wasn't being followed.

Laurel sighed. "Thank you. I believe I will, but it's got to be later tonight, then later I'll move to a hotel."

"We can talk about that part later," Agnes said, "but for tonight, I'll leave the light on for you."

After leaving Maynard in the office of the large grain distributor, Ridge impatiently waited outside in hopes of riding with him to the train station. He was sorry he hadn't thought to suggest that inside. Ridge passed the time speculating about Maynard. What had caused him to flinch when Ridge indicated he hoped Sam hadn't gotten into any kind of trouble over the woman at Petersburg?

*What was it?* Ridge asked himself. *Pain? Regret? Fear? Or something else? I wonder if Griff knows what happened to Sam after Petersburg?*

Thinking of Griff made Ridge recall the letter in which he said that the local gossips still expected him to marry Varina. He didn't want to marry anyone except Laurel. But it took two to make a marriage, and she had obviously changed her mind.

Ridge briefly thought of returning to Virginia to both talk business with Griff and to try pinning Maynard down on what had happened to him at Petersburg. But that would mean leaving Laurel here when she was in danger. Even the private detective Ridge had hired to protect her had allowed an intruder to slip in and out of her room without being noticed. Maybe she was through with Ridge, but he loved her too much to be through with her.

His mind jumped to Kelly. *What could he possibly mean when he said I had been helpful to him? All I did was tell him who was at the murder scene just before he got there. Maybe if I could talk with Laurel. . . .*

He interrupted himself as Maynard and the buyer emerged from the building. Ridge hurried to meet them.

"Sorry for interrupting, Sam," he began, "but I got to thinking we could ride and talk on your way to the cars."

"I can't, Ridge. Mr. Wherry here has an appointment near there, so we're going to hail a cabriolet and finish our business on the way. Sorry. It was good to see you."

"Same here," Ridge replied. He was left standing alone, staring absently after them, his mind filled with unanswered questions.

Both Laurel's father and aunt couldn't understand why she insisted on arriving at Agnes's small home well after dark, but Laurel had prevailed. Even though she preferred to slip out quietly with only a small suitcase and her reticule, her father accompanied her in walking down the street to where she might find a passing hack.

They had only gone a short distance when she glanced back and saw someone walking some distance behind them.

Her father asked, "Nervous?"

"Not really."

"You think we're being followed?"

"I hope not."

"Look, Laurel, I'm not so sure that going off to stay with my sister is such a good idea. You'd be better off to stay with me. I had all the windows—"

"It's all right, Papa," she said quickly. "When we find a hack, I'll not go there until I've had the driver take me around until I'm satisfied nobody's following. So stop worrying."

"That's too much to ask, and you know it." His voice firmed. "I can't help being concerned when I know you're in some kind of trouble, and I hate being shut out where I can't help you."

"Please, Papa! Try to understand. There are some things that I must do on my own. I'll be careful."

They fell into an awkward silence, walking along until he found a hack. He hoisted her small bag into the vehicle after her. "Let me know if I can help," he said as the hack pulled away.

"I will," she promised, and turned to wave as the horse began moving along the darkened street. But she also looked farther back and saw a shadowy figure break into a run. She smiled, knowing he couldn't keep up that way, and his chances of finding another hack before she was out of sight were slim.

The man was pleased with himself as he rode alone in the rented buggy he had anticipated needing. She had left her father's house with a carpetbag, as he had expected. He had hurried from his room and through the night to where he had tied a rented horse and buggy a block away. He deliberately didn't light the buggy's coal oil lamps, but hurriedly took his seat and began driving along a side street toward Laurel and her father. He was in time to see Laurel getting into a hack.

As that vehicle pulled away, leaving her father standing there, the man in the buggy was startled to see someone dart out of the darkness, running toward him from the way that Laurel and her father had come.

"Hey, Mister!" the runner called. "Wait up! I'll pay you to use your rig. . . ."

Instinctively the buggy driver snatched the light buggy whip from its socket and cracked it smartly across the horse's back. As the animal leaped away, the driver turned to look back through the buggy's tiny window. The runner slowed to a stop.

The man in the buggy scowled. *What was that all about? Was it some plug-ugly planning to rob me? Or had he been trying to follow Laurel?*

The scowl deepened. The runner had offered to pay, but that could have been a ruse to get the buggy stopped. But if the runner had been following Laurel, that was something unexpected. What did it mean? Had he made a miscalculation? He reflected on that as Laurel's vehicle turned a corner.

When he reached the next street, two identical hacks were moving away, one passing the other. Which one was hers? He couldn't decide before the next corner, each turned in opposite directions. Which one? Which one? It upset him to not be in control, even from such an unexpected event.

A tiny knot of doubt nagged him as he made a choice and followed the hack which had turned right.

※

On the Sabbath, Laurel went to the church where Sarah and John Skillens had their membership. John helped Laurel meet and question the church members in a fruitless effort to learn of a possible motive or suspect. That afternoon, Laurel also interviewed Sarah's neighbors, but without discovering a single item that might help solve her murder.

Frustrated, but at least satisfied she had not wasted the weekend, early Monday morning Laurel dressed carefully and left her aunt's house, arriving at the *Chicago Globe* building shortly before seven o'clock. She found Orville Seymour standing in his office, smoking a cigar, and watching the bustling editorial staff through a large glass window. Vance Cooper stood beside him.

Seymour motioned for her to enter. She stepped inside, pulling her hoop skirt closer to her body to step through the door into his office. His hazel eyes studied her thoughtfully.

"Ah, Miss Bartlett!" he said, removing the cigar from his mouth. "All ready for your first day?"

She gave him a smile. "I'm ready."

"Good. Did you have a good weekend?"

"Yes, thank you." There was no sense in saying that her aunt and she had discussed tentative plans for Laurel to return to Sacramento with her.

"You remember Vance Cooper?" the publisher asked Laurel, jabbing toward the correspondent with the cigar. "He tells me you met a few days ago."

"Yes, we did. Good morning, Mr. Cooper," she said, giving him a friendly smile.

"'Morning, Miss Bartlett," he replied, lightly touching his heavy mustache. His brown eyes swept her appreciatively. "If you're ready, let's get started."

"I'm ready." She turned to the publisher. "Please excuse us."

"Certainly." He reached over and opened the door. "Just one final word of caution, Miss Bartlett. Remember what I warned you about Lieutenant Pierce?"

"Yes, of course. He eats correspondents. Swallows them whole."

Seymour grinned the way he had when she had replied to that statement last week. "And you told me that he may try, but he won't swallow you. See that he doesn't."

Turning to Cooper, the publisher added, "I never hired a woman before. I don't expect anything to happen that will reflect adversely on me or this paper. Do you understand that?"

Laurel thought she caught a flash of anger in Cooper's brown eyes, but there was no hint of that in his voice.

"I'll keep an eye on her, Sir." Turning to Laurel, Cooper added, "Let's get over to the precinct and find out if there's anything new on your friend's murder."

Before Ridge began his day's rounds of calling on prospective customers, he stopped in at Emory Brush's detective agency. Even before Brush invited him to sit down, Ridge sensed something in his manner.

"Something happen?" Ridge asked uneasily, locking his blue eyes on the other's almost-black ones.

Brush made a sucking sound with his teeth. "I had to let an operative go—"

"Why?" Ridge interrupted, getting to his feet in alarm. "Something happen to Laurel?"

"She slipped away from her father's house Saturday night after dark, and the man I had guarding her . . ."

"She's gone?" Ridge's voice shot up in alarm. He leaned over the desk. "You mean she disappeared?"

Brush shrugged. "I'm afraid so."

Ridge stepped back and almost tripped over his chair. "What time? What happened?" His words shot out in sharp staccato fashion. "Well?"

"She and her father left the house after nine o'clock with a carpetbag. They hailed a cab, but my man wasn't able to get one, so he tried to stop a buggy that someone was driving by. . . ."

"Never mind! What happened to her father?"

"Nothing. After she got in the hack, he turned around and returned to his home."

"Then why didn't you ask him where? . . ." Ridge checked himself, remembering that he instructed Brush to not let anyone know that Laurel was being watched. Ridge turned toward the door. "Get more men on this and try to find her. I'm going to talk to her father!"

Laurel and Cooper entered the brick building where she was

repulsed by the stench common to jails. The sergeant looked up from behind a wooden partition where he sat hunched over a desk piled high with weekend reports.

"Well, now Cooper," he exclaimed gruffly, "why are you bringing a lovely lady into this den of . . . oh!" He leaned forward to stare at Laurel. "I remember you! You sassed the lieutenant!"

Cooper said, "She sasses everybody. Sergeant, this is Laurel Bartlett. Laurel, meet Sergeant Kerston. He's all bark and no bite, but he can help us find the files that the detectives always succeed in misplacing before they go home from their shifts."

Laurel gave Kerston a friendly smile, but he again gave her an appreciative head-to-toe glance even though he was almost old enough to be her father. "How do you do, Sergeant Kerston?" she said.

"Miss Bartlett," he replied with a slight nod. "You look out of place around here, but you're mighty welcome, too." He glanced at Cooper and added in a mocking tone, "We get too many ugly kinds around here."

A feminine voice asked from down the hall behind the sergeant, "Oh, so that's how you talk about me when I'm not around?"

Laurel was pleased to see Charity Dahlgren hurry down the hallway. Her blonde hair was parted in the middle as when Laurel had first seen her, but she had created sausage curls which hung down the back of her neck. Earrings dangled from her lobes, adding emphasis to her pretty round face.

"'Morning, Laurel," she said. "It's good to see you again."

As in their lunch at the Excalibur Hotel, Laurel felt drawn to the *Illustrated Press* correspondent. "I'm glad to see you, too," Laurel replied sincerely.

"Here, now!" Cooper said with mock severity. "You two are competitors, so act like it."

"Ah, Cooper," Kerston grumbled, "leave them alone. It would

be nice to have some correspondents around here who wouldn't be willing to murder the other one for a story."

"Which is why we're here," Cooper said. "Sergeant, let me have a look at that police blotter."

"No need of that," Charity cheerfully assured him. "Not a thing happened over the weekend that's worth a column inch of type."

Laurel felt her hopes sag as Kerston spun the blotter around and Cooper skimmed it with a practiced eye.

Laurel asked, "Nothing on Sarah's murder?"

"No," Charity replied. "Nothing in the reports, anyway. But I haven't been able to talk to Kelly yet."

Laurel glanced at Charity's dangle earrings and thought about the one Sarah's widower had found in the coal scuttle. "Those are pretty earrings," Laurel paused, trying to think how to phrase her next words.

Charity lightly touched both ornaments. "Thanks."

Cooper looked up from the police blotter. "Are you going to stand there making woman talk or learn how to read this thing?"

"Sorry." Laurel stepped closer to him and looked down. "What are we looking for?"

"Anything besides arrests for drunk and disorderly, domestic violence calls, and other non-news entries. You see, Sergeant Kerston, or whoever's on duty when a report comes in, is supposed to enter the time and the incident."

Cooper's finger slid down the list. "We're looking for a robbery, burglary, arrest of someone besides vagrants. And especially if there's been a homicide. If we find something like that, the sergeant will pull the written report for us to get the details."

Heavy footsteps coming down the hall from the jail section made Laurel look up.

The sergeant said in a low voice, "Here comes the lieutenant."

Laurel sensed from his tone that the sergeant was at least a little apprehensive. She vividly recalled Pierce's curt treatment of her last week.

He strode into view, still wearing a rumpled dark suit, his eyes on a sheaf of papers in his hands. He looked up, took in all four people in a quick glance, then suddenly turned gray eyes on Laurel.

"You!" His voice was hard and cold. "What does it take to make you understand what I told you the other day?"

"I'm now working for the *Globe*," she quickly explained. "Mr. Cooper is training me to work this beat."

Cooper straightened up from looking at the blotter. "She's right, Lieutenant. Miss Bartlett started work—"

"You blasted newspaper people don't own this precinct!" Pierce interrupted, glowering at Cooper. "You want my cooperation, you play by my rules! You hear?"

Cooper's face darkened. "We're just doing our job! You know that the people have a right to know what's in public records, including police reports."

Pierce roared, "You want to get bounced out of here, too?"

"No, of course not!"

"Then don't lecture me! One more word out of you, Cooper, and you're out with her!"

Laurel's whole body flushed with mixed embarrassment and anger. "Sir, please don't shout at him because you're angry with me! I'm here on official newspaper business, so I hope we can work together. . . ."

"Do you think I'm a fool?" he snapped, thrusting his face toward her in his fury. "You're here only to get inside information about your friend's murder! Now, step outside so the rest of us can get on with our work!"

His discernment of her real motive unnerved Laurel, but she

kept her eyes locked on his, hoping he had not read the truth in them. "All right. I'll do that for now, but I'll be back."

His face contorted in wild rage as he drew back his right hand.

Laurel involuntarily drew back, but he abruptly spun around and stalked down the hallway toward the jail section.

For a moment, nobody moved. Then Laurel swallowed the ire that nearly choked her. She included Cooper, Charity, and Kerston in a quick glance. "I'm truly sorry about this," she apologized. "I'll wait outside."

Cooper bobbed his head. "All right."

Charity said, "Wait, Laurel. I'll go with you."

She was so distressed that she would really have preferred to be alone, but she nodded. The two women walked out into the sunny summer morning.

"I'm so embarrassed," Laurel confessed, walking down the five short steps before turning to the other woman. "I have never had anyone speak to me like that!"

"He wasn't always like that." Charity glanced up and down the street. "You want to walk? Sometimes it helps me to do that when I want to slap somebody silly and can't."

In spite of how she felt, Laurel appreciated Charity's efforts to lighten the mood. "I guess so."

Charity turned to the right, giving Laurel a moment to join her. "I'm sorry neither of us got to speak to Kelly about any progress on your friend's case."

"Me, too." Laurel didn't want to dwell on the subject because it only riled her emotions. She glanced at Charity's earrings and posed the question she had wanted to ask inside. "You have many pairs of earrings?"

"Oh, several. Why? Don't you like them?"

"I think they're very pretty, but I don't wear them very often. I just never got into the habit, I guess."

"I've used them for years. The trouble is, I'm always losing them. I sometimes pull one off, then lose it because I can't remember where I left it."

Laurel mulled her next question carefully. "Have you lost one lately?"

"Matter of fact, I did. How did you guess?"

Satisfied that she had solved the mystery of the earring John Skillens had found, Laurel asked, "Did it have a black stone?"

"No, I haven't had one like that in years."

Laurel's eyebrows shot up in surprise. "You sure?"

"Positive." Charity stopped walking and looked hard at Laurel. "Why did you think I'd lost one like that?"

Disappointed, Laurel shrugged. "Nothing important."

"I'm not so sure. From the look on your face just now, I get the feeling that you know something about an earring that's more important than I can imagine."

Laurel held the other woman's gaze for a long moment, wanting to trust her, to share confidences with her as she had once done with Sarah. As Laurel hesitated, she heard a horse pull up to the curb.

A male voice called, "Charity!"

Both women turned as a man in his late twenties struggled to lift a heavy camera and wooden tripod from the cabriolet.

"That's Darius Barr," Charity told Laurel in a low voice. "I want you to meet him. The police department recently started taking pictures of murder scenes. Maybe you saw him taking photographs at your friend's house?"

Laurel's stomach gave a violent lurch. She had been vaguely aware that a photographer was present at the time, but she had not really noticed the man. Now she did, sensing something in Charity's voice and manner that indicated Darius Barr was somehow special.

Taking a good look at him, Laurel was aware of his dark wavy hair and full black mustache. The hair was worn long and bushy in back. Only half of his ears showed on the side. His mustache stuck out a good inch beyond both ends of his mouth. He had a square chin with a deep dimple in the middle.

Charity whispered, "You want to know anything about photography, ask him." She smiled when he turned from paying the driver.

He returned the smile, glanced at the camera and tripod he'd set on the sidewalk, then walked eagerly toward the women. Laurel felt very uncomfortable, aware that he had pictures of Sarah as vivid as her memories of that terrible murder scene.

She suppressed a shudder, glad that she was not a photographer assigned to take grisly pictures.

# Chapter 11

When Maggie opened the door, Ridge wasted no time with formalities. "Do you know where Laurel went?"

The matronly housekeeper cocked her head and demanded, "Who wants to know?"

"I do! Maggie, don't exasperate me! Where is she?"

She replied impertinently, "I heard you two arguing after the burglary. If she didn't tell you where she's gone, I ain't going to, neither."

She started to close the door on him, but Ridge stopped it with his foot. "Maggie, she may be in danger! I've got to find her, and fast!"

For a second, Maggie seemed uncertain, then she shook her graying brown hair. "No. Now take your foot out of this door or I'll stomp on your toes!"

Ridge grabbed her by both shoulders. "I am not going to stand here arguing with you. Where's her father?"

She drew back her right hand to slap at him, but his grip prevented her from reaching him. She yelled, "No Rebel can lay a hand on me! . . ."

Laurel's father opened the door to his library and stepped into the hall. "What's going on?"

"This Rebel wants to know where Laurel is!"

"Well, tell him!" Bartlett started down the hallway toward

the front door. "And don't call him names!"

"I will if I want," Maggie said defiantly. "If you want him to know, you tell him, because I ain't going to!" She hurried past her employer, heading toward the kitchen. He turned to follow her with his eyes, muttering under his breath.

Ridge hurried to meet the older man. "Where is she?"

"Went to stay with Aunt Agnes for a couple of nights."

Ridge momentarily closed his eyes and threw his head back to sigh heavily with relief. "Oh, thank God!"

Bartlett added, "But she's probably at the *Globe* by now, starting her new job." He paused before asking, "How did you know she wasn't here?"

Ridge hesitated, grateful that Laurel was all right, but in his concern about her, he hadn't thought through what his appearance here would mean. He had already refused to tell Bartlett or Kelly what Laurel and he knew about her belief that Sarah's murder was tied to their war-time activities.

If Ridge now declined to say that he had hired a private detective to protect Laurel, it could jeopardize his relationship with the older man. Ridge didn't want that even though Laurel had broken their engagement.

"You've asked a hard question," Ridge said quietly.

"I'll try to make it easier for you. Let's go into my library and I'll listen to whatever you have to say."

Ridge followed Bartlett down the hall, trying to think how much he should disclose.

Laurel's initial thoughts about Darius Barr's grisly work vanished as she acknowledged the introduction by Charity.

Laurel showed her instant favorable impression of him by

doing what she rarely did: extend her right hand to him. "How do you do?" she asked formally.

He gingerly gripped her fingers and grinned at her. "Glad to meet you. Charity told me about having lunch with you the other day. I'm sorry about your friend."

"Thank you." Laurel commented, "You two seem to be good friends."

"Good enough to be betrothed," Charity said, lightly touching his forearm.

He added, "Only we're not ready to tell her folks yet. They don't like me being a policeman. They say it's too dangerous. We just can't seem to make them understand that mostly I just take pictures of crime scenes. . . . Oh, I'm sorry!" He slapped his palm against his forehead. "Me and my big mouth!"

"It's all right," Laurel assured him.

"Thanks." He turned to look toward the police building. "Well, I've got to get to work before the lieutenant has my head on a platter." He hurried to retrieve his tripod and camera.

"And I've got to dig up something for my paper," Charity said. "Say, Laurel, a bunch of us usually get together for lunch. You want to join us?"

"Oh, thanks, but I'm with Vance Cooper, and I'd better not do anything until I check with him."

"He usually eats there, too. Place called the Fog Horn, near the *Globe* building. I hope you can make it."

"So do I." Laurel added sincerely, "Thanks for being here with me just now."

"My pleasure." Charity joined Barr who had both arms filled with photography equipment. They entered the police station together.

Laurel stood alone, knowing that this had not been the time to bring up her idea with Barr. Maybe later.

Bartlett sat down in his leather wingback chair in front of the glass door bookcase and motioned for Ridge to take the matching chair opposite him.

Ridge glanced around the room, still undecided as to how much, if anything, he should tell the older man. Ridge recalled when he and Laurel's father had been here before. Later, Kelly had privately questioned Laurel and Ridge in this room.

Bartlett prompted, "You were going to tell me how you knew she wasn't here."

Ridge's eyes met the other man's. "Fair enough. I hired a private detective agency to protect her around the clock. This morning they told me that she had fooled one agent by leaving the house with you and going off in a hired hack."

"Ah!" Bartlett exclaimed. "That explains why I saw someone running after her hack Friday night. It must have been your agent. In fact, he tried to stop a passing buggy—hoping to follow her, I'm sure—but it didn't work."

He added, "I don't know whether to be angry with you for thinking I couldn't protect my own daughter, or to be grateful that you're concerned enough about her to have hired around-the-clock security for her. But he must not have been on duty when the break-in occurred."

"He was, but he failed. Anyway, Mr. Bartlett, I didn't mean any disrespect toward your ability to take care of Laurel. I love her, and since I couldn't be with her all the time, I did what I thought was the right thing to do under the circumstances."

Bartlett's eyes narrowed thoughtfully. "Even though she broke the betrothal?"

"I'm not giving up on our getting married. We've broken up before and gotten back together."

"Do you know why you have this tension between you?"

"I think so. She's afraid that other people won't let us be happy together. It's like the way Maggie treated me just now."

"You'll have to get used to her. I know she's a trial, but she's been with me since the girls were little. I'm sure she thinks she's protecting Laurel."

"I can understand that. But it's also a cultural aftermath of the war. When Laurel went down South, she felt the same resentment, although nobody's been as openly antagonistic as Maggie. Still, it hurts Laurel, and I don't want her to be hurt."

"Have you thought of moving out west?"

Ridge shook his head. "No. Even though my present work is there, I have plans to build a grand house for us. When Laurel was in Virginia that short time, I showed her plans I've drawn up. I'll soon have enough money from my business venture to build that house."

"I understand that your family's land was seized in the war under the Union's Confiscation laws. You can't build that house there unless you petition the President for amnesty and he grants it, restoring the property. Is that right?"

Ridge nodded. "Yes, it is. I suppose you could say that stubborn pride has kept me from applying so far. However, I'm considering changing my mind. If amnesty is granted, that will give me more flexibility for some plans I have."

"That's a start, Ridge. Compromise is a big part of marriage and life. Whether you live in Virginia or out west, I prefer that Laurel live near me. But I know that she must go where your work requires you to live."

Ridge met the older man's eyes, but didn't answer him directly. "I'd better go. I'm glad that Laurel is all right."

Bartlett rose from his chair. "Thanks for caring enough about her to do what you did. But we both know that all this is somehow related to the break-in. That's why she moved to my sister's place in the night."

Ridge got up and walked around in back of the chair, aware of the faint, pleasant fragrance of fine leather. "I've thought a lot about that, and now feel that you should know. However, she doesn't, and I don't want to betray her trust. Can you understand that?"

"In a way, I suppose I can. But I've also thought a lot about everything, and I think I see something."

Ridge waited while Bartlett walked around to stand by Ridge's empty chair.

"Take those two letters, well, envelopes, that came," Bartlett began. "Laurel opened the first one in front of all of us, but wouldn't say what was in it that frightened her. Later, Maggie told me that she had seen what it was that upset Laurel: a piece of newspaper with only a date on it of April 3, 1865. That's the day Petersburg and Richmond fell."

Ridge nodded, recalling how Laurel had shown it to him after he had taken her outside, away from her family.

"The second envelope," Bartlett continued, "was empty. She opened it at the cemetery after Sarah's funeral. I think that's related to whatever's going on, too, like the break-in. Ridge, this has something to do with the war when Laurel was absent for short periods of time, and never has said why. But I think you know."

He looked at Ridge who dropped his eyes.

"I thought so," Bartlett mused. "Now I'm rather fond of you, and think you'd make Laurel a good husband if she ever comes to her senses. But . . ."

He paused, his voice firm and louder. "If anything happens to her that I could have prevented if I had known what you do, then you'll understand that I'm going to hold you responsible!"

Laurel was getting impatient when Vance Cooper exited the police station and approached her. She said, "I guess I was wrong about not letting the lieutenant eat me alive."

Cooper grinned appreciatively at her. "He sure tried, but when you told him you'd be back, I think you gained his respect."

"Oh? How so?"

"After he calmed down, he came out to the desk and said he'd give you another chance."

Laurel's face lit up with delight. "Really?"

"Really. But you'll have to watch your step around him. Kelly, too."

"You saw him?"

"He came in the back way, but there was nothing new on your friend's murder."

"I had hoped there would be," Laurel said.

"These things take time. Incidentally, Kelly asked me if I knew what you and your beau won't tell him. I told him I didn't know a thing."

Laurel realized that Cooper's statement was meant as an opening for her to tell him more, but she wouldn't do that. She said, "That has nothing to do with our work."

"I see. Well, I didn't get enough news from here to even fill a column inch, so we'd better head over to the firehouse and see if we can do any better there."

"The fire department is also part of your—uh—our beat?"

"Sure is. If there's not been a fire of consequence, we can do a feature about the firemen, their horses, or something. By the time we finish there and get back to the paper to write our stories, it'll be lunch time."

"Oh, good. Charity said that sometimes all of you eat at a little place near the *Globe* building. Do you suppose we could join her?"

"We can if we don't get involved in something too pressing. But remember: she's competition, so don't mix friendship and work. If she gets a story ahead of us, Seymour will have you and me drawn and quartered and our heads hung on a pike."

Laurel made a face. "That's a terrible expression."

"Newspaper people, like coppers, sometimes talk a little on the rough side. Anyway, as I was saying, we could have lunch with Charity, but frankly, I was looking forward to just the two of us having that time to get better acquainted."

Laurel tried to keep a light tone. "We'll do that as we work together."

Cooper's voice dropped. "When we're working, it's all work. But I haven't forgotten what I told you the other day."

She put a little chill in her reply. "You mean your false accusation that I used my looks to get this job?"

"No, not that. I've thought about it. I have to admit that you were clever to think of a way to bypass the lieutenant so you can help find your friend's slayer. But see how discerning he is? He had already figured you out real fast. Anyway, we won't work all the time."

She frowned, not sure what he meant.

He reminded her, "Charity had put you up to asking my thoughts on what kind of a person killed your friend."

"Oh, yes. I'm interested in your theory about what goes on in the mind of a killer. It might help to find whoever murdered Sarah."

"I think it's more than a theory. After all, I've had occasion to interview several convicted killers and to cover stories about their victims. There's a kind of similarity to them even though I've never been able to get a detective to agree with me, not even the lieutenant or Kelly."

"I'd be very interested to hear more about your idea, Mr. Cooper."

"Vance. If we're going to work together, we'd better be less formal. Agreed?"

"Agreed. Call me Laurel."

"Good! We're making progress." His eyes swept her from head to toe. "So are you willing to make the trade I suggested?"

"Mr. Cooper," she said coolly, understanding what he meant, "you told me . . ."

"Vance," he corrected.

"You told me, Mr. Cooper," she reminded him with a tone meant to stop the direction of his comments, "you'd only do that if I went to dinner with you, and I told you that I'm betrothed. . . ."

She left the sentence dangling, knowing that was no longer true.

He reminded her, "Yes, and I told you that as long as you weren't married, I was going to keep asking."

"As you said a moment ago, when we're working, we're work-ing. I'm ready to learn more about my new job."

He shook his head. "Well, I'll have to try again. But for now, we'll work. Let's get back to the paper."

"Sounds good," Laurel replied, but she knew she now had more to contend with than just Lieutenant Pierce. *Not that it's a problem,* she told herself, *Ridge and I are through, so maybe . . .* She left the thought unfinished because even thinking of Ridge's name made her hurt.

Ridge knew he should be making calls, but his mind wasn't on business. He took a cabriolet from the Bartlett house back to his hotel. In his eagerness to see Emory Brush earlier, Ridge had not stopped at the front desk to check for any business notes or telegraphic dispatches from his Omaha office.

The hotel clerk reached into the pigeon hole behind him and handed him several wires. Ridge carried them to an upholstered chair in the lobby and glanced through the sheets. All but one was from his field manager in Omaha. Ridge laid them aside and read the one from Virginia:

*Imperative you come soonest. Griff.*

Ridge frowned, re-reading the terse words again. *Why didn't he explain?* Ridge wondered. *Must be personal, but whatever it is, he could have given me a hint.*

With an annoyed sigh, Ridge turned to the other wires from his Omaha manager. Each wire was encouraging, reporting a new and significant land sale along the line of the coming transcontinental railroad, but each message also asked for a business decision. They all ended the same: Can you come soon?

"No, I can't!" Ridge muttered, crumpling the last sheet in his hand. He glanced around, hoping nobody had overheard. He returned to contemplating Griff's cryptic message.

*But I can't!* Ridge told himself. *I can't leave Laurel now, even if she did say we're through.*

His thoughts jumped back to Kelly. *What did he mean when he said I'd been of great help to him? All I did was mention the newspaper people who were at the murder scene. How could that be helpful in solving Sarah's murder?*

Ridge sat quietly for several minutes, looking through the lobby window at the passing pedestrians, saddle horses, carriages, and dray wagons, yet not really seeing them. His mind whirled.

If he went to Virginia, he could not only see what Griff wanted, but he might also be able to talk with Maynard. Ridge was confident that Sam had not killed Sarah or was a threat to Laurel.

Still, Ridge was a little uneasy about the look he had seen on Maynard's face when asked if he'd gotten into any trouble over the girl he knew as Charlotte Wilson.

Ridge also needed to be in Omaha. The wires from there indicated that the business was growing so fast the manager couldn't handle it alone. Decisions had to be made, and that required somebody with time to think them through before acting correctly.

*I need a partner,* Ridge silently admitted. *Griff would be ideal in all ways except mobility. Still, even though he can't get around in that rolling chair, he's got a good head. He could make decisions and wire them to Omaha. That would leave me free to do what I do best: get investors interested in opening branches out west.*

He tapped Griff's wire. *I should go to Virginia right away. Laurel would be safe if she went with me. But how can I get her to do that when she walked out on me?*

With a heavy sigh, he shoved the messages into his pocket and stood up.

As Laurel and Cooper entered the *Globe's* front office, they were told that the publisher wanted to see them. That was an unusual summons because the editor was their normal contact. Laurel hoped she wasn't in any trouble for standing up to the police lieutenant.

"Sit down," Seymour said by way of greeting. He put his cigar into the ash tray as they eased into the two chairs opposite him. He reached into his desk and handed a letter across to Cooper. "Both of you," the publisher said soberly, "this just came. Read it together."

They leaned forward and spread the single sheet on the front part of the desk. Laurel skimmed the first few words: *Dear Mr.*

*Newspaper Man, I killed that Skillens woman. . . .* Laurel sucked in her breath and stopped reading.

Seymour asked impatiently, "What do you think? Is it genuine, or just from a publicity seeker?"

Laurel realized the question was intended for the veteran correspondent, so she waited for him to reply.

He turned the page over, examined the envelope, then handed both across the desk. "Publicity seeker."

Laurel cried, "How can you be so sure?" Then she glanced at the publisher and saw a slight frown of disapproval on his face. "Sorry," she apologized.

"It's all right," Seymour replied. He shifted his gaze to Cooper. "That was my question, too."

The correspondent leaned forward to face the older man across the desk. "This letter writer offers no details that haven't been written up and published. If he were the real perpetrator, he would have offered some proof, like something that hasn't been reported."

"Such as?" Laurel asked, then clamped a hand over her mouth. "Sorry again," she told Seymour.

"Again, a good question," he replied, picking up his cigar. "Cooper?"

"As you know, Mr. Seymour," he began, giving Laurel a knowing look, "the police often ask us to hold back some bits of information. We did that, so if this letter were written by the man really responsible for that woman's murder, he would have given some little tidbit in his letter to prove it."

Laurel felt her hopes fall. This had seemed like the first and only break in Sarah's murder, but it was just a cruel joke.

"Makes sense, Cooper." The publisher took a quick puff on his cigar and stood up. "All right. Give this letter to the editor for his records, but don't run the letter or even mention it."

"Uh . . ." Cooper began, also standing. "Could I make a suggestion?"

Laurel couldn't imagine what he had in mind, but she sensed that the veteran had an idea which might help solve Sarah's murder. This time, she didn't blurt out anything, but turned to Seymour and waited for him to ask the logical question.

He did. "What kind of a suggestion, Cooper?"

"Well, I've told you about my theories on those unsolved murders in New York, and that I think there may be some connection with this one."

"So?" Seymour said impatiently.

"So let me show this letter to Kelly and the lieutenant, and if they agree, let me write a story and include the points I just raised. If the real person responsible sees this, and he is the kind of person I think he is, he won't stand for someone else claiming responsibility. In order to prove that this letter writer is a fraud, the real perpetrator would logically have to give us some detail that hasn't been published."

The publisher looked doubtful. "I don't see how that will—"

Cooper interrupted, "Every little thing the police can learn about this killer will bring them that much closer to catching him. Letting me run this story can't do any harm, and it might provide just enough new information for Kelly to make an arrest."

Laurel nodded approvingly but didn't speak as the publisher stood in thoughtful silence.

Cooper added, "Why not give it a try? Right now, the police aren't making any progress. But if I'm right about the way this killer thinks, it's logical that he would write a rebuttal to this first letter in care of the *Globe* because that's the only place this story will run."

"That has some merit," Seymour mused, fingering the letter. "If your theory is right, it would boost our circulation to have a part in breaking this case." Waving his cigar, he added, "All right, Cooper. Run this by the detectives. If they approve it, we can still make the late edition."

"Thanks!" Cooper grinned broadly at Seymour and grabbed Laurel's hand. "Come on! Now you're going to see why covering the police beat is the most exciting and rewarding part of being a newspaper correspondent!"

He almost dragged Laurel out of the room, but she didn't mind. For the first time, there might be a break in solving Sarah's murder. Laurel would do anything she could to make that happen, and fast.

That night, the man entered his room carrying a folded newspaper. He laid it on the foot of his bed but didn't light the lamp because it might show him as he peered out the window. There he swore softly under his breath. Her bedchamber was still dark as it had been since Saturday night. He was still upset with himself for having followed the wrong hack that night.

He had hoped to learn something of her whereabouts at noon. He often overheard bits of minor gossip at the Fog Horn, but the usual correspondents and detectives weren't there. Only the pretty blonde woman reporter and her police photographer beau had shown up. They were so interested in each other that they had not noticed him, eating alone.

It wasn't too unusual for some of the regulars not to show up, so he consoled himself that they would be there tomorrow. Then he would find where she'd gone.

He walked back to the desk, lit the coal oil lamp, and carried it and the folded newspaper to the nightstand by his bed. He shoved the porcelain bowl and pitcher aside and placed the lamp on the end closest to the bed. He took off his shoes, stretched out on the bed, and opened the paper. The headline hit him at once:

### LETTER WRITER CLAIMS
### KILLING SARAH SKILLENS

In disbelief, he read the short story which had been squeezed onto the front page of the last edition. He re-read it again and again, resentment surging through him each time. He threw the offending paper on the floor, leaped up, and began pacing in high agitation.

An idea began to take shape in the man's mind. He liked it, rolling it around mentally, silently choosing the right words. He moved the lamp to the desk, sat down at his desk, and began to write. When he finished, he leaned back, trying to think of how to sign it.

It needed to be something intriguing and full of ominous meaning.

*Destruction! Yes, that's good!* He picked up the pen and started to write. *No, wait! That's too common. It needs to sound more sinister. What's the word in Greek or Latin?* It came to him suddenly. *It's Apollon in Greek.* He remembered because the word only appeared once in the Scriptures.

He dug in his small closet and found the Bible his mother had given him but he hadn't read in years. He flipped to the back of the New Testament and began skimming. When he found it, he gave a low, glad cry and again picked up his pen, then again hesitated.

*No, Apollon is too hard for readers to pronounce. It's easier in Hebrew.* He touched pen to paper and carefully signed it: *Abaddon.*

# Chapter 12

A cross town in a modest neighborhood, Laurel sat in her frugal aunt's tiny parlor which seemed overwhelmed with heavy rosewood furniture. The room felt especially dark and gloomy to Laurel because Agnes had lit the old-fashioned oil lamps. She resisted buying the newer and brighter kerosene lights. The only cheerful spot was a small vase of freshly picked flowers sitting on the dining table.

Agnes looked over the top of her silver-rimmed spectacles from where she was sitting in a Victorian loveseat with the popular leaf design. Her fingers continued to make the crochet hook fly in creating a doily for her new home.

"Laurel, I appreciate your agreeing to be my bridesmaid if I'll wait until you can finish your work with the *Globe*. But I've been thinking about that. I must wire Horatio of when to expect me in Sacramento."

"I can't give you anything more specific than what I've already told you: I'll leave as soon as Sarah's murderer is caught. I hope that's within the next two weeks."

"That's why I asked you to stay here instead of moving to a hotel. I suspect that this case would be brought to a quicker solution if you told that detective what he wants to know."

Laurel shifted uncomfortably in the Windsor chair. She had chosen it because the spindle back and saddle seat with raking

legs was the only item in the room which didn't seem to overwhelm her petite body.

"I'm sorry my father mentioned that to you," Laurel said,
wishing she had taken a hotel room tonight.

"You're being unreasonable," Agnes replied, her voice crisp.
"You and Ridge obviously know something about why Sarah was
murdered."

Laurel looked away, barely noticing the large mantle clock
with round gothic twin steeples and a scenic drawing of the
Potomac River under the round face. There had been a time when
she could barely stand to be in the same room with Agnes.
However, since their trip to California and back, Agnes had
changed. Laurel suspected that was because her spinster aunt had
decided to accept a marriage proposal, even though she was in her
mid-fifties. But she still had the same blunt way of speaking, and
that irritated Laurel.

She said tartly, "No, it's not obvious! It's just an idea I have,
and that's all it is."

The hook stopped moving and Agnes's piercing blue eyes
seemed to bore directly into Laurel's mind. "Let's see if that is
logical. You got two strange letters. Your room was broken into
and a sack and a photograph left on your highboy. You broke your
betrothal to Ridge. It is very obvious that you're under a great
deal of emotional stress, and probably because you think your life
is in danger."

"Aunt Agnes, I don't want to hear anymore!"

For a long moment, the older woman said nothing, but her
eyes never left Laurel's. "I believe you have just now confirmed
that I'm right about you being in danger."

Laurel snapped, "Even if I were, I can—"

"I know!" Agnes interrupted, throwing up her hand with the
needlework. "You can take care of yourself! Well, let me tell you

something that might change your mind."

There was a hint in her tone that made her niece wait without replying.

"My brother described the photograph that was in the sack," Agnes explained, "but he only got a brief look before the detective took it way, so he wasn't quite sure of some details. Tell me: was there a tree in that picture that looked like a headless person?"

Laurel saw no harm in answering that. "Yes, when we were children, we called it the Ghost Tree. Why?"

"During one of your many unexplained absences in the war, a young woman was found murdered there."

Laurel blinked in surprise. "How come Papa didn't tell me that? Or Kelly?"

"The detective and that other one, Pierce, were both away fighting the Confederates. Maybe my brother didn't remember, but I do. Her slayer was never found."

Laurel felt the skin on the back of her neck crawl. The reason for the picture being in the bottom of the sack now took on a new and sinister aspect. But she tried to sound unconcerned. "So?" she said.

"So there may be a connection. . . ." Agnes began when a knock at the door made her break off her thought.

Laurel glanced that direction, then back to her aunt. "Are you expecting anyone?"

"No, of course not. I rarely have evening visitors." She started to stand, but Laurel motioned for her to stay put, saying she would answer it.

"All right, but don't open the door until we find out who it is!"

Standing in the darkness outside, Ridge raised his hand to

knock again when Laurel's voice came through the solid wooden door.

She called softly, "Who is it?"

"Ridge. Let me in."

"We have nothing to say to each other," she replied coolly.

"Yes, we do!" He raised his voice and slapped an open palm against the door. "So please let me in."

Laurel didn't answer, but he could hear her lowered voice and her aunt's indistinguishable answer. Ridge started to knock again when the door opened.

"Thank you," he said, stepping inside and taking in the two women and the dark room in a glance. He looked beyond Laurel and said to Aunt Agnes, "Please forgive me for showing up so unexpectedly like this, but I just had to see Laurel."

"Come in," Agnes said, laying aside her needlework. "I'll fix us some tea."

Laurel started to protest, but Agnes quickly left the room, hurrying down the hallway. Laurel turned to face Ridge who was still standing.

"Please be seated," she said, trying to keep her voice from showing any of the sudden emotion his presence had stirred in her. "But I would appreciate it if you made this visit as brief as possible."

"I understand." He waited for Laurel to sit before he sank into the other end of the loveseat, away from where Agnes had left her project. "How have you been?" he asked.

"There is no point in your asking social questions," she said frostily, still trying to control her emotions. "Why are you here?"

He was annoyed by her coolness, but he determined not to let her know that. "Very well," he replied, "I don't intend to lose you, Laurel."

*And I don't want to lose you!* her heart cried, but her mind reminded her that they had too many obstacles to ever be happy together. "There is no point in discussing that."

She saw his jaw muscles twitch, but when he spoke again, his voice was calm. "You may be angry, Laurel, but I've come to tell you something I've done."

He briefly told how he had hired a detective to guard her day and night, and how he had failed when she drove away from her father's house Friday night.

She listened in silence, touched by what a sweet thing he had done, but she kept her face impassive.

He continued, recounting what Brush had learned from the discharged agent. "Someone followed you," Ridge said somberly, searching her eyes for a reaction. "The guard tried to stop a passing buggy, offering to pay to borrow the rig so he could follow you. However, that driver used the whip and sent his horse running after you."

Laurel licked suddenly dry lips. "How do you know he was following me? It could have been coincidence—"

"I didn't come here to argue with you!" he broke in, frustration in his voice. "The detective saw whoever it was follow your hack out of sight! Do you understand what this could mean?"

She understood. Even though she had not seen anyone following her when she arrived at her aunt's home, whoever it was probably knew she was here.

Ridge saw concern in her eyes. He pressed his advantage. "I got an urgent wire from my friend Griff in Virginia. He wants me to come at once. Please—come with me! You'll be safe. . . ."

Laurel's thoughts darted away. The killer had surely sent the picture as a warning to her. She was positive that it, along with the letters, the break-in, and the sack were meant to frighten her. She wondered if Sarah had any such hint of tragedy before she was struck down.

"Laurel," he said, breaking into her thoughts, "don't risk staying in Chicago; come with me right away."

"I can't leave here now for all the reasons I've already told you."

"You'd risk your life unnecessarily?"

He hoped his blunt question would make her see the sense in his suggestion, but she shook her head.

"You seem to forget that we are no longer betrothed, so why can't you accept that?"

He looked at her for several seconds before replying. "Because I love you, and always will. I know we have our problems, but we can work them out together."

"No, we can't. If it were just you and me, maybe we'd have a chance, but we don't, so we may as well face it."

"Even if I agreed with you, I can't leave you unprotected, knowing that you really believe someone is trying to kill you. I'm not going to let that happen!"

The words weakened her resolve, but she was determined not to continue with a relationship that could not end happily. She asked quietly, "Since I'm not going to Virginia with you, do you have any other suggestions?"

"Yes." He stood quickly and approached her. "Tell Kelly what you suspect. Tell him about what you and Sarah did in the war, and the two letters you received."

"No!" She cut in curtly. "I've kept that part of my life secret, and I intend to keep it that way!"

He sat beside her, his face clouded. "You're making him try to solve a murder without giving him vital facts that you possess. That's not fair to him, or to Sarah's memory. How can he do his job when he's handicapped that way? You're also risking your own life unnecessarily."

"I have risked it many times before, and I always survived!"

"Yes, but then you knew who your enemy was. Now you

don't. You don't even have a good idea of whom he might be. Laurel, I'm getting tired of trying to make you see that you're doing a very dangerous thing!"

She abruptly stood. "This conversation isn't getting us anywhere. You'd better leave!"

He challenged her with his eyes for a few seconds before slowly getting to his feet. "I don't want to do that, Laurel," he said, his voice low. "Let's talk. . . ."

"Goodnight, Mr. Granger!" She hurried to the door and jerked it open. She was breathing hard, her mind and heart in such terrible conflict that she nearly trembled.

Wordlessly, he stepped out into the night.

Laurel closed the door firmly behind him and leaned against it, fighting back tears when her aunt entered the parlor pushing a tea cart.

"Where's Ridge?" she asked in surprise.

"Gone!" She nearly choked on the word before almost running from the room. "Really gone!"

Ridge had only ridden a short distance on the rented saddle horse when he snapped his fingers. "Oh, no!" he muttered into the darkness. "How could I have forgotten to tell her about Maynard?"

He quickly thought it through. Maynard had already left for Virginia before Laurel was followed when she left her father's house. *But if I go back and tell her now, when she's feeling so stubborn, she probably wouldn't change her mind and go with me anyway. But if I wait a few days, maybe I can convince her to go with me to Virginia so she can talk to Maynard and satisfy herself that he's not the one who's bothering her.*

He hesitated, then wondered, *But what if something happens to her between now and then?* It was too late tonight to tell Emory Brush and have him assign another guard. He'd have to do that tomorrow. That left only one alternative: to ride back to his hotel, get comfortable clothing, and keep watch through the night.

The next morning went rather smoothly for Laurel, for which she was glad. Lieutenant Pierce allowed her back into the police station, but neither spoke to the other. She was glad to stay out of his way because she didn't want another scene with him.

Charity came into the precinct just as Cooper and Laurel were finishing reading the police reports of the night before.

"Lunch today?" Charity asked cheerfully, picking up the police blotter and skimming the entries.

Laurel replied, "As I said before, it's up to Cooper." She looked at him. "What do you think?"

"I think we had better find Kelly and see if he's got anything new, then we'll go cover the fire station."

As Laurel rose to follow Cooper, Charity called after them. "I'll look for you at noon."

"I hope we can make it," Laurel answered.

Cooper didn't say anything more until they stopped outside Kelly's small office. "Don't trust her, Laurel. Remember, she's competition."

"I'll remember," she promised as Cooper knocked.

Kelly called for them to come in. He sat behind a battered desk in a tiny cubicle that smelled of mildew and age. "Well," he said, leaning back and looking across the room at them, "you don't need to ask because there's not a single new lead on that murder. So, Cooper, let's hope that your idea works and that newspaper story last night stirs something up."

"It was a good story," Cooper replied, perching on the front of the desk. "I think it'll work. The only question is how long before that happens."

Laurel felt the detective's eyes shift to her. "You about to tell me what I want to know?" he asked.

She had thought a lot about that after Ridge's remarks last night, but she still held to her position. "I've told you all I can."

He asked gruffly, "Are you aware that you could be cited for withholding evidence in a capital murder case?"

She shrugged. "You're only guessing, and I doubt that you could charge me with anything on a guess."

"Don't be too sure of that, Miss Bartlett. If I don't turn up something worthwhile on this case pretty soon, and the lieutenant starts making things hot for me, I'm going to push you pretty hard."

Cooper said in a light-hearted tone, "Will you two stop quibbling? Kelly, if you don't have anything worth a few inches of copy, Laurel and I are going to the fire station. Maybe they'll have something worth printing."

"Maybe I do have something." Kelly turned to the file he had been examining when they entered. "Or again, it may be nothing. Miss Bartlett, do you remember the photograph that was left in the bottom of the sack?"

She felt herself tensing up, recalling what her aunt had told her last night about the dead girl. "Certainly."

"Take a look at this." He slid a folder across the desk toward her. "Happened during the war at the foot of that same tree that was in the photograph in the sack."

Cooper joined Laurel in glancing at the hand-written report. A seventeen-year-old girl had been found strangled early one morning.

"Never solved," Kelly said when the correspondents finished

reading. "Manpower shortage, mostly. No motive was known, and to my knowledge she was never identified."

Laurel asked, "Are you suggesting that there is some tie-in with this death and the picture that was left in my room?"

"I'm not suggesting anything," Kelly replied. "I'm just investigating, but there is one similarity. A newspaper was found next to her body."

"Just like Sarah," Laurel mused.

Cooper inquired, "Any clue with what was in the paper that might have been related to the murder?"

"Nothing in these files." Kelly looked at Cooper. "I don't hold with your New York ideas about how a killer's mind works, but right now I'm open to any possibilities."

Laurel turned expectantly to Cooper, hoping he would offer some insights into his theories which he had offered to discuss with her only over dinner.

He said, "My primary interest has been in murderers who kill more than one person and keep on doing it. I'm still sure in my own mind that those two women in New York fell victim to someone like that."

"Never mind all that," Kelly said impatiently, "just tell me again what you think."

Laurel urged, "Yes, I'd like to hear, too."

He grinned at her. "You're just trying to get out of going to dinner with me."

Kelly exclaimed, "Well, I'm not! Tell me what you think might be helpful here, or get out and let me work."

Cooper's face sobered. "Well, sometimes the killer seems to have an overpowering urge to leave some little personal sign of his work. Like a signature so people will know he did it."

"Such as?" Laurel asked.

"Could be anything. Like a newspaper, as was done at the

scene of your friend; or a piece of jewelry, like earrings. . . ."

Laurel involuntarily sucked in her breath, causing both men to glance sharply at her. "Sorry!" she said quickly. "Go on."

"In the New York cases, one earring taken from the first victim turned up at the scene of the second victim. That showed the killer wanted the police to know he had done both crimes. He also took one earring from his second victim, presumably to leave at the scene of his next crime."

Kelly made a face. "He was tormenting the police, challenging them to catch him. They never did."

"Killers can be egotists," Cooper said flatly. "And some are very intelligent. They think they can get away with murder, and sometimes they do."

"Yes, but those are rare," Kelly declared. "Most of the cases we get are done by stupid people. But I have seen a couple of very bright criminals."

"These earrings," Laurel said carefully to Cooper, "do you know what they were like?"

"It's been a long time, but as I recall, the second victim had dark stone ones a friend had given her."

Laurel tried to keep her face from showing any reaction, but both Cooper and Kelly looked at her.

"Why do you ask?" the detective asked suspiciously.

"I was just curious." She tried to sound convincing. Her training as a spy and detective had made her cautious. She kept pieces of information to herself until she had time to think about whether to share them. She didn't want them to know about the earring, not yet anyway.

She rushed on, trying to divert further questions along that line. "What else might a killer do besides leave his kind of signature?"

"Well," Cooper said, "As Kelly can tell you, sometimes a false clue is left behind to throw the authorities off."

"That's rare, though," the detective pointed out.

"What kind of false clue?" Laurel asked.

Cooper shrugged. "It could be anything, but preferably something that makes the detective think he's got something worth pursuing. While he's doing that, going off on a wild goose chase, the perpetrator is laughing to himself and the trail is growing colder by the minute."

"How about motive?" Laurel asked.

Again, Cooper grinned at her. "That's enough for now. Kelly doesn't really believe me, although I've talked to many confessed murderers and picked up some of this kind of information. And as for you, Laurel, if you want any more, you know how to get it."

Kelly grumbled good-naturedly, "Will you both get out of here before the lieutenant comes in?"

Going out the door, Cooper studied Laurel with his brown eyes. "How about tonight?"

"No, thanks." She looked more closely at his goatee. "Did anyone ever tell you that makes you look like a billy goat?"

They started down the hall toward the front of the building before he asked teasingly, "You want me to cut it off?"

"Don't do it for my sake, but you would look better if it was shaved off, leaving only your mustache."

His tone was bantering. "Have dinner with me, and I'll shave the goatee."

The sergeant stuck his head around the corner of the front office. "Hey, Cooper! The *Globe* just sent a boy over here with a message for you."

"Thanks, Sarge!" Cooper took Laurel's hand. "Keep that thought. Let's find out what's so important that a runner was sent for us." He hurried her along down the hallway toward a tousle-headed boy.

"Mr. Cooper!" he called, hurrying to meet the two correspondents. "Mr. Seymour says for you to come see him right now."

"Why?" Cooper asked, almost towing Laurel as he hurried after the boy who was already pushing through the front door.

"I don't know," the boy replied, hurrying toward a hack waiting at the curb with a driver. "But he said it's mighty important."

"Your story about the letter!" Laurel guessed, letting Cooper assist her into the vehicle.

"Sounds logical," Cooper replied, as the boy squeezed into the front seat with the driver. "Maybe we're finally going to get a break in this case."

Laurel fervently hoped so as the carriage lurched away and melded into the Chicago traffic.

❧

The publisher stood in front of the large window of his office smoking the ever-present cigar when Laurel and Cooper entered.

"Looks as if your idea might be paying off, Cooper," Seymour said by way of greeting. He waved them to chairs and returned to his behind the desk. "This came in today's mail."

Laurel felt a surge of excitement as Cooper reached out and took an envelope. He opened it quickly and spread out the single page of paper.

"You are fools," Cooper read aloud. "The letter in your paper on Friday was not written by the one who killed that Skillens woman. He's a liar, and you should have known that. That was my work, and here's proof. She was on her right side, her clothes discretely in place, and a copy of *The Illustrated Press* was at her right side."

Seymour said, "Those facts weren't in any of the local papers, so it seems as if this is the responsible person."

Laurel thought the handwriting looked the same as that on the envelopes she had received, but she couldn't be sure. Her eyes dropped to the signature. "He signed it, 'Abaddon.' What kind of a name is that?"

"I think I've heard it sometime or other," Cooper replied, "but I can't place it. Can you, Mr. Seymour?"

"No, but it does sound vaguely familiar."

"The fact that this man chose it suggests it has a bad connotation," Cooper mused. "Well, we've got Abaddon—whoever he is—communicating with us. That's a start to locating him. Since he swallowed this bait, maybe he'll go for another one and your friend's murderer can be apprehended."

Laurel eagerly asked, "Do you really think Kelly can do something with this letter?"

"Sure, if we help him." Cooper grinned and grabbed her hand. "Come on! Let's go see what he makes of this."

# Chapter 13

In Kelly's tiny office, Laurel watched with rising hope as the detective minutely examined the letter which Abaddon had sent to the *Globe*.

"What do you think?" she asked. "Does it give you an idea of who this Abaddon is?"

The heavy-set officer absently drummed big fingers on the desk. "I think the letter is genuine, and it's certainly more than we had before," he mused, pale blue eyes shifting from Laurel to Cooper. "Let's see what we can make of it before we take this to the lieutenant."

Laurel asked, "May I see that envelope?"

Kelly handed it over without a word. Getting a close look at it was all Laurel needed to confirm that it was addressed in the same handwriting as the two which had come to her father's house for her. She made her face impassive so that neither man noticed any reaction.

"I've got a couple of thoughts," Cooper volunteered. "First, we know he's very confident, or he wouldn't have written this letter."

"That," Kelly agreed, "or he's tormenting us, daring us to catch him if we can."

"Which we will," Laurel said fervently, handing the envelope back.

"Next," Cooper continued, "it's obvious that this man knew details about the crime scene that the first one didn't. But the tone of this letter indicates that the writer was maybe a little angry at someone trying to take credit for his crime."

"He seems to have a big ego," Kelly said. "Now, I don't want you to get the wrong idea, Cooper, but since it was your suggestion to plant this story, maybe some more of your beliefs about the criminal mind might be worth my time."

Cooper gave Laurel a triumphant smile. "I'm flattered, Kelly. But I'm also after a big story, and I think this case is shaping up to be just that."

"Never mind the blarney!" Kelly said quickly. "Just tell me what you think. Incidentally, if you tell the lieutenant that I said that, I'll hide every file you ever want in the future so that you couldn't write a story even if your life depended on it."

Laurel was a little uneasy about the semi-joking manner the men had adapted over Sarah's death, but she didn't want to stop the trickle of information that seemed about to begin flowing.

"Well," Cooper said, leaning back in his chair, "his ego suggests that he's either very intelligent, or he thinks he is. He's not only willing to take risks, but he seems to enjoy it."

Turning to Laurel, Cooper said, "That seems to tie in with whoever broke into your room and left that sack and the photo. He made two trips: one trip to open the window for entry, and then a return trip to actually do that. He was in your room with your father sleeping in the next bedchamber. That's unnecessary risk—unless that's why he does it. For the thrill, the chance of getting caught, but being confident that he won't be. That's also why he does the killings."

Gooseflesh suddenly erupted on Laurel's arms. "You mean he gets some kind of perverse pleasure out of . . . ?"

"Yes, he does," Cooper broke in. "During the interviews I did with multiple killers in New York, I became convinced that that is their motive, along with the sense of power it gives them."

"I can't believe it!" Laurel exclaimed.

"Oh, it's possible, I guess," Kelly commented. "I've dealt with men who loved to hurt people, just for the feeling it gave them. Strange thing, they sometimes had started out being cruel to animals when they were younger."

Cooper nodded. "I found that in some of my New York interviews, too. I also learned that many of them came from abnormal homes. You know, one or more drunken parents, beatings, that sort of thing."

Laurel protested, "But I knew of a case like that in our neighborhood, and nothing bad ever came out of it."

"Not that you know about," Kelly corrected. "When you've pounded a beat as long I did before I made detective, you'll find that there are secrets in many homes that no one outside of that home knows about. I even had a case where a preacher beat his wife, but the church members wouldn't believe her."

Laurel closed her eyes, thinking that she wasn't enjoying the police beat as much as she had enjoyed doing undercover work for big companies.

"So, Kelly," Cooper said, "let me make a suggestion. We try to find a way to keep this story alive so that the perpetrator continues to write to the paper. That'll give you something to work on, and I'll get a good story which, of course, I'll share with Laurel."

That was an offer she hadn't expected. But in her first reaction of being pleased, she was also aware it was possible that he was really just trying to improve their personal relationship. *Well*, she thought, *I'm not betrothed anymore.* She gave Cooper a little smile. "Thank you."

"Enough of this," Kelly said brusquely. "Let me get a few of these thoughts down on paper, and then talk to the lieutenant when he gets back from lunch."

"Lunch!" Laurel exclaimed, "That sounds good to me." She

turned to Cooper. "What do you think?"

"Why not? But if Charity Dahlgren is there, she's going to be a little unhappy because we got a story that she didn't."

"She seems really nice," Laurel observed.

"She probably is," Cooper replied, getting to his feet, "but never forget that she's competition. Don't trust her or anybody else with information that would give them a chance to beat you to a good story."

"I'll remember," Laurel promised, smiling good-bye at Kelly. At least there was some sign of progress in catching Sarah's killer, even if Laurel hadn't really done any effective investigating. Still, she wished it was possible to be friends with Charity, as she had been with Sarah.

Just before noon, Ridge headed for the telegraph office, feeling guilty for not promptly replying to Griff's wire of yesterday saying it was imperative Ridge come soon as possible. He struggled with his priorities of wanting to protect Laurel, the pressing demands of his thriving business, and the concern that Griff might have an urgent personal need to see him.

*I have to go see him,* Ridge told himself, *but I can't stand the thought of leaving Laurel behind. If there was just some way I could . . .*

He broke off his thought as a daring idea snapped into his mind. *She'll be furious,* he admitted, *but maybe that's what has to happen to make her come to her senses.*

He turned slowly and retraced his steps, fleshing out details of what he could say to overcome her anger and stubbornness.

The Fog Horn was packed when Laurel and Cooper arrived. There was about a fifteen-minute wait.

"Well," Cooper told Laurel, leading her back out of the way near the door, "I guess this gives us a moment to talk about something besides business."

"I'd rather talk about this murder," she replied, not quite able to let herself get interested in him even though she knew she was no longer engaged.

"We can talk about it all you want over dinner tonight."

It was flattering for him to be so persistent, but she just wasn't in the mood for that subject. She tried to think of a more neutral course. She said, "What got you interested in the mind of a killer?"

His face sobered. "My father was murdered but his slayer never caught."

"I'm sorry."

"Thanks. He and I were close. He was a railroad engineer who used to take me with him to the yards. He let me handle the controls and blow the whistle. All the things a young boy likes to do."

He fell silent, staring at the floor, so Laurel waited.

He continued, "I wanted to be just like him when I grew up, but I couldn't get a job on the railroad when I was old enough. I needed to work, and I had always liked words, so I applied to the newspapers, only they wouldn't hire me, either. Finally, I heard that the army needed engineers to run trains down through the South, and I applied there, too."

"You were a train engineer in the army?"

"No, I didn't make that, either. You see, it was very risky running trains through Rebel territory because the cab couldn't really be protected. There wasn't time for the army to train engineers, so they hired civilians like my father."

Cooper paused and shook his head. "He went all through the war, getting shot at, having the tracks torn up in front of him, all that sort of thing. But when he got home, somebody murdered him. Life is so strange!"

Laurel unconsciously laid a gentle hand on the back of his. "Yes, it certainly is."

She was aware that he looked down at their hands, so she quickly lifted hers away. "I'm still trying to understand how you got into those New York papers."

"They hired me as a photographer because they were scraping the bottom of the barrel. All the good photographers were off covering the war."

"And you never did get into the war, or become a train engineer?"

"Oh, yes, finally. The conscription act caught up with me, and since I didn't have any money to hire a substitute, the army swore me in. But not to fight. To help take pictures."

"The army had photographers?"

"Sure. Oh, I know that people like Matthew Brady get all the publicity, but there were some of us who had to do it the army way."

"But," Laurel pointed out, "that doesn't explain how you got to be a correspondent."

"I didn't like photography; that's how. I have loved to read ever since I was little, and I liked words, so working around the newspaper gave me a chance to try my hand at some no-pay stuff. Finally, I was on my way."

"Do you ever regret not getting to be an engineer?"

"All the time." He glanced around, lowered his voice, and confided, "Don't tell anyone, but I've applied to Seymour to be sent out west to cover the building of the transcontinental railroad."

Laurel pulled her head back and studied him closely. "My, you are just full of surprises!"

He grinned. "Have dinner with me and I'll give you my life's story on the condition that you first tell me about yours."

She shifted her feet, unwilling to even think about her past experiences. "I'd rather listen."

"How are we going to get to know each other better if you don't tell me everything there is to know about you?"

She had only told one man about her past, and that was only because they had expected to be married. Now that was over, and if Ridge hadn't been such an honorable man, she would have been fretting that he might betray her confidence. She wasn't going to risk telling anyone else.

The waiter came and said their table was ready. As they followed him toward the back of the long, narrow room, Cooper said, "You didn't answer my question."

"There's nothing much to know," she said evasively, and felt a twinge of conscience. Since returning to her childhood faith after meeting Ridge, she had tried hard to keep the commandments. Still, she hadn't really told a lie, she assured herself.

"Laurel! Cooper!" the feminine voice made them turn to look toward the back wall on the left. "Join us!"

Laurel was pleased to see Charity Dahlgren and Darius Barr at a table for four. Laurel was glad for an excuse to avoid any further potential personal discussion with Cooper, so she turned to him. "Let's do it."

He seemed less inclined, but graciously agreed. They slid into the chairs opposite the betrothed couple.

Charity turned mock accusing eyes on Cooper. "On second thought, I'm not so sure that I want to sit with someone who slipped a story over on me yesterday."

Pleased with himself, Cooper gave her a wide grin. "It's part of the business, you know. Always try to be one step ahead of the competition."

Barr defended his betrothed. "But you had an advantage. That letter quoted in your story was sent to the *Globe*, not to the *Press*."

"That's the way it is sometimes, Darius," Cooper said in good humor. "The breaks come to those who know how to exploit them."

Charity's eyes narrowed. "Exploit? You'd do that in a murder case involving Laurel's best friend?"

"It's my job," Cooper assured her.

Laurel saw that he was deliberately toying with Charity, delighting in seeing her discomfort over having been able to beat her to a story. At present, it wasn't really a big story, Laurel knew, but it might become one, and this was a side of Cooper she hadn't sensed.

A shadow fell across Laurel's face, making her look expectantly to see the waiter. Instead, Porter Armistead stood there, looking embarrassed.

"Oh, Porter!" she said, recovering from her surprise. "We seem to be bumping into each other a lot lately. How are you?"

"Fine." He didn't raise his eyes to meet hers. "I was just on my way out," he waved casually in the direction of the back, "and I thought I'd ask if there's any news on Sarah's case."

"No, I'm sorry to say. Oh, you've met Charity Dahlgren of the *Illustrated Press*. This is Darius Barr, her betrothed."

Armistead bobbed his head in acknowledgment but didn't do more than briefly cut his eyes in their direction.

Laurel continued, "This is Vance Cooper. He works for the *Globe*. As of this week, I do, too."

"You do? Congratulations."

"Thank you."

"Hello, Armistead," Cooper said. "I've seen you eating in

here fairly often." He glanced toward the back of the room. "You must like police officers. I've seen you before, sitting back there with a couple of patrolmen from our precinct."

"I work not far from here, and I have great respect for authority," Armistead said, his eyes briefly lifting to Laurel's face. He dropped his gaze at once, asking, "What are you doing for the *Globe*?"

"Mr. Cooper is teaching me how to cover the police beat."

"I see. That must be exciting."

"I'm just getting started, Porter. But so far I like it."

"That's good. You must enjoy being back in your father's home after your trip out west."

"It's nice to be back," she replied. "How's your mother?"

"Well enough, I guess."

Laurel's eyebrows arched. "You don't live at home anymore?"

"Not since I got back from serving our country. Well, excuse me. I've got to return to the office." He nodded briefly to everyone and left.

Laurel twisted in her chair to follow him with her eyes. Something nibbled at the back of her mind, but she couldn't decide what it was.

❧

Ridge came directly from the police station to the Fog Horn where the desk sergeant said Laurel and Vance Cooper had probably gone for lunch. He walked in slowly, noticing that most of the diners had left. Laurel wasn't in the front part of the restaurant, so he walked back until he found her sitting to one side with the others. But when he saw that they were starting to leave, he turned and walked back to the front and waited.

As the four of them headed for the door, Ridge stepped forward and nodded briefly in acknowledgment of Charity and Cooper, whom he had met.

Laurel was annoyed that he had shown up, so she briefly and coolly introduced Darius Barr, then said, "Please excuse us. We've got to get back to work."

"I need to talk to you first." His tone was flat and hard, indicating he didn't want an argument.

"Well, only for a minute," she replied. "Cooper, you go on back to the precinct, and I'll be there shortly."

"I'd rather wait," he said pointedly, his eyes locking onto Ridge's.

Ridge's opinion of Cooper hadn't changed since meeting the correspondent at the cemetery where he had insisted upon setting up an appointment with Laurel. But Ridge had come here for a more pressing cause that surpassed his feelings toward Cooper. "Suit yourself," Ridge said coldly, taking Laurel's elbow and leading her several steps away.

She said disapprovingly, "You had no business coming here."

"Oh, yes I did!" He looked down on her, his eyes firmly fixed on hers. "I've been thinking a lot about us, and what might keep you safe from whoever's after you."

"That's hardly news worth coming over here to tell me," she said tartly.

"If you're trying to make me angry, Laurel, you're not going to succeed. I've come to ask you one more time to come with me to Virginia. . . . "

"Not that, again!" She threw up her hands in exasperation. "I will not do it! How many times do I have to say that?"

"Only one more time." His tone was low, but it carried an impact that made her blink.

"All right. I'll listen this last time."

"Fine. Now, there are two parts to what I have to say. First, whoever tried to follow you from your father's house that night couldn't have been Sam Maynard."

A frown creased her forehead. "How do you know that?"

"I talked to him Friday afternoon. He was going out on the cars right after work. So that means whoever followed you in the buggy is still around."

She snapped, "You should have told me that before!"

"I probably should have. Now what I'm going to say will make you furious. You may even hate me, but I believe you're a reasonable woman under all that self-reliance."

Even though she had told herself they could never be happy together, she couldn't imagine what he could say that would make her hate him.

"It's this," he explained, "I would rather you be alive and hate me than not do what my heart and mind tell me is the only way to keep you safe."

He paused, took a deep breath, and plunged on. "You are convinced that your war-time past is somehow tied to Sarah's death and what you perceive to be your threat to life. So you must tell Kelly about . . ."

She sucked in her breath, but he gently laid strong fingers across her lips.

"Don't argue, Laurel! My mind is made up. If you don't go with me to Virginia, then . . ." he paused, removing his fingers, "then I'll tell him myself."

"You wouldn't!"

"Try me."

"But you promised!"

"And I'd keep that promise if I could see any other way to handle this. But I can't."

"You're giving me an ultimatum! That is the most despicable thing you could do!"

"It's not as bad as having you dead."

Cooper stepped close saying, "What's going on?"

Ridge rose on the balls of his feet and turned with fury in his eyes, but Laurel spoke before he could.

"Nothing I can't handle. Give us another minute."

"Well," Cooper said uncertainly, slowly backing up.

Ridge turned expectantly back to Laurel.

She stared in disbelief, her eyes and mouth open wide, and yet knowing he was dead serious.

"Meantime," he said in a gentler tone, "I've told the private investigators that you're staying with your aunt. You'll be safe there for tonight. I'll check with you there tomorrow morning at seven o'clock. After that . . . well, it's your choice. It may also be your last chance."

He started to turn away, then added softly, "Please understand how desperately I love you, or I would never do such a thing. That's how important you are to me, alive, even if we never get together."

He turned and strode away, his limp barely noticeable while Laurel still stood in stunned, speechless silence.

❦

Laurel and Cooper arrived back at the precinct after she resisted all of his best efforts to tell him what had been going on with Ridge. She struggled to control her emotions when the sergeant said the lieutenant was waiting for them in his office. She had the feeling that Cooper was preoccupied with what he had seen outside the restaurant as well, but she also sensed that he was pleased.

Pierce's office was closer to the front of the building so that the stench of the jail wasn't as offensive. But Laurel had to quickly suppress a wave of revulsion as he bent and spat chewing tobacco into the brass cuspidor located behind his battered desk.

He looked up from an open book, leaned back, and laced his fingers across his slight paunch. The fierce black eyebrows, like vultures raising from carrion, only partially shielded his cold gray eyes.

"I've just been doing some investigation on my own while you two were out stuffing your faces," he began. "That name, Abaddon, kept running through my mind until I found out what it means and where it's from."

"That's encouraging," Laurel said, trying to put her argument with Ridge out of her mind. "What is it?"

"I heard it by chance," Pierce replied, absently touching the end of his broken nose which had healed crookedly. "I was walking by that little park on my way back from lunch where I heard one of those black soap-box preachers ranting away to the drunks, who weren't paying any attention to him. I wouldn't have either, except he quoted something about Abaddon."

"It's in the Bible?" Cooper asked.

"Yes, but the old black preacher couldn't find it. In fact, I noticed he was preaching with his Bible turned upside down. He probably can't read, but he sure can quote from memory. Anyway, I had the sergeant run over to the court house and borrow the Bible they use to swear in witnesses. I finally found it. Book of Revelation, the ninth chapter, and the eleventh verse."

He shoved the open Bible across the desk toward Cooper. "It's about some locusts that look like horses prepared for battle, and their kind, whatever that means. Anyway, read that verse aloud."

Cooper cleared his throat. "And they had a king over them, which is the angel of the bottomless pit, whose name in the Hebrew tongue is . . ." he paused and looked at Laurel before finishing, "Abaddon, but the Greek tongue hath his name Apollyon."

"Abaddon!" Cooper repeated. "No wonder I couldn't place it. Even when I went to Sunday School, I don't think we ever studied Revelation. But I'm sure that some of those traveling fire and brimstone preachers must have harangued us in church about it. That's why it was so vague in my memory."

"The king of the bottomless pit," Laurel mused. "Now why would our letter writer choose that name?"

"Power," Pierce said. "At least, that's what I thought, but I asked the clerk of the court who is quite a Bible scholar. He says the word is generally understood to mean destruction. Of course, that is also associated with power or control."

"Destruction and a bottomless pit," Cooper said softly. "Our man likes symbolism, it seems. He not only destroys, but if I understand this correctly, he also thinks he sends them to hell. What power he must think he has!"

"And the arrogance to use it as his name," Pierce agreed. "So Abaddon doesn't think we'll ever catch him."

Laurel's mouth went dry, and an invisible noose seemed to encircle her throat. He figured that Sarah deserved such a fate, but Laurel knew better. She also knew this was no ordinary killer, and she was definitely on his list.

# *Chapter 14*

Laurel was quiet and thoughtful as she and Cooper left the lieutenant's office. Walking toward the sergeant's desk, Cooper returned to their earlier conversation about Ridge. Cooper vainly pressured Laurel to explain what Ridge had said that so upset her. She was so distraught over his ultimatum and Pierce's information about what the word Abaddon meant to her, that she didn't reply to Cooper.

He shrugged and changed the subject. In a bantering tone, he asked, "So you think I'd look better if I shaved my goatee?"

This time he waited for her answer.

She realized he had said something, and struggled to recall his words. Then she merely nodded, her mind still on what Ridge had said.

"Good! I don't want to look like a billy goat."

She sensed that he was trying to cheer her up, but she couldn't even smile.

He seemed not to notice. "So I'll shave it because what I think I just saw back there with him is good for me; maybe enough for dinner with a certain pretty lady."

Again she didn't answer as they approached the sergeant's desk.

Cooper turned his attention to Sergeant Kerston. "Well, Sarge, what kind of excitement did this department generate while we were in with the lieutenant?"

"Nothing. It was so quiet I could have taken a nap, except I had to book one of our regular vagrants that a patrolman brought in on disorderly conduct."

"Oh, that'll make the front page," Cooper said with mock severity.

"It might. Your paper was responsible for the fight he was in." The sergeant jerked his thumb toward the cell block. "Jay Ninian tangled with another vagrant because Ninian claimed he wrote a letter to the *Globe* which they published."

"He's the one who wrote that letter?" Cooper asked.

Laurel was aroused from her self-absorption as Kerston replied. "So he claims. It seems he uses newspapers for something besides trying to keep warm. He reads them first, if you can imagine that. Anyway, he admitted to the arresting officer that he got the idea for claiming responsibility for the murder from something he overheard on a recent sojourn in this hotel. After it was printed, he boasted to his fellow vagrants, but they didn't believe him. He tried to convince them the only way he knew how: by assaulting one doubter."

Laurel asked, "Are they certain that he couldn't have been the one who killed? . . ."

"Not a chance," Kerston replied. "Ninian was questioned as a matter of course, but he didn't have any of the crime scene details right."

Cooper yawned. "Well, if that's the most exciting news you can offer, Laurel and I had better go see if we can scrounge up something worth printing."

The rest of the day didn't get any more interesting for

Laurel, who struggled with the blunt choices Ridge had given her. She was so glad to walk out of the *Globe* after work that she didn't see Charity until she spoke.

"You got a minute, Laurel?"

Laurel glanced up. "Oh, Charity! I guess my mind was somewhere else."

"Like back at the Fog Horn after lunch?"

Laurel sighed. "Oh, that."

"Ridge looked rather grim when he said he had to talk to you."

Laurel hesitated, knowing that Charity was trying to invite a conversation without being too blatant about it. Yet Laurel was mindful of Cooper's warning that Charity was competition and not to be trusted.

"Laurel, I'd like us to be friends, but if I'm in sensitive territory, I'll understand."

"I'd also like us to be friends," Laurel admitted, "but I never had a really close friend except Sarah. Yet that's no reason why you and I can't talk. Do you have time for a cup of tea?"

In fifteen minutes of casual conversation at a small nearby cafe, nothing more was said about Ridge's grim appearance at the Fog Horn. Laurel knew that Charity was allowing her time to decide whether to again mention the noon incident. Finally, Laurel made up her mind.

"Charity, has Darius ever given you an ultimatum?"

"No, and he'd better not, either."

Laurel smiled. "Do you suppose all women feel the same about that?"

"I wouldn't be surprised. But my old grandmother used to

tell me that compromise is better than self-righteous indignation. So if I loved Darius enough, I'd probably calm down and compromise."

"But what if love wasn't enough? I mean, what if there are circumstances that are greater than love?"

"You're talking about fear."

"Well, yes, fear of circumstances, I guess."

"Saint Paul said that there is no fear in love, but perfect love casts out fear. That would have to include the circumstances."

Laurel absently sipped her tea, mulling the thought around. She asked, "But what if you could see both his side as well as yours on such a thing? I mean, if you thought he really was doing something for your own good, and not just his?"

"That would probably depend on how much I cared. If I thought he did it because he loved me, I probably would do what he asked."

That made sense to Laurel. *If I really loved Ridge as much as he loves me, then we could talk about it and probably work something out. But that's not how I think,* she admitted to herself. *I want to do things my way.*

The idea made her uncomfortable, so she shifted the subject. "You like being a correspondent?"

Charity's expression showed she wasn't ready to drop the topic of Ridge's apparent ultimatum, but she slowly nodded. "I enjoy it, but I wouldn't want to do it the rest of my life, especially now that I've met Darius."

Laurel debated posing a question that troubled her, then decided to work up to it. "Have you . . . uh . . . ever looked at any of the crime scene photos he's taken?"

"Some of them. It's a matter of not letting yourself get emotionally involved, which is what he also has to do."

"I don't think I could do that."

"I don't like it, but Darius told me that you get used to such things when it's your job, just as he says all officers have to become detached when they're working a crime scene. I'm not morbidly curious, but I learned to do it and not let myself get all torn up emotionally."

Edging closer to her goal, Laurel confessed. "I took one quick look at Sarah, then turned away in horror. But the memory won't go away. It seems burned into my brain."

"That would be a really terrible thing to have to live with. I didn't know Sarah, but I'm sure you'd rather remember her as she was in life."

Laurel shuddered. "I try to substitute some of the good memories for that last one, but it's hard."

"I'm certain it is." Charity hesitated, then added, "Darius's job is a little harder than the patrolmen who are usually first on the scene. Same with detectives who follow up on the investigation. They learn to walk away and forget it enough to do what they must. Darius's work requires him to go over photographs many times, looking for some little detail that might have first been overlooked. A couple of times, he's noticed something that he thought was probably insignificant, but he showed the detectives, who followed up and solved the case."

"So a photograph can sometimes help?"

"Yes, in some cases. Since he and I both want to help find whoever killed your friend, Darius has repeatedly gone back over the pictures he took. He's trying to see if there's anything that might be helpful. But so far, nothing."

Taking a quick breath, Laurel asked her question. "Have you helped him that way?"

"You mean, have I looked at Sarah's photographs?"

"Yes."

"I have. Is there something special you want to know about?"

Taking a deep breath, Laurel explained. "Kelly showed both Ridge and me something he said was found at the scene, but neither of us remembered seeing it, and we had no idea what it was."

"What did it look like?"

"We only saw it briefly, but as I recall, it was something made of wood and about the thickness of my forefinger." She held it up for Charity to see. "One end was rough, as if it had been broken off. The other end came to a point, as I recall."

"Oh, I know what you mean. Kelly also asked Darius about it. He examined it and said it looked like a piece off the end of a camera tripod. Kelly had Darius show him his. Kelly agreed that's what it probably was."

Laurel frowned thoughtfully, wondering when a photographer other than Darius had been in Sarah's house. *I'll have to ask her husband,* she thought.

Charity said, "What did you just think of?"

"Oh, a question I have to ask someone."

"If you mean Sarah's widower, Kelly already did that. He said Sarah had never had her photograph taken, and he was sure there had never been a photographer in their house until the police one came, meaning Darius."

Abruptly, Laurel recalled the photograph left in the sack on her highboy. Was that coincidence? Or could it mean something?

Charity said, "You did it again."

"Did what?"

"You just thought of something else, didn't you?" When Laurel hesitated and dropped her eyes, Charity said, "I just got my answer, didn't I?"

Laurel didn't answer. She asked, "Did Darius look at the date on that newspaper found beside Sarah?"

"I don't know. Shall I ask him?"

"No, don't go to any trouble. I was just wondering."

"Now you've got me curious. I'll let you know after I find out from Darius."

Laurel realized she might have inadvertently given a competitive correspondent leads which would give her a jump on a possible story. If that happened and Cooper found out what she did, he would be furious. Besides, even though Laurel thought she could mask her thoughts rather well, Charity had twice picked up on something that made Laurel a little uneasy.

It was time to end this conversation. Laurel stood. "I've got to go. I enjoyed our talk."

"I did, too." Charity rose to her feet. "I'm sure that Cooper warned you to be careful around me because I might beat him and you to a story. Naturally, if I can, I will. But I also am genuinely interested in being your friend and seeing Sarah's murder solved. So don't hold back if there's something I can do to help that way."

"Thanks. I'll remember." But as Laurel walked away, she had the uneasy feeling she should not have talked so candidly with Charity.

Ridge found it almost impossible to conduct any business that afternoon. He went through the motions of making calls and trying to persuade companies to open a branch along the transcontinental railroad route. He sent wires to his Omaha office with instructions, not sure they were really quite right. He thought of telegraphing Griff, but still didn't know what to say. Indecision was not characteristic of the former cavalry officer, and he hated himself for it. But he knew that until Laurel was safe, he could not fully concentrate on other matters.

*Well*, he told himself as he wearily returned to his hotel room, *I'll know by seven o'clock tomorrow morning whether or not she's going to quit being so stubborn.* It was going to be a long night.

❧

The man who called himself Abaddon sat in his room in darkness, which matched his mood. He often felt moody just before he struck. Afterward, he was always exhilarated. Sometimes the feeling lasted for months. It had even lasted for a year after he took his first victim right here in Chicago.

But with each murder, the sense of domination and control, of power over both the late victim and even the police, grew greater. So did the drive to strike again. They came like attacks inside his head, forcing him to move more and more often in order to sustain the feeling.

But this time, he had worked out a different strategy to heighten his final triumph. It hadn't worked out quite the way he wanted so far because Laurel had not been terrorized as much as he hoped. Well, he could change that tonight.

❧

For about an hour that night, Laurel tried to read, but Aunt Agnes's old-fashioned oil lamps made that almost impossible. Laurel would have preferred her own place with kerosene lamps, but she really didn't want to be alone, either. Her thoughts were too troublesome.

She was aware when Agnes stopped crocheting and laid her needle work down on the arm of her chair. She wiggled fingers that were showing a tendency to become stiff if she worked them too long in a repetitive movement.

"Let's talk," Agnes said bluntly.

Laurel lowered the book to peer over the top. "About what?"

"About what's troubling you."

"Nothing's troubling me."

"Nonsense! You haven't turned a page in fifteen minutes." Some of Agnes's former characteristics still remained. "You broke your engagement to Ridge, you're keeping something from that detective, and your life is in danger. So don't tell me nothing is bothering you."

Laurel laid the book on her lap. "Well, today Ridge gave me an ultimatum. He said he'd give me until seven o'clock in the morning to decide to go to Virginia with him."

"Good for him!"

"Aunt Agnes! Whose side are you on?"

"Both. Tell me exactly what he said."

Laurel repeated the conversation with him, ending with, "After he gave his high-handed ultimatum, he said something like, 'Please understand how much I love you, or I would never do such a thing. It's more important for me to know you're alive, than for us to be together.' "

"Ah, Laurel! Laurel," Agnes almost moaned, shaking her head. "Do you realize what kind of love it takes for a man to make such a statement?"

Laurel protested, "I know how it sounds, but marrying him is too big a risk—"

"That's ridiculous!" Agnes broke in, the old familiar sharpness returning to her voice. "I've watched you two in Virginia, then California, and now here. He obviously loves you. Don't you honestly love him?"

"Oh, Aunt Agnes! I don't know!" Laurel's voice shot up with a touch of agony in it. "Something always seems to happen that breaks us up!" She felt her eyelashes thicken with tears that she fought back.

"You remember in California when I told you about the mistake I made when I was about your age?"

"Of course." Until that confidential revelation, Laurel had never suspected her brittle relative had ever been wooed by any man.

Agnes continued. "I didn't marry him because his mother made life difficult for me, and I was afraid she would ruin our marriage. That was foolish of me. She has been long gone, but I'm still here, and without him, yet with a lifetime of regret."

Laurel waited until Agnes continued.

"Now, these many years later, I'm going to take a far greater risk than you face with Ridge. I'm more than halfway through my life, yet I'm going to move away from my brother, you, and the rest of what is my only family. I'm leaving my church and all my friends. So, if you think I'm not afraid . . ." her voice began to break and her eyes suddenly shone with hot tears, "you're badly mistaken!"

Laurel started to stand so she could reach out and hug her aunt, but stopped. "Of course you are," Laurel said, resettling in her chair. "But I think Horatio Bodmer is a very fine man, and you'll be happy. . . ."

"This is not about me!" Agnes said sternly. "I just used that personal illustration to make you see that you're about to make the same mistake I did. That's all."

She picked up her crocheting again. "What are you going to tell Ridge in the morning?"

"That I'm not going to Virginia with him, if that's what you mean."

"Ah! You're going to show him he can't tell you what to do, that you can take care of yourself. Well, I've lived long enough to know that there always comes a time when there's nobody to help except God."

Laurel didn't seem to hear. She was thinking of trying to bluff Ridge. She had tried on the way over to Agnes's to convince herself that he wouldn't actually go through with it if she seemed sincere enough. But her heart warned her that Ridge might call her bluff. Then what?

Laurel feared that if Ridge returned to Virginia alone, no matter how much he claimed to love her, Varina would try finding a way to dissolve his will.

Agnes interrupted her thoughts. "Please answer me: Are you going to stay up on your high horse to show him he can't tell you what to do? That you can take care of yourself, even if it kills you?"

"Well, I am not going to Virginia with him!"

"I see. Well, then what's your alternative? To stay here where someone seems determined to kill you? You'd better take my Bible and seek guidance for wisdom."

Laurel started to protest because she wasn't in the habit of praying for guidance or wisdom. But this situation was different. "Thanks. Maybe I will, but I have my own Bible."

She rose, lit a tallow taper in a hand-held holder, and walked down the hallway. Shadows leaped on the wall, great black shapeless monsters that were reminiscent of her childhood. Shadows tonight sprang out of familiar places, then silently fled as she lifted the candle high.

As she entered her small chamber and set the candle holder on the nightstand, the shadows froze when she stopped. But as she moved toward the armoire, they came to life again, moving with her. She could not escape them. They gave her a sense of foreboding.

She dressed for sleep, slid under the covers, and held her Bible close to the candle, but she did not read.

Several thoughts crowded into her mind, each demanding consideration. How could a piece of a photographer's camera tripod have been left at Sarah's murder scene? Could she have had a photographer come to the house that John didn't know about? No, that didn't seem logical.

The piece obviously wasn't from Darius Barr's tripod. So who else was there who knew anything about photography? Vance Cooper did, but he had been there without equipment except for note pad and pencil. Maybe the tripod piece wasn't really a clue from the time of the murder. Maybe it was a false clue left by Abaddon to throw the police off his trail.

Shaking that thought away, Laurel considered her idea of trying to bluff Ridge. She'd tell him she would not go to Virginia. If he started to walk out, she could try to get him to talk. She could ask for more time to think about it.

*No,* she told herself, *that won't work. He set a time limit and will stick to it. Once that limit is passed, he'll talk to Kelly then go to Virginia alone. Unless I back down.*

Her thoughts jumped back to Cooper. *He was very happy because Ridge upset me outside the restaurant. If Cooper shaves his goatee, he must be serious about me. But do I care?*

"No," she whispered aloud, her breathing making the candle flame dance and the shadows shift. "And I shouldn't care about Ridge, now that I've broken our engagement. So why do I torture myself with thoughts about Varina and Ridge? Why can't I walk away with my heart as simply as I walked away from our betrothal?"

Laurel didn't know how long she had been asleep when her eyes popped open, her heart leaping in alarm. Total darkness engulfed her aunt's guest bedchamber, but Laurel sensed someone close by.

She had never been able to explain to herself how this happened, but it had occurred twice in the war. Both times she had escaped being shot by a silent sentry.

Once, slipping through the lines after a successful mission into the Confederacy, she thought she was safely back into Union territory. Still, when the feeling gripped her, she stopped dead still and listened.

Finally, she had spotted a black Union picket directly ahead, but only when his uniform rustled where he shifted while standing against a tree trunk. Another time, it had been a Confederate soldier sitting against a stump. She hadn't seen him until he moved his rifle, and a stray moonbeam through the canopy of trees reflected a tiny pinpoint of light.

So she heeded the feeling now in the thick blackness of the tiny chamber. She lay perfectly still, moving only her eyes, but they could discern nothing. She listened, avoiding the temptation to hold her breath to better hear. She realized that if someone were in the room, he might hear her breathing, and any change in that could make him strike.

The feeling persisted even when she remembered that Ridge had hired a detective to watch outside. But that hadn't stopped the break-in at her father's house.

She had never used a weapon, but now she longed for something, anything. But all she could do was decide that if she detected any movement toward her bed, she would throw herself out the opposite side, scream in hopes of momentarily distracting him, then run for the door.

It wasn't a masterful plan, but that was all she could think of as she lay there, her heart thumping, her mind filled with dread of the unknown.

She didn't know how long she lay there, every nerve taut, every fiber of her being tense, and fear sending scalding blood pounding through her veins. The tension became so great she was tempted to sit up, to do something to ease the stress.

The doorknob turned, slowly, quietly, but she heard it. Surprised, she almost forgot to keep breathing normally. *Why is he at the door, unless he's leaving? But why would he? . . .*

Her thought snapped off as the door eased open, very, very slowly. She could barely hear it against the pounding of blood in her ears. She vainly strained to hear it close. She stared toward it, unable to determine if it was open or closed. Then, again, there was silence.

It took all her will power to stay still, fearful he might have used the door as a ruse to slip up on her in the darkness. She desperately probed the blackness with eyes that showed nothing she could identify. Neither could she hear any sound.

Gradually, her sense of alarm passed and she began to feel relieved. Still, she waited another few minutes before reaching for the matches and striking a light.

Fearfully, she swept the room, then, almost sobbing in relief, she lit the candle. She had closed her door upon retiring, but now it stood open about a foot.

Aunt Agnes! Laurel was ashamed that she had not thought of her relative's safety before.

Holding the candle high to light the way, Laurel ran barefooted across the hard wooden floor, then down to her aunt's door. She started to knock but stopped when she heard Agnes snoring.

Immensely relieved, Laurel retraced her steps and re-entered her room. The candlelight reflected off of something white at the foot of her bed. She bent to hold the candle close to a piece of paper with four words:

*Not yet. Soon. Abaddon.*

# Chapter 15

Laurel was still very distressed when Ridge knocked on the front door at seven o'clock the next morning. She hurried to answer it, reminding herself, *Both Aunt Agnes and I could have been killed last night. And his note . . .*

She shuddered. *It's a clear warning that whoever he is, he's in complete control, choosing the time of my death . . . and so far I've been unable to do a thing about it. He finds me, he slips by the guards . . . .*

She opened the door and said softly, "Come in."

He looked sharply at her. "Are you all right?"

Still unnerved, she nodded as he stepped into the parlor where Agnes surprised him by coming to him and seizing both his hands in hers.

"We are so glad to see you!" she exclaimed.

"Why?" he asked, instantly alarmed. "Something happen?"

"Yes! We could both be dead!" Agnes cried. "A lot of good your guard did last night! Tell him, Laurel!"

She took a quick breath and hurriedly repeated the night's incident. When she mentioned the cryptic note, Agnes handed it over for him to see for himself.

He read it aloud. "Not yet. Soon. Abaddon." Ridge turned to Laurel. "That settles it. You're coming with me to Virginia."

She resented his assumption, but replied quietly, "I will, if you'll wait until Friday after work."

"I can't believe you, Laurel!" His voice rose indignantly. "After what you went through last night—"

She interrupted, a defensive edge to her words. "I need to make arrangements with Mr. Seymour. It will take a minimum of three days to go and come, not to mention whatever time you'll need with your friend Griff."

"I don't want you back here alone again."

"Now look, Ridge!" she flared, but he cut her off.

"No, you look! I could have lost you last night, both of you." His voice dropped. "I'm not going to go through that again! So, all right, I'll wait until Friday after you finish work, but only if you both leave here with me now."

Softened, Laurel sighed. "So we compromise?"

His eyebrows arched in surprise, but he smiled and reached out to take both her hands in his. "Yes, we do."

He gave her fingers a quick, gentle squeeze before turning to the other woman. "Aunt Agnes, come with us."

"That's very kind of you, but I want to talk to my brother before I make any decisions. Well, except to move out of this house until this mad man is caught."

"You're a wise woman," Ridge told her. "I'd suggest that you urge your brother and the rest of the family to go visit out-of-town friends or relatives for awhile."

He didn't wait for a reply, but faced Laurel. "I don't know how, but this Abaddon must have inside information to know you'd moved here. Whom did you tell?"

"Nobody. Not a soul."

"Unless he followed you here, you must have told someone. Maybe Cooper?" When Laurel shook her head, he rushed on. "How about your friend Charity?"

"I told you: I didn't tell anybody." Some of her old spirit

returned at the hint of disbelief in his tone. "I was careful after I left Charity. Nobody followed me."

"Well," Ridge said grimly, "he not only knew you were here, but he knew how to avoid the guard stationed outside. This Abaddon is either very self-confident and fearless, or very foolish. Nothing he's done leads me to believe he's foolish. Both of you, please grab a few things, and I'll get you out of here."

"Where are we going?" Laurel asked.

"I'm not going to say." He waved at the dark walls. "Maybe they've got ears. Oh, first tell me, did you call the police, and where did he break in?"

"We didn't call the police," Laurel answered, "because whoever he is obviously was not going to return last night. We knew you'd be here early this morning."

Agnes added, "He came in a window on the south side of the house. It's overgrown with bushes, so you'll have to crawl under them to see. We found it from inside."

As the women left the room, Ridge followed them with his eyes, then closed them and whispered, "Thanks, Lord!"

❧

Ridge drove his rented horse and buggy on a circuitous route from Agnes's home. He explained that Abaddon would naturally not expect Laurel to remain at her aunt's place. However, he might anticipate that she would go to her father's home. Ridge had rejected the idea of having them at his hotel for fear that Abaddon might also be expecting that.

After Ridge was satisfied that they had not been followed, he stopped at a small hotel where he had both women register. From there, Agnes could take a hack to her brother's home, but Ridge warned her to be careful about being followed.

After leaving Agnes at the hotel, Ridge started driving Laurel to the *Globe* building, but turned off into a small, quiet city park. As the wheels crunched onto the gravel drive, she asked, "What are you doing?"

"I'm looking for a place where I can kiss you."

"You're what?"

"Goint to kiss you." He grinned at her. "In fact, I'm going to kiss you until your ears fly off!"

"Wait a minute!" The fright from the night before had faded, making Laurel more sure of herself again. "I think you misunderstand. Just because I'm going with you to Virginia doesn't mean things have changed between us."

He reined in the horse and looped the reins around the whip socket before turning to her in disbelief. "You can't be serious!"

"We still have so many problems!"

"We can work them out! With you at my side, I can handle anything."

She made a low, moaning sound. It was so tempting to believe him.

He reached out and pulled her to him. His lips closed over hers. In spite of herself, Laurel's arms went around his neck. For a wonderful moment, she let herself give in to the kiss and the safe feeling of being in his arms.

Then she abruptly pulled back. "Ridge, I don't think this can work."

He shook his head. "You are the most exasperating woman I've ever known! You're beautiful, you're intelligent, you're everything I ever wanted in a woman, and yet you are the most obstinate, unreasonable . . ."

She glared at him. "I will not be spoken to that way!"

"All right! All right!" He lowered his voice. "I apologize! Now, I'll try to watch what I say if you'll quit aggravating me. But what

I said some time ago still goes: I love you and I intend to marry you."

She softened instantly, her whole being melting into a soft, warm feeling. She admitted to herself, *I can't stand the thought of us not being together, but I have to be practical. It'll be hard enough being with him all those days and not let him see that my heart isn't saying what my mouth is. He mustn't find out.*

Ridge broke into her musings. "I'm confused. Are we going to pretend to Griff and the others that we are still betrothed?"

"Just be politely attentive but with no unnecessary display of affection."

"And you think nobody will notice?"

"Why should they?"

Ridge considered that a moment before saying quietly, "Maybe Griff won't, but Varina will."

Laurel stiffened. "Why do you bring her into this?"

"Because she's a very discerning woman, and she'll notice. Believe me."

Laurel was surprised to experience a feeling like molten liquid instantly sweep over her entire body. She knew Ridge had just spoken the truth. She had no doubt that his ex-fiancée would exploit any opportunity to get Ridge back. But Laurel could not bring herself to change her mind.

She flounced against the buggy's backrest and said coldly, "Please take me to the office, now!"

Ridge stared silently at her for a few seconds, his mouth working as though he was choking back a reply. But he reached down and untied the reins in one quick motion.

"This is going to be one miserable weekend!"

She didn't answer as he slapped the reins hard against the horse's back.

Laurel was still steaming inside when she entered the *Globe* building. She forced herself to put Ridge and Varina out of her mind as she knocked on the door to the publisher's office. He invited her in.

"Mr. Seymour," she began, "do you have a minute?"

"Only a minute," he replied, looking up from papers on his desk and placing his cigar on the tray. "What's on your mind?"

"I have a very personal problem that requires me to go out of town over the weekend. I can't get back until Tuesday morning, maybe not until Wednesday. I'd like your permission—"

He broke in. "You're a new employee and you ask that?"

"I don't expect to be paid. I just want to ask your permission to miss a day or two."

"Of course you wouldn't get paid! But what if I won't give permission?"

Laurel didn't need another heated discussion right now. She took a quick breath. "I have no choice but to make this trip, regardless of what happens here."

He picked up the cigar and puffed thoughtfully. "It would set a bad example for the others if I allow this."

"Not if they thought I was ill," she blurted, and instantly regretted it. Becoming the kind of believer who didn't tell lies or bend the truth all out of shape didn't come easily to her, in spite of her intentions.

Seymour blew smoke toward the ceiling. "You think of everything, don't you?"

She ignored the pinprick of conscience, saying, "Mr. Seymour, I'm only doing what I must."

He tapped the ashes from the cigar into the tray. "I hear good things about you from Cooper, although I suspect he's got more than a professional interest in your sticking around before he leaves for Sacramento."

"Sacramento?" she repeated, feigning surprise.

"Yes. He's been hounding me to send him west to do some stories about the Central Pacific. He wants to be there in mid-September when the last granite tunnel is expected to be completed in the Sierras."

"He told me that he hoped to . . ."

"He was in a few minutes ago," the publisher interrupted, "pushing me for a decision, so I gave him the assignment. That will create a permanent opening here, for the right person, of course."

He seemed to be broadly hinting that Laurel might be that person. Unknown to him, she was committed to doing one last detective job for Pinkerton—in California. She had expected to begin that when her two weeks were up at the *Globe*.

Now that she didn't plan to marry Ridge, she could probably stay on with the detective agency. Seymour's hint seemed to lay another unexpected problem upon her.

She veered away from the issue. "About the time off . . ."

"Take it," he snapped. "But don't tell anyone I gave you permission. Now, let's both get to work."

"Thank you very much, Mr. Seymour," she replied and hurriedly left his office.

Ridge postponed calling on prospective clients until he could regain control of his surging emotions. He stopped by the depot, bought tickets for the six o'clock Friday afternoon cars to Virginia. He then wired Griff of his and Laurel's arrival time so a carriage could be sent to Richmond for them.

He was still silently fuming at Laurel's latest surprise demands, yet he was glad that they would be together for the long train trip. Most of all, he was relieved that she would be safely out of the mysterious Abaddon's reach for a few days. Ridge hoped that by the time they returned, Kelly would have captured him.

*Maybe*, Ridge told himself as he left the telegraph office, *Laurel will come to her senses and realize we love each other and can make a marriage work. But it's going to be torture to be so near her and not be able to even hold her hand.*

Laurel found that Cooper had shaved his goatee when she saw him that morning. He asked, "Like it?"

"It's much better," she cautiously admitted.

"I could also take off my mustache as well if that would help you make up your mind to have dinner with me."

She quickly steered him away from that subject. "Mr. Seymour tells me you're resigning and heading for California."

"Sure am. Going to cover the opening of the Central Pacific's last long tunnel through the granite backbone of the Sierras."

"Very poetic," she replied. "When are you leaving?"

"Tell you later," he said as they entered the Grove Street police precinct.

Sergeant Kerston looked up from behind his desk. "The lieutenant wants to see you two right away."

"Something up?" Cooper asked.

"Plenty! Our Mr. Abaddon claimed another victim last night."

Laurel suppressed a gasp. "What? Who?"

"The lieutenant will fill you in," the sergeant replied evasively. He lowered his voice. "He was yelling so loud at poor Kelly awhile ago that the building shook. I can imagine what he's going to say to you two."

Laurel had started down the hall but paused when Cooper asked, "Why, Sergeant? What did we do?"

"You mean, what did your story do?" Kerston grinned. "You'd better ask the lieutenant. Oh, he's so mad he might not give you time to get the front door open, so I'll hold it ready, just in case."

Laurel and Cooper looked at each other in perplexity as they hurried down the hall to Pierce's office. There was no time to speculate, but Laurel didn't care. She had enough struggle controlling her feelings over the break-in last night, the quarrel with Ridge, and now this.

Lieutenant Pierce looked up as they entered, his black eyebrows knit disapprovingly over cold gray eyes. "Sit!" he commanded, turning to expectorate into the brass cuspidor behind his desk.

Before he turned back to them, Laurel noticed that the ends of Kelly's reddish mustache quivered even though he didn't speak to them. His usually flushed face was bright crimson, his pale blue eyes partly hidden under half-lowered lids. He reminded Laurel of a puppy that had been whacked hard with a folded newspaper.

"So," Pierce began, looking hard at them in turn. "Your little idea about running a story over that letter got a man killed last night. Is that what you expected, hoping to get a big story out of it?"

"Who got killed?" Cooper asked.

"Ninian." Pierce motioned toward the wall closest to the cells.

Cooper asked, "Jay Ninian, the vagrant?"

"The same," the lieutenant replied. The judge let Ninian

walk when no witnesses appeared to testify against him on disorderly conduct charges. Last night, Ninian was murdered.

Cooper asked the question that was also on Laurel's mind. "What's the story got to do with his death?"

Pierce glowered at Cooper. "Everything! He was nothing but a bummer until you came to Kelly with this idea of printing that letter. So thanks to your greediness in creating a bigger story, Abaddon killed him, probably in revenge for claiming credit for that woman's death."

Laurel didn't believe that, but Cooper spoke before she could. He exclaimed, "Lieutenant, I resent the implication that we did that to get a bigger story!"

"Resent all you want! That's my opinion. If it wouldn't raise a stink with your publisher over violating freedom of the press, I would throw both of you out of here and never let you back again!"

Laurel asked quietly, "How do you know Abaddon killed Ninian?"

"Because he was bucked, gagged, and smothered, the exact same way your friend was. A newspaper was beside the body, too, except this one was folded so that your story showed. Nobody outside this precinct knows all those details about your friend's death, well, except for you correspondents, so it had to be this man who calls himself Abaddon."

Pierce spat into the cuspidor while the other three people in the room sat silently waiting for his tirade to subside. He swung back to them.

"Kelly, you'd better solve this before anyone else gets killed. Miss Bartlett, I should never have let you back in after our first encounter. As for you, Cooper, if anyone else turns up dead because of your hair-brained ideas, I'll go see Seymour and tell him you're not welcome here. Now, all of you get out of my sight!"

Kelly turned right and continued toward his office while Laurel and Cooper moved left down the hall toward the desk sergeant's area.

He grinned as they approached. "I heard it all," he commented. "I'm surprised he let you out of there alive."

Laurel had endured enough this morning. "Sergeant," she snapped, "a man is dead, and you're smiling!"

"Miss Bartlett," he replied somberly, "a police officer gets callused to such things, or he couldn't do his job. But I wasn't being disrespectful of the dead, just enjoying seeing someone else get trampled on the way Kelly and I do ever since the lieutenant's wife died."

"I'm sorry," Laurel said. "I guess I overreacted."

Cooper looked down the hall. "Well, if we don't get that story, what Pierce did to us will be nothing compared to what Seymour will do. Besides, I don't want to lose that chance to cover the railroad story, so I'll go back and try getting the facts from Kelly. Laurel, you check the blotter to see if there's anything there." He turned and retraced his steps.

Kerston called after him, "What railroad story?" When Cooper didn't reply or stop, the sergeant repeated his question to Laurel.

"You'd better ask him," she said. "May I please see the police blotter?"

"Save yourself the trouble of looking, Miss Bartlett. We didn't even book any drunks last night."

Laurel was glad for a moment's respite. "Then I think I'll wait outside for Cooper."

She walked out into the fresh air, her mind whirling with the latest strange turn of events. She wondered, *Would Abaddon*

*actually kill a bummer just because he claimed credit for*
*Sarah's death? And why is he torturing my mind with the*
*photograph in the sack and last night's break-in? He's so*
*confident of himself. 'Not yet. Soon,' his note said. How*
*soon?*

She wished it were already Friday night. At least she would
then be safe for a few days.

At noon, Laurel was glad when Cooper announced that he
had an appointment and couldn't join her for lunch. She needed
the time alone to sort through her feelings after a very bad night
and morning. She went to the Fog Horn because it was close and
she didn't really know any other place near the precinct.

She planned to ask for a table in the back where it was quiet,
but noticed Porter Armistead sitting back there near some uniformed officers. He wasn't a part of their brotherhood, but like
many people, he obviously liked to be near them. Laurel didn't
want to chance his coming over to her table, so she turned to leave
but ran into Charity Dahlgren just entering.

"Oh, Laurel!" she cried, "I'm glad I ran into you. What a
morning! Another victim for this Abaddon."

"Yes," Laurel agreed, not sure if she was in the mood to talk
any more about Ninian's death. During the morning, Cooper had
expounded at length on his theories about why Abaddon had chosen to kill a man. So far as Cooper knew, all his possible previous
victims had been women. Cooper also was convinced that tomorrow's mail would bring a letter to the *Globe* from Abaddon.

Charity said, "Laurel? Are you listening?"

"What? Oh!" she shook her thoughts away. "I'm sorry. Yes,
I'm alone. Cooper had an appointment."

"Darius was still in the darkroom working on the photographs he took last night, so you and I can talk freely," Charity replied. "There's a table for two in that corner out of the way. I've got something to tell you, but nobody else is to know."

Ridge walked into Emory Brush's office and got straight to the point of his visit. "I know this Abaddon is very clever, but I've made other arrangements to protect Miss Bartlett, so I've come to pay you off."

The private detective stood, his dark-complected face somber. "Those were top operatives. Only a very skillful person could have gotten by both. I've never run across anyone like this Abaddon."

"Regardless of that, our arrangement obviously isn't working." Ridge reached for his wallet. "What do I owe you?"

"I can't take any more money from you, Mr. Granger." He shook his head. "This Abaddon seems to know more about what's going on inside this office than I do."

Ridge paused. "Hmm? Do your men gather after work at a certain favorite spot?"

"Of course. All coppers tend to congregate because it seems it's pretty much 'us against the world.' So they form close bonds. Why?"

"I suppose they then talk about their work? The cases they're on? That sort of thing?"

"Yes, but so does every detective and uniformed officer on the force. It's a close-knit brotherhood."

"Where is this after-hours place?"

"Not far from here. Place called the Big Rooster. But if you're thinking what I think you are, forget it. These men don't talk in front of outsiders."

"I'm not surprised." Ridge opened his wallet.

Brush said, "I told you; I can't take your money."

"No hard feelings," Ridge replied, replacing the money, then extending his right hand. He walked out with his mind already focusing on a new possibility.

Laurel and Charity briefly reviewed the known details of Jay Ninian's death, but Laurel was eager to hear what Charity had said at the door.

Laurel prompted, "What is it that you want to tell me?"

Charity glanced around, leaned across the small table, and spoke very softly. "I checked with Darius on the date of that newspaper found beside your friend's body. It was an old one. Twenty-seven months old: April 3, 1865, to be exact." Charity's gray-green eyes narrowed thoughtfully. "But you already guessed that, didn't you?"

Laurel admitted, "I'm not really surprised."

"Is that part of what you've kept from Kelly?"

"I can't talk about it."

"Do you know who Abaddon really is?"

"No, of course not! If I did, don't you think I would have told Kelly? Then that poor man wouldn't be dead this morning."

"Are you partially blaming yourself for his death?"

Laurel didn't answer, but she felt a little nudge of guilt that maybe she was somewhat responsible.

Charity asked, "Did it ever occur to you that whoever killed your friend might also be after you?"

Laurel called on her Civil War skills of hiding her emotions. "I've thought about it."

"And?"

"And I'm doing what I can to prevent that."

"So you are in danger?"

"Look, Charity, I like you as a friend. But Cooper keeps reminding me that you're a competitor, and you know I'm not going to tell you anything that I shouldn't."

"Fair enough. I'll let it drop, but I hope you're not making a mistake in keeping all this to yourself."

"So do I."

They placed their order before Charity asked, "Are you squeamish about talking of your friend at lunch?"

"I'd rather not, but I am committed to helping solve Sarah's murder. What do you have in mind?"

"Well, this morning Darius was going over those crime scene photos of your friend while waiting for those he took last night to develop. He showed me Sarah's crime scene, then said something intriguing."

"What was that?"

"He said about the second letter that came to the *Globe*, 'Abaddon's description was so exact that he could have been looking at my photographs!' "

Laurel stared at Charity. "You mean that Darius thinks her killer might have taken a picture after? . . ."

Charity broke in. "That would explain . . . no! Wait! Why didn't I think of that before? Forgive me, Laurel, but I've just had a thought, a theory. I'm sorry. I just can't say anything more."

"But . . . " Laurel cried in dismay.

"I'm really sorry!" Charity interrupted. "I've got to do a little investigating on my own. Now, we'd better have lunch so we can both get back to work."

Laurel was frustrated, but asked no more questions. However, a new thought nagged her: *What did she mean about, 'that would explain . . .' something?*

# Chapter 16

Laurel returned to the Grove Street Precinct after lunch, still trying to understand what idea had come to Charity during their luncheon meeting. As Laurel entered the police building, the desk sergeant jerked a thumb toward the back.

"Kelly told me to send you into his office as soon as you returned. Cooper's already in there."

"Thanks, Sergeant," she said, and hurried to the detective's office. He and Cooper looked up as she entered. Kelly's face was still flushed, but not as much as when the lieutenant had berated them earlier.

When she was seated beside Cooper, Kelly said, "I was just telling him that I located the retired detective who worked that murdered girl's case. Her body was found near a strange-shaped tree in an old park. You know where that tree is?"

"One shaped like a headless man?" Laurel asked. When the detective nodded, Laurel explained, "When we were children, we stopped there one time on a hayride."

"That's the same tree that was in the photograph Abaddon left on your highboy. As I told Cooper, the old detective remembered that case. The victim's name was Effie Chapman, age seventeen."

"Only seventeen." Laurel sadly shook her head. "Did you find any connection with hers and Sarah's deaths?"

"Both smothered, yet not tied up the same way. But that was just before the war when nobody had heard of such a thing as being bucked and gagged."

"That poor girl!" Laurel exclaimed.

Cooper said, "I think she may have been one of the first victims of this crazy Abaddon."

Kelly exclaimed, "Cooper, you're always full of ideas about what goes on in the mind of a murderer. Yet in this case, there is a possibility of a connection. But why was the first victim here, and then no more around here until Sarah Skillens, and now Jay Ninian?"

Cooper said, "You're the detective, so you tell me."

"Well, I figure that the perpetrator was either in jail or the military between the time of the Chapman murder and those women in New York that you're always talking about. Then he came back here and added Sarah Skillens and Jay Ninian to his list."

"Sounds logical," Cooper agreed. "Killings of those New York women began shortly after the war ended."

Laurel asked, "Are you suggesting that Abaddon used to live here, but there were no more murders after that young girl because he went away with all the other men to fight in the war?"

"It's possible," Cooper replied, "but he could also have been in prison or something like that. Eventually, he ended up in New York where he killed those others. So, yes, I think he could have lived here a few years. Or maybe he was just passing through when he killed that teenager."

"I don't agree," Kelly said flatly. "I might accept that idea if only Sarah Skillens was murdered. But the death of Ninian tells me whoever Abaddon is, he now lives here."

The detective quickly reviewed Pierce's observations that the vagrant had been bound and killed in exactly the same way as

Sarah, and nobody outside the precinct and the newspaper correspondents knew those details.

Laurel squirmed in her chair, recalling how the killer had
twice been in her bedchambers. She had slept through the first
break-in at her father's home, but she had been awake when it
happened at Aunt Agnes's. Laurel knew she should tell Kelly
about that, but if she did, he would demand to know what else she
was keeping from him.

She asked, "Is there anything new on Sarah's murder?"

"No." It was a blunt, hard statement that suggested his frustration at the lack of progress.

Cooper said, "You're forgetting about the sack she found on
her highboy."

"That sack." Kelly waved an impatient hand. "It's so common that it couldn't be traced to the seller. In fact, the perpetrator may have deliberately left it just to throw me off the track for
a few days."

"Laurel doesn't know about the latest on the chloroform,"
Cooper prompted.

Kelly said, "Our investigation and the coroner's report determined that your friend was chloroformed in the kitchen but
smothered on the back porch. But we couldn't trace who bought
that."

"Why would he have smothered her on the back porch?"
Laurel wondered.

Kelly shrugged. "Who knows? It doesn't make much sense.
There are more windows out there than any other room in the
house. Not that any neighbors saw anything because of the
hedges around her place."

Cooper suggested, "Tell her the latest on Ninian."

Kelly told Laurel, "He was also chloroformed from behind,
bucked and gagged, then smothered like your friend."

Cooper explained to Laurel, "Killers often use the same method when there are multiple victims. That's their mode of operation, like a signature I mentioned before."

Laurel's thoughts jumped back to Charity. Did she mean that Abaddon had taken a picture after Sarah's death? If so, why? And what had Charity meant when she said, 'that would explain, . . .' then wouldn't say?

"Oh!" Laurel exclaimed softly as a possible answer struck her.

Both men looked sharply at her.

Kelly asked suspiciously. "What did you say?"

"Oh, nothing."

"Don't tell me that!" Kelly growled. "What did you just now think about?"

Laurel said, "I'd better not say anything until I think about it some more."

Kelly's face blushed bright. "Look, Miss Bartlett, I knew early-on that you're holding something back about this case, but now there's been another murder. If I find out that you withheld evidence, I'll come down on you so hard you'll wish you were dead! And that doesn't count what the lieutenant will do to you!"

"I'm sorry, Mr. Kelly," she said calmly, "but that's all I'm going to say right now."

❧

In spite of the pressing business matters that seemed about to overwhelm Ridge, he was so anxious about Laurel's safety that he could not make himself work. To follow up something Emory Brush had said, Ridge located the Big Rooster. It was several blocks from the Grove Street Precinct where Laurel had her police beat.

"Sorry to bother you," Ridge said when a man claiming to be the manager came out from the kitchen to where Ridge stood at the counter. "I hired a detective from Emory Brush's agency, and he told me that some of his men eat here frequently."

"So?" The manager wiped his hands on the dirty apron that covered his paunch. His tone implied that he wasn't going to volunteer any information.

"So I just wondered if any uniformed police officers also join them sometimes?"

"What's it to you, Mister?"

"Just curious."

"Then ask them." The manager started to turn away. "You'll find them at the Locust Street station."

"Locust Street? Don't you get any customers from the Grove Street Precinct?"

"Why should I? They walk enough on their own beats to come clear over here." He stalked away.

Ridge returned to the sidewalk, nodding to himself. That narrowed the possibility down to the Fog Horn, unless there was another place near there where they ate breakfast or had coffee. He hailed a hack and headed toward Grove Street, wondering if a policeman with a loose tongue ate at the Fog Horn.

*It could be somebody inside the police ranks,* he told himself. *Or it could be a waiter, or somebody else who could overhear what they say. I'd better go see how much I can find out—discreetly.*

In mid-afternoon, Laurel met Cooper so they could walk together for a final check of the firehouse.

She asked, "When are you leaving for California?"

"Next week, I hope. I'm allowing myself a month. As you once told me, you had to change trains five times from here to Omaha. Then it was another fifteen days on the stagecoach." He smiled at her. "Time's running out for us to have dinner. How about tonight?"

Laurel didn't want to risk being out at night, not even with a male escort. She said, "I have other plans."

"I thought that when I shaved you'd stop making excuses, especially after I saw you and Granger quarreling."

"You and I are working," she reminded him of his own words, "so let's not talk of personal matters."

"Talking of dinner is not permitted, but talk of heading to Sacramento is. Right?"

"You're going there to cover a railroad story. That's business."

"Oh, you're clever," he said with a smile. "But I don't give up easily."

She returned the smile. "Tell me more about your ideas on a murderer's mind."

"That's business, I suppose?"

"Certainly."

Cooper suppressed a sigh and began. "One of the most common characteristics I found in interviewing those multiple killers—and others—is that they feel it's never their fault. They blame everything on everyone else. They are never responsible because in their view, the victim deserved to die."

Laurel thought about Sarah, who had never had an enemy or had never hurt anyone. There was only one reason that Laurel could think of why Sarah had been singled out by Abaddon. Sarah had helped Laurel with her spying missions into the South. Even if Abaddon was for the Confederacy, how did he learn of Sarah's role in the secret missions? Somehow, he had found out, and also learned that Laurel had done the actual field work. So Abaddon killed Sarah, apparently without warning. Yet he was now tormenting Laurel, letting her know she was going to die, and soon. But why was he trying to terrorize her?

"It's never their fault," Cooper repeated, "and their reason is power."

Laurel turned to him. "Why do they want power?"

"My interviews with such men showed that they generally don't think much of themselves, deep down inside. Oh, they put up a good front, a rough exterior. But if you look under the surface at what they're really saying, they feel unimportant and deficient in some way."

"You really think so?"

"Oh, I'm quite sure of it. They fantasize, dreaming about overcoming those feelings of inadequacy. Because they're often very intelligent, they plot carefully after choosing a victim and creating a reason why that person should die. When the perpetrator acts out his fantasy, he feels exhilaration. He believes that he really does have the power of life and death over someone."

"But why do they kill again and again?"

"Because the exhilaration wears off, like a drunk who can't stand being sober. The killer has to have that feeling again, so he kills again. Sometimes they can go for quite a while between murders, but usually they shorten the time between each one."

"And," Laurel guessed, "the more they succeed in getting away with murder, the more they feel safe in tormenting the police. Right?"

"It's the challenge more than feeling safe, I think. This type of man adds to his feelings of power by daring the police to catch him. Then he's in control of them, too, and not just the victim. Abaddon apparently delights in daring them to catch him. That's why he sent that letter to the Globe: to show his disdain for the police."

Laurel fell silent, realizing that Abaddon was controlling her by keeping her moving from place to place, and from showing he could enter her room in spite of guards outside. Now she was going to Virginia to escape him. No man had ever controlled her, yet this unknown one was absolutely dominating her life. Soon, he had warned, he would take that, too.

Cooper didn't seem to mind her silence. He continued, "I wondered what kind of background these men had. From my interviews with them, I found they often had a terrible childhood. Some were beaten by one or both parents. Some were neglected. They all grew up with a brooding hatred that eventually caused some to kill the offending parent. Once in a while, when the perpetrator still didn't feel powerful enough to do that, he substituted others."

Laurel guessed, "Meaning he killed those weaker than he, like that poor teenager found by the ghost tree, as we kids used to call it."

"That's the way I see it. But something puzzles me about Abaddon. While almost everyone, North or South, can quote Scripture, and tell the stories of Noah, Samson, and Daniel, for example, how many do you know who are familiar with the names Abaddon or Apollyon?"

"Not many. I didn't know it until he wrote it."

"It's supposed to mean destruction, but why did this man choose the Hebrew Abaddon instead of the Greek Apollyon?"

"I don't have any idea," Laurel admitted.

"I don't, either, but he must have had some rather extensive Bible training somewhere in his past."

"So if he had a mother or father who mistreated him, someone else cared enough to teach him Scripture?"

"Why do you rule out a parent?" Cooper inquired. "Who knows what goes on inside the average home? I've met some very strange characters who knew what the Bible said, but didn't obey it."

"I suppose. But what makes this kind of person act? What triggers him to kill?"

"I'll tell you about that over dinner, unless you let me talk about how lovely you are."

Laurel didn't answer. She found herself frowning thoughtfully as the smell of horses from the fire station informed her that she and Cooper were near there.

Ridge introduced himself to the owner of the Fog Horn who was more affable than the Big Rooster's manager.

"Sure," the proprietor said in response to Ridge's question, "we have officers in here all the time from the Grove Street Precinct. Why do you ask?"

"What do you know about each of them?"

"Good men, every last one of them." He took on a cautious tone. "You got a problem with one of them?"

"No problem," Ridge assured him. "I'm trying to locate someone who likes to be around them. For example, did the waiter asked to be assigned to their table?"

"Certainly not. Coppers usually aren't real good tippers. Besides, they torment the poor waiters so much, just having fun, you know, but that makes it hard for me to get someone to serve them without a direct order."

"I see. How about customers? Do you have any who like to sit with them or nearby?"

"Say, Mister, who are you and why are you asking so many questions?"

"Personal reasons. Very important ones."

"Well, I don't think I'd better say anything more. I don't want to do anything to upset my customers, and coppers talk among themselves. If they find out I was telling you things that are none of your business, I could lose some of my regulars. So, good day to you, Sir."

Ridge hid his frustration as he returned to the city streets, trying to think of what he should do next.

❧

Laurel and Cooper were leaving the firehouse with only a structure fire that might be worth a paragraph when they met Charity and Darius just outside.

Charity shook blonde hair away from her eyes and asked mockingly, "Did you two beat me to a big story?"

"Not today," Cooper replied. He glanced at Barr. "I know you're engaged, but what's a police photographer doing with an *Illustrated Press* correspondent during working hours?"

"Sh!" Charity whispered, glancing around in mock seriousness. "Big story about to break, but it's so secret I can't tell you. Neither can Darius."

Laurel knew she was teasing, but Laurel also knew that Charity had a theory about Sarah's murder, and that was something Laurel really wanted to know about. But this certainly wasn't the time to ask.

Cooper said lightly, "Charity, you're just upset because the *Globe* and its superior correspondents beat you to a story."

"Oh, you mean that piece you wrote that got that poor vagrant killed?" Her manner was bantering, but there was a bite in her tone. She added mockingly, "I need a big story to offset the one you two wrote about the letter that got that man murdered."

Cooper said sharply, "That story didn't cause his death!"

Charity turned discerning eyes on Laurel. "Do you agree with that?"

Darius had remained silent, but he seemed to sense that his intended bride was getting into a discussion that was not good for anyone. He turned to Laurel. "I was looking at that photograph that was left on your highboy, and I noticed something that might interest you. That shot was taken near dusk."

"Dusk?" she repeated.

"Yes. I could tell from the long shadows. Until recently, there wasn't a film out that could take good pictures without lots of light. The new film also doesn't require as long an exposure as it used to."

Laurel wasn't sure she understood what he meant. She cocked her head inquiringly.

He explained, "So whoever took that picture did it fairly recently. I don't know that it'll help you, and neither does Charity, but I thought I'd mention it."

Laurel glanced at Cooper who nodded knowingly, "That seems right in line with something else I picked up in my search: killers often return to the scene of the crime."

"They do?" Laurel asked. "Why? And why take a picture of the tree near where that girl's body was? . . ." She broke off and turned her eyes on Charity. From the way her eyebrows suddenly arched up, Laurel knew that the other woman had thought of something.

So had Laurel. If Effie Chapman's killer had returned to the scene of the crime to take the photograph near dusk, he might return again. It was a theory worth checking out, but Laurel didn't want to leave Cooper to ask more questions of Charity. Making a hasty excuse, Laurel grabbed Cooper's hand, and hurried him away.

He chuckled. "Well, it's nice to at least get to hold hands with you, Laurel. And you're the instigator, too."

"Don't get any ideas," she warned him, then fell silent, knowing that she had to grab a hack and drive out to the tree as soon as her work was finished for the day.

Ridge was waiting in a hack outside the Globe building when Laurel walked out after work. He called to her, and thought she looked disappointed when she saw him. He got out and helped her into the backseat. From her expression, he was sure she was not glad to see him.

He pretended not to notice. "How did it go today?"

"Fine." She was both flattered and annoyed that he had shown up without warning. He could have told her this morning that he planned to give her a ride back to her hotel. She resented his assumption, but quickly thought of an idea and smiled to disarm any possible suspicions.

He told the driver to just start and he'd give him the address later. As the carriage started to move through the afternoon traffic of carriages, wagons, and drivers on horseback, he leaned close and whispered to Laurel. "Can't trust anyone until Abaddon is caught."

She nodded and asked, "How was your day?"

"Oh," he said casually, "I made some calls and checked on some things. Bought our tickets for Friday night on the cars."

She tried to ignore the strange but pleasant feeling of being near him, and the unexplainable attraction she had always had for him. *Stop it!* she sternly rebuked herself. *Don't even think about it!*

She lowered her voice. "Ridge, do you remember when Kelly showed us a piece of wood that he said came from Sarah's place, but neither you nor I could identify it?"

"Of course. Why?"

"Charity told me that Kelly had also asked Darius about it. He said it looked like a piece off the end of a camera tripod, and Kelly agreed."

Ridge looked expectantly at Laurel but said nothing.

She explained, "Charity also told me that she had talked to Sarah's husband—widower—and he swore that Sarah had never had her picture taken. No photographer had ever been in that house, either. That is, until Darius Barr came as the police photographer."

Ridge said, "I'm not sure I understand."

"There's more. You remember that photograph of the strange tree that was left in the sack on my highboy?"

"Are you suggesting that photography somehow ties in with Sarah's death?"

"It's a thought," Laurel admitted. "But today at lunch when Charity and I were talking about all this, she mentioned that Darius said he had noticed something in reviewing Sarah's murder scene. As I recall, Charity quoted Darius as saying something about, 'Abaddon's description was so exact that he could have been looking at my photographs.' "

Ridge shook his head. "Did she mean Darius thinks Sarah's slayer might have taken a photo after he killed her?"

"I think that's what she meant, but that's when she suddenly said something about, 'Why didn't I think of that before?' then she wouldn't say anything more."

"A photographer," Ridge murmured. "Whom do you know who is one?"

Laurel hesitated before replying. "Only one, well, he used to be. Vance Cooper, and he seems to know more about the killer than anyone else. But it can't be him!"

She hesitated, suddenly concerned, before asking herself, *Can it?*

Abaddon claimed he wasn't feeling well so he could leave work a little early. He stationed himself more than a block away from the *Globe* building and waited for Laurel to leave. He had known she would not stay at her aunt's house anymore, so he had to follow her to her new dwelling. He wasn't surprised when Ridge picked her up in a hack. Abaddon promptly hailed a cabriolet and told the driver to follow the hack.

All went well after they left downtown until Abaddon was delayed when the near horse of an approaching heavy carriage suddenly shied at something and abruptly swerved into the cabriolet. The horse escaped unscathed, but wheels on both vehicles crunched together. Spokes on the cabriolet's lighter wheel collapsed, throwing both the driver and passenger into the street.

Neither was really hurt, but Abaddon was furious because the hack with Laurel and Ridge disappeared during the delay. Abaddon stared after them, annoyed because he didn't like it when his plans went astray. That wasn't a good sign; the second bad one, in fact. First he had been forced to turn his attention from Laurel to Ninian. That hadn't been in his plans, but he couldn't let someone else take credit for his work. Now this.

Abaddon leaped up and stormed over to the carriage to rage at the driver. The coach was empty. Abaddon stopped instantly. *Don't do anything that'll make him remember me, he warned himself. Be nice; let my driver handle this.*

Abaddon walked to the shade of a nearby tree to wait while the two drivers talked. When they were through, the offending driver offered Abaddon a ride back downtown. He accepted, leaving the cabriolet driver to deal with his damaged vehicle.

Abaddon was cordial but not very talkative on the drive. He had to find where she had moved so he could carry out his next act of terror. She had not frightened easily, but this time he would raise the level of fear.

*One more time*, he assured himself, *then it'll be time. But first, I have to find her again.*

As a lighter, faster hack passed the heavy coach, Abaddon recognized Ridge seated behind the driver. Abaddon slid down below the coach window so that he couldn't be seen and wondered where Ridge had left Laurel.

Laurel entered the small hotel and found a note from her aunt. "Have decided to stay the night with my brother. Back tomorrow."

For a moment, Laurel thought of going there, too, but decided Ridge was right. Abaddon might be expecting her to do that, so why take the risk? She started to take off her shoes and be more comfortable, then remembered that Darius Barr had said the picture left on her highboy had been taken about dusk. She looked out the window at the deepening shadows of the evening. *If I can get a hack, I can be at the ghost tree before dusk.*

Moments later, she was outside where a lone hack stood waiting for a fare. She seated herself in the back and said to the driver, "I don't know the address where I want to go, but start driving and I'll direct you as we go along."

Abaddon had the offending driver drop him off in the heart of the city, well away from his rented room. He was a careful man who had planned well. He became morose, walking casually along, mentally drifting back to how he had begun.

*Effie Chapman was pretty, and a little older than I was,* he reminded himself. *But she shouldn't have laughed when I asked if I could call on her.*

He could still see the whole humiliating scene in his mind: the seventeen year old sitting alone under that strangely shaped tree, reading, as she often did. He thought it through and returned one afternoon just before dark so that he could escape into the heavy underbrush and trees if necessary.

Now, the more he thought about it, the more he felt the need to relive the experience. It would help if he went there. He could make it just before dark, he decided, and went looking for a hack to hire.

Ridge was deep in thought when he entered the lobby of the hotel where he was staying. He had come to the conclusion that something was bothering Laurel besides her concern about disapproval from other people in both the North and South.

*Maybe,* he told himself, *it's because we're both so strong-minded. But I'm willing to meet her halfway. She still has to come to terms with what's more important.*

The desk clerk handed him a few telegrams. He carried them to an upholstered chair under a wall lamp with a brass reflector that gave more direct light on his reading. Four were business messages from his manager in Omaha. All required decisions that Ridge couldn't really concentrate on making.

The last wire was from his friend Griff. "Delighted you and Laurel are coming. Meet you in Richmond."

Shoving the telegrams into his pocket, Ridge stared out the lobby's large windows at the lengthening shadows.

*In Virginia,* he reminded himself, *I'll have to heed Laurel's edict to be politely attentive. I wonder if Griff or his parents will notice a coolness in Laurel?*

Ridge hoped that they wouldn't see Varina because he was positive she would sense the tension between Laurel and himself.

*I wish I could patch things up with Laurel!* he told himself. *Not just for appearances sake, but for all time.*

He sat for a moment, his brow furrowed in thought.

*I don't like the idea of her and Agnes being alone after someone was in Laurel's room last night, even if I did make sure that no one followed us to that hotel.*

He decided to go check on them, even if it made Laurel angry.

Darkness was falling fast when Laurel told the hack driver to stop. He was an older man with gray whiskers who reined in the horse and looked back at her.

"Excuse me, Miss, but are you sure you want to stop here?"

"I won't be long," she replied, stepping down. "Please wait."

"I don't know, Miss. There ain't hardly a living soul around here this time of evening."

"I can take care of myself," she replied with a smile intended to reassure him. She adjusted the draw string of the reticule on her right wrist and started across the deserted park.

The tree that reminded her of a headless person with arms stretched out was an ash gray. This made it seem even more like the ghost tree of her childhood. The ashen color contrasted sharply with the green leaves of the other trees and dense brush as high as a harness shed. From somewhere in the gathering gloom an owl was already uttering its plaintive "whoooo" call.

*This is later than it was in that photograph Abaddon left in the sack on my highboy,* she told herself, trying to not feel uneasy. Short years ago, she had repeatedly slipped through both Union and Confederate lines on her secret missions. Each time it had been an adventure; a time of danger and thrills, and she had not been afraid.

*So,* she asked herself as she neared the tree, *why do I feel so jumpy now?*

About twenty feet from the tree, she stopped and slowly turned, looking in all directions. She heard the hack horse blow noisily, but she couldn't see him because there was a mound of untended berry vines between them.

Satisfied that she was alone, she slowly neared the tree, trying to imagine on which side of the tree the seventeen-year-old's body had been found.

*Why was she killed?* Laurel wondered. *Who did it? Did she know him, or was he a stranger? And why did he break into my father's house and leave that photograph for me? It must mean something. But what? Unless? . . .*

She tried to snap off the thought, but it was too late. Unless he figured that I'd be so curious that I'd show up here like this sometime, and he . . .

She whirled around, her heart suddenly leaping like a surprised deer. But there wasn't another person around. There was silence except for the owl's eerie call.

She scolded herself, *Stop imagining things! Take a good look around and then get back to the hack!*

Laurel circled the tree, her eyes darting up the headless trunk. Against the darkening sky, it looked more than ever like a beheaded human. The bare limbs resembled outstretched arms, minus hands. She dropped her gaze to skim the brush and other trees.

She felt gooseflesh ripple along her arms, but she silently chided herself and turned back to the tree. On an impulse, and to prove she wasn't afraid, she sat down and rested her back against the rough, gray trunk.

Abaddon had a difficult time controlling his breathing. He

had recognized her at once, even in the fading twilight. He licked his lips, his eyes following her as she moved toward the tree.

A few minutes before, Abaddon had approached from the opposite direction after telling his driver to wait on the dirt side road. Abaddon was feeling a kind of mild euphoria from remembering what happened here when he heard wheels crunch on gravel, then the voices of a man and a woman. Abaddon had quickly entered the shelter of high brush where he crouched down and stared into the fast-falling darkness.

Even in the fading twilight, he had recognized Laurel at once, and groaned inwardly. *Not tonight! I wasn't expecting her!*

His thoughts leaped back to when he had watched her at her father's house after she discovered the photo in the sack. He had known before hand that she would then go to this tree, so was prepared and followed her. But that time she had stopped in her vehicle without leaving it, thwarting his plan to frighten her more.

Now she was unexpectedly back, and Abaddon wasn't prepared. His eyes followed her as she moved toward the tree. Even in the thickening gloom, he saw how pretty she was. He licked his lips and had a difficult time controlling his breathing.

Then he remembered what she had done, and anger surged through him. He watched as she looked around, circled the tree, then seemed to be heading back toward her hack.

*Oh, no!* He silently exclaimed. *Don't go! Not yet!*

He heaved a huge sigh of relief when she abruptly sat down on the far side of the trunk. He could only see her reticule where it rested on the ground just beyond her right hand.

The owl floated over his head on silent wings, but he didn't know it was there until it gave a wild, hoarse cry. He flinched and instinctively ducked lower, then berated himself for his reaction. The bird of prey vanished into the evening sky, giving Abaddon an idea.

*Yes!* he applauded the concept, then immediately shook his head. *No! Don't risk everything by acting impulsively! Plan it, as I've done everything so far.* He teetered between logic and emotion for a few seconds before reason lost.

It's not her time yet, but she doesn't know that. There's nobody around, so she needs some sudden terror.

He quickly pulled off his shirt and loosely draped it over his head, hiding his face but leaving an opening so he could see. He reached into his pocket for the heavy pocket knife he always carried.

Opening it, he rose on tiptoes, bent low, and stealthily crept toward her, knife in hand. Keeping the tree between them, he made only a little more sound than the owl had made until his hands touched the trunk.

Laurel started to get up. She turned to lift her reticule and caught a flash of something behind and to her right. "Oh!" she exclaimed, unsure of what she had glimpsed. She took a quick look and drew back in fright.

In the twilight, she saw the knife in the hand of a man with a huge, misshapen head. She involuntarily screamed as the knife flashed down, missing her as she fought her long skirt in getting to her feet.

Without a word, her attacker struck again. She instinctively jerked her bag up defensively. It struck the knife hand as it flashed down the third time. She saw the blade arc in the air before falling to the ground several feet away.

As her assailant leaped to recover it, she sprang to her feet, yanked her long skirts up above her ankles, and ran screaming toward her waiting hack. She dodged in and out of obstructing brush and around trees. Above the frenzied pounding of her heart, she heard heavy footsteps running behind her. He had not spoken a word.

Risking a glance back, she saw him veer at an angle to cut her off. She dared not risk him getting between her and the hack, but she could not run any faster. She lost sight of her pursuer when he ran behind a long mound of berry bushes. She continued her frenzied race toward the waiting hack.

She sobbed with relief when she saw the gray-bearded driver running toward her, yelling, "What's the matter?"

Breathlessly, she rushed up to him. "Get us out of here, fast!"

"What happened?" he asked, taking her arm and quickly guiding her toward the vehicle.

She panted, "He was chasing me!"

"Who?"

She pointed, "That . . . man." She stopped. There was nobody in sight. She scanned the darkened area with frightened eyes. "He was there, by the tree. He chased me with a knife. He was behind those berry bushes. . . ."

The driver's chuckle stopped her. "Miss, I think you scared yourself. Here, let me help you up, then I'll take you where it's light."

She looked at him in disbelief. She started to protest that she had been attacked, then changed her mind. It didn't matter if the driver believed her or not; she knew what had happened. Suddenly, she wished Ridge was there to take her in his arms and hold her safely.

It wasn't likely that Abaddon would be watching his hotel, Ridge knew, but he was still careful to direct his cabriolet driver by a roundabout way toward the hotel where he had left Laurel after work. Ridge didn't mind the delay. It gave him an opportunity to think about what he wanted to say to her.

He knocked on her second-story hotel room door, wondering how she would react to his unexpected appearance.

"Who is it?" Her voice came through the door.

"It's Ridge."

"Ridge!" He thought she sounded glad, which really surprised him. He heard her run across the floor, then stop and carefully open the door a crack.

He had never seen her looking so pale and wan. He asked, "What happened?"

"Oh, Ridge!" she cried, opening the door wide and throwing both arms around his neck. "I'm so glad you're here!"

He was so startled that he didn't say anything, but from the trembling of her body, he knew she had suffered a frightful experience. He had never known her to be so vulnerable, but he gladly pulled her close and held her tightly, content for the moment to know she was willingly in his arms. He tried not to think whether this was reconciliation, or only a frightened reaction to some horrific incident. He waited in uncertain hope for her to regain her composure.

When only an occasional shiver shook her, she freed herself from his embrace. She wearily sank onto the end of the bed and told him what had just happened.

He listened with rising concern, standing beside her and looking down at her with troubled eyes. "This has gone far enough, Laurel," he told her. "You've got to tell Kelly everything before I take you with me where you'll be safe."

His surprise at her reaction to his arrival was no greater than when she slowly nodded. "Maybe you're right about telling Kelly." She slid off the high bed. "Aunt Agnes is staying the night with

Papa. Please, can we go downstairs where we can talk?"

His arms slid around her. "Anything you want as long as we're together." He slowly bent toward her.

For a moment, she hesitated, then tilted her head back and closed her eyes as his lips claimed hers.

Abaddon still felt some residual excitement over his chance encounter with Laurel at the old tree. He did not return to his rented room, but instead went to his widowed mother's where she lived alone in the large two-story house in which he had grown up.

He took care that she didn't see him as he slipped silently through the darkness to what had been a guest cottage when he was a boy. He cautiously unlocked the door and gently pushed it open, flinching at the squeak of rusty hinges.

Everything was as he had left it, he decided after lighting a candle and holding it high. He moved a heavy chest aside and put his finger in a metal ring which had been recessed into the wooden floor. He raised the hidden trapdoor and smelled the familiar odor of moist earth which had long been denied fresh air.

Lowering the candle into the dark hole, he checked his equipment. There were two large cameras, each covered so they resembled fair-sized boxes. One was a half-plate Daguerreotype camera with a ground glass viewer. It rested on a wooden shelf beside the walnut portable tripod. He had stolen it in New York after he had been pressed into service as a photographer's assistant. But that camera was too slow for his present work, so last year he had stolen a new model before moving back to Chicago. He gingerly touched the second camera through its cover, gloating in its faster lens and film.

Soon now, he told himself. Soon. His fingers moved on to

touch the wooden mahogany tripod that he had used at Sarah Skillens's. He stopped at the tip of one leg when he felt something rough.

Holding the candle closer, he saw that a small piece was missing. *Wonder where I lost that?* he asked himself, then shrugged and turned to his carefully-boxed plates.

It was a temptation to examine them again, but he shook his head. *I'll do that when I add the next one.*

Still feeling good about frightening Laurel, and anticipating the feeling of really being alone with her when he carried out her death, he quietly lowered the hidden trapdoor and slid the chest back into place.

It was a good day, he admitted to himself, and tomorrow should be even better. *I just wish I could be at the* Globe *when the mail arrives.*

His latest letter should be included. He tried to visualize Laurel's face when she saw the page telling why Jay Ninian had been killed. But Abaddon knew that he would have to wait until noon in hopes that talkative patrolmen would discuss Kelly's and Pierce's reactions when the correspondents took the letter to them.

Abaddon blew out the candle, locked the door, and vanished into the darkness.

The air was already sultry the next morning when Laurel arrived at the *Globe* building. She walked with a light step, recalling with tingling pleasure how she had impulsively thrown her arms around Ridge after being chased by the knife-wielding assailant last night. She thrust that frightening memory aside and smiled to herself when she relived the kiss shared with Ridge.

Then she frowned, thinking of what she had to do this morning. She wasn't exactly suspicious of Cooper, but she didn't want to tell Kelly in front of Cooper about why she thought Sarah had been murdered, and that her own life was in jeopardy.

She entered the building and headed for her desk at the back of the editorial department. As she walked past Seymour's big window, he jumped up and tapped on the glass, beckoning with his cigar for her to come in. Cooper rose from his chair across from the publisher's desk and opened the door for her.

"Read this," Seymour said by way of greeting. He handed an envelope to her.

She glanced at the address and unconsciously licked her lips. The handwriting was the same as on the two letters sent to her at her father's house. Trying to hide her sudden sense of alarm, she pulled out the single sheet of paper.

Seymour said, "Read it aloud."

She nodded and began. "The man who tried to steal credit for my work has paid the price. He deserved what he got, just as Sarah Skillens did for her actions. But she did not act alone, and so you may soon expect to write another story about the next victim."

Laurel paused, feeling a constriction in her throat at the clear implication that she was that victim.

Seymour took the cigar from his mouth. "Finish it."

Laurel forced herself to read without emotion. "The police are so inept that they can't stop me." She hesitated before reading the signature. "Abaddon."

Cooper said, "The lieutenant and Kelly aren't going to like that, especially if we print that last part."

"It's our job to print it," Seymour declared. "So, take it to them, then write it. Build our circulation."

Laurel handed the letter to Cooper as they both got to their feet.

Seymour said, "Laurel, wait a minute. Cooper, she'll be right out."

When the door closed behind Cooper, the publisher looked across the desk at Laurel. "Cooper's leaving for California, and you're not experienced enough to handle the police and fire beats by yourself. So I've hired a new man. You work with him. Understand?"

"Yes."

"All right. You and Cooper go show that letter to the police and get the story back for the last edition."

At the precinct, Cooper told the desk sergeant that they had to talk privately to Kelly. He said he was in the lieutenant's office and should be out in a minute.

The correspondents entered Kelly's tiny office and closed the door.

Cooper asked Laurel, "Are you surprised that Abaddon sent this new letter?"

"I guess I shouldn't be," she replied.

"I expected it. That's typical of this kind of killer. He must feel really alive now, thinking that he can openly challenge the police."

For a moment, she thought of telling Cooper about being chased last night, but decided against it. She had begun to be a little concerned about how much he seemed to know of how Abaddon's mind worked. But after Ridge had left last night, and she was still basking in the warm glow of their reconciliation, two disturbing thoughts kept her awake for hours.

She had agreed to tell Kelly about the two letters she had received, and the two break-ins of her bedchambers. However, she was reluctant to reveal Sarah's and her clandestine war-time activities, but finally yielded to Ridge's reasoning that she must do everything possible to help Kelly apprehend Abaddon before he could harm her.

Laurel's second concern was about Cooper. He was always with her, but she didn't want him present when she confided in Kelly. She vainly tried to shake a recent feeling of apprehension about Cooper.

Laurel reasoned with herself. *Charity's theory about Abaddon has something to do with photography. The only one I know besides Darius Barr who has ever taken pictures is Cooper. But he only had a pad and pencil at Sarah's murder scene when Ridge and I were there.*

Cooper didn't have a camera when they saw him, but he could have gone to Sarah's place earlier, killed her, and taken pictures.

Laurel tried to shake the thought away, but another replaced it. *He sure knows a lot about how Abaddon thinks. No! That's ridiculous! I'm being too imaginative after the two break-ins and my experience last night.*

Cooper's voice aroused her. "Kelly's coming."

She heard the door to the lieutenant's office open and Kelly's heavy footsteps in the hall. She mentally braced herself for what he would say when he read Abaddon's letter.

Sergeant Kerston called from down the hall, "Wait up, Kelly."

His footsteps stopped. "What is it?"

The sergeant's voice got closer. "I think that Dahlgren woman is on to something you should know about. This morning she asked if I had any contacts with Federal authorities. I told her about an agent I used to know who's now with the National Detective Police. I gave her his name."

"Keep your voice down!" Kelly said in a hoarse whisper.

"Who else knows about this?"

Laurel could barely hear Kerston's next words. "Only a couple of patrolmen who were standing nearby talking. Maybe they heard, but I can't say for sure."

Laurel couldn't hear anymore, but she looked at Cooper who had obviously also overheard.

He whispered, "Do you know what the NDP means?"

She did, but didn't want to admit it. It had evolved for the Union's secret service which Allan Pinkerton had begun early in the war for General George McClellan. Her mouth suddenly felt dry as she evaded a direct answer to Cooper. She lowered her voice. "What about it?"

"Why would Charity want to contact them?"

Laurel suspected that her war-time records had probably been transferred to the NDP. What if Charity got hold of those before Laurel could tell Kelly? It had always been Laurel's personal desire to keep her spying a secret, but Pinkerton did not require her to do that. His only demand was that she not tell anyone about being one of his operatives. Reluctantly, she silently admitted that Ridge was right; she had to reveal her war-time activities to the detectives. She had to do so before Charity informed them.

Laurel's thoughts were disrupted by the detective barging into the room. He looked at Cooper and spoke bluntly. "The sergeant says you want to talk to me, but I've got nothing new for you, and I'm busy. So get out and let me work."

Cooper was unperturbed. He handed the letter across the desk. "Oh, but we have something for you, Kelly."

Scowling, the detective skimmed the letter, then his face flushed bright red. His mustache ends quivered as he glared across the desk at the reporters.

"Stay here!" he ordered, jumping to his feet. "I'll show this to the lieutenant, then I'm sure he'll want to question you both!" He hurried around the desk and into the hallway.

At noon, Abaddon sat unobtrusively in his usual back corner of the Fog Horn, eating slowly and reading his newspaper. He seemed unmindful of the three uniformed officers laughing and telling stories at their nearby table. They didn't say anything of interest to Abaddon, who kept looking toward the front of the restaurant.

*She and Cooper should have received my letter by now*, he thought. *They would take it directly to Kelly, so that's probably why they're late.*

He waited, eating slowly, working up the courage to say something casual to Laurel that would give him some clue as to where she had moved since he invaded her bedchamber at her aunt's house. He would have to be very careful, but that was part of the challenge. He would learn what he wanted and nobody would suspect him if he did it right.

A change in the tone of a uniformed officer at the nearby table alerted him to listen closely.

"What else could it mean?" the officer asked. "She's on to something that neither Kelly nor Pierce knows about. Otherwise, why would she ask the sergeant if he knew anybody at the National Detective Police?"

Abaddon was tempted to lean closer, but forced himself to appear deeply interested in his newspaper. His story about being away during the war was that he had been on detached service. Actually, he had only been a civilian clerk for the NDP. That's how he had come across two familiar names of war-time spies. By now, his own name might also be in those files.

The patrolman told his friends, "I don't know what tipped her off, but obviously, Dahlgren thinks she's on to something about who that perpetrator is. I wouldn't want to be around the lieutenant or Kelly if a newspaper correspondent—and a woman at that!—solves this case instead of them!"

Abaddon listened awhile longer, but nothing more was said of interest to him. It didn't matter, because he had heard enough. He casually got up, paid his bill and left. He was angry that his care-fully-worked-out plans were disrupted by Charity Dahlgren's snooping. Now he had no choice except to turn his attention from Laurel to deal with Charity Dahlgren—and quickly.

# Chapter 18

The noon crowd at the Fog Horn had thinned out when Laurel and Cooper finally got there. Abaddon's letter this morning made her realize that time was running out on her because she surely was to be his next victim after Jay Ninian. She didn't want to suspect that Cooper might really be Abaddon, but the nagging thought made her think of a discreet way to learn where Cooper had been the afternoon Sarah was murdered.

He seemed obsessed with talking about Abaddon's latest letter. After they were seated at a table, Cooper said, "I don't understand how Abaddon knows what's going on about things that haven't been published. For instance, how did he find out that Ninian wrote that letter claiming he had killed your friend?"

Laurel hid her real thoughts by saying, "I don't know, but you seem to know a lot about how he thinks. What's your theory?"

"He obviously must have some direct access to the police. They're the only ones who knew those details."

"Not the only ones," she corrected him. "We knew. So Charity must have known, too."

Cooper looked across the table at Laurel. "Surely you're not suggesting that she? . . ."

"Oh, of course not. I'm just pointing out who besides the authorities knew about Ninian."

"Speaking of Charity, what did you make of the sergeant

telling Kelly about her contacting the National Detective Police?"

"I don't know what to think," Laurel replied.

Cooper idly consulted the bill of fare before saying, "We both overheard Kelly telling Kerston to keep his voice down, which suggests it's got something to do with this case. I'd like to find out what it is."

"So would I," Laurel agreed wholeheartedly.

"Maybe I could nose around." Cooper turned to look toward the back of the restaurant. "Usually, there are some patrolmen back there eating. The sergeant said a couple of them might have overheard when Charity asked about the NDP. I'll ask them the next chance I get."

Laurel doubted that Charity would tell Cooper any more than she had after informing Laurel a few days ago that she had a theory. But Laurel now was really disturbed because if her name was in the NDP files, her long-kept secret could not only be known to Charity, but perhaps also circulated throughout Chicago in a story carried in the *Illustrated Press*.

She said, "Let me know what you find out."

"We'll write the story together." Cooper replied. He paused, then asked, "What did you think about today's letter from Abaddon threatening a second victim?"

Laurel tried to keep her face impassive. "He did threaten someone, didn't he?"

"He sure did. Kelly and the lieutenant said they didn't have any ideas about that." Cooper hesitated and gazed directly at her. "However, I noticed that he looked at you in a strange way when he said that."

Laurel managed to smile disarmingly. "As he said, he suspects everyone, so I guess that includes me." She added, "And you, too, I suppose." She paused briefly before asking casually, "Where were you before you showed up at the murder scene?"

He grinned. "Are you trying to incriminate me?"

"Of course not. I was just pointing out that if, as Kelly says, 'everyone's a suspect,' and you think this Abaddon has to be getting his information from someone on the inside—"

"Well," Cooper interrupted, "I was at the *Globe* writing when word came of her murder."

Laurel's smile broadened. "A room full of reporters would make good witnesses."

"It could be somebody else," Cooper replied. "Maybe somebody we haven't even thought about." As their waiter passed with a tray for a nearby table, Cooper said under his breath, "It could even be one of them."

"Or," she said quietly, "It could be a customer who overhears what the officers, or we, talked about." When Cooper nodded, Laurel abruptly made a decision about confessing what she had kept from Kelly. "After we leave here, I need to take care of a personal matter. You don't mind covering the firehouse alone, do you?"

"No. Just meet me back at the paper in time to help write the story about today's letter."

"I'll be there."

"One more thing. Since I'll soon be leaving for California, how about having that long-delayed dinner with me tonight?"

"I'm sorry, but I can't."

"That's too bad. I had some thoughts about Abaddon that can't be discussed over a short lunch."

Laurel recognized that Cooper had tossed out a baited hook. "Such as?" she asked.

"From Abaddon's letter, and what I've learned from interviewing killers in prison, I have a hunch that this man is engaging in mental torture with whoever his next victim is. Today's letter confirms that for me."

Laurel's pulse speeded up, knowing that Abaddon's letter meant she was to be that other victim. She managed to ask casually, "How so?"

"Well, when we print the story with a copy of today's letter from Abaddon, his next victim might logically read it and assume his or her days are numbered. But I don't think whoever Abaddon meant in today's letter is necessarily his next target."

That surprised Laurel. "You don't?"

"No, I don't. This kind of criminal would envision something else; something to first hurt his ultimate victim emotionally, maybe through her family. Or someone else she loves."

Laurel felt goose bumps suddenly form on her arms. She was frightened for her family, Ridge, and herself.

Cooper sighed. "Well, I guess you're not that interested, or you'd want to know more over dinner."

She had to know more, no matter what the risk. But how much could there be in a public restaurant? "What time tonight?"

Instantly, she regretted her words, but it was too late.

"I'll pick you up at seven."

"No," she said quickly. "I'll meet you. Just tell me where."

"The Silver Slipper near the lake."

She politely refused to say anything more during their meal as her emotions hastily tumbled over each other. *I need to tell Kelly right away, but on the other hand, if Cooper's right, my family could be in danger.*

Laurel decided that right after lunch, she would go to her father. She would try to persuade him to leave town for awhile, and urge the rest of the family to do the same. She blinked as a new thought hit her. *What if Abaddon goes after Ridge before Friday night when we head for Virginia?*

Ridge had a good morning, successfully signing up two large companies to buy land from him after he induced them to open midwest branches. It was the logical way to better serve the exploding influx of settlers who were already heading west to resettle along the line of the coming transcontinental railroad.

He felt great when he finally stopped for a late lunch. He still didn't understand why Laurel had suddenly reversed herself from breaking up with him. He shook his head, remembering how she had agreed to accompany him to Virginia on the condition that he be 'politely attentive' to her. When he next saw her, she had thrown her arms around his neck and returned his kiss. He knew that reconciliation had its benefits.

He told himself, *I'll surprise her by taking her to dinner tonight. I'll be at the* Globe *when she leaves this afternoon. Later, I'll drive along the lake where we can catch up on the romance we've missed out on lately.*

He smiled, thinking ahead to having her by his side on the long train ride to Virginia. By the time they reached Richmond, maybe she would agree to a wedding date and where they would live.

🐾

Shortly after she arrived at her father's home in mid-afternoon, Laurel realized she had made a mistake. She hadn't expected Emma to be visiting with their father and Aunt Agnes. In the parlor, the older sister listened quietly to Laurel's suggestion before she spoke with her usual critical attitude.

"You won't tell us why, yet you want all of us to pack and leave Chicago for awhile. Surely you don't expect any of us to listen to such a ridiculous notion?"

Laurel turned to her father. "You didn't tell her about the break-in?"

"Break-in?" Emma cried. "What break-in?"

Laurel didn't wait for her father's explanation, but looked at her aunt. "You didn't tell her about your place, either?"

"There was no need, my dear," Agnes said calmly. "My brother and I had talked it over and decided there was no point in alarming the rest of the family until and if we knew something more about all this."

Emma threw her arms up. "Will somebody tell me what's going on?"

Laurel gave her a cool but firm look. "If we do, will you stop screeching?"

"I'm not screeching!"

Her father said gently, "Yes, you are, Emma. Now sit down quietly and listen without interruption until we give you the details."

Something calmly authoritative in his voice made his oldest daughter wordlessly drop onto the Victorian loveseat beside her aunt.

Laurel quickly told Emma about the break-in upstairs and the sack with the photograph in it. Agnes helped detail what had happened at her place, and added that neither she nor Laurel had been back since Ridge arrived the morning after the second break-in.

Both Emma's hands flew to her mouth and her eyes opened wide. "But why?" she asked, getting to her feet and taking a couple of agitated steps. "Why?"

Laurel said, "I can't answer that, but I feel very strongly that all of you, including Harriet and her family, should leave town as quickly as possible."

Emma exclaimed, "Well, I refuse to believe we're all in some kind of danger because of what's happened to you! I need something more tangible than your feelings."

Laurel tried to speak patiently. "There are some other things I can't tell you that convince me that this is more than just my feelings."

Emma exclaimed triumphantly. "Now you're telling the truth! This has something to do with all those secret trips you made during the war!" She whirled to look up at the painting of her mother. "Oh, I'm glad she didn't live to see this day, and she didn't know about your illicit liaisons during the war!"

Laurel's anger exploded. "I've told you on my honor that I never did anything to bring shame on this family!"

"I don't believe that!" Emma snapped. "Neither does anyone else. Right, Papa?"

He said softly, "I believe Laurel."

Agnes nodded. "So do I."

"Well, I don't and I never will!" Emma stalked angrily across the room in front of the fireplace, then spun to face Laurel. "God is punishing you for your dark acts during the war! If anything happens to me or my family, it'll be your fault!"

The women's father said sternly, "Emma, that's enough!"

"No, Papa, it's not!" she replied. "She can fool you and Aunt Agnes, but not me! Sowing and reaping is at work here! Laurel, your secret sins will get us all killed unless you repent!"

The unjust accusation hurt Laurel more than the furious tirade. "I will say it one more time, Emma: I never did anything to dishonor myself or our family. Now, I don't know what else I can do except urge all of you to leave town for awhile."

Her father's voice was barely audible, but strong. "I believe you, and I will not only take your advice, but I'll do my best to persuade Harriet and her family to do the same. Emma, I'm asking you to join us."

"No, Papa! I will not run away from something that's not my fault!"

Agnes said sharply, "Then you're a fool, Emma! I'm soon going to California to get married, but right now, I'm going with my brother and anybody else in this family who's got any sense!"

"Thank you," Laurel said with deep feeling. "The sooner we do, the better I'll feel."

Emma shrugged. "Well, I see it differently. Laurel has always been a rebel. She refuses to be submissive to anyone: Papa, her Rebel, and even God."

Laurel smarted under the verbal onslaught, but a secret fear that Emma was right kept her from replying.

Emma shifted her eyes to Laurel's. "As you know, I don't care for your Rebel, but I hope he has sense enough to get away from you before it's too late."

Turning toward the door, Emma added, "I'm not going to stay here and argue this any longer. I'm going home to my family, and we're not going anywhere."

With her hand on the door knob, she looked back at Laurel. "You said you're afraid for those you love, but what about your Rebel? Is he in danger because of you?"

With a triumphant tilt of her chin, Emma stormed out, slamming the door behind her.

With an effort, Laurel put Ridge's safety aside, knowing they would be on their way south by tomorrow afternoon. "Papa, I'm sorry about this."

"So am I," he replied. "But I hope she'll calm down and use her common sense and go away."

Laurel took a couple of steps and kissed him on the cheek. "I love you, Papa."

"And I love you, as well as the rest of my family. But you mustn't be too upset over all this. Everyone in life has trials, yet the Bible tells us that all things work together for good to those who love God."

Laurel would have expected such a comment from Aunt Agnes. Her father rarely said much that was spiritual in nature, although he had always been faithful in church attendance. Laurel told him, "I've had enough trials lately to last a lifetime."

Agnes commented, "Believe it or not, Laurel, trials are good for you, for all of us. The struggle between faith and doubt always seems to come around again, but each time we overcome, it gets a little easier."

Those words echoed in Laurel's mind when she returned to the hack she had waiting outside. She told the driver to take her to the Grove Street police station. Then she sat back in the seat and tried to sort out her thoughts.

*Could Emma be right? Am I being punished for all the lies I told both in my missions behind enemy lines, and in letting people think I was a newspaper correspondent when I really was a Pinkerton operative? Is there really a bottomless pit where Abaddon plans to send me?*

She shook the idea way. *I've got to quit thinking like this! Abaddon is only a man, and if I tell Kelly what I know, maybe that'll help apprehend him. Then this whole thing will go away and only be like a bad memory.*

Abaddon had a difficult time concentrating on his menial office work that afternoon. He still had contacts at the National Detective Police in New York, but he dared not raise suspicion by inquiring if Charity Dahlgren had been seeking information. He must make his preventive move, but not tonight. Even though it was risky to wait, he had to finish formulating his plan. *By tomorrow night*, he assured himself, *I can do it.*

Nearing the Grove Street police station in mid-afternoon, Laurel hoped that Kelly was in a good mood. It would be hard to confess her secret if he was short-tempered. Laurel started to push the door open when it swung out. Darius and Charity stood there.

"Oh, Laurel!" Charity exclaimed with a glad cry, "I've been looking everywhere for you."

"Well, you found me," she replied with a smile, although she didn't want any delays getting to Kelly.

Charity and the police photographer stepped outside and let the door close behind them. Charity asked, "Do you have a minute?"

"Well," Laurel said a little uncertainly. "I guess."

"I'll be brief." She turned to her fiancé. "You may as well go ahead and I'll catch up with you." When he nodded and walked off with his camera equipment, Charity faced Laurel. "Kelly told me that you brought today's letter that Abaddon sent to the *Globe*. How do you think he found out that Ninian wrote that first letter?"

Laurel wished she could ask Charity why she had contacted the National Detective Police, but instead, she replied, "Cooper and I talked about that at lunch. It must be that Abaddon has some inside contacts."

"That's what Darius and I think. But is it somebody inside the police station, or a waiter where the police eat, or someone else?"

Laurel said thoughtfully, "It could be any of those, or maybe somebody like a newspaper correspondent."

Charity's gray-green eyes narrowed. "I hope that wasn't meant to be directed at me?"

"No, of course not! It was just something that was mentioned at lunch."

"Did Cooper suggest that, or you?"

Frowning, Laurel admitted, "I'm not sure."

"Sounds like Cooper. He is a keen competitor who would really like to see me out of this business."

"You don't like him?"

"Oh, we get along, but he never lets me forget that he expects to beat me to every story if possible. So far, he's done it, which doesn't make me look good to my editor, except for the afternoon your friend Sarah was killed. That's the first time I beat Cooper to a scene."

"He was at the *Globe*," Laurel explained. "He must not have been notified right away."

Charity raised an eyebrow. "He wasn't at the *Globe*."

"He wasn't?"

"No. Darius had seen him loading a camera into a buggy about an hour before I got the call."

Laurel stared at the other woman. "Are you sure?"

"Positive! Darius told me when we rode over to the scene. I remember because I was glad to get a small jump on Cooper."

Laurel scowled, shaking her head. "Where did Darius see him?"

"Not far from where your friend was killed. . . . Oh, no, Laurel! You're not thinking—"

"Oh, no! I'm just curious!" Laurel broke in quickly. She silently added, *I wish I wasn't going to dinner with a man who was either terribly mistaken or outright lied to me. Which is it?*

Laurel studied Charity for a moment before adding, "This morning Cooper and I overheard the sergeant telling Kelly that you wanted to know if he had any contacts in the National

Detective Police. Are you on to something?"

Charity smiled and shook her head. "You reminded me that we're competitors, so you don't think I'm going to answer that, do you?"

"I suppose not," Laurel admitted, "but it was worth asking."

"I will tell you this," Charity replied. "We talked that day about the newspaper dated April 3, 1865. I'm sure you know that's the day both Petersburg and Richmond fell to our armies."

"I remember. I also remember what you said about Darius thinking that Abaddon could have been looking at one of the pictures Darius took at Sarah's murder scene."

Charity's smile widened. "And I recall that's when I suddenly thought of something that I wouldn't tell you. I still won't because we're competitors."

When Laurel shrugged, Charity said, "Well, I will tell you this much: my investigation isn't complete, but I hope to have something by tomorrow. I need a big story to offset the ones the *Globe* has been getting over the Ninian letters and murder."

She paused before asking, "I have to repeat the question I asked the other day: are you in danger because of what you won't tell Kelly? I mean, today's letter warned that somebody else was going to meet Sarah's fate, and since you and she were so close . . ."

Charity left her thought incomplete as the door opened and the desk sergeant looked out. "I thought I recognized your voices," he said. "Miss Bartlett, the lieutenant wants to see you right away."

Laurel's eyebrows arched in surprise. "Why does he want to see me?"

"I didn't ask, and he didn't say. But if I was you, I'd hustle in there right now."

Laurel was glad for an excuse to break off the conversation with Charity. After quick parting words, Laurel followed Kerston inside the police station. She couldn't imagine what the lieutenant wanted, but she was sure she wasn't going to like it.

❧

When Laurel opened the lieutenant's office door at his call to come in, one look at his face told her she had been right. It didn't help that Kelly was already seated across from him, looking miserable.

The lieutenant locked cold gray eyes on her. "Sit," he ordered, motioning to the chair beside Kelly. When she obeyed, he turned in his rumpled dark suit and spat tobacco juice into the cuspidor behind him.

Laurel glanced at Kelly, but he kept his eyes downcast. The ends of his reddish mustache quivered.

Pierce turned back, absently rubbing the end of his crooked nose. "Kelly tells me you're keeping something from him about your murdered friend. Is that true?"

"That's why I came here just now," she began. "I want to—"

Pierce interrupted by slapping his open palm on the desk. "I don't care what you want! We have another victim on our hands, and Abaddon not only claims credit for killing Ninian and your friend, but warns that he's going to kill someone else. Does he mean you?"

Laurel resented Pierce's attitude, but she kept her voice under control. "I think so. That's why I came—"

"Why does he want to kill you?" Pierce broke in. "What's this all about? I warn you: I'm only going to ask you once. If you don't tell me everything straight out, right now, you're going into those stinking cells with the drunks until you do talk!"

Laurel took a deep breath and began telling the two men things that only Sarah and Ridge knew. She told of her war-time enlistment with Pinkerton's newly formed secret service under General George McClellan. Chronologically jumping back and forth, she recounted her experiences behind Confederate lines and bringing back military intelligence for Union generals. She recalled her only brother's battle death at sixteen, which had motivated her to do what she could to aid the Federal cause.

She was surprised that Pierce did not stop her or ask questions. Only when she had finished telling about Sarah's part in helping her with disguises and places to hide Confederate maps and other papers did Pierce finally say something.

"Why didn't you tell Kelly this long ago?"

"I didn't ever want anyone to know what I had done."

"Why?" Pierce's tone was gentle, almost warm. "You served the Union just as Kelly and I did in uniform, only you didn't have to, but we did. You should be proud!"

"Proud?"

"Yes, of course! Haven't you heard about all the former women spies who have written books, or gone on the stage to tell their stories for money? You're one of the youngest I've heard about. You should be doubly proud!"

Kelly spoke for the first time. "Absolutely."

Laurel looked closely at both men and saw respect in their eyes. Suddenly, she felt as if a heavy burden had been lifted from her heart. It was even more gratifying that her news had been so well received.

With a deep sigh of relief, Laurel admitted, "I never thought of it that way. I had worked in secret, and nobody knew, except Sarah and Ridge. I expected to take my war-time experiences with me to the grave. I only told Ridge so that there wouldn't be any lies or secrets between us."

Pierce's tone hardened. "I wish we had known all this before. Maybe Ninian would still be alive, not that he was making much of a contribution to society. As for your friend, I don't suppose anything could have saved her. But now . . ." His voice trailed off.

"But what?" she prompted.

"Now we've got to figure out how to keep you alive while we put all this information together to apprehend this perpetrator."

"I'm going to Virginia tomorrow evening on the cars," she said. "Be gone a few days. Will that help?"

"It'll help," Pierce assured her. "Now, Kelly, you help us go over the clues and everything else we know to this point. We're about to catch ourselves a killer!"

Laurel hoped that was true, but she wasn't as sure of that as Pierce. However, she was confident that time was fast running out, and Abaddon apparently controlled the hour and place when he would claim her life.

# Chapter 19

At the end of the day when she exited the *Globe* building, Laurel was greatly relieved by the reaction of both Pierce and Kelly at her confessed war-time role as a Union spy. She briefly wondered how this revelation might affect whatever theory Charity had formulated about Sarah's death. Laurel quickly replaced that thought with something that Pierce had suggested when she was about to leave the police precinct.

"Laurel, you're a real patriot! You should write about your spying experiences for the *Globe*. They'll make sensational reading. In fact, you could even write a book or maybe go on the stage to tell your story for money."

For the first time, Laurel wasn't uncomfortable with the use of the word "spy." She wasn't proud, and had not thought of herself as a patriot, but she was intrigued by the lieutenant's idea. Seymour would have to approve it, but she was sure he would see the probability of increased circulation if she ran a series of features.

Stepping onto the sidewalk mostly filling with men going home, she shook her head. *It's strange. Ever since the war ended, I've worked so hard to keep it all a secret. Now I'm considering writing about it. But right now, all I really want is for Abaddon to be caught before he . . .*

"Laurel! Over here!" Ridge's voice broke into her thoughts.

She lifted her eyes to see him smile and step down from a hack to the curbside.

He approached her saying, "I came to take you home."

She started to return the smile, then quickly checked it. *Cooper! I have to meet him for dinner!*

Ridge cocked his head. "What's the matter?"

"Uh . . . thanks, but I can't. I've just told the lieutenant and Kelly everything I know. Now there's something I have to do tonight."

"I'm glad you told them. How'd they take it?"

"Rather well, as a matter of fact. But I'd rather tell you what I think you should do."

"Me? Except for looking forward to our trip tomorrow night, and marrying you . . . "

"Wait! I'm serious. It may be that Abaddon will try to hurt me by . . . well, by killing my family, or someone else close to me."

"Your family should go away until this is over."

"They are. Well, most of them anyway. But, Ridge, Abaddon seems to know so much that he has probably figured out that if I told anyone about Sarah's and my war-time experiences, it would be you. So, for your own safety, I want you to leave for Virginia right away. Tonight. I'll follow tomorrow—"

"No!" he broke in. "I'm not going anywhere without you. We need to make some plans on the cars. But this is no place to talk about that. I'll take you home. . . ."

"I told you I can't!" She hadn't meant to sound so sharp, but she couldn't back down. "Now, please, think about what I said, and let me go about my business."

His jaw muscles twitched in frustration, but he answered quietly. "All right, I'll leave you alone for tonight and I'll be careful. But I'm not leaving for Virginia without you. We'll ride down together tomorrow, and I'll expect an explanation." He turned and entered the hack.

Laurel sighed. She hadn't wanted this to happen.

❧

Abaddon returned to his rented room shortly after dusk and moodily sat on the bed without lighting the lamp. He removed his glasses and closed his eyes to work out details of a new plan while fuming at the unexpected complications Charity Dahlgren had caused.

*Three, no, soon four murders within as many weeks or less will have the city in an uproar. If I didn't have to finish with Laurel, I'd leave town right after Charity. But I can't do anything to make the police suspect me.*

His anger surged because she had interfered with his plan. *Well, tomorrow night she'll regret that.*

❧

At her hotel room, Laurel hurriedly bathed and dressed for her dinner with Vance Cooper. She was nearly ready when Aunt Agnes arrived with news about her brother and the rest of his family.

"They all left to visit your dad's cousin in Wisconsin for awhile. Emma fought tooth and nail against the idea, but I think she was really frightened, which is why she went with her brood."

"I'm very glad. But why are you still here?"

"I've changed my mind," Agnes declared. "I'm going to stay here with you so you and I can go to California together."

"Oh!" Laurel exclaimed, her eyes widening in concern. "That could be dangerous!"

"I've considered that, but it's less so for me than for you.

Besides, my mind is made up. I'm staying."

Laurel impulsively reached out to hug her aunt, then stopped herself. Instead, she said softly, "I'm touched."

"No need to be. Now, finish what you're doing."

Laurel checked her reflection in the mirror. To discourage any of Cooper's romantic notions, she had parted her hair in the middle and pulled it back behind the ears. She knew this wasn't flattering, but neither was the simple pleated skirt and bodice or white collar buttoned just under the chin.

Agnes mused, "Ridge isn't going to like that attire."

"He's not going to see it." Laurel picked up her reticule and hurried from the room.

❧

Ridge picked up the daily telegrams from the hotel desk clerk and carried them up to his room. He didn't open the wires, figuring they were all from his Omaha manager who wanted answers to pressing problems.

Ridge dropped heavily into the one upholstered chair by his bed and scowled, wondering why Laurel refused to see him tonight. He hoped she wasn't going to change her mind about their marriage. He eagerly looked forward to their long ride on the cars where they could finalize their future.

He was pleased that she had told the authorities of her spying background and possible tie-in with Sarah's murder and the threats to her own life. Most of all, he was glad to get her beyond Abaddon's reach for a few days. She might now be in a better mood when he told her that he was finally willing to swallow his pride and petition President Johnson for amnesty. That was the first step necessary to regain the Granger family plantation. But if she didn't want to live in the South, he was agreeable to wherever she would be happy as long as they could be together.

His thoughts leaped to their brief meeting outside the *Globe* building this afternoon. *She acted strangely, saying how much she worried that Abaddon may be trying to kill me to get at her, then refusing to even tell me why I couldn't come talk to her tonight. I don't understand.*

He shook his head and tried to shift his attention to the telegrams. He began opening one, then stopped.

*She's always saying she can take care of herself. Could she possibly have some kind of a lead as to Abaddon's identity? Could she even be thinking about meeting him? . . .*

He abruptly dropped the wire and stood up. He did not think she would be home, and finding her in the city of Chicago was almost impossible. But maybe her aunt knew where Laurel had gone and why.

❧

Laurel and Cooper were seated at a reserved table in a quiet corner of The Silver Slipper overlooking the lake. Just enough moonlight showed to reflect off the water. Instead of sitting across from her, he chose to sit on the same side, explaining that this way they could both watch the waves.

He commented, "I like the view here."

"It's a beautiful spot," she admitted, taking a more careful look at his attire. He wore a plain bow tie, dark blue suit with a hint of lighter stripe over a matching vest. Without his goatee, she was aware that he looked quite dashing. This was confirmed by surreptitious glances from three young women dining at a nearby table.

"I'm honored to have your company, Laurel," he said, turning to look at her face in the light of two tall tapers. "I hope this will be the first of many evenings together before I leave for California."

She moved to head off further romantic comments. "When do you leave?"

He grinned at her, the candles reflecting humor in his brown eyes. "You're good at steering the conversation off on an angle. But as I told you before, I'm a patient man." He ran fingers along his clean-shaven cheeks and ended with a slight flip of his heavy mustache. "I leave next week for Sacramento."

"I hope you have a good trip, and that you get some very good stories about the opening of the Summit Tunnel."

"Thank you, but I'd like it better if you were going to be there, too. We could write some great stories."

She let that pass without comment, knowing that she had promised Allan Pinkerton that she would work on one more detective case for him out of Sacramento.

Cooper shrugged. "All right, you don't want to talk about that. Now, I know our original agreement was that if you'd have dinner with me, I'd tell you more about what I have learned about the way a killer's mind works. But I can't believe you really want to do that now."

Privately, Laurel agreed. She glanced beyond the candles to the moonlight on the lake and wished Ridge were here with her instead of Cooper. She took a tiny sip from her crystal goblet but didn't answer.

He shook his head. "I'm not doing very well, am I?" He paused, but when she took another sip, he continued. "All right, here's a safe subject. In talking casually with one of the patrolmen today, I learned that Charity received a reply wire from the National Detective Police."

Laurel lowered her goblet and turned quickly to face him. "How does he know that?"

"He didn't say and I didn't ask, but an officer's job is to be observant. He also noticed that the wire had something to do with your friend, Sarah." He paused for a second before adding, "And you."

Laurel glanced away to avoid any possibility of her face disclosing her sudden concern. Whatever Charity's theory was, she was certainly on to something. *Well,* Laurel told herself, *it won't matter so much now that I've told Pierce and Kelly what she and I did in the war, but I still don't want that story spread all over the pages of the* Illustrated Press.

She rebuked herself. *Just a little while ago I was thinking of doing the very same thing for the* Globe, *but I still would rather keep it all secret.*

Cooper broke into her meditations. "Why do you suppose Charity is checking out you and Sarah with the NDP? Something to do with why she was murdered?"

Laurel became cautious. She was suspicious of him because he seemed to know more about Abaddon than even the police. Also, Cooper had either lied to her or been mistaken in telling her where he had been just before Sarah's death, and why he arrived late at the scene.

"Let me ask you a question," she said. "I talked to someone who had seen you with a camera not far from Sarah's house shortly before Ridge and I found her body."

"I still take photographs now and then."

"But you told me you had been at the *Globe* where all the editorial people had seen you."

His eyebrows slid down and the humor left his eyes. "Are you suggesting what I think you are?"

"I'm not suggesting anything. I'm just being what you taught me to be: a correspondent who asks questions to clarify things."

For a moment, his expression didn't change. Then he laughed lightly. "You're a saucy one, all right." The humor returned to his eyes as his voice dropped and he leaned toward her. "I've never wanted to kiss a woman in my life as much as I want to kiss you right now!"

She drew back. "Mr. Cooper, please!" She glanced around the restaurant. "You know I'm engaged to Ridge."

"So you've told me before, but I also saw that little spat you two had the other day. I think there's a lot of doubt in your mind about marrying him."

"There is not!"

His grin reappeared. It was almost mischievous. "There's one way to find out, Laurel." He slowly leaned toward her. "One kiss can't hurt, and it might help you."

"I don't need any help!" She started to pull back, then hesitated. She didn't want him to know she was suspicious that he might really be Abaddon.

He misunderstood her hesitation and quickly leaned toward her, gently placing both hands on her cheeks. "Oh, Laurel," he said huskily, "you are so beautiful!"

His lips touched hers, gently at first, then more firmly. She caught the quick intake of his breath and felt his hands tremble on her cheeks. But there was no magic for her. It was about as romantic as pressing a couple of pieces of bacon rind against her lips. The ridiculous thought almost made her giggle.

He drew back sharply, his hands sliding from her face. "Am I that bad?"

She tried to pretend innocence. "What?"

"Don't play coy with me, Laurel! I sensed your reaction and didn't find it a bit flattering!"

"Please! Don't be upset!"

"Well, I am!" He threw his napkin on the table and stood up. "You insisted on meeting me here instead of letting me pick you up. I assume you can return back home the same way!"

She watched him storm out and heard the three girls at the nearby table tittering. Laurel felt her face flush hotly. Vance Cooper was the one man in the world she did not need to have angry with her, especially if he really was Abaddon.

Agnes's voice came through her hotel room door in response to Ridge's knock. "Who is it?"

"Ridge. I'd like to speak to Laurel, please."

Agnes opened the door. "She's not here."

He frowned. "You mean she went out alone?"

"Yes, but I don't know where."

"She shouldn't have done that! I know she thinks she can take care of herself, but she also knows that Abaddon plans to kill her, so why would she go out alone at night?"

Agnes shrugged. "When I got home, she was all dressed and ready to leave."

Ridge's eyes narrowed. "Was she dressed up?"

"No, in fact, she looked rather plain. She had pulled her hair back in a way I've never seen her wear it before. She wore a plain blouse buttoned to the chin, and a simple skirt. I told her that you weren't going to like her attire, but she said you weren't going to see it. Then she left."

"That's all she said?"

When Agnes nodded, Ridge was both angry and concerned. He left, stopping at the desk to ask the clerk if he had seen Miss Bartlett leave. Yes, alone in a rented hack. The driver had not returned, so Ridge couldn't ask where he had taken her. He debated about searching for her. Chicago was too big, yet he couldn't just go back to his room and forget it. He said a silent prayer and hailed a hack to begin what he suspected would be a useless investigation.

Laurel returned home early, to her aunt's great relief. She didn't volunteer where she had been or with whom, and Agnes didn't ask. But when Agnes told Laurel that Ridge had been here, she warned that Ridge would surely be back early tomorrow morning. Laurel agreed, but didn't want to get into a discussion about tonight until she and Ridge were on the cars where he would have time to cool down after she told him.

To avoid confrontation the next morning, she arose early, had breakfast near the *Globe* building, and was at the newspaper's door when Seymour arrived with the key.

"I'm glad you got here early," he greeted her. "I need to talk to you."

She thought he sounded rather serious, but he said nothing more until they had passed through the silent offices to his private one. He reached for a fresh cigar, but paused before lighting it.

"I'll come right to the point," he said. "I've hired a replacement for Vance Cooper on the police beat. Name is Irvin Usher. He's highly experienced, but when I told him about you, he flatly refused to work with a woman."

Laurel's face grew warm with indignation. "In time, I could be as good a correspondent as any man!"

"I don't doubt it, but I need this man, especially with these murders to cover, and you're not experienced enough to do it alone. So I'll move you to another beat."

Laurel took a slow, deep breath, knowing that she had to leave for California on a Pinkerton assignment. She had also investigated Sarah's murder as best she could. She had told the police everything she knew about why she thought Sarah had been killed. Maybe it was time to leave Chicago before Abaddon carried out his threat against her own life.

She forced herself to speak calmly. "Thank you, but you know I took this job on a temporary basis. I am very grateful for the opportunity you gave me, but I don't want to transfer to another beat."

"Don't be hasty, Laurel! In spite of the way some of the men have reacted to you, I think it's been good for the paper to have you on staff. Take an extra day or so in Virginia. After you return, I hope you'll stay on."

There was no harm in that, Laurel reasoned, and maybe Pinkerton wasn't ready for her just yet. But she had used up almost all the time he had given her.

Laurel nodded. "I appreciate the offer, Mr. Seymour. I'll check with you when I return."

Cooper was quiet, almost sullen, Laurel thought as they left the paper for the police precinct. He didn't mention their tense parting last night, and neither did she. It was going to be a long day, but at least tonight she would be on her way to Virginia with Ridge. She guessed he would be at the Fog Horn at lunch, wanting an explanation for last night. To avoid a possible scene there, she had decided to eat someplace else, preferably not too close by.

Sergeant Kerston looked up from his desk when the two Globe correspondents entered the front door. "Oh, Laurel, the lieutenant wants to see you right away."

Cooper asked, "What about?"

"He didn't say, but he's waiting in his office for her."

Cooper asked, "What about me?"

"He didn't mention you."

Laurel sensed that Cooper resented being left out, and was

also probably suspicious of what was going on with a junior reporter and the lieutenant.

Laurel excused herself and went to see Pierce. Kelly was with him when she entered.

"Please sit down," Pierce said pleasantly. "We want to review all the clues and any evidence in this case, then discuss a suspect list Kelly's worked out."

"Anything to help," Laurel replied, feeling relieved that since her confession yesterday, both detectives seemed to have softened their attitude toward her.

It took a couple of hours for Kelly to present each clue found at Sarah's home, at the break-in at the Bartlett home and Aunt Agnes's, and the vagrant's crime scene. After he had completed his presentation, Kelly turned to the lieutenant to draw conclusions.

"The use of chloroform at both murders suggests that the perpetrator might be a small man who doesn't have the strength to overcome a woman," Kelly began. "When your friend regained consciousness, he had bound her. He must have made her move under her own power to the back porch where she was killed. We have a theory about why he chose that spot with windows where he could have been seen by a neighbor in spite of the hedges."

Pierce shifted the wad of chewing tobacco to the other side of his mouth. "The small object which neither you nor Ridge Granger could identify had come from a tripod tip. This leads us to believe a camera was used on the back porch. He needed extra light for his photograph. But we don't know anyone with much knowledge about cameras."

Laurel thought, *Yes you do: Cooper!* But she didn't want to accuse him based only on her suspicions. Instead, she asked, "What about the sack left on my highboy?"

"A distraction, we think," Pierce replied. "Abaddon used the sack to hold the photograph of that strange tree, and to make us waste time checking it out. The tree, on the other hand, was where that teenage girl was killed. We think she was probably Abaddon's first victim, and he wanted us to make a connection with your friend Sarah. So far, we haven't been able to do that. But we suspect that the killer lived here then, and now he's back."

The lieutenant turned and spat into the spittoon before continuing. "The newspaper found at your friend's side was dated April 3, 1865. That's the day both Petersburg and Richmond fell, virtually ending the war. Kelly and I would like you to tell us what you think that has to do with either you or Sarah Skillens."

"I had been in Petersburg," Laurel explained, "and obtained military intelligence from a young Confederate officer. I passed it on to my Union contacts."

"Kelly checked that out yesterday after our talk, and confirmed that this information was what helped our troops to breach the Rebel lines. You did a great service to our country. In a minute, we'll need the name of that young officer and any other suspects you might think of. But first, let's finish with the evidence as we know it. Is there anything else that we should know?"

Laurel glanced at both men. "Yes. I received two envelopes in the mail, and I'm sure the handwriting was the same as that of those letters Abaddon sent to the *Globe*. I still have those envelopes if you want them."

"We do," Pierce replied. "Anything else?"

"John Skillens gave me a black stone earring he found in the coal scuttle at their house. When Cooper described the one found at the murder scene of the last woman killed in New York, I knew this one was its mate."

"An earring?" Pierce's eyebrows shot up. "You have a piece of evidence that links this murder to New York and didn't tell us?"

"I'm sorry," Laurel said hastily. "I should have."

"You certainly should!" Pierce snapped. "Do you still have it?"

"Yes, I can take a hack at noon and get it."

"Good! Bring the envelopes, too," the lieutenant said. "Now, you must have thought of possible suspects. Tell us who they are."

She shifted uncomfortably in her chair. "I'm very reluctant to even mention—"

"You've got to tell us," Pierce interrupted sternly.

Still feeling averse to say anything, she told about Sam Maynard, but noted that he had left town before the vagrant had been slain.

Pierce asked, "Do you know if he really left town? Or if he did, how do you know he didn't come back?"

Laurel admitted, "I don't know."

"All right," Pierce said, "anybody else?"

Laurel looked around to make sure the door was still closed, then she lowered her voice. "Vance Cooper seems to know more about Abaddon than anyone else. And he was a cameraman in New York before he became a reporter."

"Oh, that's right!" Pierce exclaimed. "Kelly, we should have remembered that. And he's leaving for California soon, so we'll have to move fast. Now, Laurel, who else do you suspect?"

"That's all. Oh, one thing I'm curious about. The other day Charity Dahlgren was talking to me at lunch when she suddenly stopped, saying she had a theory. She wouldn't say anything else. But I heard that one of the officers here saw a wire she had received from the National Detective Police. It had both Sarah's and my name in it. Why would she research Federal files unless she's guessed something about this case?"

Pierce looked at Kelly. "Check that out with her and see what she says." He turned back to Laurel. "From all you told us, it seems you would be a lot safer if you left town until we catch this perpetrator."

"I'm leaving for Virginia with Ridge right after work today. Except for my aunt, the rest of my family has also gone out of state."

"Good!" Pierce nodded approvingly. "We'll need your testimony after we apprehend Abaddon, so stay well."

"I intend to do that," she said, and left, dreading having to answer Cooper when he asked what the detectives had talked about with her.

Laurel had only walked a few steps away from Pierce's office when Cooper hurried up to her. He jerked his head toward the lieutenant's office and bluntly asked, "What was that all about?"

She debated how much to tell him now that she had mentioned him to the detectives as a murder suspect. From the frosty way he had treated her so far this morning, he was still smarting from her reaction to his kiss last night. Being excluded from her meeting with Pierce and Kelly had undoubtedly made him more agitated.

She finally answered honestly, "I don't know if it was confidential or not. Maybe I'd better ask them. . . ."

"Never mind!" he snapped, eyes glittering angrily. "You go on over to the firehouse to see if they've got anything worth writing about."

"Please don't be angry. . . ." Laurel left her thought unspoken as Cooper irately turned on his heel, stalked down the hall, and went out the front door.

Sergeant Kerston raised his eyebrows. "What's the matter with Cooper?"

"You'll have to ask him," she said evasively. "Has Charity been in yet this morning?"

"No, and that's not like her to be late. She hates to risk having Cooper beat her to a story."

"When you see her, tell her I'd like to meet her for lunch at the Excalibur. I'm going to the firehouse."

Laurel had decided to take a direct approach with Charity. She planned to tell Charity what the patrolman had said about her receiving a wire from the National Detective Police. Laurel felt she had a right to know, because both Sarah and she were mentioned in it.

Laurel opened the door just as Darius Barr came in, loaded down with his heavy camera and tripod. "Here," she said, "I'll hold that door for you."

"Thanks." He eased through with his cumbersome load. "I had to take a few shots of a carriage wreck."

"Anything serious?"

"Not really. Where's Cooper?"

"He went off alone. Say, have you seen Charity yet?"

"No." Darius shifted the camera in his hand. "Hasn't she been here already?"

"The sergeant said she hadn't."

"She probably overslept. She's been putting in a lot of extra hours lately. She was probably overtired."

"Well, if you see her before the sergeant does, tell her I'd like to meet her for lunch at the Excalibur."

Laurel headed toward the firehouse, thinking of how she might placate Cooper. She looked up as a buggy pulled up to the curb.

Allan Pinkerton smiled through his full beard. "I'm glad I ran into you," he said without preamble. "Get in. We need to talk."

"I'm working," she replied. "On my way to the firehouse for a possible story."

"I'll drive you there."

Laurel nodded and accepted a hand up. She settled on the

seat beside him. "I think I can guess why you want to see me."

He guided the horse away from the curb. "So you remember our arrangement?"

"Of course. I had two weeks to help find out who killed my good friend Sarah. Then I was to report back to you to work on my final case."

"It's in California," he reminded her. "It's urgent, so I need you to leave right away."

"I'm leaving tonight for Virginia—"

"Cancel it," he interrupted. "A railroad client came by my office first thing this morning with a problem that requires an operative to be in Sacramento within a month. That's you."

"But I can't do it, Mr. Pinkerton!"

"You must. You could probably have until Monday to start and still make it, but no longer than that."

Laurel kept her annoyance from showing. Silently, she reviewed her situation. *Seymour says the new man won't work with a woman. I don't want another beat, although I like being a correspondent. I need to keep earning a living. But Cooper's also going to be in California covering the opening of the Summit Tunnel. Maybe he's not Abaddon, but I don't want to take a chance.*

*Ridge and I are supposed to leave tonight for Virginia. I don't want to cancel on him. I wonder if he would go to Sacramento with me if I can get Pinkerton to give me until next weekend when Ridge will be back from Virginia?*

Her thoughts jumped. *Ridge is going to want to know where I was last night.*

"Well?" Pinkerton prompted. "How about Monday?"

"I don't know. What kind of a case is it?"

"I'll tell you after I get your decision."

"That sounds as if it's dangerous."

"No more dangerous than any other case you've gone on, and no worse than what you did during the war."

Laurel was apprehensive. "I need time to think."

"I'll expect your answer this afternoon. You owe me this one, and I'm counting on you."

Laurel anguished over this unexpected complication as Pinkerton drove her to the firehouse. There she got the facts about a couple of minor dwelling fires.

On the short walk back to the *Globe*, she brooded over the many complexities which kept ensnaring her. No matter how hard she tried to sort them out, the more complex they became.

*Like Ridge*, she thought. *He's probably planning on catching me at the Fog Horn to ask about last night. That's why I asked to have Charity meet me at the Excalibur.*

Heading for her desk at the back of the editorial department to write her fire story, she noticed Seymour standing at his big window. As he often did, he was smoking a cigar and watching the activity.

An idea made her impulsively turn toward him. He motioned for her to come in. Sooner or later, she had to go to California for Pinkerton. His rule that agents must not reveal their true status meant she would again need some way of keeping that confidential. Her faith prohibited lying, but she had an alternative possibility that only troubled her conscience a little.

"Mr. Seymour," she began, stepping through his office door as he seated himself behind his desk, "I must return to California with my aunt who's going there to be married. So how about letting me write for the *Globe* while I'm there?"

He waved the cigar smoke away with his hand. "That's a surprise request, Laurel. You know I'm already sending Cooper to cover the opening of the Summit Railroad Tunnel."

"Yes, I do, but I'll cover other aspects of railroading. That is,

I would write feature stories instead of hard news so that I wouldn't interfere with what you're paying Cooper to do."

The publisher puffed thoughtfully on his cigar, which indicated to Laurel that he was intrigued with her suggestion. She added quickly, "I would do that on the same arrangement as before: being a stringer instead of a staff correspondent."

Removing the cigar from his mouth and blowing smoke toward the ceiling, Seymour commented, "That's an even stranger request because you won't get a regular salary that way."

"I know. But I'd prefer being a stringer. Besides, Cooper probably would prefer to work alone out there."

"Did something happen between you two?"

She raised an eyebrow. "Why do you think that?"

"Because he came in this morning and said he didn't want to work with you anymore, and he wanted to leave for California right away. That's a switch from the way he was looking at you when you first started here."

She saw the suspicion in Seymour's eyes. "It's not important," she said. "But as a stringer, I'd naturally not write about anything that Cooper prefers to cover."

The publisher stood. "All right, Laurel, you're my California stringer. When do you leave?"

"I'll let you know."

Things were happening more rapidly than Laurel liked, she realized as she went to her desk. Aunt Agnes would probably be glad to know she could wire Horatio Bodmer of when she would arrive in Sacramento for their marriage.

Laurel wrote her fire story and filed it, her thoughts jumbled with all the ramifications Sarah's murder had caused. Laurel deeply regretted not having really done much of value to find the killer, but maybe Charity could shed some light on that if she showed up for lunch.

Laurel left the *Globe* shortly before noon and took a hack the short distance to her hotel. She checked that nobody seemed to be following her. Telling the driver to wait, she hurried inside and asked her aunt if she was agreeable to shortly head for California. Agnes was, saying that she would have to wire Horatio Bodmer of when to expect her so they could set their wedding date.

Laurel opened the drawstring on her reticule and placed both envelopes from Abaddon inside, along with the black stone earring found in Sarah's kitchen. Laurel hurried back to the waiting hack, planning to turn the items over to the detectives after lunch.

She arrived at the Excalibur Hotel a few minutes past twelve o'clock, but instead of Charity waiting, she was surprised to find Ridge.

"I had to talk to you, Laurel," he said without a greeting. "I went to the precinct and learned you had left messages with both Darius and the sergeant of where you'd be about now."

Laurel glanced around. "Have you seen Charity?"

"No, but I just got here. I want to know about last night. Then I'll leave and you can have lunch with her."

Laurel hesitated, torn between her responsibility to Pinkerton and his urgent California assignment and Ridge expecting her to accompany him to Virginia tonight.

Stalling, Laurel told Ridge, "This isn't the time or place to talk about it. Besides, something else came up just a short time ago."

"I guess I can wait until we're on the cars. But before Charity arrives, let's take a table and you can tell me what just came up."

Seeing no logical alternative, and eager to avoid any possible conflict with him, Laurel agreed. They took a table where they could watch the front entrance.

After ordering, Laurel lowered her voice and leaned across

the table so nobody but Ridge could hear. "As you know, my leave of absence from Pinkerton is up, and he wants me to go to California no later than Monday."

He drew back. "You can't! We won't be back from Virginia until Tuesday or maybe later!"

"I know, but I owe Pinkerton a lot for giving me a couple weeks to work on Sarah's case. Besides, this is my last assignment. Then I'm through as an operative."

Ridge shook his head. "I don't want you to go to California without me, and I absolutely must see Griff to work out some business plans. So come with me tonight, and we'll talk about California on the cars."

"It's not that simple. Pinkerton wants my answer today, so I need to head over to his office this afternoon."

"What are you going to tell him?"

"I'm going to ask for a postponement until we get back from Virginia."

"What if he won't grant it?"

Sighing softly, Laurel evaded answering. Instead, she said, "There's something else. Cooper resigned and is heading for Sacramento. His replacement told Seymour he won't work with a woman."

Ridge mused, "That means you're out of work unless you take Pinkerton's assignment."

"Well, not entirely. Seymour says I can still be a stringer for him out in California. That will provide the cover I need for Pinkerton's work."

"Wait a minute! When are we going to get married?"

Laurel met his eyes. "This isn't the time to discuss that, either. I don't want Charity to interrupt us." She glanced beyond Ridge and waved. "Here comes Darius, but I don't see her."

The photographer approached, looking troubled. "I knew

you'd be waiting," he said to Laurel, "so I came to tell you Charity hasn't come to work yet."

Little tingles of alarm made Laurel's heart speed up. "She hasn't?"

Darius shook his head. "I'm on my way over to her place right now. I didn't want you sitting here alone, but I see that you aren't," he finished, smiling at Ridge.

Darius paused, then added, "Well, I've got to get over to Charity's place."

As he turned away, Laurel told Ridge, "I've got an uneasy feeling. I think I'll go to the precinct and wait for Darius to return with her."

Ridge vainly tried to talk Laurel into eating, but she told him she had the earring and two envelopes to give to Kelly.

Ridge reluctantly said, "All right, but I'm going to plan on us being on our way to Virginia tonight."

"Oh, that's putting me in a terrible dilemma! I just don't know what to do!"

She left Ridge and started for the police station.

Armistead took his usual table at the Fog Horn, unnoticed by the nearby uniformed patrolmen who discussed their various activities with lots of laughter and crude humor. He saw Cooper eating alone across the restaurant. *But where's Laurel?* Armistead wondered. He had heard about Cooper going to Sacramento to cover some railroad event. But that didn't explain why Laurel hadn't shown up. Any departure from people's usual patterns was one of the subtle signs Armistead had learned to look for in his precarious double life. Such anomalies often meant something was going on that he should know about.

He was apprehensive because he had been forced to turn his attention from Laurel to deal with an unexpected interference. He had never liked having to deviate from his carefully-worked-out plans. After considering every possible thing that could go wrong, he agonized that he might have overlooked something.

He wondered, *Have I done that? Is that why Laurel isn't here? Or am I borrowing trouble?*

He ate slowly, picking at his food, then taking lots of time with his newspaper. Only when the officers had gone and just a few patrons remained did he reluctantly give up, pay his bill, and leave.

Laurel asked the desk sergeant about Charity and learned that she still had not been in. He told Laurel that Kelly was still at lunch, but the lieutenant wanted to see her in his office.

When Laurel knocked at Pierce's door, he looked up from his desk and asked, "Did you bring those items?"

"Yes." She handed him the two envelopes and the black stone earring before sitting down across from Pierce's desk.

He compared the handwriting on the two envelopes Laurel had received with the two that had come to the *Globe*. "No doubt about it," he concluded. "Your two and the one that came after Ninian was murdered were written by the same person. But this other," he tapped it with a finger, "must have been written by Ninian, taking credit for your friend's death. That was an expensive boast, costing Ninian his life."

Laurel nodded but said nothing while Pierce carefully examined the earring.

He laid it on his desk and glanced across at her. "I think I should show this to Cooper since he mentioned seeing a similar earring in New York."

"Lieutenant, what's your honest opinion? Are you going to be able to solve Sarah's murder, and Ninian's?"

"Like most departments, we have a few unsolved homicides, but I don't think this will be one of them. You see, most criminals are downright stupid, although Abaddon isn't like that. Sooner or later, though, he'll make a mistake, and when he does, justice will be served."

"I hope you're right." Laurel cocked her head at the sound of voices down the hallway. "Could that be Charity?" she asked.

"Not with those big feet," Pierce replied with a wry smile. "That's Kelly. Would you mind opening the door and calling him in so he can see these exhibits?"

Kelly silently scrutinized the items. When he finished, he said, "I'll get a wire off to New York to ask for a detailed description of the earring they found there. See if it matches this one."

"I figured you'd do that," Pierce replied. "Although I don't have any doubt that there will be a match."

Laurel asked, "What about the envelopes? Any way to trace them?"

"We tried with the two that came to the *Globe*, but without any luck. We'll still check on yours."

"Speaking of the *Globe*," Laurel said, "I guess you know that both Cooper and I are leaving."

"You, too?" Pierce asked in surprise. "I'd heard about Cooper. He's been twisting Seymour's arm for months to get to cover that train tunnel opening in the Sierras. But why you?"

She said with a sardonic little smile, "The new man doesn't want to work with a woman."

"So what are you going to do, Laurel?" the lieutenant asked.

"I'm in quandary about that."

Kelly guessed, "I'll bet you're going to give up work and get married."

Before Laurel could answer, she heard the sound of the front door being opened quickly and Darius's voice. It was high and panicked.

"Sergeant, where's the lieutenant?"

Laurel leaped to her feet, but both detectives were ahead of her. They jerked the office door open just as Darius cried out in a voice choked with emotion.

"Charity's dead! Murdered!"

"Oh, Lord, no!" Laurel whispered, her hand flying to cover her mouth. But she knew the truth even before she ran down the hall behind Pierce and Kelly to the distraught young photographer.

Her mind screamed, *She's dead, and I'm to blame!*

❧

The rest of the afternoon raced by in a furious flurry of questions to Darius, then barked orders by the detectives to uniformed patrolmen. They rushed off to secure the scene until the detectives could arrive and begin their preliminary investigation.

Laurel choked back her own grief and shock to learn the details from Charity's fiancé. Then she wrote a brief note to Seymour, ran outside and gave it and a coin to a young boy, telling him to run right over to the *Globe* and give the note to Cooper or Seymour.

Returning to the lieutenant's office, she listened to Pierce quiz the distraught young photographer.

"No," he said, his voice thick with pain. "She wasn't like the others. She wasn't tied or gagged. Her place was all torn up. Drawers pulled out and dumped on the floor, cupboards opened, clothes closet ransacked, even the flatware and the dishes . . ."

Kelly broke in. "Doesn't sound like Abaddon's work. It could have been a burglar, and she surprised him. . . ."

"Or maybe Abaddon really did it," Pierce replied, "and didn't want credit for it. He's smart enough to think of that. It could draw us off of Abaddon's trail because he's never torn up a place or robbed the victim."

Pierce frowned before adding, "I think Abaddon is our perpetrator, and it has something to do with these other murders. He just tried to disguise his handiwork."

Laurel silently agreed. She had absolutely no doubt that Abaddon had killed Charity because she had somehow learned something that made him afraid. She might have been about to discover his identity, tying him with threats to her, and Sarah's murder. To keep that from happening, he had killed Charity.

*But*, Laurel asked herself as the interrogation continued, *how could Abaddon have possibly known what Charity wouldn't even tell me? Well, except that she had a theory. Something to do with a photograph. . . .*

She frowned, trying to remember exactly what Charity had said that day at the Fog Horn.

Pierce's voice broke into her thoughts. "Kelly, you go on over there and get the investigation started." Turning to Darius, Pierce asked kindly, "Do you have a friend or pastor or someone you'd like us to bring in?"

Darius didn't seem to have heard. "I just can't believe it. It can't be real. It just can't be!"

Laurel reached out and gently touched his arm. "If you'd like to talk about it when you're through here, I'll be around."

He looked at her with eyes dulled with grief. "Thanks. Charity liked you. She . . ." he turned away with a sob, and ran down the hall to Kelly's empty office.

Laurel heard him close the door before she recovered sufficiently to dig a pad and pencil from her reticule and begin furiously making notes.

When Cooper arrived in response to the message she had sent, she was so preoccupied with the horrible situation that she forgot about their unhappy parting last night and his cool treatment of her so far today.

They walked outside the station where it was quiet. She filled him in from her memory and notes. He frowned when she mentioned that Kelly didn't think the crime had been committed by Abaddon.

Cooper asked, "What time did it happen?"

"They don't know yet. That'll have to wait on the coroner's report, but it was sometime last night."

He looked at Laurel. "Maybe even while you and I were having dinner?"

She wondered if he was reminding her so that he had an alibi, but that would be true only if Charity was killed early in the evening. What would his defense be if she had lost her life after he left Laurel?

Laurel told him, "I'll get back to the paper and start putting my notes in order. I'll hand them over to you when you're ready to write the story."

"You don't need to do that. You're on staff, so you're entitled to write your own story. You like features; do it that way. I'll do the straight news."

"All right, thanks." She briefly thought about going back in to try comforting Darius, but decided that he would probably prefer to be alone right now. She turned and walked toward the *Globe* building.

Ridge was so eager to have Laurel alone for a couple of days on the cars that he made his last business call and quit early. He hired a cabriolet to take him by Laurel's hotel to pick up her carpetbag.

Agnes gave it to him saying, "I hope you and Laurel have a good trip."

"We will. You sure you won't go with us?"

"You two go ahead. I'm going to write a long letter to Horatio and tell him more than I could in a wire. Don't worry about me. I'll be all right."

"I'd feel better if you came along."

"At the risk of sounding like Laurel, I'm going to say, 'I can take care of myself.' "

"See that you do." He reached for Laurel's bag. "You might like to know what I'm going to tell her on the cars: I've decided to swallow my pride and petition the President for amnesty."

"Good for you, Ridge! But what if you get your land back, and Laurel doesn't want to live in Virginia?"

"Then I'll sell the land because I don't care where we live as long as we're together." Ridge kissed Agnes on the cheek, returned to the cabriolet and gave the driver directions to his hotel so he could pick up his own bag.

In about an hour, he reminded himself, *Laurel and I will be on our way. I wonder what she'll say when I tell her that I've changed my mind and will ask President Johnson for amnesty so I can get the plantation back?*

Laurel had written a moving first-person account of her brief friendship with Charity Dahlgren. As Laurel finished it, she felt warm tears sliding down her cheeks. She absently brushed them away and glanced around the city room. For the first time, she was aware that the entire all-male staff was watching her. As one man, they turned away, but she didn't care.

*I couldn't save her life*, Laurel thought grimly, *but at least I can let the* Globe *readers know what kind of a woman she was.*

Guilt overwhelmed Laurel. She dropped her head and closed her eyes for a moment. Then she straightened up and determinedly lifted her chin.

*Well, he's not going to get away with this! If it weren't for me, Sarah and Charity would still be alive! Abaddon has to be punished for what he's done!*

She heard a couple of footsteps as someone stopped at her desk. She looked up, dabbing at her eyes. Through the mist, she saw the publisher without his cigar.

"Laurel," he began quietly, "I heard. I'm sorry. Is there anything I can do? You want to leave early?"

"Oh, no, thanks," she said, reaching into her reticule for a tiny handkerchief. "I'll be all . . ."

*Pinkerton!* she thought. *I promised to give him my answer this afternoon.* She glanced at the roman numerals on the weight-driven hexagon calendar clock hanging on the far wall. "Oh, yes!" She stood up quickly. "If you don't mind, Mr. Seymour, I'd like to leave right now!"

She composed herself as best she could, turned in her copy at the desk, and hurried outside. She could see the all-seeing-eye sign down the street which marked the headquarters of the Pinkerton Detective Agency.

*If I hurry, I can tell him and still get back before Ridge* . . . Laurel was startled by the sight of him stepping down from a cabriolet at the curbside.

He started toward her with a welcoming smile, but it froze instantly. "What's the matter?" he asked, rushing up to take both her hands.

"Charity's dead!" She blurted, "Murdered!"

"What?" Ridge exclaimed. "Charity? When? How?"

Laurel briefly repeated what Darius had told Kelly and Pierce. She concluded, "The lieutenant is sure that Abaddon did it."

Ridge shook his head in disbelief. "It's a terrible thing, really terrible. But that's all the more reason we need to get you safely out of town before this crazed killer gets you."

Laurel fought to control her emotions so she didn't create a scene in the street. She pulled her hands free from Ridge's and said softly, "I can't go! Not now; not after this!"

"You must! If Abaddon killed Charity, you know he'll be after you next! Now get in and we'll get you away where you'll be safe!"

She shook her head. "No," she said dully, "she's dead because of me, and so is Sarah! They must have justice!"

"Don't be so stubborn!" Ridge exclaimed, taking her arm. "You need to get away, and I absolutely must see Griff or I might lose everything I've built up so far!"

"I'm sorry, Ridge," she said defiantly, pulling her arm free. "You go to Virginia, but I'm staying here!"

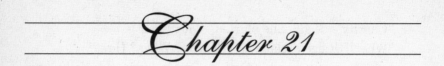

In deep shock over Charity's murder and in emotional pain over another break-up with Ridge, Laurel forgot about going to see Pinkerton. Instead, she made her way back to the police station. There she numbly listened to what little had been learned since she left earlier.

Lieutenant Pierce explained, "Kelly sent a patrolman back with preliminary investigation results. Like the others, Charity was suffocated. We won't know until we get the coroner's report if chloroform was used. But otherwise, there's no similarity to what Abaddon did before. He never ransacked a victim's place before, but I still believe he's responsible."

"If Abaddon did this," Laurel said dully, "it's my fault, and I'm sick about it. Maybe I also caused Ninian's death, and I'm sure about Sarah's."

"Don't blame yourself, Laurel. This is the work of a madman."

"I think there's more to it than that. I know that Charity had some kind of a theory about this case. When she asked Kelly if he had any contacts in the National Detective Police, I was sure she would contact them and that would turn up what Sarah and I did during the war."

"Speaking of the NDP," Pierce said, "Kelly reported that the one who killed Charity took every scrap of paper from her room.

So if it was Abaddon, he must have been looking for correspondence or any notes she might have made."

Pausing, the lieutenant added, "But he overlooked a wire that had slid under a sofa. It was from the NDP and mentioned Emory Brush."

Laurel blinked in surprise. "The private detective?"

"He's the only Emory Brush I know about."

Laurel frowned. "What was said about him?"

"I don't know yet. Kelly didn't tell the patrolman."

Laurel's frown deepened as she recalled how Ridge had hired Brush to protect her, and yet Abaddon had twice slipped by to torment her. *But what's the connection between a private detective agency? . . .* "Oh!" she exclaimed, remembering Pinkerton. "I have to keep an appointment. I hope I'm not too late."

She was out of Pierce's office before he could ask any questions.

Ridge boarded the cars for the long, slow trip to Richmond. The wood-burning locomotive's speed of about thirty miles an hour gave him plenty of time to reflect on his unhappy parting with Laurel.

He hated to leave her alone to face the aftermath of Charity's death, but he had to see Griff about working out a partnership. Otherwise, he faced the possibility of losing all that he had made on land speculation. As for Laurel's stubbornness, he wondered if she would ever be willing to compromise as any marriage required.

*It was never that way with Varina*, Ridge reminded himself. He hadn't meant to think about her, but he was so upset over this last break-up with Laurel that it was natural for him to make comparisons.

*Varina and I never really quarreled*, he recalled, staring out the window as the cars began moving away from the Chicago depot.

*Growing up together, everyone was sure she and I would marry. But after we were engaged and I went off to fight the Yankees, and she married that older man, well, that hurt. But she must hurt worse because he's dead and now she's a pretty young widow in desperate financial circumstances.*

Ridge remembered how Varina had openly tried to win him back when he had brought Laurel to see where his family plantation had been before the invaders burned it. Varina didn't give up easily. Sighing, Ridge wondered if maybe he should let Varina try to help him forget Laurel.

❦

Laurel breathlessly alighted from a hack as Pinkerton was locking the door under the all-seeing-eye sign. She rushed up, exclaiming, "I'm sorry! I almost forgot because a friend was murdered, and then I couldn't find a hack."

"Who was murdered?" he asked.

"Charity Dahlgren. I recently met her—"

Pinkerton broke in. "The correspondent for the *Illustrated Press*?" When Laurel nodded, he unlocked the door and led the way back into his office while Laurel briefly began repeating what she knew.

Pinkerton motioned her to a chair and seated himself behind his desk. He listened in silence until she had finished. Then he asked, "So you're sure she was about to uncover your war-time experiences?"

"Yes, but Pierce already knew about that. I had to tell him

because of the threats against my life."

Pinkerton said through his full beard. "So I heard."

Laurel wasn't surprised. She was often impressed with his uncanny ability to know about people and events that others did not.

"Well," he said, "I suppose you've come to say you can't take the California assignment."

"Everything's happening so fast," she replied, "but on the ride over here, I thought that if you can wait until after the funeral, I might be able to make that trip for you."

He raised one eyebrow. "Alone?"

"No, my aunt would accompany me, as she did before."

"So what you're not telling me, Laurel, is that your beau boarded the cars alone a few minutes ago because you and he have broken up again?"

In spite of herself, Laurel stared in surprise. When he waited without speaking, she explained. "He insisted that I go to Virginia with him, but I couldn't under the circumstances. He had an important business appointment down there, so I pressured him to go even though he didn't want to leave me, especially now."

"Any regrets?" Pinkerton asked quietly.

Laurel knew that it was a leading question, but she chose not to answer it. She reasoned, *Ridge undoubtedly is tired of my independent ways. I can't blame him. When he gets to Virginia, I'm sure Varina will be there to comfort him.*

Laurel asked. "Can your railroad client wait until sometime next week before I leave for Sacramento?"

"Don't you want to stay here and help solve all these murders?"

"I'd like to, but there are practical reasons why I want to head for Sacramento. For one thing, I need the income. Also, getting away from Chicago may help me stay out of Abaddon's reach."

"Or," Pinkerton astutely observed, "you may think the person you suspect is also going to California, and you can follow him and try to prove your case. Right?"

Laurel was confident that Pinkerton knew more about this whole situation than she had told him. Even the newspaper stories about the first two murders didn't have any mention of what the founder of the detective agency seemed to know.

"Maybe," she finally admitted.

"Suppose you're right, but he carries out his plan against you out west? Isn't that foolhardy?" When she again didn't reply, he added, "You'd better tell me the whole thing."

Laurel hesitated, thinking rapidly, then nodded. She told Pinkerton why she suspected Cooper was responsible for all three murders. She concluded, "He's the only logical suspect, but neither Pierce nor Kelly agrees with me. So if you're agreeable, I'll do your client's assignment as my job and do my private investigating on my own time."

"Suppose Pierce and Kelly are right, and Cooper is not your man? Failing to think of other suspects could get you killed while you're watching Cooper."

"I'll keep an open mind."

"You say it, but I'm not sure I believe you."

Laurel flared, "That's your right! Now, all I need to know from you is whether we've got an agreement?"

"We have, but it won't do any of us any good if you're wrong about who killed those people."

Abaddon, as he now preferred to think of himself, bought the latest afternoon newspaper edition, but there was only a small item squeezed in the front page: "A third murder victim in less than two weeks was discovered early this afternoon by police. No details were available at press time although the victim is believed to be a young woman."

Swearing softly to himself, Armistead tucked the paper under his arm and realized what must have happened. He had struck after midnight, assuming Charity's body would be found sometime early this morning. However, the patrolmen conversing at lunch had made no mention of a murder. That, and the brief news item, meant that the body had not been discovered until just before press time. Tomorrow there would be screaming headlines and front page details.

Abaddon had an uneasy feeling about this delay. It suggested that he had acted too soon after the Ninian and Sarah Skillens slayings. Three victims so close together would really have the populace howling for an arrest.

*But,* he admitted to himself, *I can't let Laurel go unpunished, especially after all I've done to frighten her. I've got to move against her, and yet something tells me now is not the time. But what else can I do?*

❦

Laurel wearily inserted the key in her hotel room door and heard her aunt's voice.

"Who's there?" Agnes demanded.

"Laurel. Who else would you expect?" she asked with annoyance as she pushed the door open. Her aunt had snatched up an unlit kerosene lamp from the nightstand. "Did I make you mad enough to hit me with that?" Laurel asked, forcing a weak smile.

Agnes replaced the lamp with a relieved sigh. "What are you doing here? Why aren't you with Ridge?"

Laurel tossed her reticule on the bed. "Because I told him to go on without me."

"Oh, no!" Agnes sank into the overstuffed chair. "Not again!"

"It was mutual this time, and I'm not in the mood to talk about it." Laurel headed for the wash basin. "It has been a day of nothing but bad news."

"Well," Agnes replied with a disdainful sniff, "I don't know what kind of bad news you had, but the day wouldn't have all been bad if you'd gone with Ridge."

"I don't want to hear about him right now."

"Suit yourself, but I can't help but wonder what your reaction would have been when he told you about his plan to apply for amnesty."

"Amnesty? How do you know that?"

"He came by to pick up your carpetbag this afternoon and told me. But you sent him off alone to Virginia and that . . . that woman."

"Varina," Laurel said absently while her heart leaped with anguish. She poured water from the ceramic pitcher into the matching bowl. "I have a headache and I don't want to hear anything more about anything." She dipped a cloth in the water, placed it on her forehead, and sat on the edge of the high bed.

Agnes rose and crossed to stand in front of Laurel where her feet dangled above the floor. "One more question, then I'll leave you alone. What happened besides you and Ridge quarreling again?"

Laurel had to fight to control the sudden return of overwhelming grief. Her voice broke as she said, "That nice woman correspondent I told you about—Charity Dahlgren—was murdered, and it's my fault!"

She closed her eyes and dropped her head while the mourning shook her entire body. She felt Agnes's arms circle her shoulders and pull her close.

"Let go, Laurel," she whispered, "go ahead and let it all out!"

The unexpected comfort of arms from a woman who didn't like to be hugged was too much for Laurel. She broke down and wept, broken with sorrow for all the terrible things that she knew she had brought on herself.

❧

The next morning, after staying up to carefully read all of the papers he had taken from Charity Dahlgren's room, Armistead tore every incriminating document into tiny pieces. He placed these in three separate sections of yesterday's newspapers and put them in a large sack.

He carried them downtown on his way to breakfast. He congratulated himself on what he had learned from wires and other documents taken from Charity's room.

The National Detective Police confirmed that Laurel had been a Union spy and Sarah had helped her, he mused. *But my name wasn't mentioned anywhere. That should mean she had not learned my connection to the NDP.*

He carefully dropped each section of crumpled newspaper in a different public trash receptacle on three streets. He bought the morning paper and hurriedly skimmed the front page story.

There were two stories. The first was a straightforward news piece. The victim's name, age, and occupation were given, along with a few details which the police had released since yesterday. There was nothing that Abaddon did not already know.

There was something new to him in the second story about police theories. These were included in what was more of a feature than a straight recitation of facts. It had a more emotional tone, making Abaddon guess that it had been written by Laurel. In that piece, Charity Dahlgren became more of a likable person instead of a murder victim, as the first story suggested.

Abaddon thoughtfully read about one unnamed detective who had expressed belief that the slayer was not the same one who had murdered Jay Ninian and Sarah Skillens. However, another detective believed it was the same perpetrator who had tried to disguise his work in ways the paper did not explain.

Abaddon stopped reading without turning to the inside page where the longer story was continued. He carried the paper to his table at the back of the Fog Horn. The place was quiet, which wasn't unusual for a Saturday, but the policemen who worked seven days a week weren't at their usual table.

Abaddon asked the waiter, "Where is everyone?"

"Most of our regulars have already been in, except for the police. The city fathers are in an uproar over this string of murders, and irate citizens are demanding an arrest. So every copper is looking for whoever he is."

Abaddon was disappointed that he would not be able to overhear whatever loose police talk might give him some information lacking in the papers. Still, he didn't want to arouse suspicion by leaving without eating.

He ordered breakfast and opened the newspaper to where the murder story continued on an inside page. The last line made Abaddon blink, then read it again.

"Police refused to confirm rumors that a telegram of unknown content had been found under the victim's sofa. The wire apparently went unnoticed when the killer made off with the rest of the victim's personal papers."

For a long moment, Abaddon stared at the words, reading them over and over again. He swore softly under his breath, took off his glasses and absently polished them with his handkerchief while his mind raced.

*What does that mean?* he asked himself. After a few

moment's reflection, he shrugged. He had always outwitted the police, so there was no need to concern himself with whatever the telegram contained. *Still*, he reminded himself, *it might be well to have a contingency plan.*

🐚

Laurel had risen early after a restless night. She found it difficult to dress and groom herself because Ridge had picked up her carpetbag with her toiletries late yesterday. He surely wouldn't have taken it on the train with him, so she expected he would have paid someone to deliver it sometime today. That didn't help now in trying to comb her tangled hair.

Agnes knocked on the adjoining hotel room door, then entered. "Here's your bag," she said. "A boy just delivered it to my room. There's a note with it."

Laurel gave up fighting with her hair to take the bag and open the note attached to the handle. She read it silently: "I'm sorry, Laurel. I wish you happiness."

*It sounds so final!* she thought, closing her eyes to hold back sudden hot tears. She quickly turned away so her aunt couldn't see.

Agnes commented, "You look a fright. Up all night?"

"I slept some," said Laurel, placing the carpetbag on the high bed and retrieving her brush and comb. "Mostly, I did a lot of thinking."

"You want to talk about it?"

"No, not really." Laurel turned to face the mirror before adding, "But you should know this: I've decided to return to Sacramento right after Charity's funeral. So next week you can wire Horatio Bodmer that we're coming."

Agnes came to stand behind Laurel and look at her reflection in the glass as she brushed her hair. "Now that I'm committed to this marriage," Agnes said softly, "I'm a little nervous."

"Don't be." Laurel lowered the brush and turned around. "I saw how Horatio was with you when we were there. He obviously loves you. He'll make you happy."

"We'll make each other happy. But I wish you and Ridge could settle your differences and be happy, too."

"Our differences are settled, Aunt Agnes. He's gone for good this time. I'll be fine."

"God ordained the family, Laurel, and that starts with the right partner. We all make mistakes, just as I did many years ago in losing the man I loved. I don't want you to make the same mistake and end up alone."

"I can always get an admirer. You know that."

"That's not the same as a man who loves you as much as Ridge obviously does."

Laurel's insides suddenly lurched at the thought of Varina having Ridge to herself while he was vulnerable. She tried to tell herself that she didn't care, but she knew that wasn't true. President Johnson would almost surely grant Ridge's amnesty petition to regain his family's property seized during the Union occupation.

He had told Agnes that he intended to rebuild on the site. Laurel remembered the plans for the great house he had shown her. If he arranged a business partnership with his friend Griff, there would be plenty of money to create a manor house and grounds in the grand style of the antebellum South.

*But I won't live there with him*, Laurel thought. *Varina will.*

To cover her feelings, she said a bit sharply, "Aunt Agnes, I've got to finish dressing and go find out more about Charity's death."

The older woman nodded and walked to the adjoining room door. "I understand. But I hope you'll remember what I said. Also, after living more than half a century, I know that faith grows stronger through trials. I have struggled with my own faith and my doubts, spiritually and humanly. You've lost your man; don't lose your God."

Laurel stood with brush in hand after the door closed behind her aunt. *That's unfair!* Laurel thought. *Yet my prayers certainly are not being answered.*

From her Sunday School days, she suddenly remembered a quotation from the story of Samson and Delilah: "And he wist not that the Lord had departed from him."

Laurel forced the words to the back of her mind, but new ones crowded in. *What have I accomplished?* she asked herself. *Sarah and Charity are dead because of what I did. I have lost Ridge to Varina. Am I really able to always take care of myself?*

She hurriedly finished dressing and left the hotel, but for the first time since she was a teenager, she had a true sense of uncertainty.

🌹

Ridge's turn to enter the cramped washroom on his car finally came. Shaving with a straight-edge razor was risky because the car bucked and swayed, but he always felt dirty until shaved. He lathered up with the brush, then braced his feet as best he could. He cautiously proceeded to shave while rebuking himself for leaving Laurel alone.

*She was really suffering over Charity's death. I should have stayed to comfort and protect her even if she does always insist she can take care of herself. I hope she's right.*

*But if I don't promptly enter into a partnership with Griff, I could lose all I've worked for since the war ended.*

The car suddenly jerked, causing the razor to nick Ridge's chin. He dabbed at the blood with his washcloth, thinking, *bleeding. That's the way I feel about leaving Laurel alone, but she had to have her own way again.*

At the police station Lieutenant Pierce briefed Laurel on the investigation of Charity's murder. Her parents had been notified in New York. The funeral would be delayed until they arrived.

"Speaking of New York," Laurel said, "did you get a report on that earring I found?"

"Came this morning." Pierce pointed to a telegram on the desk. "Just as I thought. It matched the one the last victim had been wearing when she was killed."

Laurel slowly nodded, then asked, "Do you have the coroner's report yet on Charity?"

"Only his preliminary one. He set the time of death at somewhere between Thursday midnight and the pre-dawn hours of yesterday."

*Well after the time Cooper left me*, Laurel realized.

She asked, "Any new clues or suspects?"

"No. If this is Abaddon's work, as I'm sure it is, he left nothing we can use except that telegram Kelly found under her sofa. It wasn't much help, although it did mention Emory Brush. When we checked with him, he said Charity had hired him to look into the NDP files for yours or Sarah's names. You know the results."

"They found our names and what we did in the war, but was there anything else?"

"No. Brush said that's all he has."

"I think I'll go see him."

"Don't," the lieutenant said. "That could be considered interfering with a murder investigation."

"I'm not going to interfere!" Laurel exclaimed. "I'm trying to help."

"Then you and Cooper go write your stories, omitting the parts I told you are still confidential. Leave the rest to us."

Laurel rose to leave, but Pierce stopped her.

"What puzzles me," he mused, "is how this killer seems to know what's going on inside my precinct."

"I had discussed that with both Charity and Cooper," Laurel replied. "We figured it could be someone in this station, or maybe a waiter where the police eat. We even wondered if it might be one of us correspondents. But it certainly wasn't Charity."

Pierce also stood. "If you want to investigate something that won't hinder our work, try figuring out which of those—if any— is responsible. But it had better not be anybody under my jurisdiction."

"I'll do that," Laurel said, and headed to the *Globe* where she could write one of her final stories.

She passed Cooper's desk on the way to hers. He looked up at her with cold eyes.

"You're late," he said without greeting her.

"I was at the police station."

"You should always come here first. Sometimes there's information that would be helpful when you do get to the station."

Laurel tried to not take offense at his reprimand. "Thanks. I'll remember that." She again started toward her desk, but his voice stopped her.

"In case you're wondering, yes, I know about the coroner's preliminary autopsy report. I was in bed asleep shortly after I left you at the restaurant. I was there all night, alone."

"I didn't ask you anything about that," Laurel said.

"No, but I know what you're thinking."

"Just as you know so much about Abaddon!" she shot back.

"I know lots of things," he said, his face grim. "I also hear things. That's my job. Now, go do yours!"

She felt a flush of anger sweep over her, but she didn't reply. She hurried to her desk, telling herself, *I'm glad I won't be working with him much longer. I wish things weren't so tense between us. But if he really is Abaddon, he's not going to change his attitude toward me. So I've got to keep a sharp eye on him in California.*

Armistead returned to the Fog Horn for lunch and was pleased when two uniformed patrolmen took their nearby table. There was no doubt that they would discuss the latest murder. Armistead held his newspaper in front of him and seemed to be reading it through his spectacles.

He heard the tall, slender officer comment, "If this murder spree keeps up, heads will roll at the precinct."

"This is the one time I don't mind pounding a beat," his stocky companion replied. "I sure wouldn't want to be the lieutenant or Kelly if there's not an arrest soon."

"You can't arrest without suspects. I've gone door-to-door around this Dahlgren's neighborhood, but nobody has seen or heard anything. My feet get so tired I'm glad when it's quitting time these days."

"Speaking of quitting, did you hear that both Cooper and Laurel Bartlett are leaving the *Globe*?"

"Yes, but Cooper's just going to cover some kind of train tunnel opening in California, then he'll be back. But she's giving up the newspaper to be her aunt's bridesmaid in Sacramento."

The information so surprised Armistead that he jerked the paper. Peering over the top, he saw both men glance at him, then away. They resumed talking together.

Armistead's calculating mind instantly began processing a new idea. *So she's going to California, hm? The authorities are so stirred up here that it would be less risky if there wasn't a fourth murder. Yes, that makes sense: finish her out west. But first, I'd better do some misdirecting to fool the detectives, not that they're smart enough to catch Abaddon.*

Smiling with satisfaction, he hoped Laurel would come in for lunch so he could start that process.

Laurel tried to tell herself not to be more nervous about her own peril since Abaddon had killed Charity, but she felt tense when she returned to the police station in the early afternoon. The sergeant told her that Darius Barr was in his darkroom, so she went there to offer her condolences.

He came out wearing an India rubber apron. Strong chemical fumes followed him, causing Laurel to jerk her head back. He noticed and suggested they talk back by the cells, which were empty. She couldn't decide if his red eyes were caused by weeping or the acrid chemical vapors.

Forcing her own anxiety aside, she expressed her sympathy to Darius, saying, "You shouldn't be working now. Don't you have anyone? . . ."

"I only had her, and I've got to work or I'll lose my mind!" His voice was thick with emotion.

Feeling uncertain and guilty, Laurel volunteered, "I'm here if it would help to talk about it."

"Right now I hurt so much that I don't know what I want, except for her killer to be caught!"

"I know." *Oh, how I know!* she added silently and with strong feelings. She fought down the knowledge that if he wasn't apprehended soon, she might be dead, too. Laurel paused before adding, "I keep remembering that day at lunch when Charity said she had a theory about Sarah's killer. Did she ever say anything to you about that?"

"No. She didn't talk much about her stories."

"I know it's really not the time to bring this up, but I'm leaving for Sacramento next week. If I can, I'd like to help solve these murders before I go. I'm sure her theory had something to do with a photograph. Do you recall commenting that the killer might have been looking at the same photograph you took of Sarah for police records?"

"Yes, but we never discussed that, either."

Asking questions in pursuit of discovering more about Abaddon made Laurel's own fears recede into the background. She persisted, "Do you suppose she knew of some photographer we don't, and she maybe went to his place looking for the photograph or the plate?"

"I don't think so. Look, all I really know is that she sent some wires to New York, and she hired a local detective agency to check on some things. I don't know the details; we mostly talked about wedding plans."

"Forgive me for asking those questions, and I'm really sorry about Charity." She accompanied him back to the dark room where he insisted he wanted to be alone.

Returning to the lieutenant's office, Laurel learned that there was nothing new from Emory Brush or the NDP. She asked the same question she had posed to Darius, finding that concentrating on detective work helped her feel less concerned about herself.

Pierce scowled thoughtfully. "Where could she have looked? Kelly checked on Cooper, the only other photographer we know, and he was clean."

"You mean Kelly didn't find any evidence. But I still think Cooper's a logical suspect."

"If it'll make you feel any better, Laurel, I'll have Kelly interrogate him again before he leaves for California. We don't want to overlook any possibility. But I think you're wrong on Cooper."

She briefly wondered, *Is it possible that I'm overlooking someone else who could be a suspect?* She shook her head. *No, it's Cooper, and I've got to prove it, even though I put myself at greater risk by following him to Sacramento.*

❧

The long train ride bored Ridge. He didn't feel like making idle conversation with strangers. Instead, he stared out the window and reviewed his objectives in Virginia. Based on what Griff had told him earlier, Ridge was confident that they could form a profitable business partnership. But Ridge could not guess what surprise his long-time friend had alluded to in his wires.

Ridge really didn't need to see Sam Maynard about his presence in Chicago. It was obvious that he could not have been the slayer of two more people after Sarah. Yet, Ridge still wanted to ask Sam some questions.

Varina posed a problem for Ridge. He really had no reason to see her, but what if he ran into her? That brought back a collage of memories that made him sigh heavily.

❧

Laurel returned to the *Globe*, grateful that Cooper wasn't around. A note on her desk read: Dahlgren funeral Monday at two, Evergreen Cemetery. Cover it.

She had expected to attend, but not in an official capacity. Sighing, she wrote and filed a brief updated story based on what little more she had learned.

Laurel sauntered out of the building, glad the work week was over. Even though God didn't seem to hear her prayers, she considered attending church tomorrow with her aunt.

She silently asked, "Lord, would it do any good? I mean, would my prayers be any more effective in church than they've been up to now?" She cocked her head as though listening for an answer, then shrugged. She made her way toward the curb, easing through pedestrians, her mind preoccupied.

Laurel looked for a hack or cabriolet while passing a lamp post and suddenly collided with someone stepping out from behind it. She caught her balance before recognizing Porter Armistead with his spectacles askew.

"I'm sorry, Porter! I didn't see you."

"My fault! Sorry!" He readjusted his specs. "Are you hurt?"

"No, I'm fine. How about you?"

"The same. Can I get you a hack?"

"No, thanks. I'll manage."

He dropped his eyes and his voice. "I'm sorry about your newspaper lady friend. She seemed very nice the day you introduced us."

"She was a fine woman." Laurel didn't have much to say to Porter Armistead just now. She looked around for a hack.

Armistead said, "It was nice seeing you."

"You, too."

"I guess this will be the last time," he told her, starting to turn away.

"What?"

He turned back to face her. "I have accepted a promotion in New York. I leave tomorrow."

"Oh. Well, congratulations. I wish you well."

"Thank you, Laurel. Now, please excuse me. I have an appointment." He rapidly walked away.

Laurel watched him go, wondering what kind of a promotion he had received in New York. She would have to ask at the police precinct. Porter might have said something to some of the patrolmen at noon because their tables were always so close together.

❧

While Laurel and Agnes headed for church the next morning, Armistead boarded the first of five trains required to reach Omaha. He settled down into a back seat, a faint smile on his face.

*She believed me. This is turning out to be even more satisfactory than I originally thought.*

Out of habit, he reviewed everything. His precious camera and other necessary equipment were carefully padded and secured in a stout wooden crate in the baggage car. He had chosen a new name for himself: A.B. Abbott. It was ironically close enough to Abaddon to suit his fancy. Even if Laurel somehow heard the name, she would not connect it with Porter Armistead. All he had to do was stay out of her sight until he was ready.

He didn't look out the window, but gazed unseeingly at the back of the seat in front of him. Anticipation always made him think of the first victim. He had watched Effie Chapman with slightly older boys slipping off into the brush near the tree where her body had later been found.

That was sinful, as he was certain Laurel had been when she was absent for various periods during the war. She had also been a spy against the South. He, a secret Copperhead who couldn't openly support the Confederacy, had determined her punishment the day he came across her name in the NDP files where he worked.

So far as he knew, Sarah had never been wanton, but she had helped Laurel in spying. They were good friends, so Sarah's death would hurt Laurel and begin to instill a sense of terror in her over what fate she faced.

Armistead's anticipation grew as the cars slowly followed the rails toward Omaha.

On the third Monday after Laurel and Agnes returned to Chicago and Sarah was found murdered, Laurel arrived early at Allan Pinkerton's office.

She had not given much thought to Armistead telling her that he was moving to New York, but now that she was within days of leaving for California, she did have some misgivings about Cooper also being there. If he really was Abaddon, as she suspected, she would try to avoid him. If not, she was confident of her ability to take care of herself.

She and Pinkerton talked briefly of the murder cases and Charity's coming funeral Then Pinkerton said he had a busy morning and handed Laurel a packet.

"This is an easy assignment," he told her. "In fact, if he wasn't a big railroad client, I wouldn't take this case. It's not our usual kind. Anyway, in this envelope you'll find everything the client wants to know. That includes attending the opening of the Summit Tunnel east of Sacramento. Wire it all to me the next day."

Laurel cocked her head. "That's all?"

"That's all. When you've finished, you've met your commitment to me. You were a good agent, Laurel. I'll miss you."

She thanked him and left, but chided herself. *If I'm such a good agent, why can't I solve these murder cases?* She paused just inside the door to the street and opened the package. She started to skim the first page to get an idea of the assignment, then looked again in disbelief.

*Nitroglycerin? He said this case wasn't dangerous!*

Two days after writing her final story about Charity's funeral, Laurel and her aunt left Chicago on their second trip west. Since they had made the journey before, they knew about the train changes to the Missouri River, the boat ride across it, then fifteen days and nights in a cramped stagecoach.

Those were known risks, as was following Cooper in a continued effort to prove he was really Abaddon. But Laurel had only a vague idea of the risks involved in getting information about the highly volatile and powerful new explosive, nitro.

She was sick at heart because of her failure to solve Sarah's murder and probably causing Charity to also lose her life. Laurel had sought solace in church on Sunday. She enjoyed the choir, but the sermon had not reached her. Her thoughts kept veering off to touch on the nitro, Cooper, and Ridge.

Remembering her silent sidewalk prayer, she closed her eyes and slightly bowed her head. *Lord, I'm here in church. Will You hear me now and answer my prayers?* She didn't consciously form the words, but her thoughts about Cooper and Ridge were meant as prayers. When she had finished the brief meditation, she felt better, even though she didn't see that anything had changed. Still, she had prayed again, and that was comforting.

After services, she carefully read the data Pinkerton had given her about her assignment. She followed that by vainly searching for current periodicals and books on nitro. Now she couldn't learn anything more until Sacramento. Against her will, her thoughts drifted to Ridge.

It was useless to remind herself that they had parted for the last time. She fought down images of what he and the beautiful, charming, and gracious Varina might be doing since he had returned to Virginia alone.

It had been a year since Ridge had sat in a fan-backed chair under hundred-foot-tall tulip trees across from Jubal Griffin, Jr., his childhood friend. Both were about the same size, build, and age.

He asked Ridge, "Well, how does it feel to be back?"

"It's different. Not like coming home after the war. It's somehow not the same this time."

Griff leaned forward in his rolling chair where he had been confined since he received a Yankee bayonet wound near the spine. "Maybe that's because Laurel didn't come along."

"Maybe," Ridge admitted, glancing from the solid manor house. It was one of the few not vandalized by the invaders whose officers had quartered themselves there.

"Or," he continued, looking back to Griff, "it's because I'm not sure I really belong here anymore."

"Don't tell me you like the west more than this?"

"I'd never thought about it. Anyway, I'm restless, and should get back to Chicago as soon as possible. So let's discuss this possible business partnership."

"I took the liberty of drawing up a tentative agreement based on what we talked about last year and your telegrams." Griff reached for a packet slipped in between his right hip and the arm of the rolling chair. "I think it covers everything. I'll put up the gold we kept hidden from the Yankees and manage the Omaha office so you can continue traveling. . . ."

"You'll do what?"

Griff smiled. "That's part of the surprise I mentioned in my wires. The other part is that I'm getting married."

"You are? To whom?"

"Faith Webster. Remember her?"

"Of course. I haven't seen her since before the war, but the last I remember, she was a skinny little girl."

"She's now a beautiful young woman, and she says she would rather have me with this chair than any man in the world. She even likes the idea of Omaha. I asked her to come by this afternoon so all of us could talk."

Ridge reached over and heartily gripped his friend's right hand. "Congratulations, Griff! I'm happy for you."

A few minutes later, Griff rolled himself back to the house where he lived with his parents. Ridge strolled down to sit by the river's edge and read the agreement that Griff had drawn up. It was close to what Ridge had in mind. He started to get up but suddenly stopped and sniffed. The fragrance of lilacs wafted to him, which was so reminiscent of Varina.

"Good morning, Ridge."

He whirled around. She stood before him, holding a small parasol. Taller than Laurel, Varina was strikingly beautiful in a short-sleeved white dress that cascaded from her tiny waist and hips to flare out gracefully at the bottom. Her long golden hair was parted in the middle and tied in braids, reminding Ridge of a drawing he had seen of a mythical goddess.

"Well," she said with a teasing smile, "it's considered proper to return a greeting."

"Oh, good morning!" The old familiar emotional tug drew him physically to step toward her. "Sorry, Varina. I was deep in thought."

"I noticed." The smile softened as her pale green eyes swept him from head to toe. "You look well, Ridge."

"I am. And you, you look . . ." He checked himself and added, "I trust you're well, too."

She laughed, a low, throaty sound which stirred old memories of when they were engaged.

"I hope you don't mind," she told him, her words soft as a dawn breeze. "I had come to call on Faith Webster just as she was leaving to come see Griff. She asked me to ride along."

Ridge felt a tingle of doubt about that. The news of his coming had surely been passed along by Griff's mother. Varina certainly heard of his arrival and planned this meeting to appear almost accidental. Ridge knew she was a very determined woman capable of scheming. She had surely learned that Ridge had come alone. But she was also a vision of loveliness whose invisible signature of lilac scent lingered in the air and his memory.

"Well," she said, twirling the parasol, "do you want to run away or shall we talk like old friends?"

Ridge thought of Laurel and their last parting. He inhaled Varina's faint lilac fragrance. "Let's talk."

She smiled warmly, slipped her arm through his, and turned to stroll with him along the shore.

❧

Laurel and Agnes had twice changed trains, giving the women plenty of time to discuss all manner of topics. One of those greatly troubled Laurel.

"If Cooper isn't really Abaddon, as the lieutenant thinks, and I'm making a mistake, I just can't figure out how Abaddon knew what Charity had figured out."

"I wish I could help you."

"I'm just thinking out loud. It's obvious that Charity had some idea of who killed Sarah and was threatening me. But how did Abaddon find out?"

Agnes shrugged. "I don't have any ideas."

"The only possibility—if it isn't Cooper—is that Abaddon knew of an information leak."

"Could he have overheard somebody talking about it?"

"I suppose, but Charity didn't even tell her beau, so I doubt she said anything to anyone else."

Laurel continued to ponder that as the cars rocked and swayed along the tracks leading west.

That night, Ridge lay in the second-story bedroom of Brickside Manor and tried to sort out his feelings toward both Laurel and Varina. He had no doubt that he loved Laurel, but she was so unyielding in her self-reliant manner that she refused to meld as one in a marriage.

Varina was the epitome of cooperation. She had been reared to use her beauty and charm to win a respectable man who was either rich or had the capability of becoming so. Her life was to be his life so they were one. That wasn't true of Laurel.

*That's enough!* Ridge chided himself. *Think about something else.* He forced his mind to focus on what he must do tomorrow: see Sam Maynard and complete the redrafting of the business agreement with Griff. And stay away from Varina! He just wasn't sure he could do that.

The next afternoon Ridge met Griff and Faith under the trees outside of Brickside Manor. Although Ridge remembered Faith as several years younger, she was now a buxom young woman with a sturdy build and quiet demeanor. It was obviously clear that she adored Griff and that his handicap didn't detract from her love.

When Ridge and Griff finished examining the final draft of the business agreement and were about to sign it, Faith went back into the house to get refreshments.

Griff followed her with his eyes. "Isn't she wonderful?"

Ridge grinned at his friend. "Yes, I would say so."

"Now that you and I have firmed up our partnership, Faith and I will get married and take our honeymoon on the way to Omaha."

"I'm sure you'll both be very happy."

Griff hesitated before asking, "What about you?"

Ridge didn't want to discuss his situation, so he didn't answer directly. Instead, he said, "Thanks for the loan of the carriage today. It was good to visit some old friends. I even looked up Sam Maynard."

Griff commented, "You and he were never close."

"That's true, but I had some concerns going back to the war. I'm satisfied they were groundless."

"What kind of concerns?"

"Oh, I saw him in Chicago a few weeks ago and wanted to talk, but he was on his way to take the cars home."

Griff nodded but asked no more questions.

Ridge was grateful that his friend sensed it was a personal matter. Ridge had steered the conversation with Sam back to something he had once said to Ridge about a young woman who called herself Charlotte Wilson. They had met briefly at Petersburg just before it fell.

Sam had thought Laurel looked familiar when they met on her last trip to Virginia, but Ridge was now satisfied that Sam did not think Laurel and Charlotte were the same person. Neither had Sam been punished for any military infraction.

*Not that it matters now*, Ridge told himself, *but if I ever again see Laurel, I can assure her about Sam.*

Griff's voice roused Ridge from his reverie. "Now that you and Laurel have changed plans, what are you going to do about your family plantation?"

"I'm going to apply for amnesty."

"Then what? Rebuild?"

"What do I need with a fine new home when my work is out west? Besides, a man alone doesn't need a big house."

"Faith told me that when she took Varina home yesterday after you talked that she thinks you've come back to live."

"What gave her that idea? We talked about all kinds of things, but nothing was said about coming back."

"Faith understood that Varina invited you to supper tonight."

"She did, but I didn't say I accepted."

"From what she told Faith, Varina thinks you did."

Ridge studied his friend's eyes for awhile. "Would you mind if I borrowed the carriage again?"

❧

*This is foolishness*, Ridge told himself as he drove toward Hunter's Grove. He arrived just before sunset and stopped the horse on the gravel driveway under the war-shattered oaks. The two-story manor house showed only minimal deterioration. But the peripheries had all been burned or torn apart and not rebuilt, mute testimony to Varina's financial situation.

He tied the horse to a hitching post and started toward the unadorned door in the middle of the lower floor. He started to pull the bell when he caught the fragrance of lilacs. He turned as

Varina came around the corner wearing a wide-brimmed white hat which seemed to be the same one she had worn when he saw her months ago standing by the river, looking across it.

"Oh!" she exclaimed with a glad smile and tossing her long golden hair which she wore loose. "I was just enjoying my garden. Won't you come in?"

Ridge heard faint singing from inside and suspected that Tessie, Varina's former slave and now a free servant, was responsible. "I'd like to talk to you out here, alone, if you don't mind."

"Of course. Shall we stroll along the river bank?"

Ridge nodded, struck by her beauty, yet recalling that she had broken her war-time promise to wait for him.

As before, she slipped her arm through his and glided toward the river behind the house. She remarked on the weather, but he didn't really listen. *Intoxicating*, Ridge thought. *That's what she is. And she's not stubborn or self-reliant to a fault.*

He realized she had fallen silent. He glanced down at her face, perfectly framed by the hat. He said in a husky voice, "You are truly beautiful!"

"And you are the handsomest man I know." She leaned slightly toward him, knocking her hat off. She let it fall, her face upturned to his. "Oh, Ridge! I have missed you so!"

He didn't answer, but stared at her face, soft and invitingly close.

She whispered, "Do you miss me?"

He hedged, saying, "I've thought about you a lot."

She tilted her chin up slightly. "Have you thought about how our lips used to feel so right together?"

His voice dropped. "I remember."

She waited a moment but when he didn't move toward her, she asked with a throaty laugh, "Well?"

He kissed her gently, hearing her sharp intake of breath and feeling her arms possessively encircling his neck.

He felt the pressure of her lips as she responded with passion, but he didn't react the same way.

She pulled back, her eyes bright with concern. "What's the matter?"

He looked down at her flawless face and saw everything there that he wanted in a woman. But there was no mystical enchantment, no spark of something he had only known with one other woman—Laurel.

"Varina," he said firmly, drawing back. "I wish you a world of happiness, but . . . whatever we once had is gone. I'm sorry!" He strode away and didn't look back.

D ays later, Ridge entered Emory Brush's Chicago office and faced the dark-complected former detective.

Ridge looked in the big man's eyes and said, "When I stopped by the Grove Street police station, the sergeant said you wanted to see me. That true?"

Brush motioned Ridge to a chair across from him. "It's true. I know you must not have much respect for me or my men after we failed to do what you hired us to do. I hope I can somewhat make amends for that by passing on something that will be helpful to you."

Ridge sat uncertainly. "How so?"

"Before you left for Virginia and Miss Bartlett headed for California, Charity Dahlgren had retained my agency's services."

"Yes, I heard that."

"I wouldn't ordinarily do this, but under the circumstances, I'm going to divulge some facts which this office turned up during that case."

"If you mean that Laurel's and Sarah's names were found in the National Detective Police war-time files, I also know that."

Brush leaned across the desk, his dark, almost black eyes locked onto Ridge's. "But I don't think you know some facts about Porter Armistead."

Ridge frowned. "What's this got to do with him?"

"We found that Armistead had not served in the military during the war, or been in detached service as he told his old Chicago friends. He drifted from job to job, including being a relief railroad telegrapher and photographer's assistant."

"Photographer?" Ridge repeated, instantly sensing where Brush was going with his remarks.

"An assistant, but he certainly could have learned how to take photographs. That was before he worked as a clerk in the NDP files department."

Ridge stiffened. "There he must have seen Laurel's and Sarah's names. . . ."

"Absolutely! We believe that when he somehow learned that Miss Dahlgren was checking into the NDP, Armistead guessed that she would also come upon his name. To protect himself, he killed her."

Ridge was stunned. "So Abaddon is really Armistead?"

"Yes, but now he's out of this jurisdiction. Some of the uniformed officers who eat at the Fog Horn heard him tell the waiter that he was going back to New York."

Ridge took a deep breath, ready to sigh in relief, but before he could let it out, he saw something in Brush's eyes that made him hold it.

"He lied," Brush said flatly. "Our informants positively identified him as boarding the Omaha train the day before Miss Bartlett left town."

Leaping to his feet, Ridge exclaimed, "Laurel! She's heading into a trap!"

"I'm afraid so. We tried unsuccessfully to wire a message ahead in hopes it would reach her on the train. Since we didn't get a confirmation back as requested, we assume she didn't get our warning."

Ridge spun to reach for the door. "Thanks. Keep trying to

reach her on the cars. I know the hotel where she stayed before. I'll wire her there, and then I'll get there as fast as I can!"

After reaching Sacramento the last of August, Vance Cooper lost no time in getting acquainted with officials of the Central Pacific Railroad. His credentials with the *Chicago Globe* and his obvious interest in railroads got him an invitation to ride a work train up to the Summit Tunnel site.

There, in the high Sierra Nevada Mountains, with the tunnel as a target, he lugged his bulky camera and tripod around immense slabs of slick, glistening granite which were everywhere. There he took photographs and gathered background material for stories he would wire to Chicago before the tunnel opened in the middle of the month.

One of the human interest stories he wanted to check out concerned reports about the countless deaths of Chinese workers who were building the CP's rail line, including the celebrated Summit Tunnel.

It was an incredible undertaking which started in mid-summer, a year ago. The quarter-mile bore through the granite backbone of the Sierra Nevada Mountains was made at the rate of about eight inches a day. Hand tools and black powder were used until recently when a new, much more powerful but unstable explosive called nitroglycerin had been tried.

What the news correspondent found interesting was that contracts for the Chinese workers required their bones be shipped back to their homeland for burial if they died in California. The work was so dangerous that ten tons of the workers' bones were reported to have been returned to China.

*That's a feature story that Laurel would enjoy writing,*

Cooper thought. She liked doing features more than hard news. He shook his head, remembering how any possibility of a relationship had deteriorated after he kissed her in Chicago. *Why am I wasting time thinking of her?*

He had ducked under the black hood over his camera to check his picture composition. He emerged again at the rumbling of wheels and horses running. He glanced down at the narrow dirt road below as a six-hitch stagecoach lurched and rumbled into view. One male passenger wearing spectacles stuck his head out the window and craned his neck up to better view the tunnel.

Cooper squinted for a closer view. *That looks like Porter Armistead. No, it can't be. Before I left Chicago, Kelly said that Armistead had told some patrolmen he was going to New York.* Cooper returned to his camera.

🐎

That afternoon Armistead stiffly climbed out of the stagecoach where it stopped at the end of the line.

During the tedious two weeks of day and night travel, he had often reflected on those women whom he had punished for their wrongdoing. He had been badly frightened after Effie Chapman, his first. He had told himself he wouldn't do it again, and eventually moved to New York in hopes of putting her memory away.

There he kept remembering the surge of pleasure he had experienced in punishing her for her indecency. She had done wrong, and someone had to punish her. He felt the same way in New York where he meted out his form of justice to the first "soiled dove." He was less frightened this time, and got a perverse pleasure in the afterglow of having punished her. When that good feeling wore off, he was not afraid to strike the third time, then twice more in New Jersey as his boldness grew.

He had returned to Chicago to dispense retribution to a couple of women. The one woman whom he felt most deserved punishment was not for debauchery, but for cruelty to him. However, as since childhood, he was still afraid of his mother, and couldn't bring himself to rise against her power.

He wasn't afraid of Laurel, whose war-time absences had to have included licentiousness. Besides that, she had helped bring down the Confederacy which he supported as a Copperhead.

He anticipated the sense of power he would have over Laurel when he finally ended the little game he had played with her. He just had to wait until she arrived in Sacramento where she expected to be safe.

Leaving the stagecoach, he took a room at a cheap hotel, changed clothes, and went job hunting. When he returned to his room at dusk, he had been hired as a relief telegraph operator under the name of A.B. Abbott, lately of New York.

During the long overland trip, he had carefully worked out his final plans for Laurel. He knew she expected to be at the formal opening of the Summit Tunnel. The first chance he got, he would explore that general area for the perfect place to punish her for what she had done.

On his first shift at the telegraph key, he felt good. He anticipated the way he would feel really alive when he had her trussed and was ready to take her last photograph.

His musing was broken by the clicking of an incoming message in Morse Code. The first few dots and dashes seemed routine, then Armistead jerked as if hit by an electric spark. The message was for Laurel from Ridge:

*"Danger. Armistead really Abaddon. Avoid him. I'm coming fast. Love."*

Armistead studied the words, then looked around to make sure nobody was watching. He lit a match, burned the message and dropped the ashes into the spittoon.

After fifteen days and nights on stagecoaches, Laurel and Agnes arrived in Sacramento. Horatio Bodmer met them. A widower in his fifties with a full head of silver hair, prominent nose, and standing just over six feet tall, he reminded Laurel of the late President Lincoln.

Bodmer said, "I apologize for not being able to provide you with better accommodations. So many people are arriving for the tunnel opening that the best I could get was the Traveler's Hotel where you stayed before."

Agnes said, "I'm so happy to be off that stage that any place will be wonderful."

Laurel told them, "It's early enough that after we register, I think I'll run over to the *Sacramento Enterprise* and see if Mark Gardner is still there."

Agnes asked, "Wouldn't you rather bathe and rest on a real bed first?"

"Of course, I'd rather, but I've got a lot to do before the tunnel opens in a couple of weeks. You go ahead with your wedding plans. I'll be back later."

Ridge had previously traveled on a stagecoach partway to California, but he had forgotten how slow five miles an hour was. Averaging a hundred and twenty-five miles every twenty-four hours seemed reasonably fast, but not when Ridge didn't know if Laurel had received any warning of the danger she faced from Armistead.

He didn't visit much with the eight other passengers squeezed into the coach. Instead, he discouraged conversation by staring out the window at the vast expanses of nothing and fought with himself.

*I should never have let her go to California without me! I was afraid of losing my business, and now I'm afraid of her losing her life. And I can't do a single thing except pray.*

Ridge had grown up in the church but hadn't done much praying during the war where he lost his faith. He had regained it after he met Laurel and learned that her spying was responsible for his leg wound and the death of his brother. It had not been easy to forgive her. Yet, in a crisis, he had asked God to forgive him for what he had done. Then he had sought Laurel's forgiveness, and she had granted it. He was still young in his renewed faith, and praying was not easy. Still, for Laurel, he closed his eyes.

*Lord*, he silently prayed, *I can't help her, but she means the world to me. So please take care of her until I get there.* It was a simple, honest petition from his heart, completing all he could do.

He had already done all the practical things possible. In Omaha, he had approached the telegraph office and asked if there were any messages for him. There weren't. That meant Laurel had not received his wire from Chicago. It also meant something more ominous: she was unaware of Armistead's plans for her.

Before boarding the stagecoach, Ridge sent another wire to the Traveler's Hotel in Sacramento where he knew Laurel had stayed before. She might not be there, but there were too many hotels of unknown names to send wires to all of them.

He valiantly tried to shift his thoughts from Laurel's dangers to his less stressful areas. *If . . . I mean, WHEN I find her safe, and President Johnson grants me amnesty, I'll give her the choice. Rebuild on my family's plantation, or sell it and live wherever she wants. Just so we're together.*

He tried to assure himself that he would get to her before Armistead did, but doubts nagged at him. *What if I'm too late?*

The familiar smell of ink and newsprint greeted Laurel when she entered the front door of the *Sacramento Enterprise*. Upon learning that Mark Gardner still worked there, she sent word that she was here.

A nice-looking man in his twenties and of just above average height, he rushed out and broke into a delighted grin. "Laurel! You came back to me!"

She smiled fondly, noticing that his blond, wavy hair was almost white, but otherwise, he hadn't changed. "You are still incorrigible!" she said with a laugh.

"No, I'm Mark Gardner. Incorrigible resigned and moved to Chicago or someplace." He seized her hand as he had done a year ago when they first met. "Come on! I haven't risked being discharged all day, so now's a good time to start."

"Wait!" she pleaded as he almost dragged her outside in the September heat. "I can't move that fast!"

"Want me to carry you?" he teased.

"I never met anyone as brash as you. What will people think, dragging me along the street like this?"

"They'll think I'm the most fortunate man in the world. And I am." He swept her with appreciative eyes.

She couldn't be annoyed with him because that's the way she remembered him: impulsive and impertinent, yet a really fine correspondent who knew everybody in the capital city. "Where are you taking me?" she asked.

"Our favorite place, The Brown Jug. Remember?"

She matched his bantering tone. "How could I forget?"

The Brown Jug was a small, informal café tucked into a niche between two retail stores off an alley. Gardner did not release her as he called to the man behind the counter, "I've just met the girl who's going to marry me, so don't bother us for a year or two."

She protested, "You said almost the same thing the first time you brought me here."

He kept her hand firmly in his as he led her through the narrow building toward the back. "Speaking of marriage, I assume that you didn't marry that former Confederate cavalryman?"

"No, I didn't."

Gardner grinned. "Are you betrothed to anyone?"

"No," she said soberly. "But I didn't come here to talk about me."

"That's all I needed to know!" he exclaimed, the smile reappearing. "Well, except why are you here?"

"I need your help to get some information."

"You've got it. I get paid to know everything about everybody, but I give that information free to the prettiest girl I know."

She smiled at his impertinence. "You are without doubt the most unusual man I've ever met."

"Flattery will get you everywhere," he shot back. "So ask your questions."

Armistead couldn't believe his luck when he was again on telegraph duty and Ridge's second wire came through. Armistead scowled, knowing that Ridge was getting closer. He thoughtfully calculated that Ridge could not get to Sacramento before Laurel paid with her life for her transgressions. But Armistead could not let her know about Ridge's warning telegram, either. As with the first one, Armistead surreptitiously looked around, then burned the message.

❧

Dusk was settling when Laurel reached the Traveler's Hotel. It was an old structure, and the lobby was filled with heavy dark furniture. From her last visit, Laurel knew it had been shipped around the Horn. She wrinkled her nose at the smell of dead cigars and brass spittoons.

A man stood at the front desk with his back to her as she approached to make sure her aunt had registered for her. The man looked up as she stopped behind him.

Vance Cooper looked at her with frosty eyes. "Well, Laurel, I knew you were coming to Sacramento, but I did not expect to see you."

"Good evening, Vance," she said formally, aware of their last tense encounters in Chicago.

He asked bluntly, "Do you still suspect me of being Abaddon?"

Flustered, she tried to think how to respond, but he quickly spoke again. "I could tell from your manner in Chicago before I heard what you said to the detectives."

Her eyes widened at that. "How did you? . . ."

He interrupted, "I told you at the *Globe*: 'I know lots of things. I also hear things. That's my job.' In fact, any good correspondent has to do that."

"I see," she said uncertainly.

"Seymour told me that you switched from staff to stringer status to cover the opening of the tunnel."

She sensed a way to possibly placate Cooper. "I did not want to compete with you on hard news, so I'll only do features. Maybe something about how many Chinese it took to build the tunnel, that sort of thing."

Cooper nodded approvingly. "Good idea, not that I consider you competition, you understand."

"I would never consider myself your competitor," she assured him with a tentative smile.

"Thanks." His countenance softened slightly. "Well, I guess I'll see you at the tunnel."

"I suppose so."

He turned away, then stopped. "Laurel, I really regret that things didn't work out for us back east."

He walked away, leaving Laurel wondering if he meant that sincerely, or if it was a veiled Abaddon threat. She turned to the clerk. "Is he staying here?"

"Not now, Miss. He did when he first arrived in town, but then he moved out. He just came to see if any late mail had come for him. I'm sorry he didn't leave a forwarding address."

Laurel hesitated, aware that Cooper knew where she was staying. *Well,* she thought, *I'm not going to hide again. I'll just have to be more careful.* Still, she wondered where he had found new lodging so she could avoid that area if possible.

When he wasn't working, Armistead twice managed to ride a work train up to the Summit Tunnel area. He told the other employees that he was there to locate the best places for a telegraph unit. Word could be flashed nationwide as the opening ceremonies progressed.

He casually wandered away from the tunnel until he located an abandoned one-room shack. It was tucked back in a clearing behind immense monolithic outcroppings of granite. The cabin was perfect because there was no evidence of human tracks near it, and the roof had been partially collapsed by heavy winter snows. This allowed extra light into the room. He needed that in the same way he needed daylight on Sarah's back porch.

It would cost some money to rent a horse and buggy, but he couldn't risk taking his heavy camera equipment up on the railroad's work car. The equipment could be hidden under a portion of the collapsed cabin roof. Chloroform, which deteriorated in light, would have to be carefully wrapped and personally carried up on the day the tunnel opened. The colorless liquid would be in a container made to prevent the heavy, ether-like odor from being detected.

Satisfied with his preparations, including how he would lure Laurel into helping him in his plan, Armistead rode the work train back to Sacramento. Now all he had to do was wait for the opening ceremonies.

Nearly a week after arriving in Sacramento, Laurel returned to her hotel after a full day of work. She knocked on her aunt's adjoining door and invited her to come into her room.

"I apologize again for not being more of a help in your wedding plans."

Aunt Agnes dismissed Laurel's concern. "I understand that you have many things on your mind. I just want you to be careful in case Cooper is really Abaddon."

"I am careful, believe me!" Laurel removed her bonnet and dropped into the chair, settling a handful of notes on her lap. "But I'll be glad when this tunnel is open. It has given me a lot of good stories for the *Globe*." She added silently, *Plus meeting the requirements of Pinkerton's client.*

"What kind of stories?" Agnes wanted to know.

"Well, for one, this will be the last railroad tunnel ever built by black powder and hand tools. I had an interview today, thanks to Mark Gardner's suggestion, with a chemist who's working with a new European creation that is eight times more powerful than black powder. It's known as 'blasting oil,' but really is called nitro-glycerin."

"Oh, yes. Horatio told me about that. When the Central Pacific first tried it, there was an accident. One man lost an eye, so the construction superintendent refused to use it anymore."

"That's changed," Laurel explained, consulting her notes. "Nitro has three ingredients: glycerin, and nitric and sulfuric acids. Together, they're highly sensitive and dangerous. But shipped by themselves, they are safe. So each day a chemist mixes up only what's needed that day. Twice as much work is now done on the tunnel."

"Well, I'm sure that's all very interesting to some people," Agnes commented. "But I'd rather talk about marriage plans. It's only a little over a week away."

"Of course," Laurel replied, and concentrated on her aunt's arrangements for the day after the tunnel opened.

❧

The vast, seemingly endless desert that Ridge could see from the stagecoach window tortured him. He hated being powerless to help Laurel in her danger. Then he squinted through the shimmering heat and saw in the distance what appeared to be a mountain range.

*No, it must be another mirage*, he thought, leaning back in disappointment. But he kept his eyes on the horizon and slowly nodded. *That's no mirage! Those are the Sierras!* He was getting closer, but was it too late? His emotional torment continued, but he said a silent prayer and dared to hope as the coach lurched westward.

Armistead was working a relief shift at the telegraph office when a brash young man walked in and introduced himself.

"I'm Mark Gardner, correspondent for the *Enterprise*. I heard you were new in town. I like to know everyone, so maybe I could do a little story about you."

Armistead tried to hide the panic that seized him. Then he relaxed and shook hands. "I'm A.B. Abbott," he said. "But there's nothing about me that you'd want to write about."

"I usually can find a story in everybody," Gardner replied cheerfully. "How about setting a time when we can get together?"

Stalling, Armistead said, "Well, it would have to be after the tunnel opening. I'm really busy until then."

"That's when we'll do it," Gardner replied.

After he had gone, Armistead remembered what had been said about knowing everyone. As pretty as Laurel was, Armistead was positive the good-looking reporter must have already met her.

Armistead later saw Laurel and Gardner enter The Brown Jug, smiling and laughing together. Armistead's resentment against her flared up stronger than before.

*There's no doubt that she's a wanton woman*, he told himself. *In Chicago, she was courted by every male, but when I finally got up the courage to ask if I could call on her, she refused. Oh, she was polite, but I'm sure she told her friends and they all had a good laugh about it. She also had many dalliances with soldiers during the war.*

His anger bubbled into a full and furious boil, making him eager for their final meeting. Then she would find out that he was more than the most intelligent boy in their school. He had real power, no matter what they thought of his small stature and mild demeanor.

He had proved that power because he was more intelligent than any of them; more than Laurel, who didn't suspect him; more than the Chicago authorities whom he had openly taunted with letters and misdirected clues. He also outwitted the correspondents until Charity Dahlgren's poking into the NDP threatened to betray him.

*It's all really Laurel's fault,* he assured himself, *starting with Effie. But in a few more days . . .*

He frowned, wondering how far away Ridge's stagecoach was. *Well, it may be close, but he's going to be too late to save her.*

🐾

Among the questions Mark Gardner had answered for Laurel was where Vance Cooper was staying. Gardner had not known offhand, although he had met the correspondent shortly after he arrived in Sacramento. Later, Gardner reluctantly provided the address and volunteered the information that Cooper was leaving Saturday afternoon for the tunnel area. He wanted to be there early to take photographs of dignitaries arriving for the celebration.

Cooper had rented what had once been servant's quarters behind a large, two-story home situated on a spacious lot overgrown with trees and shrubbery.

Laurel casually walked that area until she saw a stray dog slip through a hole in the backyard fence which ran along a little-used alley. He saw her, tucked his tail between his legs, woofed at her, and ran off.

Content for the moment, Laurel continued her routine. She

kept remembering Charity's comment that Sarah's killer might have been looking at the same photograph of the murder scene that Darius Barr had taken for the police.

If Charity was right, Laurel had decided, then Abaddon might keep photographs or plates of his grisly work. *If Cooper is who I think he is, then maybe he brought some pictures with him. He would have to keep them where he lives.*

She was watching from a distance when Cooper emerged from his quarters Friday afternoon, carrying a duffel bag. She gave him a five-minute start. Then, after making sure that nobody was in sight or watching her, Laurel slipped through the fence.

She knew that the chances of entering the little house were slim. But if she couldn't enter, maybe she could look through the windows and see if there were any photos. She doubted there would be any incriminating ones in sight, but she had to make sure.

As twilight softened the shadows and darkness began to settle, she moved across the silent backyard. She was not afraid, but her heart still speeded up as it had on her spying missions.

She reached the back window. She placed her hands on either side of her forehead to cut down as much outside light as possible. Carefully, she started to peer in.

The sound of a gate opening toward the big house made her freeze in place. She strained to listen and heard footsteps coming around the side of the main building. Footsteps coming toward her.

Laurel whirled and ran on tiptoes toward the back fence, keeping the little house between her and whoever was coming.

Breathing a little hard, she slid though the fence and into the alley just before she heard a key in the lock. She waited until she heard the sound of the door opening, then, ignoring her racing heart, she walked away as casually as possible. *I'd better not risk that again!* she warned herself. *But I had to try.*

In frustration, she headed back to her hotel knowing that the tunnel opening was tomorrow.

# Chapter 24

Laurel joined railroad dignitaries, the press, and the general public on the excursion train from Sacramento. All were in a festive mood when they disembarked near the Summit Tunnel where banners and flags were flying and a brass band was playing. Spectators quickly sought the best vantage points to watch the official opening of the Central Pacific Railroad's incredible Summit Tunnel.

Below the tracks, a few observers had ridden saddle horses or carriages on the narrow stage road. It had no shoulders, so the vehicles and animals were left in the roadway, which rarely had traffic. These onlookers had brought picnic baskets and were prepared to enjoy the day, even though they had to look up at a difficult angle to see the ceremonies.

Laurel seemed to be the only one who was not in a high state of excitement. Personal problems kept trying to dominate her thoughts, although she wanted to finish the job she had been sent to do. In preparation for this, she had carefully researched the pertinent tunnel facts.

At more than seven thousand feet above sea level and only 124 feet below the peak of Donner Pass, thousands of Chinese laborers, working day and night for two years, had cut a twenty-foot bore through almost seventeen hundred feet of the mighty Sierra Nevada Mountain's solid granite spine.

Laurel, at barely five feet in height, didn't want taller people blocking her vision. She moved away from the crowd, seeking a place on the high side of the mountain for an unobstructed view of the ceremony. It was rugged terrain, with immense outcroppings of glistening granite which had been fractured over the centuries by alternating melting snow and summer heat. Long-ago earthquakes had lifted and twisted the giant slabs where some stunted conifers clung to life after taking root in the cracks where poor soil had collected.

After another glance at the stage road below the railroad tracks, Laurel turned away and continued to look up the side of the mountain above the tunnel. It was rough and uneven terrain, but she saw a few men up there, so she lifted her long skirts above her ankles and continued to work her way upward.

In passing two excited railroad fans, she heard one say, "You've got to admit nobody thought those Chinese workers could get this job done."

"I never expected it to happen," his companion replied, "especially when they used nothing but hand-held iron drills and blasting powder, plus two groups working at opposite ends until they met in the middle."

The first man mused, "I heard they used 500 kegs of powder a day. But if they had used that new blasting oil, it would have gone much faster."

"It's called nitroglycerin," his friend said. "But it was too unstable and dangerous. Anyway, the tunnel's done, and they'll have rails laid by November."

"Then," the first man declared, "you watch the Central Pacific race across the deserts to link up with the Union Pacific. Then we'll have our transcontinental railroad for sure."

Laurel didn't hear any more as she passed out of their hearing and saw Vance Cooper setting up his big camera on a sturdy wooden tripod. She was relieved that he didn't seem to notice her as he ducked under the black hood and aimed his camera at the tunnel opening.

A distant jangle of harness chains and the drumming of horses' hooves drew Laurel's attention back to the stage road below. A six-horse hitch pulling a westbound coach slowed at the unusual traffic. Laurel was surprised when the driver stopped the coach and passengers began to disembark. It was obvious that the unscheduled halt was to allow everyone to take a look at the tunnel which had received nationwide press coverage.

Laurel was about to turn and get as far away from Cooper as possible but still keep him in sight, when she saw the last person step out of the coach. She sucked in her breath and stared.

Ridge? It was too far away to be sure, but he had a slight limp when he walked over to the edge of the road and looked up toward the tunnel.

Laurel's heart leaped as she silently tried to decide if it was Ridge. *No, couldn't be*, she assured herself, *he's in Virginia, with Varina*. Sighing, Laurel resumed her climb up the mountainside.

Ridge was glad to have a chance to stretch his legs. He walked up beside a fellow passenger who was scanning the tunnel area with field glasses. Ridge barely noticed.

After taking trains from Chicago to Omaha, he had boarded the stagecoach and rolled west at five miles an hour. After fourteen days and nights of this, he was grateful to be within hours of reaching Sacramento. But would Laurel be safe? He berated himself for letting her go off alone, yet, except for sending a wire warning her about Armistead, there was nothing Ridge could do to protect her until he reached Sacramento.

He had often prayed that his telegram had alerted her to the fact that Armistead was really Abaddon, and that he had not gone to New York as he had said. He now had ample time to carry out his murderous plan.

Ridge idly scanned the crowd above him, then the few people higher up on the mountainside. He noticed a slight, slender woman moving away from the excursion train and tunnel. Ridge blinked in surprise, then spun toward the man with the field glasses.

"Please, sir, let me borrow those for one moment."

When the man complied, Ridge hurriedly adjusted the glasses and focused on the woman. "Laurel!" he exclaimed aloud. Then, in doubt, he lowered the glasses and quickly returned them to his eyes. "It is Laurel!" he cried.

Laurel stopped to catch her breath and look for the easiest way to climb up just a little higher. As her gaze moved on, she suddenly stared.

*That's Porter Armistead!*

She watched him standing alone by a small gulch that cut through the jumbled outcroppings. He didn't seem to notice her before he casually turned and was lost to sight in a crevice between the monoliths.

*Strange,* Laurel thought, *he told me that he was going to New York. So why is he here?*

Her curiosity aroused, she headed toward the spot where he had vanished.

Through the field glasses, Ridge first saw Cooper as his head emerged from under his black camera cloth. Past him, higher up on the mountainside, Ridge located Laurel, then shifted focus from her to the area above.

"Armistead!" Ridge exclaimed aloud. He watched the man who called himself Abaddon disappear among some monolithic granite knobs. Ridge added in amazement, "And she's following him!"

Ridge hastily handed the glasses back to their owner, saying, "Tell the driver this is as far as I'm going. I'll pick up my bags later at the terminal!"

Running as fast as his lame leg would permit, Ridge left the stage road, heading for the railroad tracks. He wanted to shout to Laurel, but the distance was too great, and he would never be heard above the brass band.

"Oh, Lord!" Ridge prayed, frantically scrambling after Laurel as she disappeared into the crevice where Armistead had been seen. "Don't let him harm her!"

❧

Now very curious, Laurel followed the gully, her eyes probing ahead for any sign of Armistead. There was none when she reached the area where the ravine widened out into a small clearing. She looked in every direction, but he was nowhere in sight.

*Where did he go?* she asked herself. At the same moment, she felt little tingles of alarm like those she had experienced during the war when a sentry was about to fire upon her.

For a moment, Laurel considered turning back, then glimpsed what seemed to be a small, tumbled-down cabin tucked away among some trees. This elevation was higher than gold miners had come, but perhaps a trapper or recluse had erected it long ago. The roof had partially collapsed inwardly. The rock chimney at the near end was sturdy, but the walls wearily sagged from neglect.

*Maybe that's where he went*, she thought. *But why? And why am I feeling this way about someone I've known since we were children?*

In spite of her reasoning, ripples of gooseflesh skittered along the back of her neck and down her arms. Stepping quietly on tiptoes, and with the greatest caution, Laurel kept close to one weakened wall and slid toward a single small window with the glass broken out. She crouched low, making sure that her shadow didn't fall across the opening and betray her. Staying below the window sill and to the right, she warily straightened up until only her right cheek and eye were beyond the frame.

The far side of the roof had fallen in, but the part nearest her still clung tenaciously to the top of the wall. She held her breath, and with one eye quickly scanned the rest of the interior. The partially open door at the end of the cabin farthest from the chimney drooped on what was left of leather hinges. There was no sound except for a blue jay with a topknot that flew over and screamed alarm at her presence.

After another more careful sweep of the interior, Laurel drew back from the window. *He's not there. But where could he have gone?* Pressing her back against the cabin wall, she hurriedly searched the surrounding giant slabs of granite now glistening like polished marble in the sunlight. She ignored the jay's raucous racket and ducked under the window so her shadow wouldn't show inside. She eased on around toward the door.

Without touching it for fear it might squeak or even fall from its hinges, she peered inside. The broken remains of a wooden bed frame still held pieces of rope which had once supported the occupant's pallet. A wooden keg which might have served as a chair had dried, letting the staves fall from the rusted metal bands. The thing was almost buried under dust from the dirt floor.

Laurel could not see what, if anything, was under the portion of collapsed roof, but she got a whiff of dust and rodents. She wasn't afraid, but considered that there might be a rattlesnake coiled up under there.

*Well, Porter's not here, so I should get back to the ceremony*, Laurel told herself. Before turning away, she again let her eyes skim the interior. They darted around, seeing nothing she hadn't seen before. But as she was about to give up, she saw something black and square in the far back corner by the fireplace.

*A camera?* she asked herself in disbelief. It was partly covered by a black cloth, but the lens stuck out enough that she was almost sure of what it was. She gently squeezed by the partly-open door without touching it. Concentrating on the unbelievable sight in the corner, she took one step toward it.

A slight sound behind her made her whirl in fright, but before she could turn, she glimpsed a white cloth in a hand strike from behind. She caught the ether-like odor of chloroform and tried to turn her head away, but the cloth clamped down hard over her mouth and nose. Wildly fighting the burning sweetness of its taste, she tried to twist free. Her willpower and physical strength quickly drained away. She felt herself growing weak, and then she knew nothing.

❧

Ridge had frantically pushed through the crowd of spectators whose attention was now entirely on the start of the ceremonies. Sick with fear for Laurel, he had reached the area where he had last seen Laurel and Armistead. The footing had become very treacherous because of the highly polished granite outcroppings.

His war-wounded left leg did not fully obey his mind, resulting in his foot sliding out from under him. He glanced down and saw where he could end up in a broken heap at the bottom. But driven by desperation, he grabbed at a scrub of tree and stopped his descent. He dropped to hands and knees and clawed his way up, grabbing a finger hold in the crevices and ignoring the pain from the young conifer limbs that managed to cling to life.

Panting from exertion and fear for Laurel, Ridge managed to scramble up a monolith which had been polished to a smooth slickness by countless centuries of melting snow. Suddenly, his left foot again slipped and he slid face down and backwards, wildly trying to stop himself.

He came to a jarring halt at the bottom, his hands bleeding and torn, his face skinned, and his clothes shredded. Quickly checking that there were no broken bones, Ridge looked around and saw a little ravine between two polished monoliths. Forcing himself to his feet, he aimed his aching body toward the gorge.

*If he's harmed her*, he silently vowed, *I'll . . . I'll . . .* He didn't finish, but gritted his teeth and forced his body upward to where he had last seen Laurel. But when he got there, he saw only a small open area with nothing but untamed wilderness.

*Where did she go?* he asked himself, vainly casting about for some sign. *And where's Armistead?*

❧

Laurel regained consciousness with a headache and the faint, lingering heavy smell of chloroform. She was on her right side, her right cheek in the dirt and the other partly turned toward the sky. She could see it through the collapsed roof. For a moment, she didn't remember what had happened, then it hit her. She frantically tried to sit up, but couldn't.

She was almost in a fetal position on the floor, bound and gagged. Shifting her gaze, she faced a tripod supporting a large camera. A black cloth loosely covered all except the front of the lens. The cloth moved as Porter Armistead's face appeared from under it.

Adjusting his glasses, he stepped around the tripod and came toward her. "So, Laurel," he said in his rasping voice, "you always could be depended upon to do what I expected. All I had to do was let you see me out there, then walk away. I knew you'd follow."

He reached down and helped her to a sitting position. Only then did she realize that she was bucked and gagged, exactly as Sarah had been. Laurel tried to speak, but only mumbling sounds came through the gag.

Too late, the awful truth slammed into her heart. She had been wrong to suspect Cooper was Abaddon.

"There now," Armistead said calmly, stepping back to look critically at her. "You're about ready to have your picture taken. Oh, you don't need to ask questions. I know what you're trying to say through that gag. I'll be glad to answer them for you, but first, I need to make sure of the lighting."

Laurel vainly struggled against her bonds and tried to work her gag free as he put his head under the black cloth. For the first time in her life, Laurel realized that she couldn't always take care of herself. Aunt Agnes had been right: there comes a time when there's nobody to help except God.

And, Laurel realized with a silent groan, *I haven't been on very good terms with Him, either!*

She was tempted to make promises to Him for His help, but resisted. She was in this trouble because of her own strong-headed thoughts and actions. She had been so blinded that she had failed to even consider Armistead as a threat. A fine detective she was!

Her thoughts rushed on, pouring over each other in fractions of seconds. *I should have listened to Ridge when he tried to protect me in Chicago. If I hadn't been so stubborn, we could have worked things out.*

She had long struggled between faith and doubt about her spiritual life and love life. Now, suddenly, when she was no longer able to care for herself, she realized that her faith had grown stronger in both her God and her man. *The Lord knows,* she thought, *but Ridge never will. He's with Varina. . . . No, don't think about that!*

She frantically looked around for some way to help herself. But she was totally helpless.

With his heart bursting with concern for Laurel, Ridge had to resist shouting her name, not knowing where she or Armistead had vanished. Ridge held his breath and listened, hearing only a jay scolding something off to the left. That stopped, and there was only the lonely sighing of the wind in the conifers. Abruptly, there was a flutter of wings and Ridge glanced up as the jay flew over him, a strident cry announcing to other wild creatures that there was an intruder below.

Ridge turned away, ignoring the bird as it lit on a granite ledge to loudly and harshly protest his presence. Ridge hastily whirled around, remembering times in his Confederate cavalry days when birds had either given away his position or that of Yankees lying in ambush.

That way, Ridge decided, turning in the direction the jay had come. He must have been screaming at one or both of them a few minutes ago! Cautiously, Ridge worked his way through the out-croppings until he saw a small cabin with the roof fallen in. *Is*

*Laurel in there? Maybe Armistead? Or maybe both?* Wishing he had a weapon, Ridge warily approached the cabin.

The black camera hood over Armistead's head reminded Laurel of drawings she had seen of executioners from the Middle Ages. Her captor's voice was calm, emotionless.

"To answer the questions I know you're wanting to ask," he said, "the first is, 'why?' Well, it goes back to when we were in our teens and I asked if I could call on you. You rebuffed me. Oh, you said all the polite things, but I knew what you meant, and it hurt me."

Laurel tried rubbing the gag against her shoulder in hopes of dislodging it. When that failed, she attempted to spit it out, but it didn't move. Frustrated, she cried out, but it came through as a muted mumble.

Armistead shook his head. "My, my! You just can't stand to not have something to say, can you? Well, this time I know you won't turn me down because the gag stays where it is. But I'll answer your other questions."

His voice had begun to lose its calmness as he returned to stand behind the camera. "You're wondering if your rebuff of me back then led to this moment. The answer is 'partly.' It started with that girl, Effie Chapman. She shouldn't have laughed at me. I'm aware that you already guessed that I killed her because I chased you at the tree where you were snooping around. But I just wanted to scare you; it wasn't your time yet. But today . . ." He left the words dangling and fell thoughtfully silent before again stooping to put his head under the black cloth.

While painstakingly circling the cabin at a safe distance, Ridge heard a man's voice. But whose? And if Laurel was inside with him, why couldn't she be heard? The only way to find out was to get near enough to look in. The sagging door might be watched, and so could the single small window on the side.

Ridge hoped to find a chink in the ancient wooden walls that would allow him to peek inside. He approached the cabin from the blind side, stealthily slipping past the outside stone chimney to the back wall. A cursory examination showed no holes or cracks between the boards. Still hearing the voice but unable to understand the words, Ridge bent low and inched along the side wall toward the broken window.

Just before he reached it, he was rewarded by finding a small knothole just about hip high. With great care, Ridge brought his right eye toward the hole. For a moment, he saw nothing but the partially collapsed roof. Then a movement caught his eye. He focused sharply and sucked in his breath.

Armistead had just emerged from the hood. He stood to the side of the camera and looked down at Laurel. She was seated on the dirt floor, her back to Ridge. But he could see that she was bucked and gagged. So that was why he had not heard her voice.

Four years as a captain in the Confederate cavalry had conditioned Ridge to make quick assessments and form a strategy of attack. He was taller and heavier than Armistead, but Ridge was unarmed, and he couldn't tell if the other man had a concealed weapon. Ridge's left leg would be a liability unless he exploited the element of surprise to the greatest advantage.

The sagging door might slow Ridge if he charged through it, but the window was too small. It would have to be the door, and the best time for that was when Laurel's captor again placed the hood over his head.

*But*, Ridge asked himself a question he could not answer,

*will he try to kill her before or after he takes his photograph?*

Armistead popped back under the hood, his voice rising slowly with emotion. "You look good in here, Laurel. Upside down, of course, or don't you know about cameras? Anyway, you wonder about Sarah. She hadn't done anything except help you with your spying, but it was enough."

Emerging from the hood, he continued, "Oh, I know it must sound callous, but her death would hurt you very much, and I wanted to hurt you as you had hurt me."

He tilted his head toward the sky. "I've got more light here than she had on her back porch, but with some of the new film and a faster lens, I got good shots of her. I wanted you to have a most unique 'going away' experience, so when I learned that you would attend the ceremony for this tunnel opening, I had to find a place that would suit my purposes. I was really pleased to find this shack. All I had to do was let you see me, and your curiosity did the rest."

Chuckling, Armistead gently touched the camera. "You didn't know that I learned to take photographs during the war. I was an assistant to a photographer in New York where I learned more than he did. When he got sick, I took over, but I kept that part of my career secret.

"You're wondering how I got on to you, aren't you? No need to nod; I'll tell you. I wasn't in the military, even though I told people I had been in mufti. Actually, when most men were away fighting, I got work as a clerk in the Union Secret Service. It's now called the National Detective Police. Anyway, they hired me, and why not? I had nothing against my name. I was a nice Chicago boy who was always quiet and never got in trouble."

Armistead squatted down in front of Laurel so he was even

with her face. "That's where I accidentally came across yours and Sarah's names, and what you did against the South. You probably heard that I was a Copperhead, but you didn't know how keenly I felt in sympathy with the Confederacy. Lincoln's tyrannical treatment of the South was too much like the way my mother treated me all those years of growing up."

Laurel noticed that his tone had taken on a hard edge and his voice rose with growing excitement. She steadily met his eyes, trying to hide her fear, but she sensed that her time was running out, and she was totally helpless. There was nobody to help her; nobody knew where she was. Even Cooper had not seen her start following Armistead.

"Well, Laurel," Armistead said, standing again. "I think I've answered all the silent questions you've been asking. Well, except two, or maybe three.

"Why did I send you that envelope with a piece of newspaper dated April third, 1865? You may remember that the Union blockade had cut off supplies to the South so that some newspapers there were down to a single sheet toward the end of the war. However, I saved a couple of Union papers from that infamous day when Petersburg and Richmond fell."

Armistead's voice took on a bitter quality. "The Petersburg defense lines were breached, partly because of your spying activity. The Confederate capitol also fell that day. I hold you responsible for your part in both of those tragic events."

He rose from in front of Laurel and walked back behind his camera. He took a deep breath and exhaled loudly before continuing.

"As for how I learned that Charity Dahlgren was contacting the National Detective Police, that was from my eavesdropping on patrolmen talking at lunch. Of course, I couldn't let her tell what she had discovered."

Laurel wasn't really listening anymore. Knowing that she had very little time left to do anything, she tried to think of some desperate action she could take to save herself. She considered trying to kick over his tripod to give her a few more moments to try something else. However, even if she could roll awkwardly toward him, the camera was too far away.

From where he stood behind it, Armistead added, "You must also wonder about those women in New York and New Jersey. They were immoral, which is the other reason I mentioned about you awhile ago. Before I found your files, I, along with the rest of those who knew you, believed that your frequent and unexplained war absences were from illicit dalliances with troops. That drove me mad! You wouldn't even let me call on you, but you had no such scruples with total strangers! I hated you for that!"

Laurel closed her eyes, unable to deny the gross error which had driven him to this moment.

She heard him say, "That's right. Keep them closed. Think of all you've done that deserves retribution. But know this: because we had known each other most of our lives, I thought you deserved to have some experiences of growing terror before your punishment. Oh, I admit you didn't scare easily, but perhaps you should have. Maybe, just maybe, if you had, you might live to see the sun go down today. But now that your questions have been answered, it's time."

There was such finality in his voice that Laurel fiercely shoved his words into the recesses of her mind. She was naturally tempted to make promises to God if He would help her, but she could not do that.

*I got into this mess because of my own strong-headed actions.* She wasn't sure if she was praying or just talking to herself, but it didn't matter. She went on. *I was a fool not to have suspected Porter instead of Cooper, but it's too late now. Too late for everything, for Ridge, or our happiness together. We could have worked things out so we could be together always. It doesn't really matter where we live, if we could just have been together, husband and wife . . . a family.*

A half-sob escaped her before she realized how deeply emotional she felt.

Armistead asked mockingly, "What's the matter, Laurel? You suddenly afraid to die?"

She opened her eyes and locked them challengingly on his. She shook her head vigorously. Not afraid of that, she realized. *I've long struggled between faith and doubt about my spiritual life and love. Now, in these final moments of life, I clearly realize my faith has grown stronger by testing. So has my love for Ridge, even if he's with Varina.*

Armistead mimicked Laurel's head shaking. "I don't believe you," he said. "Death makes us all afraid."

Again, she vigorously shook her head. She didn't want to die, but she believed that she had triumphed her one major character flaw. And, in her heart, she had faith that God knew that, although Ridge never would.

Armistead shrugged. "Then that makes you the only one who was not afraid. I don't like to fail, but I only failed in frightening you the way I intended. Well, it's time to take your 'before' photograph. You can watch that one, but obviously, not the 'after.'"

She suppressed a shudder as he placed the hood over his head. Laurel closed her eyes and her lips moved in a brief, silent prayer. *Lord, I am so sorry. . . .*

The sound of the door crashing made her eyes pop open. Armistead frantically tried to jerk the hood off of his head just as Ridge's fist sank deep into his middle. The air exploded from him as he tried to fight back. But Ridge was upon him with teeth bared, black fury in his eyes, and both arms clamped tightly about his adversary. They crashed to the floor, sending up clouds of dust. Ridge came out on top with his fist drawn back.

Armistead stopped struggling, threw both hands protectively over his head and tried to roll into a ball. "Don't hit me anymore, Ma! Don't hit. . . ."

"I'm not your ma," Ridge said, rapidly checking Armistead for weapons. "But you just told me a lot."

Moments later, with Laurel's gag removed and her bonds untied, she cried, "I've been such a fool!"

"So have I," he said gently, taking her into his arms. "But that's over for both of us. Just as tomorrow always promises to be there, in faith, you and I can now look forward to a lifetime of happiness together."

"Oh, yes! I believe that!" she whispered and closed her eyes as his lips claimed hers.

On May 10th, 1869, when the Central Pacific and the Union Pacific locomotives gently touched cowcatchers at Promontory Point, Utah, Mr. and Mrs. Ridge Granger and their young son were there.

After being granted amnesty by President Johnson, Ridge sold the family plantation property in Virginia and relocated to San Francisco where there was more tolerance for both former Union and Confederate supporters.

When the UP made its first run to support its boast of the "railroad from the Atlantic to Pacific" and "from Omaha to San Francisco in less than four days," the young family was aboard. Laurel realized her long-ago dream of being the first woman to make that historic journey, and she believed that hers was the first family ever to ride a train across a country united by shiny iron rails.

# Chapter 24